Ghost Centurion

GHOST CENTURION

Ronnie Evans

First paperback edition 2024

Book design by Push Publishing.

978-1-80541-429-2 (paperback)
978-1-80541-430-8 (ebook)

Index

CHAPTER 1

THE CURSE

MARCUS LOOKED INTO the mirror. It was a ritual he carried out at the beginning of each month. He rubbed his hand along his smooth chin. No need to shave; there was no stubble, not even the slightest trace of hair. He looked at his clear bright eyes, then at his thick black hair: not a sign of any grey, or even of a receding hairline.

He turned away from the mirror. He sat at the kitchen table staring straight ahead, wondering why he did this to himself. As he sat alone, he glanced round at his room, sparsely furnished with a small table and four wooden chairs. There were no paintings on the walls and the whole house was devoid of photographs. There were no wedding photographs, or photographs of laughing children, nor were there any old grainy photos of relatives long gone.

In the hallway was a full-length mirror. He had no idea why he had bought it. It had just seemed a good idea at the time. It had a plain wooden frame which fitted in perfectly with the drabness of the house. He hoped,

1

secretly and stupidly, that one day the mirror might be a messenger of salvation. He knew, however, that the mirror did not lie. The bare walls without photographs did not lie; the whole house screamed the truth! He was no more than a vapour, which came into people's lives for a short while and then was gone.

Marcus tried to ignore the mirror. His face, after all, had not changed in two thousand years. In fact, his body had not aged in any way since the day of the curse, a day that now came to his mind with increasing clarity and regularity. Why this should be so, he could not understand. He knew that after all this time, it was pure insanity to believe that one day, he would glance in the mirror and see some change. He turned to face the mirror, smiled, and said, "One day… one day, you will see…"

CHAPTER 2

FIRST ENCOUNTER

THAT DAY, IN first-century Jerusalem, was a day which had started out not unlike any other day in that damned city, in that cursed country, with its incomprehensible and strange religion. Marcus gazed around at the soldiers on guard, awaiting his instructions.

Marcus was a Roman Centurion and his assignment on that day was the execution of three scoundrels. It was a role he neither liked nor disliked. He was totally indifferent to the suffering of others. He was an arrogant and cruel man. As he approached the crucifixion site, he laughed when he recognised one of the men he was about to crucify. It was the Nazarene—a man he personally disliked. He had nothing to fear from this so-called God-Man, or Man-God, or whatever he called himself.

As a Roman, Marcus was not unfamiliar with the concept of a man being a God. The Roman Emperor, Caesar Augustus, was, in fact, a God. There were temples dedicated to him across the world. As for the Nazarene, Marcus was far from impressed. There was no warhorse

3

and no chariot! In fact, there were no horses at all. Marcus laughed! Who had ever heard of a God who walked?! This 'God-Man' did not have an army. He surrounded himself with the most appalling people—beggars, prostitutes and thieves. Now, here he stood, delivered to this place by his own people and at the mercy of Marcus and his small troop of Roman soldiers.

Marcus thought back to his father and his grandfather, who both believed that Julius Caesar was a God. In addition, his grandfather had actually counted Julius Caesar as a personal friend! Marcus, however, was not quite so sure that Julius Caesar would have held the same opinion of the friendship as his grandfather, who even had a small shrine dedicated to Julius Caesar! When times were hard, he would say, "I will go and pray to my friend, the great Julius Caesar."

Marcus laughed again: this crucifixion certainly deserved special treatment. He always liked to put on a show for the family and friends of the condemned men, when they came to watch their friend or family member being executed. Why they would want to witness such a gory spectacle and the suffering of someone they loved was a complete mystery to him, but he was always glad they were there. He loved to see the look of shock and horror appear on their faces. In fact, the more they wailed and cried, the more he felt it demonstrated the power of Rome. He believed absolutely that power and fear were synonymous.

As he finished enjoying the evening at the expense of the Nazarene, he turned to look at the horrified expressions on the faces of the Nazarene's friends and family. A young woman, probably in her early twenties, stared at him. He was pleased to see the expression of anguish on her face and the tears running down her cheeks. There was, however, something else. He did not know how he knew this, but what stunned him was that the tears were not solely for the Nazarene, but also for him! For the first time in his life, he felt ashamed. He turned away, dropping his instrument of torture.

Marcus removed his heavy helmet and placed it on the ground. He could feel the warmth of the sun carried on the breeze, bathing his face with wave after wave of uncomfortable heat.

The sweat ran like tiny streams, flowing down his brow into his eyes, and stinging like a thousand hot needles. He cursed beneath his breath, removed his small bright red scarf and mopped his face. Marcus hated being on crucifixion duty because it took so long for the prisoners to die. Marcus watched as his men gambled, laughed, and cursed—anything to relieve the boredom. As one of the men started to sing a more raucous song, Marcus cringed. "By the Gods, stop that noise!" he shouted. "You sound like a cat with his foot caught in a trap."

The man who had been singing looked genuinely offended, and glanced around at his companions, hoping for support. One of the men invited Marcus to join them in their game. The others, all talking over each other, joined in. Marcus, however, declined. He never gambled with the men. He felt that if he won, it would only cause resentment, and if he lost, it could encourage mockery. Marcus would not be mocked. He shook his head and turned to face the city. The men resumed their noisy banter. One or two of the soldiers were quite relieved by Marcus's refusal.

Marcus looked at the great city laid out before him. He continued mopping his face, then picked up a flask of water, took a long drink and poured some of the water over his head.

It was at this moment that a young man came over to him and said, "Hello, Centurion... or may I call you Marcus? I have a feeling that we will become good friends." Marcus turned around to look at the individual who had moved towards him. He did not like the way the man had approached him. He was obviously very wealthy and appeared to have an extremely arrogant attitude. Marcus felt a shiver run down his spine when the young man smiled at him. His smile reminded Marcus of a snake, with its tongue darting in and out of its lips, hunting for prey.

"Who told you my name?" Marcus asked, without looking at the man, who responded laughingly, "Come now, don't be so modest. Everyone knows the brave Centurion, the war hero." Marcus grunted and turned his back on the young man.

Wherever Marcus was posted, he automatically disliked and looked down upon the local people. As far as Marcus was concerned, they were a conquered people and, therefore, inferior. He had no wish to befriend any of them. For that reason, Marcus took an immediate and particularly strong dislike to this young man. Yet Marcus knew it was more than that—it was the man's arrogance, his snake-like smile, and his whole demeanour which made Marcus uncomfortable. "No!" he answered abruptly. "I am not your friend, and no, you cannot call me Marcus."

The young man smiled and responded, "I just want to congratulate you on doing such a fine job here." The young man waited as if he was expecting Marcus to answer him. Marcus said nothing. "How...however," stuttered the young man, "I know this man and, believe me, he has had it coming for a long time. I'm Flavian, by the way." Marcus ignored him and continued putting away the tools he had used for the execution. "I was wondering," Flavian continued, "if you would sell me those tools and your spear?" "What on earth would you want them for?" Marcus demanded. Flavian replied, "It would be a little memento to remind me of this day" . Marcus continued to ignore Flavian, and, taking another mouthful of water, he swilled it around his mouth and spat it out at Flavian's foot. "No!" Marcus answered without even looking at Flavian. Now, go away, little man. I will not sell tools belonging to Rome to the likes of you."

Flavian turned around to look at the Nazarene on the cross. As he turned around, he saw Flavian's face become pale and turned to see what had caused such a reaction. To his surprise, a young woman stood in front of the Nazarene. Her arms were crossed in front of her as if she was hugging herself. She stood silently, looking up at the Nazarene.

Marcus was surprised that he had not noticed her before. He watched as the young woman turned around. He stood, transfixed. She was, without doubt, the most beautiful young woman he had ever seen. She smiled at Marcus, and he thought to himself, "She is only a girl."

She then turned to look at Flavian. Marcus saw a look of fear appear on Flavian's face as he quickly turned away, adding, as he hurried off, "I must go, Centurion. But we will meet again."

Marcus watched in amazement as Flavian scurried away like a rat. He turned to look at the young girl, but she was gone. Marcus looked around, but he could not see her anywhere. He asked his companions if they had seen which way the young girl had gone. They looked at each other, puzzled, and then one said, "A young girl?" One of the other men answered, "This is no place for a young girl. I think we would have noticed if one had been here."

Marcus looked upwards as the sky darkened, but still, he felt no fear. He merely said to himself, "Perhaps not such a small God after all?"

CHAPTER 3
THE SCARS

MARCUS LONGINUS was born on the banks of the River Tiber, in the sprawling cosmopolitan city of Rome. His grandfather and his father had been Centurions before him. His grandfather had ridden with Julius Caesar and was by his side when he crossed the Rubicon. Following in their footsteps, Marcus had proudly joined the Roman Army at sixteen years of age. As a soldier, he was efficient and totally ruthless. He exemplified all that was Rome.

Marcus had made a name for himself in his very first battle. He remembered being terrified as the Legionnaires lined up, in ranks six deep and five hundred abreast, facing thousands of mad Syrians. Each one of the Legionnaires was armed with a javelin and a sword. As the Syrians charged forward, the Legion Commander would shout "Release". The first rank would throw their javelins; five hundred javelins hurled into the charging Syrians had a devastating effect. Then the front column of legionnaires would turn round and make their orderly way between the ranks to the back of the Company.

The second column of Legionnaires would then hurl their javelins into the Syrian army and turn to make their way to the rear of the column of Roman soldiers. This was repeated by the third rank, and then the fourth rank. When the Syrians were upon them, the Legionnaires drew their swords. Each Legionnaire was trained to hold his sword in his right hand and his shield in his left. He would then be able to slash, stab and cut the man on his right; the man directly in front of him was attacked by the Legionnaire to his left.

Marcus was in the fourth rank when a Syrian swordsman, a giant of a man, over six feet tall, ran forward, jumped up and landed with his feet squarely on the shields of Legionnaires in the front rank. The sheer force of the Syrian swordsman's attack caused three Legionnaires to fall backwards.

The Syrian jumped from the shield. His arms looked the size of tree trunks! Marcus felt the soldier next to him pause in shock and then hesitate. It was a fatal mistake. With one swing of his sword, the Syrian cut off the head of the soldier, and the same blow carried the sword onwards, cutting through Marcus's scarf and his leather neck-guard. Marcus felt excruciating pain as the sword cut deep into his neck. He fell onto his knees and, instinctively, pushed his sword upwards. He was fortunate—his sword thrust was true. It cut into the Syrian's stomach and up behind his ribs, killing him instantly. The dead man fell on top of Marcus, pinning him to the ground. It took three soldiers to pull the dead Syrian away from Marcus. Marcus was covered with so much blood that when the battle was over, his fellow Legionnaires stared at him in disbelief, astonished that he was still alive. The battle left Marcus with a terrible scar on his neck.

Two years later, Marcus was wounded again when a mass of flaming arrows struck his shield, causing it to burst into flames. Marcus was forced to throw his shield to the ground. As he bent down to pick up a shield from a nearby dead soldier, a flaming arrow hit him on his hand. He pulled the small red scarf from around his neck, using it to put out the flames. He snapped the arrow in half, pulled it out of his hand and threw it away. He wrapped his hand in his scarf and carried on fighting. At twenty-two years of age, he was already a legend.

As Marcus looked out of the window of his house in London, more memories of his past life came flooding back. It always surprised him that he remembered his past with such clarity. It was as if it were only yesterday.

In 1670, he had moved to London whilst the city was being rebuilt after the great fire. He had changed his name many years earlier from Marcus Longinus to Marcus Albright, a nondescript and easily forgotten name. Most of the people he met on his travels probably thought he was boring and easily overlooked, which is exactly how he wanted to be remembered, if he was to be remembered at all!

For some reason, which he could not quite understand, his mind kept drifting back to that cold evening in first-century Jerusalem when he had been promoted to the rank of Centurion. He was ten years younger than his father had been when he was promoted to Centurion, a fact that made him extremely proud.

Marcus, like every soldier who had ever lived, loved nothing more than spending time at the end of the day with his friends, drinking and sharing stories. Although he normally felt neither pity nor remorse after he had been on duty at a Crucifixion, as Marcus made his way to the inn near to the barracks which was frequented by soldiers, many of them from his Legion, his intention was to get as drunk as was humanly possible.

He was with his two closest friends, Cassius and Septimus. Cassius was two years older than Marcus and Septimus was the youngest of the three, but he outranked both of them; he was a Centurion and his Command, at that time, consisted of eighty men.

Although they had been friends for years, in truth, they had both always been afraid of Marcus. He had a fierce reputation, renowned for his strength and his skill as a soldier, but also his discipline. He would ensure that a Legionnaire was severely punished for the slightest misdemeanour. Neither Cassius nor Septimus was confident that their friendship would ever protect them.

They made their way through the narrow winding city streets. The air was full of intoxicating aromas from the numerous market stalls. The streets were filled with individuals playing instruments, but, to Marcus's surprise, all were out of tune. He smiled to himself when he heard the revelling crowd mocking the death of the Nazarene.

They arrived at the inn, which was popular with the Legion, and, also frequented by senior ranks. It was good to be seen there. The inn was well-known for its excellent wine, good food and available women. It also had a talented young man who played the lyre and whose repertoire was wide and included many bawdy soldier songs.

As they approached the inn, it appeared as if the evening was in full swing, although to Marcus, it was as though the music was somehow off-key. As they got closer, Marcus turned to his companions. "What the hell is that?" They turned to him confused. Marcus pointed in the direction of the inn. "By all the Gods, can you not hear that dreadful, appalling, apology for music?" Cassius looked puzzled and shrugged his shoulders. "Sounds good to me," he said. The three friends descended the stone steps into the inn. Cassius and Septimus were laughing and singing before they got to the bottom of the steps. Marcus followed them, gazing around as if he had stepped into another world. They made their way across the room to an empty table.

Marcus glanced around the room. There must have been fifty men in the room, most of whom were already drunk and singing. Marcus had spent enough time with soldiers of all ranks to know that they were, normally, far from melodic when drunk, but tonight, they sounded particularly appalling and the music was starting to hurt his ears. His friends had eyes only for the girls, who danced between tables and flirted with the soldiers. Marcus managed to catch the eye of a girl going through the room filling the soldiers' cups with wine. He watched, fascinated, as the girl, who was no more than five foot two inches in height, came towards him carrying the most enormous pitcher of wine with what appeared to be seemingly little effort, before she banged it on their table. While Cassius paid (Marcus never paid first), the girl poured out the wine, at the same time expertly avoiding the grabbing hands of the laughing soldiers around her. Septimus quickly picked up his tankard and drank it straight down, swallowing the contents in one mouthful. Cassius laughed.

Marcus reached for his tankard, but before he could take a drink, a young girl came and sat on his lap, running her hand through his thick black hair. She noticed the scar on his neck; "I wager that could tell a story," she said. Marcus ignored her comment. He took hold of her by the waist, lifting her up off his knee, and pushed her away. Cassius put his hand on his shoulder. "That's not like you, brother. A pretty girl like that one!" The noise was now unbearable to Marcus. He grabbed hold of his cup, hoping the wine would give him some release, but as the cool liquid touched his tongue, his eyes bulged. He felt he was about to throw up. He put his hands tightly over his mouth, but there was no stopping the vomit projecting from his mouth.

Septimus jumped up. "What the hell was that?! Are you ill?" Marcus was bent over, spitting the taste of vomit from his mouth. "No, it's that damned wine. It's poison, damned poison." Cassius looked into his own empty cup. He picked up Marcus's cup, looked into it and took a sip. "Tastes all right to me!" he said, then passed it on to Septimus, who did the same, smacking his lips slightly, before passing it back to Marcus. He reluctantly took it back, stared into it, and took a small sip. He felt his stomach heave. He spat out the offending liquid. His head was banging as the singing of the soldiers increased in volume, sounding like a chorus of croaking frogs and screeching birds of prey.

Marcus stood up. He needed to get out of the inn. As he left the table, his friends called out to him, but Marcus totally ignored them, pushing to one side the servant girl, who was on her way to clean up the vomit, and moving up the steps as quickly as he could before scrambling through the door.

He was met by a cold wind blowing in his face. It felt wonderful. He leaned back against the outside wall of the inn, breathing heavily, wondering if he had contracted some dreadful Hebrew disease. The streets were crowded with Pilgrims from across the world who were in Jerusalem for the Passover. Some stared at the Centurion who was behaving so strangely. But as Marcus waved his hands in the air, swearing at them, they scurried away. Marcus moved quickly through the busy streets. He desperately needed to get away from the inn and from the sound of the music, which had become an even louder, more discordant, and painful noise.

When he was well out of earshot, he stopped to try to make sense of what had just happened. His mind began to clear now that he was away from the inn and the noise had quietened. He decided he needed something to eat.

It was common to find street traders selling food in the streets of Jerusalem, which was true of most of the cities in the ancient world. Marcus went over to where an elderly man was selling hot chicken from a small stall near the grand Jewish Temple. Marcus held out his hand and gestured to the old man, who promptly placed a large portion of meat in his hand. He moved towards the old man with the obvious pretence of paying him. The man shouted to Marcus, "No pay… No pay." Marcus turned away. His attitude was that he was a conqueror and should not be required to pay.

Marcus took the meat and sat down on the Temple steps, gazing at the Temple Gate. It was an enormous solid gate, decorated with a great golden vine covered with huge golden grapes. He wondered why Rome had not taken the gold away. Perhaps Rome was going soft? He laughed at that very thought. He glanced up at the night sky. It was a beautifully cold but clear night. There was a full moon, but it seemed bigger than he had ever seen it before, and it took his breath away! His reaction surprised him. In the distance, he heard a cock crowing.

Marcus stood up and watched the crowds walking past, oblivious to his presence. He felt the chicken warm in his hand, which was good on a cold night such as this one. He pulled off a small piece of warm meat and placed it in his mouth. Before he had the chance to taste it, he quickly pulled the meat out of his mouth, looking at it in disbelief. The chicken was warm in his hand yet cold in his mouth. How could that be so? He spent what seemed to be an age examining the small piece of meat between his fingers. "It is warm. It is warm," he repeated. He gingerly stuck out his tongue and, again, gently placed the small piece of meat on it. He pulled the meat away. It was cold! It felt cold in his mouth, and it tasted a little like stale bread. He spat it out.

People in the passing crowd were outraged that he was spitting on the temple steps. He ignored them. His attention was totally focused on the meat. He transferred it from one hand to the other, lifted it to his nose, and smelt it. When he had completed his examination, once again, he took a small bite. It tasted like cold stale bread! He threw the remainder onto the floor, away from the direction of the Temple, and he held out his arms, shouting, "Are you satisfied now?" As he strode away, Marcus struggled to get rid of the lingering, dreadful taste in his mouth. He pushed his fingers into his mouth and scraped his tongue, but it had no effect. He ran back to the old man's stall, grabbed a pitcher of water, poured it into his mouth, gargled and then spat it out.

As he walked away, his appetite now completely extinguished, he looked up at the Roman Fortress with its four huge towers. The Fortress had been built to protect the Temple. Marcus had to admit to himself that the two buildings together looked magnificent. He looked up at the walls of the temple and noticed dozens of large black crows, perched along its length. The crows seemed to be watching him. He shouted a series of expletives. People in the crowd with families admonished him. Marcus swore at them. He looked again at the mass of crows high on the temple wall. They had grown in number and as he watched, more crows landed, and they too seemed to be watching him. Marcus decided it must be his imagination and he turned back, away from the Temple. After walking a few paces, he looked back over his shoulder. The crows were still watching. He felt a shiver move down his spine.

As he walked through the gates of the Fortress, the two soldiers on guard saluted him. He suddenly felt safe. It was a strange feeling, because in his whole life, he had never experienced a time when he had not felt safe. Even in the height of battle, he had always felt in complete control and he was always calm. He remembered the Syrian swordsman. It was only his own ability to remain calm, even in the most terrifying of situations, that had saved his life. Whenever he was with the Legion, he had never felt that he was merely in a fort, in a barracks or out on manoeuvres. He always felt as though he was where he belonged, and the Legion was his actual home. Although it had not been that long since he had left his barracks, it felt to Marcus as though it was a lifetime ago. He thought to himself that today had been a really strange day.

Marcus climbed the stairs, making his way to his room, thankful that as a Centurion, he had his own private quarters, away from the soldiers' dormitories. His quarters were in the West Tower and had a small window overlooking the Temple. He sat down on his chair, looking below at the hustle and bustle of the crowd. He watched for some time before getting up to drink water from the pitcher near his cot, in an effort to wash the still-lingering taste of stale bread from his mouth. He lay on his cot and fell into a deep sleep.

Marcus woke early. He had not slept well. For some reason, the crucifixion on the previous day had disturbed him. Normally, he would not have given an execution a second thought. However, the strange appearance of the young girl and how she seemed to strike fear into that horrible man, Flavian, mixed with the event at the inn had been disturbing. He shook his head, trying to shake the memories from his mind.

He noticed that Addayya had been in his room. It had been cleaned and the equipment used for the crucifixion had been neatly packed away and stored in a leather bag. Marcus had to admit, reluctantly, that Addayya had done a good job. He had also taken his uniform, cleaned it, returned it and laid it out neatly on the chair in the corner. There was a tray on the table, and fresh water for washing. Addayya had been out and purchased some fresh food—bread, which was still warm, olives, a little fresh fish, and cheese, together with a small flask of wine. Marcus smiled to himself; all that hard work and effort in training him was finally paying off. He poured the water into the bowl. All the turmoil of the previous day was forgotten. Marcus had just put his hands into the cool water when he was interrupted by Addayya, who was bobbing up and down, apologising for the intrusion.

Are you ready for a shave, Master?" he asked. "Oh! Sorry, Master, I see you have already shaved." "What are you talking about?" Marcus asked. He could see the fear in Addayya's eyes at the sudden change of mood.

Marcus quickly moved his hands to his face, muttering, "Not possible. Not possible." He stared into the mirror; his face was smooth. Marcus had black hair and a dark complexion, so he had been shaving since he was sixteen, long before his friends of the same age. Indeed, by early evening on most days, he would shave again. He turned to Addayya and shouted, "Get out!" Addayya ran.

Marcus glanced at the tray of food. He was hungry, but, almost too afraid to taste it. He picked up the bread. It felt fresh and warm. He tore off a small piece and held it to his nose. It smelt good. He hesitated for a second, and then put it into his mouth. It was cold and stale. He spat it out. He picked up an olive, and then tried the fish, followed by the cheese, all with the same results; they felt cold and tasted stale. He took the flask of wine and, nervously, put the tip of his finger into it and tasted it. To his horror, it tasted like vomit. Marcus sat staring at the tray of food for what seemed to be an age.

Marcus was not prone to panic. First, he had to be certain that this was not some strange illness. Perhaps he had been poisoned? That seemed the most likely expla-nation. He tried to think of anyone who would try to do such a thing. Yet, apart from the taste of food and wine, he felt perfectly well, although he could not imagine an illness which would prevent the hair from growing on

23

his chin. He considered various ways to make enquiries around the camp. The Legion's Physician seemed to be a good choice to approach to make discreet enquiries. Marcus had known him for years. It was the Physician who had taken care of Marcus after he was wounded. Marcus knew that the Physician had a great deal of respect for him.

He made his way out of his room into the large corridor on his way to the Physician's Surgery. His room was high up on the third floor and as he made his way down the stairs, he could hear the noises coming from the soldiers' dormitories. They were not quiet, but rather places full of shouting, swearing and often fighting. Marcus was thankful to have the rank of Centurion as this meant he had the privacy of his own room.

On the ground floor was the garrison Mess Hall. There were ten huge tables, each one big enough to accommodate at least twenty men. The men worked and ate in shifts. It seemed as if the Mess Hall was aways full. Marcus looked into the hall. Several of the men noticed him and shouted for him to join them. He was tempted as he had not eaten. Marcus laughed, shouting across in response, "This is the last place on earth I would eat with you rabble." One of the men gave a large belch, then laughed and asked, "What's wrong with us?"

At the far end of the yard were the stables. There was a warm breeze which carried the strong smell of the horses to every area of the barracks. It was the first thing he noticed when he woke up, and the last thing he noticed before he retired for the night. Just near to the main gate was a group of women with some large wooden bats stirring a container of boiling water with the Legion's dirty washing. An older lady, who oversaw the small group of women, smiled through broken teeth, and shouted across at Marcus, "Hey, beautiful! Would you like to fill up my pot for me?" She then held up the pot that was used to collect urine for the washing. This brought a roar of laughter and whistles from the soldiers. Marcus just grinned. He and all the soldiers were well used to the washer women and their coarse sense of humour.

As Marcus made his way across the yard to the Physician's room, he paused for a moment and watched as a troop of soldiers came in through the main gate. He waited as they came to attention and were then dismissed. As the men passed him on their way back to the barracks, they clenched their fists and slapped their breastplates in salute and, in unison, called out, "Centurion." Marcus returned their salute and continued onward towards the Physician's quarters. He knocked on the door and entered without waiting. The Physician was an elderly man who had the habit of mumbling to himself. Several soldiers were waiting to see the Physician, who was attending to a soldier's wounded leg as Marcus walked into the room. The soldier, on seeing Marcus, tried to sit up, then gave a cry of pain. The physician looked at Marcus then growled at the soldier, reiterating, "Didn't I tell you to keep still?" Then turning to Marcus, he said, "Well! We are honoured! What can I do for you?"

Marcus answered, "Speaking hypothetically, have you ever heard of an illness with these symptoms?" Marcus listed the symptoms. The Physician scratched his head, and answered, "That's a new one on me. Why do you ask?" The wounded soldier interrupted Marcus, "Sounds like a curse to me." Marcus immediately reacted and hit the soldier hard across his face, knocking him to the floor. The man screamed in pain. Marcus's eyes were blazing. "If I ever hear you suggesting for one moment that I am cursed, then I will have you flogged. Do you understand?" The soldier nodded. Marcus screamed, "I said, Do You Understand?" "Yes, Centurion," the terrified soldier said weakly. Marcus, his face like thunder, turned to the Physician, giving himself a moment to compose himself.

"Well, to be honest, I am not sure who said it, but have you heard of such an illness going around?" The Physician shook his head, then answered, "No, I have not heard any reports of an illness matching your description." Up to this point, Marcus had not considered the possibility of being cursed. The idea terrified him. He tried to act nonchalantly. He attempted a smile, but the best he could manage was a sort of half grimace. For a second, it looked like the Physician was about to speak again, but Marcus turned and quickly left. It was vitally important that no one suspected anything. It could be very dangerous if someone even thought that he was cursed. It could end in a very messy death.

Before any battle, the Roman army would slaughter an animal and inspect its entrails, looking for omens to see if the Gods were angry with them. He knew of a case when, after losing a battle, the defeated General, bizarrely, blamed it on one of the Vestal Virgins. They entombed her alive in the centre of Rome. Her cries could be heard for days. Marcus's father had been the Centurion in command of the Arresting Party. He told Marcus that it was not always easy being in the service of Rome. Marcus remembered vividly his father's account of the arrest. He and a dozen men had charged into the temple of the Vestal Virgins and dragged the poor girl

27

out. She screamed her innocence and begged for mercy. It was reported that she had had an affair, which was forbidden for a Vestal Virgin. Marcus's father did not believe the accusation for one minute. He knew the General who had lost the battle; he was arrogant and useless. His father said the two normally go together. The soldiers took the girl to a house in the centre of Rome. The house had a deep cellar. The girl was unceremoniously thrown down the stairs into the cellar and the entrance was bricked up.

Marcus's father served in the legion for thirty years and had many terrible experiences, yet he would say that the entombment of the poor girl was the incident that disturbed him the most. Twenty years later, he would say that he could sometimes still hear her pitiful screams. The story left Marcus claustrophobic, a condition he hid from in the Legion. He remembered serving in Gaul, where they were searching through the caves in the hills for rebels. As the Legion entered the dark, forbidding caves, he was, in truth, terrified, and at one point, was on the verge of panic, but, fortunately, the Commander called them all out of the caves. In the whole of his life, he had never been so relieved.

Marcus knew he needed a plan and that he had to continue to act normally. He forced himself to eat. Even though all food tasted the same, exactly like stale bread, he could just manage to eat it providing that he drank copious amounts of water at the same time. Looking as though he was enjoying the meal was difficult, and he was not sure how long he could keep it up. Drinking wine was impossible. He just could not keep it down. He would try drinking in the privacy of his Quarters, but the wine tasted so vile that no matter how hard he tried, it was always with the same result—projectile vomiting, which he would then have to remove. He dared not tell Addayya to clean it up. Slaves were bigger gossips than Senators' wives.

He decided he would have to fabricate some excuse for not drinking wine, which should not be too difficult, but he knew he could not keep it up indefinitely. Marcus had heard that sometimes, curses did not last for a long period of time, and it depended entirely on the power of the witch who had cast the curse. He decided that there was nothing he could do but wait it out._

CHAPTER 4

JUSTIN AEOLUS

Unfortunately, as Marcus discovered, life is never that simple. Several days later, Marcus was preparing to go out on patrol with a small troop of soldiers when he was summoned to his Senior Officer's Quarters. Marcus knocked on the door and waited. After a short time, the door was opened by his Senior Officer, Justin Aeolus, who impatiently waved him in. Marcus stepped into the room. Although it was a room he had seen many times before, it never failed to impress him. Justin Aeolus was a member of one of the wealthier families of Rome. Everything about him spoke of his power and wealth. Most officers would sit behind a simple table, but Aeolus sat behind a huge desk on which were some parchments and a silver frame, with a small painting of his family. The floor of his office displayed a fabulous mosaic depicting a hunting scene. In the far corner of the room sat two hunting dogs, who eyed him suspiciously, as if he was to be their next meal! On the wall hung a tapestry of a woman and two children. Marcus recognised the figures—they were the family of Justin Aeolus. The tapestry had gold thread running through it, which glinted in the sunlight. Near the window, Aeolus' armoured breastplate hung on a specially made stand. It was draped with a scarlet cloak.

Marcus waited patiently whilst his commanding officer shuffled through some parchments on his desk, selecting one which contained a particular name and address, which, he handed to Marcus. "Arrest everyone on that property. If they resist, kill them all," Aeolus said, adding, "but do not kill the owner of that property. Not this man." He pointed to a specific name. "I want him alive. Do you understand? This man is a rebel leader and is a damned clever one. He will not be easy to capture. You will have to take him by surprise. He is damned slippery. Damned slippery." Justin Aeolus then sat down and started looking through some more parchments on his desk. Marcus realised that the meeting was over. He saluted Justin Aeolus, who responded with a grunt. Marcus turned and left the room.

Marcus returned to barracks and called his Troop together. They assembled in a large room leading off the fortress courtyard. Even though the room had a huge heavy door, which blocked out the light for defensive purposes, there were only two small windows, both with heavy shutters. Once the door was bolted, it would be very difficult for anyone to gain entry to the fort. However, this meant that even with the door open, there was very little in the way of light to illuminate the room, making it necessary to have four large lanterns lit in the corners of the room, casting eerie shadows around the walls. Marcus picked up one of the lanterns and placed it on the table, where he had a large map of the city laid out. The Troop gathered around the table. As they leaned over to examine the map, Marcus looked across at the men as the flickering light danced across their faces. He could see that they all looked eager and were ready for anything! They had absolute confidence in Marcus as a leader.

Marcus said, "We have to arrest anyone found in this building," pointing to a building on the map. He continued, "I am told this man, the Rebel Leader, is dangerous and clever. He will almost certainly have lookouts, and so we will casually walk around this area." Marcus pointed to an area about a mile from the building. He continued, "Remember, take your time. Stop and talk to people. If you see any children, be friendly. Ruffle their hair, pat them on their head… Anyone watching will think it is just another routine patrol. We will not be wearing any heavy armour and will be carrying only light shields.

When I give the command, 'Run', then run as if your life depended on it. We have got to get to this man's hideout before anyone can warn him."

Marcus looked at the faces of the men in front of him and he could see that they were all keen and ready to go. Marcus was aware that soldiers hated being part of an Occupation in any city, with its endless mundane Patrols amongst a people who hated you. They longed for some action to break the monotony. Marcus continued, "Right then, go and get ready, and remember that you are going to have to run fast for at least a mile, so dress accordingly."

CHAPTER FIVE
THE DOGS

As Marcus made his way, together with the patrol, through the narrow winding streets of Jerusalem, he felt glad to be undertaking some real soldier's work. He was hoping that they would meet with some resistance. He knew that he was taking a risk instructing his men to wear only light clothing, but he knew if they were to wear full armour, they would have little chance of getting to the building in time to stop the occupants from dispersing. Besides, Marcus had every confidence that even lightly armed, his men were more than a match for any rebel gang.

Marcus saw an old lady struggling to carry some heavy copper pots. He approached her and saw the fear in her face as he came closer. "Are you alright with that heavy pot?" he asked her. "Would you like me to get someone to help with that?" He saw the fear in her face. She shook her head and scurried off into the crowd. The Patrol came across a small group of children chattering loudly to one another. When they saw the soldiers, they became silent and stared at the Patrol. One of the men reached out to pat one of the boys on the head. The boy stepped back, then turned and ran away. Marcus could see that his men were starting to feel uncomfortable; the crowd around it was growing.

As they turned a corner, Marcus could see that there were only a few people scattered around ahead of them. He shouted, "Run!" They ran, shouting for the people to get out of their way. Marcus, as he had expected, was soon ahead of his men. He did not slow down but kept running as fast as he could. When they arrived at the building, he briefly stopped at the door, and his men close behind him, running and pushing people out of the way.

Marcus raised his foot and kicked the door down. As it burst open, in front of him was the Rebel Leader. Marcus smiled. His plan had worked. The Rebel Leader was taken completely by surprise. The man turned and ran towards the back door. Marcus laughed and shouted after him, "You are going to have to run fast to get away from me." As Marcus gave chase, he turned to his men and shouted, "Kill everyone in the building."

As Marcus started to chase the Rebel Leader, he heard a noise that chilled him to the bone. A pack of large angry dogs came around the corner, howling and barking as they closed in. Marcus drew his sword ready for the onslaught, but as the dogs reached him, they came to a sudden halt. The two dogs at the front slid across the tiled floor. The two behind them crashed into them and they rolled over each other, smashing into a small table and sending a vase flying into the air. It landed on the ground and broke into pieces just a few feet in front of Marcus. Marcus raised his sword and the dogs retreated yelping and crying. Their previous ferociousness lost, they ran into the back room and tried to hide under the table, shivering in fear.

As he went through the door, chasing after the fleeing rebel, he heard the men entering the building. Then he heard the dogs. They were no longer afraid! With the barking of the dogs and the screaming of his men ringing in his ears, Marcus gave chase to the fugitive.

Marcus soon outran the man, knocking him to the ground and standing over him with his sword at the man's throat as he waited for his men to catch up with him. Suddenly, a young man jumped onto Marcus, knocking him to the ground. Fortunately, he managed to hold onto his sword. Marcus rolled over quickly and pushed his sword up into the man's chest.

Marcus was soon on his feet. The Rebel Leader was now standing up and Marcus could see that he was trying to decide whether to run or fight. He chose to run. He had, however, hesitated for too long. Marcus hit him hard on the top of his head with the handle of his sword and the man fell to his knees. Marcus looked around. A small crowd had started to gather. They were shouting and cursing. Marcus thrust his sword into the rebel's shoulder and the man screamed. Marcus turned to the crowd and twisted the sword. The rebel let out an ear-piercing scream.

The crowd became silent. Marcus thought to himself, "There are no heroes here!" He shouted towards the crowd, "Leave here now or I will cut his arm off." He leaned across so that his face was near that of the rebel and, through gritted teeth, whispered, "My orders are to bring you back alive, but not necessarily in one piece!" The crowd, reluctantly and slowly, started to step backwards.

After what seemed like an age, two of his men appeared, and Marcus withdrew his sword from the rebel's arm. He could not believe his eyes! The men were covered in blood! Marcus said, "What happened to you? Where are the rest of the men?" One of the men answered, "Most of them are dead; the rest are badly injured." The rebel lying on the ground said to Marcus, "Why did the dogs not attack you? What did you do to them?" Then he shouted, "The Devil… the Devil… You must be the Devil!" The crowd started to gather closer to the three soldiers. They were clearly amazed at the sight of the two soldiers covered in blood and the man on the floor shouting "The Devil… the Devil.!"

Marcus told the two Legionnaires to put the prisoners in chains and take them back to the fort. He added, "I will wait here with the injured men. Tell the Surgeon to get here as soon as he can." The two men hesitated, looked at the crowd, then looked at each other. Marcus had seen that look many times, but only after the most vicious of battles. The men were clearly in shock. Marcus said, "Listen, I don't know what went on in that room and clearly it was terrible, but the men need help and only you can do that."

Once again, Marcus turned to the crowd. "Get out of here! I will not tell you again." The three soldiers watched as the crowd nervously looked at one another, then slowly started to disperse. Marcus waited for a few minutes, watching the mob breaking up into small groups and disappearing in the small winding streets and alleyways of Jerusalem. When he was convinced that the danger was past, Marcus put his hand on the shoulder of one of the men and said, "You are not far from the Fort. Make your way as quickly as you can. You will be alright." The two men nodded, one of them wiping his face with his left hand which only succeeded in leaving an even larger bloodstain on his face. Marcus could see that the man was trying desperately to hold himself together. Marcus said, "Take the prisoner and go. We need help and we need it now." The two men once again looked at each other, then grabbed the prisoner and, without a word, turned and started back to the Fort.

Marcus made his way back towards the rebel's hideout and was met with the most horrendous sight he had ever witnessed! The floor was covered with so much blood that as he walked along the hall, the blood splashed up onto his legs and as he brushed against the walls, his tunic became covered in blood. Marcus stepped over the mangled remains of his comrades. It was clear that the dogs had been trained to attack and go for the throat.

Suddenly, Marcus turned as he heard a moaning sound coming from the back room. He picked his way through the bodies of his men and some of the dogs, making his way to the back room where he discovered two of his men lying alongside the remains of two dogs. Marcus knelt next to his men. They were badly injured, but Marcus was thankful to see they were still alive. He took off his cloak, tore it into strips, and used it as bandages.

It was over two hours before the surgeon arrived accompanied by at least one hundred legionnaires. The Surgeon was not normally a man to show any emotion, but Marcus could see the anger on his face as he surveyed the carnage around him.

He waited a few moments then shook his head before he spoke to Marcus, "Where are you wounded, son?" Marcus said nothing. The Surgeon repeated, "Where are you wounded?" Marcus looking at what remained of his troop said, "It is not my blood, and where the hell have you been?" The Surgeon, looking around at the bodies of the soldiers, angrily replied, "What were you thinking of, sending these men into this butcher's yard without any heavy armour or javelins?" "How could I know that there were damned attack dogs here?" Marcus said. The surgeon shouted, "You are supposed to know! You are supposed to damned well know. Damn you. Damn you. It is your job to know! Now, damn well get out of my sight."

Marcus went outside and was surprised at how many soldiers there were gathered in the courtyard. They were heavily armed and stood in four ranks around the building. "I am surprised at such a show of force," Marcus said to the Centurion who was watching the crowd gathering. The Centurion looked at Marcus as if he had gone mad. "Have you any idea what's going on?" he asked. "The men that you sent back with the prisoner were attacked. One was killed. The other only made it back by the skin of his teeth, and the prisoner has escaped.

They are calling you the devil!" the Centurion continued. "It will not take much for the whole of Jerusalem to go up in flames. If that happens, a hundred men won't be enough."

Marcus's eyes followed the gaze of his fellow Centurion and saw men scrambling on the rooftop. They were carrying slingshots. The Centurion ran into the building and shouted, "Pick those injured men up. We will have to carry them. We are leaving NOW."

Marcus heard a noise that always made his blood run cold—it was a loud whirling sound… the sound of dozens of slings spinning, ready to release their lethal projectiles onto the ranks below. It was then that Marcus needed all his experience as a Centurion. "Shields up!" he screamed.

Within a few moments, they were running through the streets of Jerusalem with their shields held above their heads. They had the appearance of a giant tortoise with stones raining down on them. Fortunately, they made it back without any additional loss of life. Once they were back inside the Fort, the crowd started to disperse. Marcus made his way back to his quarters, shocked and bewildered.

The next morning, Marcus was called in to see his Commanding Officer. As he was entering his office, Justin Aeolus screamed at him, "What the hell did you think you were doing?! Seven men killed. Explain yourself, and it had better be good!"

One of Marcus's greatest attributes was that he had the ability to remain calm whenever he was under pressure. This ability had never served him better than at this moment. He was fully aware that he could lose his rank, that he could be flogged, or even executed. Marcus calmly explained why he had believed that speed and surprise were the only way to catch the rebel. Marcus pointed out that the plan had worked, but that they had been let down by poor information. He was told where the man was, but there was no mention of him having four attack dogs.

The Commander stood and said, "I hope you are not suggesting that it is my fault?" "No, Sir," Marcus answered, "That is why I said we were let down." The Commander thought for a moment, "What is this about these attack dogs running away from you, and that Rebel shouting that you are the devil." "Well, as I said, Sir, we caught them by surprise. A fully armed Roman soldier crashing through the door with his sword raised gave them a shock, and by the time I ran out of the back door, they had recovered! No big mystery, and as for being called the Devil, it is nothing new for Roman soldiers to be called a devil."

The commander looked unconvinced. "I must tell you," he said, "that it is your reputation alone that spares you on this occasion. Rome does not take kindly to this type of failure. Do you understand?" Marcus nodded. "Now, get out!" his Commander said angrily. Marcus saluted and left. Marcus had almost convinced himself that the dogs were simply taken by surprise, but he still could not get out of his mind the image of the terrified attack dogs cowering under the table.

It was clear to Marcus that he was under a very powerful curse. In addition, he was now being watched and talked about. He had to be careful. He could not have another incident such as the one with the dogs.

CHAPTER 6

MARY

Marcus knew that he needed to establish who would have cast the curse on him. He then had to ensure that the curse was lifted. He sat at the table looking out of his window. Who could possibly be responsible? He looked back over the past few weeks. Had anything happened that might result in how he now found himself? Suddenly, it came to him. A few weeks had passed, but it was definitely the day of the Crucifixion. That was the day when his whole life came crashing down. Marcus went through the events of the day; was it that worm of a man? What was his name? … Flavian, that was it, but why would he curse me? Surely not because I wouldn't sell him the Crucifixion tools. If that was the case, he would somehow have got word to him offering to remove the curse in exchange for the tools. No, not Flavian, but who? He cursed and shouted aloud, "It was that girl! That is what she was doing. She was a witch! It must have been her. It must have been! She must have put this terrible curse on me." What should he do now?

He had to find her! He knew that it would not be too difficult—after all, he was a Roman Centurion. It was routine. It was part of his duties to find individuals who were wanted by Rome.

As he expected, it took only several enquires and two days. He was told Patrols often saw her out on the western side of the city. He was asked if he wanted her to be brought into the barracks, but he told them he would deal with it himself. He knew he would have to be very careful. Finding her would be the easy part: getting her to lift the curse—that would need to be handled delicately. He could not threaten her. She would know he dared not kill her, because then, he would never be free of the curse. Alternatively, if she heard that he was coming for her and she ran, he might never find her. Marcus was told that she was often seen buying fish from the market stalls, mid-week, around noon.

It was the busiest market day of the week. He arrived just after noon, and the marketplace was already very crowded and full of street traders. People eyed him suspiciously. He felt like a hyena among a herd of wildebeest! As he wandered around the stalls, he noticed people looking at him, whispering to each other, then disappearing down the tiny streets and alleyways. It was about an hour before he saw her. She was looking at fish laid out on a stall. He quickened his step. When he was within a few yards, he shouted, "Hey, you, girl. Stop there!" in a booming voice that startled those around him. The girl froze. He thought she must be terrified, which pleased him and gave him a feeling of power. Experience had shown him that people were much more compliant when they were afraid.

The girl stood with her back towards him. He slowly walked around to face her. He expected to see her shaking with fear and with a look of terror on her face. She was, instead, completely calm, showing not the slightest sign of concern. He was considerably proud of his self-control, but, at that moment, he had an overwhelming desire to knock her to the ground, to kick her, and to beat her. The girl was in her early twenties and she was beautiful. She was about five foot six inches tall with long black hair, which she wore looped to one side, over her left ear. She was standing with her hands on her hips, looking at him.

In his rage, he wanted revenge for what this girl was causing him to go through, but he knew that would have to wait. He decided the best strategy would be to attempt to befriend her, although, as she had witnessed his more brutal side, it did seem unlikely that she would believe his change of behaviour.

Approaching the girl in a calm manner, he looked down at the fish on the market stall as if he was interested. The crowd around him were now paying more attention to him. He overheard someone say, "Centurions don't buy fish" . Marcus had always been confident that being a Roman soldier was enough to guarantee his safety, but after the trouble with the dogs and the attack by the crowd, he was now not quite so sure. He knew he had to be careful. He looked at the girl out of the corner of his eye, smiled and said in a friendly voice, "Hello. We meet again. Do you remember me, girl?" He spoke as gently as he could. He smiled inwardly; he thought he sounded like a loving father. She nodded. "Yes. I do remember you. It was you—you are the one who tortured Yeshua." "Yes, Yes", he replied, tersely. "It was my job. I know I may have, perhaps, gone too far and I do regret it," he lied. "Look, I am sorry! All right? I am really sorry, but do you not think that I have been punished enough? Anyway, are you people not supposed to forgive? I have apologised. Now, will you please lift the curse?"

She looked at him, puzzled. "What are you talking about?" He stared at her. "You put a curse on me, at the

Crucifixion." "I am not a witch, and I did not put a curse on you," she responded sharply. Marcus stared at her. He was angry, totally dejected, and he could feel his hope slipping away. The proud arrogant soldier disappeared. What was left was a man almost at breaking point. Weeks of living with the curse and fear of discovery had taken its toll. However, Marcus was very good at reading people and he knew the girl was telling the truth.

For one of the few times in his life, Marcus was speechless and totally lost for words! He genuinely did not know what to do. He tried to speak, but all that came out of his mouth was a stuttering, "…but who… what… how….?" He turned away. He was no longer afraid of the crowd. He pushed a young man out of the way and started to walk through the mass of people. Some individuals in the crowd started to react angrily. The girl held up her hand and said, "It's alright. He is going now. There is no need for anyone to get hurt." The crowd went quiet. Marcus thought to himself, "Who is this girl who can influence such a crowd?" She gently took hold of his arm and turned away from the crowd, saying, "No, wait. I know someone who may be able to help. Come tonight." She turned and pointed; "Come to that building over there. Come tonight." As she started to leave, Marcus asked, "Wait, before you go, what is your name?" "Mary of Magdala," she replied. "They call me Mary Magdalene."

Marcus walked away from the crowd, feeling utterly dejected. He found it extremely difficult to come to terms with the fact that he, a strong, independent, and powerful Roman Centurion, had virtually placed his life in the hands of a young Hebrew girl. However, he had no alternative. There was absolutely nothing more that he could do.

That night, Marcus made his way across the city, not knowing what to expect. He wondered, momentarily, whether it was a trap. He dismissed that idea because, strangely enough, he actually trusted Mary Magdala. Marcus stood outside in the dark shadow of the building that Mary had pointed out to him. He waited beside the large wooden door, uncertain whether to knock and ask for help or to go back to the barracks. He shrugged his shoulders. He had no alternative but to knock on the door and wait. He knocked on the door. The door was opened by an angry-looking young man. He stared at Marcus then turned away without speaking and went up the stairs. Marcus followed him.

At the top of the stairs, there was a large bright room with a long table set against the back wall and four smaller tables scattered around the room. There were approximately fifteen men and six or seven women present. Mary stood in the corner talking to a small group of women. Most of the men were in conversation at the other side of the room. Mary looked in his direction and briefly acknowledged him. Marcus continued to stand near the door for what seemed like an age before a young man, who was sat at the large table, looked up and waved him over.

As Marcus approached the table, the young man stood and apologised for leaving him unattended. He introduced himself. "Hello. I am Y'hochanan (John) . Please join us. You have already met Cephas, and this is Ya'aqov (James). You know Mary. Tell me about this curse." As John listened intently, Marcus slowly and carefully explained the effects of the curse in great detail, one by one—his problem with music, food, drink and his feelings for women. Almost as an afterthought, he mentioned that he no longer needed to shave. This seemed to raise John's interest. He held up his hand to stop Marcus from talking. "No, wait. When did you last shave?" Marcus answered, "About four weeks ago." John leaned over and rubbed his hands through Marcus's hair. Marcus sat back in surprise. John said, "Your hair is very thick. When did you last have it cut?" Marcus ran his fingers through his hair. It was thick but short. With a look of realisation on his face, he exclaimed, "My hair! It is not growing!" John was quiet, considering what he had just heard and seen. He answered, "My friend, I am afraid it appears that you are quite right. You are cursed."

Marcus was silent. He had heard much of these men, that they had special powers. He had no doubt that what they were telling him was the truth. Cephas stood up and banged on the table. He leaned across towards Marcus and said, quietly but angrily, into his face, "Justice. Justice at last."

John went back to his seat and sat down. Marcus watched as Cephas continued angrily pacing up and down the room, whilst, at the same time, muttering to himself about consequences, justice, and why Marcus would think that they could, or would, be willing to help him.

Looking at Marcus, John spoke kindly to him, which made Cephas even more agitated and angry. "Please forgive my friend. He tends to get a little over-excited." "What did you say?" Cephas exclaimed, pointing at Marcus. "Him! He is to forgive me... forgive *me*! Are you serious?" John turned to Cephas. "Have you learned nothing over these last three years, Cephas? Believe me, people with far worse things on their conscience than this man has on his will join us and be welcomed." Cephas hesitated before turning away, looking chastised.

Marcus looked from John to Cephas, fascinated and yet bewildered by the conversation between the two men. Marcus continued: "Well, how can l get this curse lifted?" John looked across at Marcus, placed his hand gently on his arm and answered, "I'm sorry to have to tell you this, but you cannot." Marcus looked around the room, and at the faces of those sitting around the table, searching for a sign, a look… something that might offer him hope, but he could see none. John continued; "Why is it, do you think, that your hair does not grow?" Marcus just shook his head. John continued, "It means that you are not ageing. Your body will always remain the same." Marcus, continuing to shake his head in bewilderment, responded, "What… what are you saying? You are telling me that l am going to live for—how long—forever? Is that what you are telling me? I cannot live like this. I would rather fall on my sword than live one more day like this."

James, who had remained silent until this moment, quietly said, "You cannot kill yourself. If you do, then you will spend the rest of eternity in hell, and, believe me, you do not want that to happen!"

John continued; "You will have to leave the Army." Before he could speak again, Marcus jumped up, and, banging the table with both fists, shouted, "Enough,

enough!" He started walking around the room, cursing and swearing, and then came back to face John. "I can't do that, do you understand? I can't do that." John answered, very quietly and deliberately, "You cannot die. You will be in battle and a thousand arrows will be fired at you, and they will all miss. Your enemy will try to stab you and they will miss. Wild animals will not attack you because you are protected, and you will not grow old." John continued; "How long will it be before anyone notices? As you are now, so you will always be. You will not be permitted to get involved in politics, nor lead an army. You will not be permitted to kill anyone, to save anyone, or to perform an exorcism. You will go through life as if a ghost."

Marcus staggered back to the barracks as if he was drunk. He cursed the Hebrews, he cursed Jerusalem, he cursed Israel and as he passed the Temple, he cursed the Temple Guards, and he cursed their God who had done this terrible thing to him.

For the next few weeks, Marcus tried to adapt to his new life in the Legion. He would volunteer for night patrols, even though he hated night patrols. It was the only way he could think of avoiding time spent in the inn and getting drunk with his friends. It was also a good way of avoiding crucifixion duty. Strangely, he had lost his appetite for killing, which was a definite disadvantage for a Roman soldier.

He was worried he was becoming paranoid. He would see soldiers talking quietly to one another and becoming silent when he looked across at them. For the first time in his life, he felt friendless and alone. As time moved on, he became distant and fearful that soldiers suspected that he was cursed.

Marcus sat at the table in his room, idly looking out of his window, watching the great crowds of people milling around the Temple. When he heard a banging on his door, he ignored it. He just wanted to be left alone. He then heard the voices of his friends, Cassius and Septimus, shouting, "Open the dammed door, will you?" At the sound of their voices, Marcus immediately felt better. He stood up, and laughing, shouted, "All right. All right. Give me a minute." Marcus opened the heavy door. His two friends, who had obviously already had a drink, stood with their arms around each other. Cassius said, "Marcus, you are in great danger of becoming a miserable pig… So…. we have invited all your friends in the Legion to your favourite inn, where we can get drunk." Marcus put his hands on his friend's shoulders and said, "I am sorry. I would love to come with you, but I have a bad stomach, and the surgeon has told me to drink only water" . Cassius said, "No! No! You have to do better than that. We are not going to take no for an answer." Septimus interrupted; "Anyway, you can drink water if you want to!" Turning to Cassius, he then said, "We will drink the wine" . Septimus laughed as if it was the funniest joke in the world. Marcus replied, "Alright… alright, I will come, but you must understand that if you force me to drink wine, I will vomit all over you." Septimus grabbed Marcus's head, pulled him forward, kissed him on the forehead and said, "Lovely fellow!" Cassius laughingly added, "Come on… Come on… You are wasting time. We don't want to be the last people to arrive there."

Marcus, accompanied by his two rowdy friends, made their way out of the barracks. Once again, Marcus was happy to be with his friends. He thought to himself, "If it all goes well tonight, and they don't mind me drinking only water, then maybe, just maybe, this might work. This could be the end of the nightmare."

They went past the brightly lit Temple, ignoring the totally disinterest guards, and made their way down the small, cobbled street that led to the inn. As they approached the inn, Marcus began to feel uncomfortable; something was wrong. He looked at his friends, who, until now, had been laughing and talking at the top of their voices, but who were now completely silent. The sound of their boots hitting the cobbles was the only sound that could be heard. As they reached the door of the inn, his two friends hesitated. Cassius looked at Septimus and said, "It's a bit quiet, isn't it?" Septimus said, unconvincingly, "You know the lads… They are probably hoping to jump out and surprise us."

The three men descended the stone steps into the inn, with the sound of their boots echoing throughout the rooms, which, apart from the innkeeper, were completely deserted. On the counter, there was a cat, which, upon seeing him, stood up, arched its back, hissed, and ran out of the room. Marcus said to his friends, "Look, I know that you meant well, and I am really grateful, but I don't think that this is a good idea." Cassius said, "No! Don't be silly. The night is young, and half of the Legion will be here soon."

Marcus reluctantly followed his friends across to the counter. Cassius ordered the drinks and said, "Where is everyone? Where is the music man and the serving girls?" Septimus noticed that whilst Cassius was ordering the drinks, the innkeeper did not for one moment take his eyes from Marcus. The innkeeper replied, sharply, "I don't know! They just didn't turn up." Septimus said angrily, "I do not know what you mean! You don't understand why your staff and all of your customers just failed to turn up?! Are you really telling me that you have no idea why?" Septimus looked across at Marcus, then at the innkeeper, who was still staring at Marcus. Septimus shouted, "By all the gods! Why are you staring at him?" The innkeeper was now starting to look a little nervous. He turned his eyes away from Marcus and said, "Look, lads, I don't want any trouble. All I know is that when you came in earlier and were asking people to come and drink with your friend... I'm sorry." He turned to Marcus and said, "I'm truly sorry but people are afraid of you." Marcus said nothing, He sat down and looked around at the empty inn. Marcus's friends were speechless. The innkeeper broke the silence and repeated once again, "I'm sorry, lads." Cassius turned to face Marcus and said, "Well... to hell with them all. The three of us will drink together." Cassius turned to the innkeeper and said, "So, we will have two cups of your finest wine and a cup of water for our friend here, or are you too afraid of a stupid curse?" The innkeeper started to pour the wine from a large pitcher. Cassius could see his hand shaking. The innkeeper said, "There is no charge, but please, only one." Septimus picked up one cup of wine and threw it at the wall. Marcus watched the wine running down the wall. He knew that there was no coming back from this.

After the incident in the inn, he found it was becoming more and more uncomfortable to be in the barracks and he would spend most of his time wandering around the city. Quite often, he would see a patrol on duty, and he would avoid them, disappearing down one of the many narrow streets of the rabbit warren that was Jerusalem. He knew, however, that he could not continue living this way. He knew it was madness.

One day, quite by chance, he found himself outside Mary's house. He tentatively knocked on the door, waited, and then knocked again. He heard the sound of soft footsteps on the stairs, then the door opened a few inches and a voice asked, "Who are you? What do you want?" The voice was unknown to him and appeared to be that of a young girl, whom he had no recollection of having met previously. Marcus, answered quietly, "My name is Marcus. I am a friend of Mary." He glanced up and down the street. He knew it would not be good to be seen entering a Christian household. The girl peered around the door but did not respond. He waited and watched as her eyes moved up and down, examining him from head to foot. "Stay here", she said, as she closed the door. He heard her footsteps hurriedly running up the stairs.

Marcus waited, wondering what on earth he was doing. Why was he here? What did he expect from these people? If they asked what he wanted and why he was knocking on their door, what could he say? What answer could he give them? He did not know. He decided it was a bad idea. He turned to leave.

"Hello, Centurion! You are not leaving already, are you?" Marcus turned back to face the door. It was Mary! Her smile immediately warmed him and he relaxed. He felt welcome. She added, "It's very good to see you again. Come in, please. Come in!" She turned and made her way up the stairs. Marcus followed her. When he reached the top of the stairs, he paused. The room was full of men, women and even children. They all seemed to be talking at the same time. Marcus felt awkward, as if he was intruding.

Suddenly, out of a crowd of people gathered together around a table at the other side of the room, he saw John coming towards him. He could not believe it. John greeted him as if he were an old friend and then invited him to join him and his friends who were seated around the table. As Marcus followed John through the crowd, John said, "Well, my friend, what is it that is troubling you?" Marcus answered, "Friend… Friend! How can you call me a friend? You know what I am, and you know what I have done." John replied, "All of the people in this room are your friends." Marcus looked in particular at the four people sitting around a table, which included Cephas and Mary, who were all looking at him intently, whilst gently nodding their heads.

Marcus followed John through the crowd, then sat down at the table. He looked at the other occupants for a few moments, unsure what to say. The friends waited. Marcus then told them about the inn and how, for some reason, he could not get out of his head the image of the wine running down the wall. John said, "Well, you know what I am going to say, don't you?" Marcus nodded. John said, "You need to leave the Legion, and you need to leave soon."

Marcus said nothing. He leaned back in his chair, staring into space. John added, "You are welcome to stay here until you decide on your next move." Marcus stood and thanked his friends for their advice, then added, "I need time to think things through." He saw his friends nodding. John said, "Take as long as you need. You know where we are."

Once back at the barracks, he climbed the stone steps leading to his room and stood near to the window, trying to make sense of the great changes in his life. Marcus had, until now, not fully realised how tough and difficult his life had become. Thinking of the Legion, the Legion he loved, now filled him with a feeling of fear and foreboding. Most of his friends had deserted him. He knew that should he make one mistake, or encounter one piece of bad luck, then, knowing Rome as he did and no matter how innocent he was, there would be no forgiveness.

CHAPTER 7
LEAVING

As Marcus entered the fort after completing his Night Patrol, he felt weary, not merely in body, but in spirit. His Patrol had spent the night silently touring the streets and alleyways of Jerusalem. Although the men would not say one word to him, he knew that they were muttering to each other and that they felt uncomfortable with the idea of being in a Patrol led by Marcus. Any sudden noise made them edgy. In one of the alleyways, a dog barked at them, and the men completely overreacted, forming a circle with their shields and drawn swords. Marcus shouted at them and told them not to be so stupid. One of the men responded with, "Sorry, Centurion." They no longer called him Marcus.

Marcus lay down on the cot in his room and fell into an exhausted sleep, but he did not sleep for long. He sat up on his cot, covered in sweat, and screamed, "Addayya, Addayya, where the hell are you?" Addayya came running into his room, shouting, "Yes, Master. Yes, Master," with a look of panic on his face. Marcus screamed, "Get me some water, damn you." Addayya poured out a cup of water and handed it to Marcus. Without comment, Marcus splashed some of the water onto his face and drank the rest. He then turned to Addayya and said, "Get out!"

The following morning, as Marcus stood nervously outside the door of Justin Aeolus's office, he felt like a small boy who was about to be disciplined by his teacher. He knocked on the door of the room and then knocked again. He waited, then he heard the Officer shout impatiently, "Come in, come in." Marcus opened the door, stepped into the room and stood in front of Justin Aeolus's desk. Justin Aeolus looked up from the documents he was studying and seemed surprised to see Marcus. He put the documents to one side and said, "Well, Centurion, what can I do for you?" Marcus had rehearsed in his mind what he would say when he spoke to his Officer, but now the time had arrived, it was as if the words had just stuck in his throat. He put his hand across his mouth and coughed. Justin Aeolus, said, "For God's sake, man, spit it out." Marcus saluted and said, "I am sorry, Sir, but I wish to request your permission to leave the Legion."

What Justin Aeolus said shook Marcus to his core. The officer looked down again at his documents and simply said, "Yes; anything else?" Marcus stood as if in shock. He had expected the officer to say no. He had expected him to say that Marcus was the best soldier in the Legion and that he could not possibly do without him. Marcus, completely deflated, replied, "Thank you, Sir." He then turned around and walked to the door. As he was about to leave the room, Justin Aeolus said, "It is for the best. I heard about the night in the inn. All this talk about the curse! Well, if you stayed, it would have ended badly." Marcus nodded quietly and left the room, hoping he would be called back, but Justin Aeolus said nothing!

Marcus felt lost as he made his way to his room. It was as if he was in a dream. He thought, "What on earth have I done?" He could not contemplate life outside the Legion. When he arrived at his room, Addayya saw the look on his face, and said, "Is everything alright, Master?" Marcus stood looking out of the window and, without looking at Addayya, said, "No". Marcus turned around and left the room. As he left, he heard Addayya shout, "Master! Master! What is wrong?" Marcus made his way along the winding corridor from his room with the sound of Addayya's plea echoing behind him.

Marcus made his way across Jerusalem, through the crowds of people, towards Mary's house. Of all the cities Marcus had visited, he had always found Jerusalem to be one of the noisiest, and the closer one came to the

Temple, the more the noise was greatly amplified. There were always trumpets blowing around the outside of the Temple building, in addition to people shouting and the noise of sheep and cattle who seemed to sense that their journey to the Temple was not good news for them! On this occasion, however, Marcus was completely unaware of any of the noise around him. He was locked entirely in his own thoughts. At one point, he was almost run over by a cart, pulled by two large oxen. The man driving the cart swore at Marcus, but Marcus did not hear him.

When he arrived at Mary's house, he felt naked. Although he still wore his full uniform, he knew that it was for the very last time. Marcus was startled to hear Mary's voice. He could not remember knocking at the door. Mary said, "Are you alright, Marcus?" Marcus gave a forced grin and nodded. Mary said, "You had better come in." Marcus climbed up the stairs to the upper room where he was met by Cephas, who, when he saw Marcus's face, said, "So! You have done it! I am surprised that it took you so long." Marcus sat down next to Cephas and said, "Is it that obvious?" Cephas laughed and said, "Well, by the look on your face, either your favourite horse has died, or you have left the legion. My guess, as you don't have a horse, is you have left the legion." Cephas let out a roaring laugh then slapped

Marcus on the back. Cephas then leaned closer to Marcus and said, "Listen, Marcus, there is life outside the legion."

Marcus had a long talk with Cephas and told him that he had decided to accept John's offer to stay with them. Cephas smiled, which made Marcus nervous. He asked Cephas, "What is the matter?" Cephas answered, "What are you going to do about your slave, Addayya?" Marcus thought for a moment… in truth, he had not even considered him. Marcus answered, "I have no idea. I might give him to one of my friends in the Legion, or I could sell him. I do not think I would get much for him. He is totally useless and I think a hard day's work would probably kill him."

Cephas looked across at Marcus, and said, "Set him free" . Marcus answered, "Are you serious? Set him free?! Why should I do that?" Cephas answered, "I do not want you to think that it is a condition of you coming here, nor of our friendship. I would say, however, that if you were to do this, it would make me extremely happy."

Marcus was quiet. He did not have any particular opinion regarding the use of slaves. Their role and the way that they were used was, to him, all part of the way of life. As a Centurion, he was often allowed to keep a number of prisoners for himself, which he would sell as slaves. He would make a considerable amount of money, selling a whole family without a second thought. Although it was not unusual for Romans to set a slave free, it would only occur, if at all, after years of loyal service. Marcus certainly would not put Addayya in that category.

Marcus remembered when in his childhood, a young Hebrew girl was brought into the house to look after him. He remembered, fondly, their time together. Her name was Hannah. She taught him Hebrew and they became inseparable. It soon became clear that Hannah was not to be harmed in any way, even though Marcus was, approximately, only ten years old. He was, however, strong for his age and also fearless. He was too young to carry a sword. However, he always had a dagger in his belt. No one was in any doubt that he would use it. There was a particular incident in the Market Place when Hannah, inadvertently, stepped in front of a Roman Citizen—Roman slaves always gave way to Romans. The man pushed Hannah to one side and then screamed I will have you flogged. Before he could say another word, Marcus pulled out his dagger and with frightening speed, held it to the man's throat, saying, in a calm but friendly voice, "How would you like me to cut out your windpipe and flog you with it?" The terrified man looked into

Marcus's eyes which looked unblinking and cold, leaving the man no doubt that Marcus meant what he said. Marcus pushed the dagger into the man's skin, drawing blood, at which point Hannah pulled Marcus away, profusely apologising. The man scurried away into the crowd, without saying a word. Marcus shouted after him, "That is right…..Run away you coward." Hannah pulled him back, saying, "Marcus, you cannot do that." She turned to a man pulling a donkey and said, "You see that man with the donkey?" Marcus, looking unsure, nodded. Hannah continued, "It is his donkey, his property. That donkey has more value than me. You need to understand, you cannot protect me like that." They walked home in silence. When they arrived back at the villa, Hannah kissed Marcus on his forehead, saying, "Thank you, my little gladiator." Marcus looked at Cephas's smiling face, and answered, "All right, all right, but I am bringing him here, and do not tell anyone what I have done. I have a reputation to consider."

CHAPTER 8

STEPPING OUT

As Marcus packed his few belongings into his bag, he took one last look around his room. He found it hard to believe that he would never set foot in the barracks again. As he made his way to the door, without thinking, he stopped and turned around. He went over to the corner of his room and picked up the bag which contained the crucifixion equipment.

Marcus had felt that he was fully prepared to leave the Army, and, in fact, he was looking forward to starting his new life. He looked upon it as a great adventure. However, when the actual day arrived, he felt lost and alone, and, more strangely, he felt frightened. He had a real feeling of panic. He was glad that Addayya had accompanied him because that way, he had to put on a show of strength. He would never allow the slave to see him show any sign of weakness.

He remembered the day he had purchased Addayya. On the way back to the barracks from the slave market, Addayya, who was approximately fourteen at the time, wailed and cried the whole way. When they arrived, Marcus explained what was expected of him and Addayya, much to Marcus's relief, finally stopped wailing, but it was, however, replaced by an annoyingly quiet sobbing. Marcus had said to him sharply, "This is the luckiest day of your life, boy. You could have been purchased by a cruel man and sent to work down a copper mine. That really would have given you something to cry about. If you behave yourself, I will hardly beat you at all." At this, Addayya started wailing again. Marcus ignored him and left the room, thinking to himself, "Slaves, slaves. Who could ever understand them?"

Marcus considered himself to be a merciful man, although, in reality, there was very little evidence to support his belief! Up to this particular period of his life, he could recollect having performed only one act of mercy. Even now, he was puzzled and amused at the act, as it was, for him, totally out of character. His legion had been ordered to wipe out a village that they believed was responsible for the killing of a Roman citizen. Whether the village was guilty or not was irrelevant; someone was guilty of killing a Roman citizen, and an example had to be made. As brutal and unfair as this appeared, it always had the desired effect. Rome's concern extended only to its own citizens.

During the destruction of the village, Marcus had broken down the door of a house, only to find a young girl, approximately twelve years old, hiding in a cupboard inside the main room. He raised his sword, then, inexplicably, thought of his own daughter. He spoke to the girl as quietly and as gently as he could. He said to her, "Listen, you must be very, very brave and stay here until it is safe to come out!" The young girl put her arms around Marcus and hugged him tightly. She whispered, "Please, please, do not leave me." Marcus answered, "I will stay outside the door for as long as I can. You must wait until it is dark and then you should be able to slip quietly away from your house and the village." Marcus added, "You will see some terrible things when you get outside of the house, but you must keep moving as quietly as you can and remember, you must be very, very brave." Marcus gently unlocked her arms from around him, and then quietly closed the cupboard door. Looking around the house, he found the bodies of the girl's family outside the back door. Marcus stood in the doorway directing soldiers away, telling them that the house was empty. He stayed there for as long as he could until he was eventually ordered elsewhere.

Marcus had no concept of the profound effect the events of that day would have on his life. He never forgot the girl in the cupboard. Without that memory, he could never have looked Cephas or John in the eye. The girl in the cupboard was his grip on sanity. It was his way of saying, "I am not completely lost. I risked everything for a girl that I did not know."

CHAPTER 9

THE TERROR OF THE TOMB

THE MOST HEART-BREAKING day of his life so far was the day he left the Army. It was much more than a career to him; the Legion was his family, his life. No wife or lover could possibly understand the relationship or even love that soldiers have for one another. They live together, fight together, and die together. When they are ill, they nurse each other. When they receive bad news from home, they comfort each other. Marcus could not count how many times he had risked his life for his brothers-in-arms, nor how many times they had risked their lives for him.

He knew the last few weeks had been hard, but now, as he was leaving, the feeling of emptiness was overwhelming. Marcus walked through the huge gates of the fortress, nodding goodbye to the guards as he left. He carried a bag containing all his worldly possessions. He was out of uniform. For the first time in his life, he felt naked and vulnerable.

Marcus pushed his way through the large crowd milling in the Temple Square. It was always a chaotic place. As he moved through the mass of people, beggars were trying to grab the hem of his garments. There were food stalls selling everything from hot chicken to small roasted mice on long skewers. There were countless animal pens filled with sheep, goats and even bulls. There were stacks of bird cages crammed with doves, sparrows, and canaries, but there was something strange. Marcus could not quite put his finger on it. He heard Addayya say something, but his voice was carried away by the noise of the crowd.

Marcus saw a group of men arguing fiercely over the price of some sheep. None of the men looked at him. Marcus glanced around at the heaving crowd. He realised why he had such a very strange feeling. He was out of uniform. He was now invisible. He was just a man in the crowd. He turned to Addayya and, through gritted teeth, said, "Come this way. Follow me" .

Addayya walked a few paces behind him. He had not told him that he was going to set him free. Probably, the very idea would have utterly terrified him, or he would have thought that it was some kind of a trick. The two men made their way through the city until they arrived at a blacksmith shop. Addayya stood outside whilst

Marcus spoke to the blacksmith. After a moment, the blacksmith called Addayya into the smithy and cut off the slave collar.

Addayya stood perfectly still as the collar was removed, before asking, "Master, Master, what is happening?" Marcus answered, "Oh, just shut up and come with me". They walked to Mary's house and were greeted by a smiling Mary, who gave Addayya a hug, which both startled and terrified Addayya. Nobody hugs a slave! Mary explained to Addayya that he had been freed and was no longer a slave, and was welcome to stay with them. Addayya continued looking at Marcus whilst Mary was talking. When she had finished, Marcus just nodded. Addayya wept. Marcus said, "Oh, for goodness's sake," and went and sat down.

It took a long time for Addayya to adjust to his freedom. He seemed to be in a constant state of terror, always looking at Marcus for some type of assurance. Marcus thought that he looked like a frightened rabbit. Mary would often scold Marcus, telling him that for the first time in his life, Addayya did not have a Master and it was now Marcus's responsibility to help Addayya to adjust to his new life. Marcus did not agree but kept his opinion to himself. He decided that it was easier to do as Mary said and help to support Addayya as he adjusted to his new life. However, Marcus found it very hard to treat Addayya in the same way as any other free man would be treated, but to his surprise, in a very short time, he noticed a change in Addayya. He was starting to look more confident and although Marcus hated to admit it to himself, secretly, he felt pleased, and even a little proud with the change he could see in Addayya.

A lot had happened during the weeks following the execution of the Nazarene. Marcus had met John and Peter a number of times. They got on well together and had become friends. He was relieved when John had invited him to stay with them. The truth was that he had nowhere else to go.

Marcus was gazing through the window, lost in thought, when Mary, who was very perceptive, sat down next to him and asked, "What is the matter?" Marcus had always kept his feelings to himself. He thought that to show any type of emotion was to show weakness. Marcus told her how he missed his family who were in Rome, and that he could never see them again. He would never see his children grow up. He explained that he had a wonderful wife, Lydia, a beautiful daughter called Marcella and a son called Gnaus. Mary asked how long it had been since he had seen them, so he told her that it was over two years since he had last been in Rome.

Marcus did not know how he would have got through those first few weeks at the house without Mary, Cephas and John. He particularly struggled with Addayya no longer being his slave. He would look at him sitting at the table, drinking wine with Mary or Cephas, and he had to fight the urge to go over and kick him. One evening, Cephas asked Marcus if he would mind getting him a cup of wine. Marcus looked stunned, as he realised that in the whole of his life, he had not once served anyone. He looked at Cephas, and Cephas smiled. He looked around the room where there were approximately twenty people sitting, deep in conversations, all totally oblivious to Cephas's request. After a short pause, Marcus slowly stood up and went over to the table, where he poured out a glass of wine and took it to Cephas. He then sat down at the table. Cephas said, "Thank you." Marcus nodded his head in acknowledgement. Cephas continued, "My brother, I think that Addayya would also like a cup of wine."

Marcus saw that Addayya was about to say something, but Cephas held up his hand and Addayya remained silent. Marcus leaned across and whispered in Cephas's ear, "But he is just a slave… and an Egyptian." Cephas responded, "But, my friend, did you not set him free?" Marcus said, "Yes, but…" Cephas continued,

"And, as for being an Egyptian, what are you?" Marcus responded, "Roman, of course." Cephas continued, "And what makes you Roman?" Marcus, who was by now totally bewildered, answered, "I was born there, of course" . Cephas continued, "What if you had been born in a tent on the banks of the Nile; would you be a different man, an inferior man?" Marcus sat silent and speechless for a few moments. He was aware that Cephas's eyes were fixed on him. He stood up, walked across the room, poured out a cup of wine and took it across to Addayya. As he sat down again next to Cephas, he turned to Cephas and said, "Are you happy now?" Cephas responded, "It is not about me, Marcus, it is about you, and how you feel. Are you happy now?" Marcus looked at a smiling Addayya and realised that he felt good. He nodded and said to Cephas, "You know what, Cephas? Yes, yes, I do feel good."

After a short time, everyone moved across into the other room, leaving him alone with Mary. He was aware that Peter and John were now more and more in demand. What had once been a small group of individuals had grown larger and larger and was now numbered in the thousands. They were given the derogatory name "Christ fanatics", or "Christ-ians". Marcus had expressed concerns to Mary that it could only end very badly.

Later that evening, when Cephas and John returned, they spoke of a very dangerous and unpleasant man called Saul, who was, apparently, trying to have them arrested. Marcus listened intently and then realised that he knew the man they were talking about. He knew him to be a very unpleasant man. Marcus, seizing the opportunity to repay his friends for their kindness, said, "I know this man. Do not worry. I will deal with him, and he will not trouble you any longer." Marcus looked around at the shocked faces of all those in the room. He continued, "I will throw his body into the rubbish dump just outside of the city. I can guarantee he will never be found, and it will never be traced back to you." Marcus looked across at John who had an enormous grin on his face. John said to Marcus, "I think you and I should sit down and discuss this matter." The two men moved across to a table at the other side of the room. John then explained to Marcus about the concept of a whole new way of life, which, to Marcus, sounded like the most fool-hardy thing he had ever heard. Marcus was quiet for a moment, studying John's face to see if he was serious, and then said, "Do I understand you correctly? You would rather die than let me take care of this despicable man?" John answered, "My friend died for me." Marcus said, "I do not think that I will ever understand you people, but if you want this Saul to live, then so be it. I am telling you, though, you will regret it."

Much to Marcus's surprise, he was actually enjoying life at Mary's house, until one particular day, when his whole new life came crashing down. He heard a banging at the door. It was a Roman patrol. Marcus saw the fear in Addayya's face. He said to Addayya, "Hide. I will go down and see what they want ." As Marcus got halfway down the stairs, the soldiers came bursting through the door. One of them shouted, "There he is—grab him" . Marcus protested, "What do you think I have done?" The Roman Commander leaned forward, spat into Marcus's face, and said, "What have you done? What have you done? You have put a curse on the Legion. Twenty men were killed today by the rebel that you let slip through your hands." The. Soldiers put Marcus in chains and dragged him outside, where they placed a chain around his neck and pulled him—in the same way they would have dragged a dog—all the way to the Roman fort. Marcus continuously fell to his knees, but the soldiers, using the heavy chain, dragged and forced him to his feet. All the way back to the barracks, the soldiers were shouting about a patrol being massacred outside the city, blaming him, and shouting that he had cursed them.

When they arrived at the Fort, they threw him into the dungeon. He pleaded with them to allow him to speak to the Fort Commander. The soldier who had previously spat on him said, "Speaking to the Commander will do you no good. It was him who ordered your arrest." As they left the cell, Marcus shouted after them, "Why do you think that I caused the curse?" The reply chilled Marcus to the bone—"The dogs… what you did to those dogs. It just wasn't natural."

Marcus spent three days locked in the cold, damp, and miserable cell. Twice a day, the little hatch at the bottom of the door opened and some food would be passed through. As bad as things were, Marcus could not help but laugh when he saw what they were actually giving him to eat. Cold, stale bread. Each time the food was delivered, Marcus would plead to be allowed to see the Commander. Each time, his pleas were met with silence. It was late in the afternoon on the third day when the cell door eventually opened. Marcus hoped that he was going to be released, but his hopes were dashed when he saw that one of the soldiers was carrying heavy chains. As they locked the chains around his hands and feet, Marcus begged them to tell him what they were going to do to him and where they were going to take him. His request was met with silence.

They took him out of the fort. For several dreadful moments, Marcus thought that they were going to crucify him, but when they came to the place of execution, they carried on walking.

Marcus was mystified as to where they were going. He knew this area well. He thought and really hoped that they were, after all, going to set him free. He was puzzled. He knew that there was nothing here in this area except for some old Jewish tombs. Marcus suddenly had a very bad feeling. He could feel the panic building up inside him. He turned to the soldier nearest to him and asked, "Why are we going towards the tombs?" The silence continued. Marcus screamed, "Why are we going to the dammed tombs?" Again, silence! Marcus tried to turn and run, but in his panic, he forgot the chains that bound him to his Guards and they merely pulled him back. He shouted, "You cannot lock me in a tomb. I will be there forever." Again, his pleading was met with silence.

Marcus then did something he could not remember ever doing in his life. He wept, and then begged and pleaded with the Legionnaires. One of the Legionnaires then leaned across and whispered to Marcus, "You are supposed to be a war hero. Die with dignity!"

Despite the terror within him, and the horror that he could not possibly describe and which no one would be able to understand, he knew that the soldier was right. Marcus did not want to be remembered like this. He wanted to be remembered as Marcus, the hero and fearless Centurion. Marcus stood straight and walked onwards towards the place of the tombs.

It took over twenty minutes for Marcus and the troop of guards to make their way up a small track on the side of the hill. Standing outside the entrance to one of the tombs were more soldiers and other individuals who were there, seemingly, waiting to seal the tomb. Marcus had to put all his strength into keeping himself from shaking.

As he drew closer to the tombs, he was relieved to see that the man in charge of sealing the tomb was his friend, Septimus. Marcus turned to where his friend was standing and said, "You know me. You know that I am innocent." Septimus answered, "I am sorry, Marcus, but you know that it does not matter what I think." The guards led Marcus into the tomb. As they were about to leave, Septimus said, "No, wait, you can take off the chains. He is not going to be able to get out of here."

As they were taking off the chains, Marcus looked around the tomb and saw there were dozens of small stone boxes. He was aware of the Jewish tradition which entailed returning to the tomb several years after the entombment of a loved one and placing the bones in a stone box. Marcus looked around to see if any of the corpses were old, and that maybe, in a short time, someone would come to place the bones in a stone box. He was dismayed to see this was obviously an abandoned tomb, which had not been used for a long time. He felt the full horror of the realisation that he could be in there forever.

As the guards left the tomb, he was alone with Septimus. Marcus said, "Septimus, please listen to me." Septimus looked nervously at the guards waiting at the entrance of the tomb, and said, "Marcus, you know that I cannot help you." Septimus signalled to one of the guards who came in with a small lamp and some oil. Septimus, handing the items to Marcus, said, "There is probably enough oil here to last a couple of days, and I have left you some water. I would advise you, however, not to drink it. You will die quicker without water. If I were you, and before the oil runs out, I would advise you to bang your head against the wall; end it quickly." Marcus replied, "Septimus, please, please, listen to me. Just for one minute." Marcus whispered to ensure that the guards could not hear what he was saying. "Septimus, you know that I cannot curse anyone, but I am, myself, cursed. Part of the curse is that I cannot die. I will be alive forever."

Septimus started to move away, saying, "Goodbye, Marcus." Marcus said, "No, please wait. Do you know why I stopped drinking with you? It is because of the curse. I cannot drink anything other than water. I started to eat on my own, purely and simply because I find all food now tastes so dreadful and appalling. Also, why did those dogs run away from me?" Marcus continued to plead with his friend; "Please, Septimus, you have to believe me." Septimus replied, "I am sorry, Marcus. Please take my advice and smash your head on the wall. Do not wait for the light to go out or you might fall in the dark. The very last thing you want is a broken leg." As his friend left the cell, Marcus fell to his knees and watched as the men sealed the tomb. He was left with only the dim shadow cast by the lamp.

Marcus started to walk around the tomb, saying to himself, "Keep control, keep control." He repeated it over and over again as he walked around the tomb. The more he repeated it, the more he felt the panic growing within him, and the louder he shouted, "Keep control." Marcus stopped suddenly. He had an idea. He went over to the stone boxes, lifted one up and dropped it. Marcus stood back as the contents of the box tumbled out onto the floor. He had to kneel down for a moment as the panic within him was making him breathe so hard that he was beginning to feel faint. Marcus started to take long slow breaths whilst repeating, "Keep calm… Keep calm…"

Marcus lay down on his back and said to himself, "No one is coming. I am going to have to do it myself." He leaned across to look at the contents of the box, which were now spread out across the floor. He shuffled through the bones without any thought about whose body they had come from. Whether they were from a man or a woman, it made no difference to him. After a short period of time, he found exactly what he was hoping to find. He was reasonably sure that he had found a leg bone, but it did not matter what it was; all that mattered was that it was strong enough to be fashioned into a tool.

Marcus did a quick search of the tomb. He soon found what he was looking for—a rather heavy rock that had a flat surface. Marcus said to himself, "This will do nicely." Marcus felt better now that he had a project. Although the fear still remained, always lurking at the back of his mind, he was determined not to let it overwhelm him. He again repeated to himself, "No one is going to help you" . Marcus took the stone, smashed the leg bone and thought to himself, "I have done that a few times in my life." He then shaped the bone into a chisel. When he had finished his work, he examined it, and said, "Not bad, not bad at all."

Marcus took hold of the flickering lamp and placed it near the sealed entrance to the tomb. He put his ear against the rocks, wondering if they had placed a guard outside. Marcus listened, but there was merely silence.

He knew that there could be a number of reasons for not hearing anything. The rocks might be too thick for noise to penetrate, or the Guards may be placed away from the tomb. The absence of noise did not actually tell Marcus anything. Marcus took hold of his precious stone and started tapping it against the stones. He knew that if there were guards at the other side of the stone entrance, then they would definitely tap back in response. From experience, he considered guard duty to be probably the most mind-destroying, boring job in the world. No guard would be able to resist tapping back. There was silence; beautiful silence. The last thing that he needed was to remove a stone and find a Roman soldier staring at him.

Marcus took his bone chisel and started to scrape away the mortar from between the large stones. He was dismayed at how hard the mortar had set. He seemed to be scraping for hours and yet he had hardly made any impression on the stone wall. Looking at his flickering lamp, he knew that it was unlikely he could get through the wall before he ran out of oil. He could not imagine how he would be able to continue working in the dark. The mortar was so hard that often, his bone chisel would break, which would delay him, whilst he smashed open another box to obtain more bones. He continued working until he was completely exhausted. Marcus extinguished the lamp to save oil while he slept, ensuring that he kept his flint handy, and could find it in the dark.

Marcus was again filled with terror when the tomb was plunged into darkness. He was grateful that he was so tired and hoped that in sleep, he could find refuge from the dark. He curled up in the foetal position, repeating over and over again, "It is only the dark. There is nothing of which I need to be afraid." Marcus fell asleep, but it was not the sleep that he had hoped for as he constantly woke up throughout the night. Even though the tomb was cold, when he awoke and opened his eyes, he was covered in sweat and all he saw was darkness. When he awoke, he assumed it was the morning! In truth, he had no idea how long he had slept nor whether it was still the middle of the night or early in the day. Marcus groped around for the flint that Septimus had left for him and lit his lamp. The lamp flickered into life, casting eerie shadows which only served to remind him of the nightmare that was now his life.

Marcus made his way to the entrance of the tomb and started scraping at the mortar with his bone chisel. He was pleased with his progress, and was actually allowing himself to become quite hopeful, when disaster struck! His lamp started flickering and he realised it was running out of oil. In his hurry to refill the lamp in the fading light, he knocked over the bottle that contained the oil. Marcus screamed, "No… noooo!" as he tried to grab the bottle, but he was unable to save his precious oil. Marcus sat, in shock, staring at the empty bottle. The light flickered for a few moments before he was plunged into darkness, a darkness without light, and, far worse, a darkness without hope. Then the demons came!

Marcus crawled on his hands and knees. He remembered what Septimus had said, that he must be careful and not fall and injure himself. He propped himself up against the wall of the tomb. He had always wondered about the girl that his father had imprisoned in the tomb in Rome all those years ago, and how she had felt when she finally gave up all hope of being rescued. Well, now he knew! He felt numb and empty. In the dark, he saw nothing, he heard nothing and he felt nothing. Then he heard a sound… a voice. He thought to himself, "…and now comes madness."

He was convinced he was hallucinating. He knew that he should just ignore the voice, but somehow, he felt compelled to listen. Initially, the voice was very quiet, but gradually, it became clearer. He realised someone or something was calling his name—"Cen…. tur…ion, Cen…. tur….ion." Marcus could feel a cold chill run down his spine. Marcus shouted, "You are not here! You are just an hallucination—a figment of my imagination." The voice responded, "Oh! I am very much here. Very much indeed!" Marcus could hear the voice moving nearer and becoming even louder. "Cen… tur…ion." Marcus shouted, "WHO ARE YOU? And what do you want?" The voice replied, "Oh, but you know who I am. Look around and what do you see?" Marcus whispered, "Nothing, just darkness." The voice said, "Well, there you have it. That is who I am: Darkness; the Prince of Darkness! I could have called myself 'King', but it would have been a little pretentious, do you not think? Humility; that is my weakness!" Marcus heard the voice give out a loud sigh, and then it continued, "Oh well! We all have to live with our weaknesses, do you not think? As for what I want, I want the tools." Marcus shouted, "Are you mad? I have not got any tools. Just these dead men's bones. If you want them, then just take them."

The voice responded, "Mad! No... I am not mad, but you? Ah, but you, very, very soon, will be mad. I could have waited a hundred years and then come by to visit you. Tell me, do you think anything other than madness awaits you? I have admired your optimism, and your ingenuity, making a chisel out of those bones. Who knows? You may have chiselled your way out of here." There was a pause; Marcus thought that the voice had gone. Then the voice returned and said, "I feel the need to apologise. After all, if we are going to be friends... I am sorry I accidentally knocked over your bottle of oil. So, now we have got that out of the way, let us get down to business. The tools I am talking about are the tools that you used to crucify the Nazarene. Well, this is how it works! I get you out of here, you get the tools, and give them to me. Simple. Everyone is happy."

As Marcus was considering the offer, since he had little choice, suddenly there was a loud booming voice. It was like the roar of a thousand lions. He felt his hair move as if blown by a strong wind, then he put his hands over his ears to protect himself from the deafening sound echoing across the cave—"GET OUT!" The whole tomb was suddenly filled with a brilliant light. Marcus quickly covered his eyes with his hands, and, as he started to get accustomed to the light, he gingerly moved them away. To his astonishment, he realised that this was no ordinary light. The light did not seem to have a single source; instead, it seemed to flow from everywhere. There were no shadows! There was a large slab in the tomb which was used for laying out the bodies and Marcus noticed that even under the slab, which would normally be in shadow, the light shone brilliantly. The cracks in the walls of the tombs were illuminated, and the rocks and stones on the floor were lit on all sides. Nothing was hidden from the light. Marcus gazed into the light in the direction of the voice, and, to his amazement, he could just make out a face. It was the face of a young girl. Marcus stood startled and speechless. Then he heard a beautifully soothing voice which seemed to come from all around him; from behind him, in front of him, to his left, and to his right, but, strangely, it came from inside his head. The voice said, "Marcus, you must never give that Thing those tools. They are for you to guard. You, you alone are the Guardian of the Artefacts" . Marcus answered, "But he said he could get me out of here." The voice said, "Be patient; you will not be here for long." Then the light was gone and Marcus was once again plunged into darkness. He was now totally convinced that he was going mad.

CHAPTER 10

SEPTIMUS

SEPTIMUS HAD WAITED outside the tomb for Marcus to arrive with his guards. He had been given the task of the entombment of his friend. He had requested that he be excused, but it had been refused. Now, as he stood waiting, he was glad that it was him. Marcus deserved to be with a friend at the end. Other than himself, there was little chance of that happening as the mood in the barracks towards Marcus was one of hatred. Septimus had, initially, tried to defend his friend, but was threatened and told to keep his mouth shut. The story of the dogs had been exaggerated to ridiculous levels. At first, there were four dogs, then six, then ten. He had even heard that the dogs' eyes glowed, that they were dogs from hell with enormous fangs and Marcus was their master.

Septimus oversaw the removal of the bodies of the so-called demon dogs and pointed out that there were definitely only four dogs and they had normal teeth! However, he knew the truth could never compete with a lie that people wanted to believe, and demon dogs made for a much more interesting story.

Septimus privately wished that Marcus had not sent those men into that house without heavy armour. A lot of good men died that day. However, the soldiers would soon tire of that story and turn their attention to something else, as soldiers do. That would have been the end of it, except for the massacre of the Roman column just outside the city. Even then, Marcus would have been safe had it not been that the Leader of the Rebels was none other than the man who escaped from Marcus. This time, there was no forgiveness. A search was mounted throughout the city, and to make matters worse, he was found in the company of Christians.

Septimus waited outside the tomb with a small group of soldiers. He watched as Marcus and the Guard to whom he was chained made their way along the narrow winding path that led up the hill. He found it hard to watch whenever Marcus fell to his knees and was roughly pulled up to his feet by the chains around his neck. When Marcus arrived at the tomb, Septimus could see in his face a glimmer of hope when he saw him. It was heart-breaking for Septimus to have to tell his old friend that he could not help him. Marcus tried to put on a brave face and said that he fully understood.

Septimus led Marcus into the tomb. He looked around. It was cold and dark, even before they sealed the entrance. Septimus thought to himself, "By the Gods, this is an awful place to meet your end." Septimus had been ordered to remain outside the tomb until it went dark. He watched in silence as the stone masons went to work. Then, when they had completely sealed the tomb, they started mixing some more mortar. Septimus said, "What are you doing? The tomb is sealed. Why are you mixing more mortar?" The stone mason said, "That is what we were told to do. They said that the poor man in there was very resourceful and so we were to double-seal the tomb."

Septimus was a few years younger than Marcus. He remembered when he first joined the Legion. They were in Gaul at the time. He was only seventeen but looked much younger. He sat around a campfire with a group of Legionnaires, Marcus being one of the group. Septimus had heard of Marcus and was excited to meet him. The Legionnaires started to mock Septimus because of his youth. A rather scary-looking Legionnaire said, "Oh! What do we have here? Does your mother know where you are?" which caused everyone to laugh. Septimus felt humiliated, and foolishly said, "I may look like a boy, but I am more of a man than you." The scary-looking man stood up, his face like thunder. He was about six foot four and looked as strong as an ox. Septimus felt sweat running down his spine, but he knew that he had to show absolutely no fear.

The Legionnaire continued, "On your feet, boy. Let's see how much of a man you are." He unsheathed his sword. Septimus nervously got to his feet. Marcus said, "That's enough, children. We have a battle to fight in the morning, so let us have an early night." The man said, "But Marcus, I can't let a boy insult me like that." Marcus answered, "Sheath your sword and sit down, or I will stand and unsheathe mine and we will see who is left standing." Septimus looked at Marcus, who was calm and looked unconcerned, but he could see fear in the face of the big man.

Marcus continued, "Tomorrow, when we do battle…" Marcus turned to Septimus and said, "What is your name, soldier?" Septimus looked at the group sitting around the fire and said, "Septimus; my name is Septimus." Marcus said, "It is good to see you, Septimus. Let me introduce you to the big ugly beast," which caused everyone to roar with laughter. Marcus continued, "Septimus, meet Cassius. Tomorrow, you will fight together and perhaps you will learn that Legionnaires fight for each other and not against each other." Marcus then turned back to Septimus and said, "Tonight, as you sit here, you are a boy, and Cassius has every right to say so, but tomorrow, after the battle, if you survive, then and only then can you call yourself a man. Now, all of you, get some sleep."

Septimus never forgot that day, the day when Marcus saved his life. It was not the only time that Marcus had saved him, and he knew that it was not only him that Marcus had saved! He swore that Marcus had virtually won a few battles on his own. He had never seen such a Warrior. Innumerable times, soldiers would say, "By the Gods, I am glad you are on our side." Now, Septimus was walking down the path in the night, after leaving his friend alone in the tomb. Septimus made himself a promise that tonight, he would drink and drink and get more drunk than he had ever done in his life. Somehow, he had to get the image of Marcus, alone in that dark tomb, out of his head.

During the first hour in the inn, Septimus and Cassius said nothing. Their thoughts were on their friend. Cassius was the first to speak. "I pray that he has killed himself by now. There is no point in prolonging the agonising wait for death in a pitch-dark tomb." Septimus looked around the room. He noticed the servant girl. It was the same girl who had sat on Marcus's knees, and whom Marcus had, uncharacteristically, pushed away.

Septimus turned to Cassius and said, "Do you remember the last time we were here with Marcus?" Cassius said, "It is no good torturing yourself. You need to try to forget Marcus." Septimus said, "No, no. I was looking at that servant girl over there. Do you remember how Marcus pushed her away?" Cassius said, "Yes, but I don't understand. What is your point?" Septimus said, "Do you not remember how strange Marcus's behaviour was on that night? And that was not the end of it. He never came in here again. In fact, we have hardly spoken since that night. He had changed."

Cassius said, "Well, you know Marcus. We never really knew what was going on in his head." Septimus looked around, moved closer to Cassius, and whispered, "When I was in the tomb with Marcus, he told me things. Strange things." Cassius said, "He told you what? Where?" Septimus answered, "In the tomb. In the tomb. Marcus said that he did not curse the Legion, but he himself was cursed." Cassius said, "Have you gone mad? What are you talking about?" Septimus said, "I know it is hard to believe, but the one thing I am really sure about is that Marcus himself believed it."

The two friends sat silently for a moment, drinking their wine. Septimus was the first to speak. "Marcus said he was cursed, and that he could not enjoy life. He could not taste any food and he could only drink water. But... and here is the strange part... he cannot die, which means he will be in that tomb, maybe forever." Cassius leaned back, took a long look at his friend, and said, "Surely, you cannot believe that?" Septimus answered, "It was not what he said, but it was the way in which he said it. He was pleading with me to help him. I mean, he was begging. He was actually begging! You know Marcus. Have you ever met a braver man? Does that sound like Marcus? He is a man who would look death in the face and spit in its eye." Cassius said, "Suppose what you say is true, and I am not saying for one moment that I believe it; what can we do about it? We certainly cannot go down there and rescue him. They would crucify us and maybe even our families." Septimus said, "I have got an idea. Marcus has got friends outside the Legion. We could tell them where he is entombed, and they could rescue him." Cassius answered, "Leave it a week. If he is telling the truth, he will still be alive. We owe Marcus that. If he is dead, we will offer a sacrifice to the Gods for him, then return here and drink to remember our friend."

Septimus offered to go to see Marcus's friends because Cassius looked too intimidating, and agreed that they would wait one week before they made their move. Both raised their cups of wine and drank to Marcus. Septimus said, "May the Gods be with Marcus in that hellhole of a tomb."

The two friends hardly spoke to each other during that painfully long week. They would eat their meals together in total silence, each lost in their own thoughts, and each trying to block out the vision of Marcus alone in the darkness.

When the day finally arrived, Cassius went to see Septimus to wish him luck. He was surprised to see him dressed almost like a beggar. Septimus explained, "The people I will meet are strange people. They are more likely to listen to a beggar than to a King." Septimus shrugged his shoulders and said, "Who can understand these Christians?"

Septimus made his way through the streets of Jerusalem with a sense of relief. He knew he would no longer have to think about his friend in that terrible tomb. He would either be dead or he would be free. Septimus had lost friends before. This was the way it was in the Legion. Soldiers died. You grieved for them, and then drank to their memory. Then you just carried on. He knew that although soldiers died, the fate that had befallen Marcus had affected him and Cassius to such a degree that for the whole week, they had hardly thought about anything else.

Lost in his own thoughts and quicker than he expected, Septimus, found himself outside the house where Marcus had been arrested. He knocked heavily on the door then waited impatiently for a few minutes. He was about to knock again when a young woman answered the door. He later found out that it was Mary Magdalene. She looked at Septimus, then looked up and down the street, and said, "You are a friend of Marcus?" Septimus answered, "How do you know that?" Mary answered, "Only a Roman would wear such a ridiculous disguise." Mary then turned and walked up the stairs, followed by Septimus, feeling rather foolish.

As they reached the upper room, they were met by two men. Mary explained to them who he was. One of the young men, who introduced himself as John, asked, "Do you know what has happened to our friend?" Septimus answered, "That is what I have come to talk to you about." John gestured to Septimus to sit down.

When Septimus was seated, he said, "I want you to realise that it is very dangerous for me to come here. Some would say it is almost treason, but I think I owe it to my friend, who has saved my life on more occasions than I can count." John answered, "Your secret is safe with us." Septimus continued, "They took Marcus up into the hills to the place where you people have dug tombs in the hillside." John said, "Yes, I know the place that you are talking about." Septimus continued, "Well, they put him into one of those tombs and sealed it. I was there at the time, but before I left him, he told me that he could not die, and he would be alone in the darkness forever."

Septimus searched the faces of Marcus's friends to see their reaction. Then he shouted, "By all the Gods, it is true! I can tell by the look on your faces. How is this possible?" John did not answer, but simply asked, "Which tomb?" Septimus, still in a state of shock, did not answer. John repeated, "Which tomb?" Septimus replied, "Marcus has been in that tomb, without light, or food or water, for a week." John replied, "We can get him out tonight as soon as it gets dark, but we need to know which tomb." Septimus answered, "It is at the very top of the hill. I remember that there was a big olive tree just outside the tomb. You cannot miss it. It is easy to spot. You can see that the tomb has been freshly sealed." John stood up, put his hand on Septimus's shoulder and said, "Well, young man, you have done your part. We can take it from here. You have served your friend well. You should go now." Septimus got up from the table and simply nodded to John. The truth was that there were simply no words he could say. He turned around and made his way back to the barracks.

It was early evening when John, Cephas and a small group of friends made their way silently along the small winding track up the hill. Inside the tomb, Marcus sat with his back against the wall. Unsurprisingly, he had completely lost all track of time. He was not sure if he had been in the tomb for a day, a week, or a month. He also was not sure if he had gone mad.

He would listen, straining his ears for the voices. He would shout "Speak to me", but his pleading was only met with silence. Marcus would think of his wife and have long conversations with her. He would remember battles and previous glories and he shouted out orders to imaginary soldiers. Then, in the silent darkness, he would whisper, "You said you would come. You said you would come." He knew, of course, that the voice, and the promise of salvation, was a mere illusion, a figment of his imagination, and the first sign of the inevitable madness that was certain to come.

It was then he heard a noise; a loud banging noise. He assumed the voices had returned and shouted, "Oh, you are back, are you? Well, you are wasting your time. You are not having them." It was then that a memory came back to him. Marcus said, "Wait a minute. Wait one damned minute. It *is* you. It is that little worm from the crucifixion. You tried to buy the tools of execution, and you ran away from a little girl." Marcus roared with laughter and continued, "And... you ran away again. Here, in the tomb." As the banging on the sealed tomb increased, Marcus started singing, "You ran away...You ran away from a tiny little girl." He laughed out loud and sang again. "You ran away, you ran away from a little girl." It was then he heard Cephas's voice. Cephas said, "Hello, my friend." Marcus pointed into the darkness and said, "He ran away," then he whispered, "He ran away from a little girl!"

Marcus turned around. He could just see a small light and a group of men making their way into the tomb. Marcus shouted, "Oh good! You have brought some friends. Come in...Come in... Sit down! Let us have a little chat." Then he heard Mary's voice, saying, "Marcus, Marcus, it is all over. We really are here! It is not your imagination. Come... Come... Let us get you home." Marcus could feel hands gently lifting him to his feet. Marcus then shouted into the dark corner of the tomb, "Thank you, little girl. I knew you would come."

John and Peter each put an arm around Marcus and helped him walk towards the entrance to the tomb. As he left his prison, he noticed a small group of men who were obviously there to reseal the tomb. All Marcus could manage was a weak smile and a nod to say thank you.

It seemed to take forever to get down the hill and into the city. When they arrived at a small house at the edge of the city, Cephas apologised and said, "It would be much too dangerous to take you back to Mary's house. Stay here for the night and I will come back tomorrow morning." Marcus could feel a panic starting to build up deep inside him. He said, "Do not leave me here on my own, please, please, and let me keep the lamp lit." Cephas answered, "Do not worry. We are going to leave some men here, and Mary is going to sleep on that cot over there in the corner."

Marcus fell asleep from sheer exhaustion, but it was not a good sleep, Mary wept as Marcus talked, shouted, and screamed in his sleep. Throughout the rest of his life, Marcus never lost his fear of the dark.

Early next morning, Cephas arrived and said to Marcus, "Come with me. Come quickly." Marcus followed Cephas out of the door to be met with the sight of a large cart pulled by two huge horses. On the cart sat a man, a woman and four children. Marcus looked down the street and saw four more carts. Cephas explained, "You are going to Philippi. It is safer for you if you travel together with these people. They are good people and will look after you."

Cephas pulled back a large sheet on the rear of the cart and put two bags in the back. He then instructed Marcus to quickly get into the cart and under the sheet. Marcus looked into the dark space under the sheet, stepped back, shook his head and said, "I am sorry. I appreciate all that you have done for me, but I am not getting under there." Mary came to his rescue. She said, "Here, put this on," holding up a large cloak. "Keep the hood up over your face. No one is looking for you. They think you are dead." Mary was right. They passed through the gates of Jerusalem without incident and were soon on the open road to Philippi.

CHAPTER 11

PHILIPPI

FOR THE FIRST two weeks of the journey, Marcus stayed close to the young men who were travelling with him. It was almost as if he was afraid to be alone, which, of course, was the case. Before he went to sleep, he would build up the fire and then sleep as close to the fire as possible. Fortunately, Cephas had told the group of Marcus's experience in the tomb, because he knew it would take time for Marcus to get over his ordeal. In truth, there was a part of Marcus which would never recover.

Marcus had always considered himself to be a brave man, but now, he was afraid of becoming the type of man that he had always looked down upon and treated with contempt. Each night, as the sun was setting, he started to sweat and tremble. He was torn; on the one hand, he didn't want to be alone, and on the other, he didn't want anyone to see him like this. No matter how hard he tried to control himself, as it became darker, his body began to shake, and as he tried to sleep, the night terrors would always visit him. He had left the tomb but it would be a long time before the tomb left him.

Marcus arrived at Philippi in the spring of AD34. He found lodgings in a small but comfortable inn on the outskirts of the city. The innkeeper was a jovial man, who also respected people's privacy, which suited Marcus well as he was finding it difficult to adapt to his new life. Normally, he would love to talk about his life in the Legion, but he now realised that even though he was assumed dead, it was wise to keep himself to himself. He always wore a small scarf around his neck to cover his scar. The scar, which had once been a mark of pride, could now betray him. He knew that if he was discovered, this time, there would be no Septimus to come to his rescue.

Marcus had a problem; a serious problem. Since his experience in the tomb, he found it difficult to be alone, and yet he had a fear of talking to people, lest he should inadvertently say something that would reveal who he was, his true identity. He was fortunate in choosing this particular inn for his lodgings, as the innkeeper just loved to talk to his customers! Marcus spent hours in his company, sitting at the bar, drinking his water. When the innkeeper said, "Why is it that you only drink water?" Marcus answered, "I have a bad stomach. If I drink anything other than water, it makes me ill." The innkeeper answered, "By the Gods! That's terrible. You have my sympathy." The innkeeper paused for a moment, then said, "Wait a minute. I know someone who may be able to help you." Marcus said, "No, no, you don't need to go to any trouble." The innkeeper said, "It is no problem. I know a man who comes in here with his friend at least once a week. His wife is amazing with herbs. Once, I had a terrible headache and she made a potion from the bark of a tree. Within an hour, it was completely gone." Even though Marcus knew that there was no cure for a curse, he felt he had no choice but to agree to the innkeeper's suggestion.

A few evenings later, the innkeeper introduced him to Cato and Domitian and explained to them Marcus's stomach problem, which made Marcus feel very uncomfortable. Cato told Marcus to sit down and said that his wife, who was excellent with potions, would be pleased to help him.

Marcus was normally suspicious of strangers, but, unusually for him, he liked Cato and Domitian immediately. They sat together, then Cato, pointing to Domitian, said, "What do you think of this clown?" Domitian said, "Oh by the Gods, give it a rest." This started Cato roaring with laughter, which was infectious. Marcus started to laugh and said, "Why, what has he done?"

Cato said, "Well, we went to watch the gladiators fight at the circus and Domitian said he didn't think that the bull looked that tough." Marcus looked shocked and said, "What, the Bull—the most famous gladiator outside of Rome?" Cato, still roaring with laugher, said, "Yes, yes; now tell him what you did!" Domitian held up his hands and said, "All right, all right, I surrender. I bet a lot of money against the Bull, and my wife will kill me." Marcus said, "How much did you bet?" Domitian took a large drink from his cup, said, "A lot!" then burst out laughing. They talked until late into the evening. His new friends told him that they were looking for a partner, as they planned to buy some land and run a farm. They saw that Marcus looked a little doubtful. When they asked what was troubling him, he told them that he had no experience of any kind in farming, which caused the two men to burst out laughing. Cato said, "How much experience do you need to muck out a stable?" Marcus laughed. The three men decided to meet the next day to discuss and plan what they would do next. It was early next morning when Cato came to see him. Cato said, "I have just come to give you that potion." Marcus thanked him.

Marcus saw a lot of Cato and Domitian and would quite often be invited to their homes. Cato's wife, Octavia, asked him if his stomach was any better. Marcus answered, "Yes, thank you. That potion worked fine." Octavia said, "But you are still drinking only water." Marcus was glad he already had his answer prepared. He said, "Actually, I would rather drink water, but, as I have said, my stomach is great now, thank you." Marcus saw Octavia give Cato a quizzical look, but he was thankful that the subject was not mentioned again.

After a few weeks, Cato and Domitian came to see Marcus at the inn and told him that they had found the perfect plot of land. They were so excited that they insisted they should ride out immediately to view it. They rode for approximately thirty minutes before they came to a river. Cato and Domitian dismounted and said to Marcus, "What do you think?" Before Marcus could reply, Cato said, "From the river here and as far as you can see, and then over the hill beyond to where the farmhouse is situated. All this land could be ours." Domitian pointed to a wood that they could see in the distance. He said, "That would be a perfect place for you to build a house for yourself." Cato said, "We have already met with a builder, who is coming to meet you at the inn tonight." Marcus dismounted, slapping the two men on their backs and shouting, "Yes...Yes... Great... Brilliant."

As Marcus did not have any idea at all about the value of land, nor how to run a business, he left it entirely to Cato and Domitian to negotiate the purchase of the land and it turned out to be an excellent decision! They managed to purchase the land at a far cheaper price than he would have thought possible, and, within a short time, they were the proud owners of their own farm. Marcus would ride out each day to check on the progress of the farmhouse he was having built. He was excited at the prospect of moving in. Each day, the builders would tell him that they could not go any faster! Marcus would apologise and say he was not trying to rush them. He just wanted to see his new house!

Marcus enjoyed working on the farm with his two friends. Cato and Domitian were both married to wonderful women, who were an enormous help in the business. Marcus and his partners were able to purchase a large herd of cattle. Each morning, the two wives would milk the cows and sell the milk throughout Philippi and the neighbouring villages. They were also very good at making cheese. Marcus remembered Cato coming to him one evening as he was finishing putting up additional fencing. He had worked hard all day and was proud of the miles of fencing he had erected over the last few weeks. Cato had a huge grin on his face. Marcus smiled and asked him why he was grinning. Cato answered, "I have a great treat for you, brother." He then produced a large piece of cheese and announced, "This will make us a fortune!"

It transpired that his wife, Octavia, was excellent at making cheese. Unfortunately, Cato insisted that Marcus should taste the cheese immediately. Marcus tried to put Cato off by telling him he was not hungry, but that he would take it home and eat it later. However, Cato looked so disappointed that Marcus did not have the heart to refuse to taste it. He broke off a large piece and put it into his mouth. He chewed on the cheese; "Hmm... that is lovely. The best cheese that I have ever tasted," he said, trying desperately to look as though he was enjoying it, whilst at the same time, trying to hold back from spitting it out of his mouth. When he had swallowed the cheese, he said, "You are correct, Cato, that cheese will be extremely popular." Cato, to Marcus's dismay, then handed him the rest of the cheese! Marcus tried his very best to look delighted with the gift! He smiled, took the cheese from Cato and ate it. Cato, looking very pleased with himself, mounted his horse and said, "Mark my words, soon, we will be very rich." He rode away laughing. Marcus felt sick.

Octavia, Cato's wife was a lovely woman, but she could not understand why Marcus was not married. She frequently invited him to dinner. He very soon established that she was doing this in order to introduce him to a series of young women whom she had also invited into her home. Octavia invited young ladies to dine with them on a number of occasions and always seemed extremely disappointed when, at the end of the evening, Marcus did not make arrangements to meet with any of the ladies again. Octavia found this especially annoying, as it was becoming more and more difficult to get Marcus to agree to come to dinner at all.

Marcus was starting to relax in his new life. It had taken many years, but the night terrors were becoming less and less frequent. However, night terrors or not, he still had a fear of the dark. He always slept with the window open and kept a lantern lit throughout the night. He was well aware that the local people knew of his fear of the dark. The light from his room could be seen for quite a distance and some would occasionally make jokes; "Oi, Marcus, it's getting dark; light your lantern!" Marcus knew it was just friendly banter and took it in good spirits. He would smile and wave his hand, whilst thinking to himself, 'You would have a lantern too if you had been sealed in a tomb with a mad demon."

Whenever Marcus was feeling depressed, which was happening with increasing regularity, he would ride to the inn, even though he could only drink water. He thoroughly enjoyed the company of the individuals he met there and as he had been away from his Regiment for many years, felt that it was now safe enough to make friends among the local people. He always ordered a meal. Even though he had no desire to eat in the company of others, he felt it kept the landlord happy, and he made sure he bought plenty of drinks for the locals.

Marcus enjoyed the atmosphere and joined in with the banter. Today, the men in the inn were in particularly good form, and as Marcus ate his meal, he began to feel much better. Good company and laughter seemed to put all his problems into prospective. The landlord's daughter, a pretty young thing about twelve years old, would often help out in the bar, cleaning tables and serving drinks. She was well-liked by everyone. Marcus smiled as he saw her come around the bar with a pitcher of water. Marcus appreciated that he did not need to ask for more water and that she had seen him empty his cup. However, he had a strange feeling that everything was not quite as it should be. He could not put his finger on what was wrong. He smiled at the girl and she smiled back. Marcus froze! Then it hit him like a club to the back of his head. The girl smiled, but it was not her smile. The girl's smile was more like that of a snake, in that her lips barely parted, and her tongue flicked out of the small gap between her lips. As she approached his table, she placed one hand on his shoulder, leaned forward and whispered in his ear. The voice he heard was that of Flavian. "Hello, Centurion. Nice to see you again. It took me a long time to find you and here you are, the great Centurion disguised as a peasant. Who would have thought that!" Through gritted teeth, Marcus replied, "Flavian, leave me alone."

Flavian said, "Oh, but I will, dear boy! Believe me, I want you to take no notice of what that silly girl said in the tomb and give me the artefacts." Marcus noticed that Flavian then looked nervously around the room before continuing, "I will give you two days; just two days." Unconsciously, Marcus grabbed the girl by the arm, and snarling, said, "Or what…?" Flavian replied, "Before friends start dying."

Marcus screamed, "You had better leave my friends alone," then, without thinking, threw the girl to the floor. The girl cried out. The inn fell silent.

After what seemed an eternity, Marcus was the first to speak. He looked down at the girl on the floor and said, "I am sorry; I am so sorry." The girl rolled over onto her hands and knees and moved as quickly as she could to the safety of the men at the bar, who stood there with a look of shock on their faces as if they could not believe what they had just witnessed. A large overweight man with a heavy beard smiled then licked his lips and shouted, "How dare you lay your hands on that young girl." Then the smile was gone but was replaced with a look of rage. Marcus noticed that the man next to the large man now wore the same smile, the same licking of the lips, the wild eyes. Then he screamed, "We are going to teach you not to come in here assaulting our children." Then the smile was gone. Marcus saw that the next man now had that same terrible smile, and he realised that Flavian was moving from man to man, turning the crowd in the bar into a murderous mob. As Marcus stood up to leave, one of the screaming mob threw his tankard of beer at him. It missed him, but the beer poured over his head. Another tanker was thrown, then another; all the tankers missed, but left Marcus soaking wet from head to toe with foul-smelling beer. He saw the landlord making his way around to where he sat, carrying a large club. Marcus ran towards the door. In front of him stood an old man who smiled at him, displaying a row of broken teeth. Marcus paused, then the man licked his lips. Marcus hit him hard in the face. The man screamed.

Marcus pushed him out of the way and ran out of the door. Marcus felt a little guilty because he knew the man was innocent and that he was only being used by Flavian, but by the Gods, it felt good.

Marcus managed to jump onto his horse before the raging mob could get through the door. Some of them still had pots in their hands and threw them at him. In fact, they threw anything that came to hand—knives, brushes and even a hammer. Marcus thought, "Where the hell did they get the hammer?" Marcus galloped away, but after a short while, he stopped to check whether the mob had followed him. When he was sure that it was safe, he rode at a leisurely pace, trying to make sense of what had just happened. He still could not get out of his mind the image of Flavian jumping from body to body. He kept trying to convince himself that what he had witnessed was impossible and that it must have been his imagination. However, even though Marcus, similar to a large number of people, was an expert at self-delusion, he knew that his encounter with Flavian, and the threat he posed, were very real.

After riding for approximately twenty minutes, he crossed a small stream. Marcus was now on his own land and immediately felt safer, although he knew that his assumption made no sense in that he was aware he was still in great danger as Flavian would not respect boundaries. Marcus looked ahead and saw an older woman leaning on the fence. She was chewing on a piece of grass whilst staring into his field through a gap in the bushes. Marcus stood up in his stirrups trying to see over the bushes, but the bushes were too high. As Marcus drew closer, he recognized the woman, who occasionally helped out with milking the cows. As Marcus drew closer, he dismounted his horse, and said to the woman, "Hello, is everything alright?" She said nothing. As Marcus got closer, he looked through the gap in the bushes to see what had captured the woman's attention. He thought to himself that maybe she had seen a herd of deer. At first, he thought it was an empty field, but then his eyes focused on some shapes lying on the ground in the long grass. There were at least twenty shapes. Marcus let out a loud gasp as he recognised the shapes; they were his cows, and they were dead. As Marcus climbed over the fence, he heard Flavian's voice. He looked back. The old woman smiled, and said, "Just a warning, Centurion. Two days, two days." She turned around, still chewing on her blade of grass.

Marcus had an overwhelming urge to run after her, but he knew that she was just an old woman. Flavian had gone. Marcus made his way around the field, checking each cow in turn. There were twenty-two cows in all. Not one of the cows had a mark on them. It looked as though they had all just dropped down dead. Marcus knew that there was nothing that he could do. He knew that he needed to talk to his partners, but first, he needed time to decide what he should do. However, time was the one thing of which he had very little. Marcus mounted his horse and rode to his farmhouse, which was only a few minutes away. He slowly dismounted and washed his face in the cool stream which ran along the side of his home. He lay back in the grass trying to think of a plan, but he knew that there was only one solution—he had to leave.

Marcus was relieved when he went to see his partners. They were already aware of the dead cows. Cato seemed to be the most upset. He kept repeating, "I don't understand it. How did they die? There was not a mark on them." Domitian was the more thoughtful one. He listened in silence as Marcus and Cato talked, whilst Cato continued to pace up and down the room, sitting for a moment, before continuing walking, repeating, "It couldn't be wild animals. There was not a mark on them."

He continued to repeat this again and again. Then Domitian said, "Listen, there is no use crying about it.

We will probably never know how the cattle died, but what is done is done. We have got plenty of cattle, so let us count our losses and move on."

Marcus then took a deep breath and told them that he planned to leave. The two partners looked at each other in disbelief. Cato said, "What… what… are you serious? You are leaving because of a few dead cows?" Marcus tried to assure them he was leaving anyway, and that he had been on his way to tell them his plans when he saw the dead cattle. Marcus hated lying to them, but he could hardly tell them the truth.

He could see they were very angry and upset. They had been together in partnership for more than ten years and they were much more than merely partners; they were good friends.

Cato said, "What about the business opportunity we discussed? It will make us very rich." Marcus told them that he did not want any money for his share of the business. They looked at him as if he had gone mad! Domitian said, "No, no. You must take your share. You have worked too hard to walk away with nothing." Marcus could not tell them that there was no point in them giving him money. He was aware that because of the curse, he was unable to accumulate wealth; it would only disappear.

He told them that he had more than enough money for his needs in his strongroom, which was partly true! Marcus was quite moved because his friends seemed genuinely upset that he was leaving. When they realised that they could not persuade him to stay, they refused to let him give away his share of the business. They told him that when he came to his senses, he should come back to Philippi and his business would still be here.

Marcus comforted himself with the thought that he really could not have stayed very much longer. He and his two friends were about the same age, and he was aware that they were starting to look older than him. He consoled himself with the thought that his move was for the best. Marcus had learned to overcome disasters in his life, which was one of the main reasons he was able to carry on. He decided there was only one place to which he would move, and that was Rome.

Marcus was sad and disappointed that his business venture had not succeeded in the way he had hoped it would. Even though John had made it perfectly clear to him that he could never have any more money than he actually had at the time of the curse, Marcus, like many individuals, tended to ignore any information that he did not like! He now had to live with the reality that no matter how hard he worked, nor how long he worked, he would never be any richer than he was now. Marcus thanked the Gods that he had quite a lot of money on the day that he was cursed. He could not imagine how he would survive if he had been poor.

Marcus loved Rome and was excited to be returning to the city. He had not been home for nearly fifteen years! But, more importantly, Marcus needed help. He knew that he was way out of his depth and he needed to speak to Cephas. If anyone in the world knew what to do, it would be Cephas. Before he left for Rome, he went to say, goodbye to his friends. They had invited him to a farewell meal at Cato's house.

When he arrived, he found Octavia crying and his two friends looking upset. He asked them what had happened. They told him that a close friend had fallen on hard times. Marcus asked them the name of their friend and they told him that he was called Maximus. Marcus knew Maximus. He had once been a Legionnaire. Marcus did not know him very well, but from what he remembered, he appeared to be a pleasant individual and seemed to have many children.

Marcus could see that Octavia was becoming more and more upset and asked her what the problem was. Cato explained that Maximus, who had always worked very hard to support his family, had, through no fault of his own, got himself into debt with his employer, a man named Yusuf. He added that this man—who owned the neighbouring farm—was not noted for being a good person. Because of the problems, and the situation in which he now found himself, Maximus had been forced to sell himself and his family into slavery for ten years. Even though this was not an unusual occurrence, Marcus was enraged that Maximus, who had been a Legionnaire and appeared to have always worked hard to support his family, had found himself in this situation.

Cato agreed with Marcus and said that he understood how Marcus felt, but that there was nothing that could be done. Marcus glared at Cato and answered, "I think that we shall really have to see about that!" Marcus left the house, went across to where his horse was tethered, mounted it and galloped away.

Maximus's house, if it could be called a house, was more like a pigsty. As he approached the house, he saw several horses tethered to the rail outside. Marcus could feel his anger increasing. As he dismounted from his horse, he took a deep breath to calm himself. He stood outside the door for a moment and waited for his anger to subside. When he felt in control of himself, he pushed the door open. As he entered, he saw the shocked faces of the members of the family who were in the room.

Maximus was holding his wife, who was crying. The farm owner, Yusuf, who had two strong-looking men with him, was startled at the arrival of Marcus. Yusuf asked Marcus, "What are you doing here? Can I help you?" He then looked nervously at his two companions. Yusuf was aware of who Marcus was and knew of his reputation.

Marcus looked around the room. He was not impressed. He saw a small hole in the roof and the house smelled of damp. There were obvious signs of vermin. Marcus asked, "How much do you want for the family?" Yusuf looked at Maximus's wife, smiled, and replied that they were not for sale. Marcus offered double what the price would be for all the family of slaves, but still Yusuf refused. Marcus was angry. The old Marcus, the Centurion Marcus, would have killed all three of the men where they stood, but he knew that because of the curse, he could not do that. He simply said, "I challenge you to a sword fight. If I win, I will pay you for the family. If you win, you will take my share of my business." Yusuf replied, "That is a very good offer, but who could better you with a sword? Your business is of no use to me if I am dead." Marcus replied, "A stick". Yusuf said, "What do you mean—a stick?" Marcus repeated what he had said, spitting out the words with contempt; "A stick. You can have a sword and I will have a stick". Marcus pointed to a broom handle in the corner of the room and said, "That stick". He continued, "That stick and me. Me and that stick against the three of you."

Marcus saw a smile spread across Yusuf's face, but there was also a hesitation and a sense of fear. He was in turmoil. Marcus knew, however, that whenever there was a battle between greed and fear, greed would always triumph! Yusuf replied, "I will need this in writing, because, if you die here…"—he then corrected himself and said, "*When* you die here, who will believe me when I make a claim on your property?" Marcus pointed to Maximus and said, "You have witnesses." Yusuf laughed and replied, "Who would believe them?" Marcus could feel his anger mounting. He took a deep breath. He knew that it was a bad idea to fight in anger. Marcus said to Yusuf, "You are not fit to lick that man's boots." Yusuf opened a large leather bag which was on the table, took out a sheet of papyrus and a pen and started writing. When he had finished, he handed it over to Marcus for him to sign. Marcus took the document, read it, and then signed it. He said, "Are you satisfied now?" Yusuf smiled.

Marcus took the stick from the corner of the room and turned towards Maximus and his wife. He said to them, "Start your packing. This will only take a minute and you are not spending another night in this pigsty."

Marcus opened the door and stepped outside. He turned to one side of the doorway, out of sight of Yusuf's two men. As they came out of the house, Marcus struck the first man hard on the side of his head. He fell down in a heap on the ground. Marcus then spun his stick around and poked the second man hard on his forehead. The man's legs buckled beneath him, and he fell down onto the ground. Yusuf came through the doorway, stepping over the unconscious bodies of his men. Marcus could see that he was about to surrender. Marcus thought to himself, "No... No... Oh no you don't!" as he hit him as hard as he could on his kneecap. Yusuf collapsed in agony. Marcus bent down, putting his face close to Yusuf's face and said, "I am guessing that I won." Yusuf cried, "Take your filthy family. I never want to see them again." Marcus stood up and said, "Well. That is very kind of you!" As he stepped over the two unconscious men, he muttered, "Damned amateurs."

He noticed that Maximus only had a small cart on which to pack all his worldly goods. As Marcus watched the family preparing to leave, he realised that the cart was actually easily large enough to carry their meagre belongings.

Marcus helped Maximus to load the family's few belongings into the cart. He told them to make their way to his house. Marcus stood and watched them leave. He then pulled the two still-unconscious men away from the house. Marcus stood over the screaming Yusuf and asked him, "Can you walk?" Yusuf replied, "Of course I cannot walk. You have broken my knee-cap." Marcus grabbed Yusuf by his shirt and pulled him away from the house, which caused Yusuf to let out a loud scream. Marcus said, sarcastically, "I am sorry. Did that hurt?"

Marcus set fire to the house and stood, watching it burn. Yusuf cried out, "You have no right. That house belongs to me." Marcus picked up his stick which was lying on the ground and said, "Would you like to challenge me for it?" Yusuf quickly answered, "No, no, no. Just do what you want to do and leave me alone."

Marcus sat down on the grass as the house burned. He saw some rats scurrying from the burning house. One rat ran quite close to Marcus. Marcus quickly picked up his stick and flicked the rodent in the air. It landed on Yusuf's chest, which, unsurprisingly, caused Yusuf to scream, "Get it off me! Get it off me!" Marcus, who was pleased with his aim, said, "As you already said, this is your house, which makes that your rat!" Marcus watched as Yusuf wailed and screamed trying desperately to remove the rat. He was quite disappointed when the rat ran off into the long grass.

Marcus waited until one of Yusuf's men regained consciousness before he mounted his horse and made his way back to his farmhouse. When he arrived home, he was met by Maximus and his family. Marcus told them that he had burned their house to the ground and said, "Good riddance to it." Maximus's wife cried, "But where are we going to live and what will become of us?" Marcus said to Maximus and his wife, "Do not worry. I am going back to Cato's house and when I return, I will sleep here, on the couch. You and your family can take the bedrooms. In the morning, I will be leaving for Rome, and I will not be coming back here. Therefore, the house is yours." As Marcus opened the door to leave, he turned to Maximus and said, "In the morning, go to Cato's house. I will tell him that you will take my place in the business as a partner." Marcus looked at Maximus and his wife and said, "Get some rest now. In the future, you will no longer have anything to worry about."

Marcus left the house. He could hear Maximus and his wife crying. He thought to himself that he could never understand people crying when something good happened. Marcus mounted his horse and made his way to Cato's house. To be truthful, he was not looking forward to the evening. He hated goodbyes.

When Marcus arrived at Cato's house, he could see the anxiety on the faces of his friends. As he related to them what had happened, Marcus said, "I gave my house to Maximus and I know I said that you can have my share of the business, but, if you do not mind, I would like to give it to Maximus." For an uncomfortable moment, there was silence.

Then his partners' wives came over to Maximus, hugged him and kissed him on his cheek. Octavia said, "What a wonderful idea."

Cato said, "It would be good to have a partner who is not completely useless for a change!" This made everyone laugh. Even though Marcus joined in the laughter, he felt a deep sadness. He knew that he was unlikely to ever have such good friends again. They all sat down and had a wonderful meal together. At least, it looked wonderful! Marcus tried his best to look as though he was enjoying the meal and even asked for more.

As he was preparing to leave, he noticed that the girls were packing lots of food into a large bag. They saw him looking at what they were doing and said, "It is for Maximus and his family. They are probably starving."

Marcus saw that his friends and their wives were becoming emotional as the time for his departure drew near. He went around the room and hugged each of his friends, picked up the bag of food they had provided for Maximus and his family, and left as quickly as possible.

Marcus made his way back to the farmhouse, to find Maximus still awake and waiting for him to return. Marcus put the bag of food on the table and began apologising to Maximus, saying, "If you do not mind, I have a long journey in the morning and I would like to sleep now." Marcus left early in the morning. He was glad he had managed to slip out of the house before anyone awoke.

In the early nineteenth century, Marcus returned to the area and found a farm shop that sold cheeses. One cheese in particular was marketed as "Octavia's Cheese". Marcus asked the staff, "Why is the cheese called by that particular name?"

The shop owner replied that he had no idea. This particular cheese had carried that name for as long as anyone could remember. Marcus left the farm shop, mounted his horse, and wept as he rode away.

CHAPTER 12
ROME

BEFORE HE HAD left the Legion and travelled to Philippi, he had asked his friends in the Legion to write to his family and inform them of his death. It broke his heart, but he felt that it was the safest thing to do. If it was ever discovered that he was cursed, his family would pay a terrible price.

Marcus had made his way very slowly to Rome. Most of the time, he just walked along at the side of his horse. After all, there was no need to hurry. Marcus thought to himself that it made no difference if it took him a month, a year, or even a hundred years to reach Rome. Being here alone, he could forget both the curse and Flavian. He hoped and hoped that Flavian would leave his friends alone. He reassured himself that, after all, as he had left, it would be pointless to harm his friends. But then again, he thought, who can fathom the mind of evil?

Out here on the Great Plains, there was no need for him to be careful with anything he said, or anything he did. As he strolled across the great plains of Philippi, he stopped to look around, remembering when he was a child, listening to the old men telling their families tales of the great battle that took place in this very spot. He was told that almost two hundred thousand soldiers had fought here. It was at this place that Mark Anthony and Octavian defeated Brutus and Cassius. It was such stories that had made him dream of one day joining the Legion.

As soon as he arrived in Rome, he sought out Cephas. He found him staying with friends on the outskirts of the city. It was there that he was introduced to Barnabas and to Paul. Marcus looked at Paul in horror. He shouted out, "Cephas! Cephas!" and, pointing to where Paul stood, bellowed, "This man is a spy. His name is not Paul; it is Saul. Do you not remember whilst in Jerusalem, the man who was trying to have you all arrested and I offered to deal with him for you?" Moving his face very close to Paul, Marcus continued, "It would have been my great pleasure to do so!"

Cephas placed his hand on Marcus's shoulder and said, "Calm down, Marcus. We know all about his past. He is one of us now." Marcus moved away from Paul, gave him a threatening look and, turning to Cephas, said, "Seriously? Do you really know who this man is?" Cephas walked over to Paul and said to Marcus, "He is our brother and our friend." Marcus looked around in astonishment and said, "Well, at last, I am no longer the worst person in the room!" This caused everyone in the room to laugh. Marcus, however, was far from joking!

Marcus always enjoyed the company of Cephas, but he was aware that like the Nazarene, he always surrounded himself with the most appalling individuals. Marcus had heard of some of the terrible things that Paul had done, but now, here he stood, with Cephas, acting as though they were the best of friends. Marcus thought to himself that these Christians really were strange people.

Marcus shared with Cephas what was happening with Flavian. He told Cephas how Flavian had attempted to purchase the artefacts used in the crucifixion. Marcus normally avoided any mention of the crucifixion as he was now deeply ashamed of his behaviour that day and he surmised that his friends, even now, struggled with the part that he had played.

Cephas listened with interest to what Marcus told him and looked across at Paul who was obviously deep in thought but remained silent as Marcus revealed that he had heard Flavian's voice in the tomb. He told them how Flavian had tried to make a deal with him, but how the young girl, on that day—Marcus preferred to use the term that day, as it was a way of avoiding mentioning the word Crucifixion—told him that he was the Guardian of the Artefacts, and he must never give them to Flavian.

Marcus paused for a minute to let the information sink in. He then told them about the incident in Philippi and the threats against his friends. Marcus added, "What I cannot understand is why Flavian wants the Artefacts and wants them so badly that he is prepared to chase me to Philippi and threaten my friends." It was Paul who was the first to speak; "He fears them." Marcus turned to Paul, and said, "Why? What can they do to him?" Paul stood up, then went over and sat next to Marcus, putting his hand on his shoulder. He looked at Paul's face; it was stern and serious. He knew that whatever Paul was about to say would have a profound effect on him. Paul said, "The Artefacts can bind him and can imprison him." Marcus looked around the room and saw Cephas nodding. Barnabas stared at Paul. Marcus said, "Surely you cannot just bind that thing—Flavian—and put it in prison?" Cephas said to Marcus, "You cannot do that, but the Artefacts can, not in a prison as you know it, but a prison in total darkness, specifically for him and his own kind."

Marcus suddenly felt a rush of excitement and said, "Great!! What is the plan? Do we lure him here, and hit him with the Artefacts?" Paul said, "No, no, he is much too clever for that. You must keep away from him." Marcus said, "What you have said does not seem to be much of a plan." Paul said, "Barnabas and I are going away for some time. Come with us and you will be safe." Marcus looked at Cephas, then at Barnabas, and then back at Paul, and said, "Safe, Safe? How is that safe? It will come, and I know it cannot harm me, but it will kill all of you." Cephas said, "That thing will not go within a hundred miles of Paul." Marcus was far from satisfied with what his friends had to say. He had not known what to expect when he told them about Flavian. He was hoping that somehow, his friends could just make his problems go away, even though he knew nothing in his life had ever been that simple.

Cephas thought it would be a good idea to lighten the mood, so he said, "How was life in Philippi... I mean apart from being chased around by a psychopathic demon?" Marcus tried to smile. It was all he could do to produce a forced grin.

The next morning, Marcus set off to find his family. He wore a long cloak with a hood. He followed the riverbank to his family's estate. It was not a very large estate, but it was quite profitable. As he got nearer to the house, he saw a huge tree. Memories came flooding back. He went over to the tree. He rubbed his hands up and down the bark. He thought to himself, "This tree... this tree was my tree." He remembered how, as a child, he loved climbing the tree. He would hide up there for hours, watching his mother going frantic looking for him. He laughed to himself and then climbed the tree.

High up and well-hidden in the branches, he had a good view into the house. He saw a beautiful young woman, approximately nineteen years old. He leaned forward as far as he dared, trying to identify the young woman. At first, he thought it was his wife, but she was far too young. He felt a shock, which almost caused him to fall out of the tree. The girl he could see was Marcella, his beautiful, beautiful daughter. She had been only five years old when he had left. Now, she was a beautiful, grown woman. He could see that she was talking to someone who was just out of his sight.

There was a large pillar in the room which was obstructing his view. He moved from branch to branch, trying to get a different angle of view inside the house. After a few frustrating minutes, he finally saw Marcella's companion. It was Lydia, his wife. He had to summon all the self-control he had to prevent himself from getting down from the tree and rushing into the house. The tree that had, at first, been a source of great joy, was now the cause of great pain. It was like looking into another world… a world he had lost. Marcus stayed in the tree for over an hour. He was unable to tear himself away. Suddenly, two young children ran into the room and flung themselves into the arms of Lydia. He could clearly see his wife laughing and kissing the children. A young couple entered the room. He recognised the young man immediately. It was his son, Gnaus. Marcus slid quietly down the tree. when he saw a young woman walking towards the villa.

Marcus asked her if she knew Hannah, she replied, "Yes, of course. Everyone knows Hannah." I am going to meet her now. Marcus, nervously, looked around, which made the young woman suspicious. She said, to him, "What is the matter?" Marcus reassuring, the woman said, "Everything is all right. Hannah is a friend of mine and I have not seen her in a long time. I want to surprise her. Could you give her a message for me? The woman, happily, agreed to do so. Marcus said, could you ask her to meet me outside the forum in two hours? The woman answered, "And your name is?" Marcus smiled and said, "Tell her, it is her little Gladiator. She will know who it is". The young woman laughed and continued to the villa.

When Marcus returned, as he told his friends about his trip to see his family, he saw them looking at each other. Marcus said, "What is it?" His friends looked uncomfortable. Marcus said, "What is the matter? Is it something that I have said?"

Cephas answered, "You must learn to be more careful. We do not know where Flavian is, but we can be absolutely certain he is looking for you. He may already have found you."

Marcus cried out, "Oh no, my family!" Marcus put his hands to his head and shouted, "No, no, no! What have I done?" Cephas said, "Calm down. We don't know where Flavian is, but we do know that he is not omnipresent." Marcus said, "Omni…. omni what? What are you talking about?" Cephas said, "It means he cannot be everywhere at once. Flavian has to search for you. Paul said he could be anywhere and so you must be careful." In a voice that was almost a whisper, as if saying it out loud would make the danger all the more real, Marcus said, "What if he is already here? What if he knows about my family?"

"Get your bag," said Cephas. Marcus went to the room where he had been sleeping. It was a small room up two flights of stairs and was shared with three other people. Marcus had a small cot in the corner. He bent down and grabbed his bag. He took the bag to Cephas. Marcus said, "What are you looking for?" Cephas answered, "We will see." Cephas opened the bag, looked inside and said, "These will do the job," then he lifted out three nails. They were obviously old and bent out of shape. Marcus said, "What use are they?"

"As we have told you, Flavian won't go near them. We have one for your wife, one for your son, and one for your daughter. If they always keep them close, they will not be in danger." Marcus answered, "That won't work. For one thing, they won't carry them around for the rest of their lives, and who is going to give them the nails? Obviously, it cannot be me!"

Marcus said, "Wait a minute. I have an idea, give them to me." He then took the nails and left. Paul and Cephas watched, looking bewildered.

Marcus made his way to the Forum. He sat on the Forum steps, taking in the great signs of Rome. It truly was a magnificent city, with its great marble temples and the greatest Coliseum in the world. Then he saw Hannah! He felt a warmth move throughout his body. A joy he had not experienced in years. Then she saw him and ran towards him. He could see that she was laughing and crying at the same time. When she was a short distance from him, she stopped, wiped the tears from her eyes, saying, "Is it really you? My Gladiator?" She then moved forward and hugged him, showering his face and neck with kisses.

She stepped back to look at him. Then taking hold of his hands, she said, "Where have you been?" "We were told that you were dead? How come you look so young? It has been fourteen years and you have not aged a day!" Marcus answered, "It is complicated. A lot has happened, but you must promise me that you will not tell anyone that you have seen me." Marcus then saw something that chilled him to the bone. It was a long, fine, silver chain and hanging from the chain was a small cross. Marcus pointed at the necklace and said, "What the hell is that?" Hannah answered, "What do you mean?" "Do you mean my necklace?" She clasped her hand around the cross as if she was protecting it. As if it was the most precious thing in the world. "It was a gift from your Mother. She gave it to me when she set me free." Marcus's face was a mixture of bewilderment and horror. He answered,"Have you any idea of what this means?" Hannah interrupted him and said, "It is all right, Marcus. I know perfectly well what it means. It means that we are Christians." Marcus answered, 'We? What do you mean—"We"?' Hannah answered, "All of us. Your wife, your son, your daughter and your mother." Hannah looked at Marcus's face. Initially, she thought that his expression was one of anger, then she realised that it was fear. Marcus's mind was racing, a million thought were racing through his mind at the same time.

However, one thought was dominant! What if they ever found out that I am the 'Christ Killer'? Hannah and my own family will hate me forever. Hannah said, "Marcus. What is. Wrong?" I have never seen you like this." Marcus was terrified of saying anything…. anything which might give away his terrible secret. However, he knew that he had no alternative. He was aware that no body knew him as well as Hannah did. Often in the past there had been occasions when it was as if she was actually reading his mind! Marcus said, "I have to go, but first, I wanted to give you these." Marcus put his hand into his bag and pulled out a small red silk bungle. In the bungle were two nails. Marcus said, "Do not look into this bungle until you get to your home." He knew that as soon as she saw the nails, she would hate him. They would all hate him. Who could ever forgive him? Marcus said, "Listen to me carefully. There are two objects in that package. One you must carry with you at all times. The other will stay in your home always. He added, "Do you understand, "Always"? Hannah nodded. Marcus leaned down and kissed her on her cheek. He said, "Good-bye', then turned and walked away. Hannah cried, "Marcus, Marcus, as he disappeared into the crown."

Marcus felt more alone than he ever had before. Even more alone than when he was in the tomb. At least then, he knew that he had a family who loved him. Now there was no-one.

Paul said, "We will leave in the morning. Flavian will not hang around in Rome. There is no point if you are not here. It is you that he is after and when he sees that you are not here, he will start looking for you."

As Marcus left with Paul and his party, he unexpectedly had a real feeling of excitement. Overall, he had been miserable in Philippi. He had worked hard with his two partners to expand the business, but he had never felt comfortable and safe in Philippi. He had always felt as if he was a fugitive, hiding out and constantly expecting someone to discover his secret. For him to be out on the road with Paul and his companions, and to be able to talk without fear, was like being set free from the darkest of prisons. His personality, his sense of humour, his wisdom and his knowledge had been held down and contained by fear, by the danger of him being exposed, so being out on the open road, with people that he trusted, was exhilarating.

Over the next few months, as he learned more about Paul, he came to respect him and became very fond of him. Even though he considered him to be the most frightening man he had ever met, they became close friends. Very soon after meeting Paul, Marcus had decided that he was also either the bravest man he had ever met, or completely mad! In whatever town or city they visited, Paul would upset innumerable people. He appeared to be constantly facing angry mobs, who either wanted to beat him, stone him, or generally do very unpleasant things to him. Marcus had long ago lost count of how many times he stood between Paul and an outraged crowd of people. Nevertheless, he always enjoyed his times with Paul. It could very often be frustrating and frightening, but never, ever boring!

One of the things which fascinated Marcus about Paul was that he would perform exorcisms on a regular basis. Marcus told Paul that when John explained the curse to him, he was told that he must have nothing to do with exorcisms, but at the time, he did not have any idea what John was talking about. Paul explained to Marcus, "It's not a trick or a show. If I am performing an exorcism, then you must keep away from me." He continued, "You must take the curse seriously. You must not ever, ever—no matter what happens—try to perform an exorcism; do you hear me?!." Then there was a long pause while Marcus waited for Paul to speak. Eventually, Paul said, "Come here; sit with me for a while." Paul wandered to the side of the road then sat down on the grassy bank and Marcus sat down beside him. Again, Paul was silent. He seemed to be looking at a flock of birds flying overhead. Then Paul turned to him, and said, "We both know this can't go on forever. Flavian will always come for you. It may take a hundred years, but eventually, he will find you… he will always find you." Marcus said, "What can I do? I can't use the Artefacts; all I can do is keep running." Paul said, "Yes, I agree, you have to keep running, but there will come a time, in the future, when you will have to stop running and fight. Marcus, you can't run forever." Marcus looked Paul in the eye and said, "But how can I fight this thing?" Suddenly, Paul's whole demeanour changed. He started to smile and his serious mood changed. He patted Marcus on the knee then stood up and said, "Sometimes we aren't given knowledge until we need it. Don't worry; I am confident you will know what to do when the time comes." With that, Paul started to walk down the road, leaving Marcus still sitting on the grassy bank. Marcus jumped up and ran after Paul. He wanted to say something, but Paul just looked over at Marcus and smiled, so Marcus knew that the conversation was over.

One day, approximately eighteen months after joining Paul and Barnabas, they explained that they had serious matters to discuss and asked him to join them. They explained to Marcus that it was now time for him to leave. Paul explained that he should go to stay with Barnabas's family in Cyprus, assuring him that he would be safe there. Marcus protested, but they simply replied that it was now time for him to leave. Marcus was already aware that it was becoming more dangerous with each day that passed and he understood their concern was in trying to protect him from danger. Marcus also understood Paul well enough to know that once he had made up his mind, then there was no point in arguing or discussing the matter any further. Marcus knew he had to leave.

Barnabas explained that it was fortunate that they were in Athens at that time because he was aware of a boat which was leaving for Cyprus the following morning. Marcus knew they must already have discussed this, and that the decision had been made. Early the next morning, Barnabas and Paul accompanied Marcus to the harbour. It was a sad parting. Once they had walked a short distance away, they turned to wave. Marcus was not to know that he would never see Paul again. The memory always stayed with him and, even to this day, fills him with sadness.

CHAPTER 13

FLAVIAN

Eventually, the boat arrived in Cyprus. Marcus disembarked and went to meet Barnabas's family. He was glad Barnabas had sent word ahead and that his family were expecting him and made him very welcome. It was a great relief for Marcus to find that they too were aware of his secret, albeit they rarely spoke about it. Barnabas's brother, Aristo, who was a master blacksmith, invited Marcus to be his apprentice. Aristo told him that he needed to be able to earn a living. This was a real life-changing event for Marcus. He would forever appreciate Aristo's good advice, as he knew that thereafter, wherever he went, he could make a good living.

Marcus stayed with the family for approximately ten years. They had a profitable vineyard and Marcus was kept very busy. He explained to them why he would only accept a very low wage. They were fascinated when he told them how his money would mysteriously disappear when he reached a certain sum. He told them he had already reached that amount. This meant he needed only his day-to-day living costs, which were not high as he did not drink or have expensive tastes. They made no comment, just shook their heads, and looked baffled.

Marcus was a tall, strong, exceptionally good-looking man, and even though he was now in his fifties, he still looked like a handsome young man in his late twenties. This was not ideal for someone who wanted to remain anonymous. Quite often, he would return to the farmhouse where he initially stayed with Barnabas's family, and there would be one, two or even three young girls visiting the family, specifically to meet Marcus. Although he would always politely refuse to engage with them, the girls were never discouraged. It saddened him because some of the girls were quite beautiful, but, unfortunately, no matter how beautiful, how fantastic, or how amazing they were, he was incapable of entering into any romantic relationship. He could recognise and even appreciate beauty in women, but only in the way one would admire a beautiful painting or an amazing view from a mountain top. He was, fortunately, not particularly concerned about this part of the curse.

After living and working in Cyprus for several years, he was able to purchase a small farmhouse of his own. He now knew that when he arrived home, there should not be any unexpected visitors!

Marcus continued with his usual practice of trying to maintain distance and not become too close to any individual with whom he came into contact through either his work or his leisure time. There were, however, occasions when he felt that he had little choice but to socialise.

Barnabas's parents were commemorating their fiftieth wedding anniversary and they invited almost everyone in Cyprus to join them in celebrating the event. Marcus was very close to both of them, and over the past ten years, they had treated him as a son. Although Marcus did not, under normal circumstances, socialise to any great degree, he would never, of course, have dreamt of not attending their celebration.

It was at this special event that Marcus met Catarina for the first time. She immediately made it very clear that she liked him! Whilst Marcus considered Caterina to be quite attractive, that was as far as his feelings for her extended.

Charis, Caterina's father, was the richest and most powerful man in Cyprus and he adored his daughter.

Marcus, however, took an immediate dislike to him. In Marcus's opinion, Charis was one of those individuals who believed that the population of virtually the whole world was inferior to him. He did, however, possess wealth beyond imagining. He also adored his daughter and there was nothing that he would not do for her.

Caterina really liked Marcus, and as the evening progressed, she followed Marcus around and even attempted to hold his hand. It was at this point that Marcus decided to leave. He apologised to Caterina, telling her that he felt unwell, and he left as quickly as possible.

Marcus stepped into the warm Cypriot night with a feeling of relief. As he made his way back to his cottage, he felt as if he had escaped a potentially very difficult situation. He comforted himself with the fact that he had been in Cyprus for almost ten years, and in all that time, he had never come into contact with Caterina or her horrible father. The probability was high, therefore, that he would never see either one of them again.

Over the following few days, Marcus and Aristo were particularly busy working in the blacksmith shop and Marcus had hardly given a thought to the evening of the anniversary celebrations. He was surprised, therefore, when a well-dressed man arrived at the Smithy and introduced himself as Julius. He explained he had come at the request of his Master to invite Marcus to dinner at his villa. Marcus asked who his Master might be. Julius was somewhat taken back and surprised that Marcus did not recognise who he was, or who he was representing. He answered, somewhat disdainfully, "Charis, of course". As Marcus politely declined the invitation, Aristo intervened and said, "Wait, wait", then speaking to Julius said, "Please thank your Master and tell him that Marcus would be delighted to attend." As the man turned away, Aristo grabbed hold of Marcus by his arm and dragged him into his shop, whilst, at the same time, thanking Julius for bringing the message.

After Julius had left, Marcus said to Aristo, "Are you mad? I cannot go to the house of that terrible man and pretend to enjoy his food and listen to him telling me how wonderful he is." Aristo took hold of Marcus by his shoulders and said, "Have you any idea who this man is? Have you any idea at all? He is the most powerful and dangerous man in Cyprus. He could easily make you, me, my mother and my father just disappear completely, without any questions ever being asked." He continued, "If this man invites you to dinner, then you go to dinner!" Marcus, albeit reluctantly, agreed to go to dinner at Charis's villa.

Marcus spent the rest of the day in an extremely bad mood, throwing down his tools and kicking his forge every time he passed it. When it came time to get ready for the evening, he sang at the top of his voice, even though his voice was painfully out of tune. For the first time since he had been cursed, he did not care how his voice sounded.

Charis had sent a carriage to collect Marcus and transport him to his home. Marcus was aware that the gesture was meant to impress him, but it did not! The carriage made its way along a mountain track to Charis's villa, which was situated high in the hills of Cyprus. When the carriage finally arrived—and even though Marcus was not easily impressed—at first sight, he realised that the villa was stunning. It was huge! He thought that there must be at least a hundred rooms inside.

As the coach arrived at the main entrance to the villa, the doors opened and he was led inside by two slaves, who were dressed in silk. As he walked through the entrance, he was amazed. Everywhere seemed to be decorated or made with gold; even the door handles were gold. Marcus was escorted through the entrance hall by the two slaves and then onto one of the terraces, which overlooked a vast expanse of land, extending as far as the eye could see. It looked as though the view encompassed the whole of Cyprus. The view from the terrace was incredible. It completely took his breath away, which, of course, was the intention. After several minutes, Charis and Caterina came onto the terrace. Caterina walked over to Marcus, hugged him and kissed him on the cheek. Marcus thought this was all so very strange as he had previously met her on only one occasion, therefore, her behaviour was completely inappropriate. She was most certainly behaving in a manner which was far too familiar.

After several moments of small talk, Charis took him into the dining room where he met Caterina's grandfather. Marcus's impression of her grandfather was that he was a kind and genuine person; an individual whom everyone immediately liked. Everyone, that was, with the obvious exception of Caterina and Charis, which became all too apparent as the evening progressed, as they exhibited a dismissive and belittling attitude towards him. Marcus could not dismiss the feeling that each time Caterina's grandfather looked at him, he appeared to be pleading for help.

The dining room, as he expected, was large and expensively decorated with frescos depicting brightly coloured scenes from Roman and Greek mythology. There were also several statues of Greek Gods and prominent Romans. Charis obviously had a fondness for Zeus, as there were at least four statues of Zeus and replicas of some of the more unsavoury characters from Greek mythology. The visitors were escorted to their seats as servants began to bring in the most lavish meal Marcus had ever seen. He lost count of how many courses were served. The food looked beautiful. He smiled and thought to himself, "If only you knew how much this food is wasted on me! You could have served me with a piece of mouldy cheese and I would not have known the difference!"

Marcus did his best to look as though he was enjoying the meal. He did, however, feel very uncomfortable when they served the wine. It was as if they expected him to say he preferred water! He was aware, of course, that the host would normally encourage a guest to try the wine, offering different varieties of wine from an extensive cellar. Charis, however, merely smiled at Marcus, nodding his head, as if in acknowledgement of his response. As he ate his meal, he looked up and saw Charis smiling at him. Marcus had a terrible feeling that Charis knew his secret, but almost immediately dismissed this idea as impossible.

As they were finishing their meal, Caterina, who was, in Marcus's opinion, sitting too close to him, inappropriately put her hand on his knee. Marcus's first instinct was to look up at her father, who seemed aware of what had just happened. Charis merely smiled at Marcus, as if it was the most natural thing in the world for his daughter to have done.

After dinner, Marcus made a point of going across to talk to Caterina's grandfather, but he was ushered away from him. Charis immediately came over and asked Marcus if he would join him on the terrace, as he wished to speak to him. The grandfather, to Marcus's surprise, was rudely ignored. Charis led Marcus onto the terrace, followed by Caterina, and behind her, an obviously very unwelcome grandfather.

Charis leaned on the terrace rail and said to Marcus, "Tell me… Look around you. What do you see?" Marcus wondered what response Charis was expecting from him. He was, moreover, beginning to feel uncomfortable. He had a very awkward and uneasy feeling about the way the evening was evolving. Marcus looked at the view from the terrace. It was amazing. It was truly amazing. He could see Pathos and also, in the distance, the harbour. It was certainly a very impressive sight. It was starting to go dark and the lights were being lit across the city, which made the view even more spectacular. Marcus turned to look at Charis and said, "It is a nice view." He could see that his answer had disappointed Charis, which was Marcus's intention! Marcus, however, had ceased playing the games of pretentious, rich men a very long time ago!

Charis said, "Cyprus. What you see here is Cyprus. I own Cyprus… and it could be yours." Marcus said, "I think there would be an awful lot of people down there who would disagree with what you have just said" . Charis laughed and answered, "Little people, with little minds." Marcus responded, "It is Rome, only Rome that owns Cyprus, and Nero owns Rome."

Charis moved closer to Marcus and whispered in his ear, "I know you, Centurion. I know all about you. Nero belongs to me. I only need to whisper in his ear and he would burn Rome to the ground." Charis smiled and continued, "I told you that we would be good friends. Do you not remember me?" Charis licked his lips. "I could be quite hurt that you do not, but it was only a brief meeting. However, I still require the tools of the execution. I know that you still have them." Marcus responded sharply, "You can't be…?" Charis said, "Oh, don't let this body fool you. I am indeed no other than Flavian, but from time to time, I have to, what should we say, 'borrow' someone."

Charis then turned around, held up his wine glass and shouted to his slaves, "Wine; bring me more wine."

As the slaves rushed around to serve Charis, Marcus stood silently, astonished, and wondering whether Charis had gone mad! Charis then walked over to Caterina, put his arm around her and said to Marcus, "Is she not the most beautiful woman you have ever seen?" Marcus answered, "She is very beautiful." Marcus was desperately trying to think of an excuse, any excuse, which would enable him to leave the company of this, obviously, crazy man. Charis continued, "When you two are married, you will rule the world. With my help, of course, Marcus, you should regard your longevity as a gift. Think of it; you and Caterina could rule forever." Marcus was completely bewildered. He looked at Caterina, who smiled at him.

Marcus said to Charis, "There is no easy way that I can say this to you, but I am not going to marry Caterina. I completely agree with you that she is very beautiful, and I am sure that she will make someone a wonderful wife." Charis interrupted Marcus and said, "I remember when you arrived in Cyprus. You looked about twenty-eight years old and my beautiful Caterina here was only sixteen. She is now twenty-six and you still look twenty-eight. I know you cannot die, Centurion, but I could tie you to an anchor and throw you into the sea. How would you like to spend eternity talking to the fish?"

Marcus responded, "I think it is time that I left." Marcus turned and looked at Caterina's grandfather, who silently mouthed, "Run!" Charis turned towards the old man, pointed at him and said, "Quiet". The old man's legs buckled beneath him. One of the slave girls screamed and ran over to him. Marcus noticed Charis and Caterina exchanging a satisfied smile. The slave girl bent down, quickly examined him and screamed, "He is dead. He is dead!" Caterina pointed to Marcus and shouted, "Murderer! You have cursed him. Guards! Guards!"

Marcus ran to the doorway, but Caterina tried to block his way. Marcus grabbed her and pushed her onto the floor. Caterina screamed loudly and the slaves in the room also started to scream. Marcus wanted to run, but he could not resist dashing over to Charis and punching him hard in his face. He was glad to see his nose explode and to see the look of shock on his face. Marcus then turned and ran for the stairs. As he was descending the stairs, he saw five heavily armed guards running up the stairs with their weapons drawn. He shouted to them, "Quickly, quickly! Your Master is being attacked." They rushed past him, nodding in acknowledgement of his forewarning.

Marcus ran outside and stopped for a moment whilst deciding in which direction he should run... up or down? He said to himself, "Should I go up, or should

I go down?" He heard the dogs barking at the rear of the house and said to himself, "I guess that means down!" He ran across the beautifully manicured lawns. There was a small wall at the end of the lawn, which he leapt over without any effort, then he carried on running until he approached a slightly higher wall. He ran as fast as he could in order to build momentum to clear the wall. He cleared it with only inches to spare. As he cleared the wall, he looked down and, to his horror, realised he had jumped over the edge of a cliff.

Marcus felt as though he was falling for an eternity! As he fell, he remembered Lydia, his beautiful wife, his son and daughter, and, strangely, the girl in the cupboard. Suddenly, he hit the ground. Marcus lay stunned and silent on the ground. He could not believe that he had survived. He looked upwards and realised he must have fallen at least one hundred and fifty feet. He struggled to his feet. Every bone and every muscle in his body hurt. He took a deep breath and even his lungs hurt! Marcus knew that feeling sorry for himself would have to come later… probably much later! He could hear the dogs barking and men shouting orders. Clearly, they had no idea where he was and how he had disappeared.

Marcus said to himself, "I outsmarted you there. You did not expect me to jump off a 150-foot cliff, did you?"

Marcus started laughing at his own joke, but it hurt! He knew that even though he was in a lot of pain, he had to run. He had to get to Pathos Harbour before Charis's men arrived there. He knew that Charis would close the whole island and he fully believed Charis's anchor threat. Marcus ran into the woods. He knew his cottage was approximately twenty minutes away if he ran! He had to go to his cottage first in order to get his money, for he knew his chances of escape without money were very poor.

As Marcus made his way through the woods to his cottage, he had to hide as he heard Charis's men approaching. There seemed to be approximately twenty men on horseback. Marcus watched, nervously, as they dismounted their horses. They were led by an older, rough-looking man who gathered the men around him. Marcus was fortunate that he could hear very clearly everything that the man was saying. Marcus smiled when he heard him say that as Marcus was on foot, and they were on horseback, he could not possibly be in front of them and so, they must somehow have missed him. The man said that he must be still in the woods near to the villa. They quickly mounted their horses and galloped back the way they had come.

Marcus realised that falling off the cliff had actually been quite fortuitous. Hopefully, it had given him enough time to get to the harbour. He managed to reach his cottage without further incident. Marcus entered his cottage. It was pitch black. He hesitated as he felt a cold sweat creeping along his back. He dared not light his lantern, which meant that he had to grope around in the dark until he located his table. He said to himself, "Do not be stupid; there is nothing here of which I need to be afraid."

He reluctantly got onto his knees and felt along the floor until he came to the floorboards under which he had hidden his money. Pulling up the floorboard, he lifted his bag out of the hole and made his way out of his cottage. He then fell to his knees panting, and saying to himself, "Well, you did it; well, you did it." He vomited on the ground and then he ran!

Even though he knew it was a foolish thing to do, he ran to the home of Barnabas's parents. He could not leave without telling them. When he arrived, he banged on the door. Barnabas's father opened the door with a worried look on his face. He invited Marcus in and as quickly as possible, Marcus explained his dilemma. It was heart-breaking to see the concerned look on their faces. Marcus tried to assure them that he would be able to escape. He promised them he would send word to them as soon as he was safe. Marcus hugged them both, but they told him to stop wasting time and to just go.

Marcus stepped out of the door and ran towards Pathos Harbour, which was approximately two miles away. Although he was completely exhausted, he knew that he had to keep on running. He reached Pathos Town and made his way through the narrow winding streets to the harbour. As he approached the docks, he prayed to every God that he could bring to mind! He prayed to Augustus, he prayed to Zeus… he even prayed to the Nazarene! "Please, please, please, let there be a ship ready to sail. Preferably somewhere civilized and warm."

He thought to himself, "Not far now… not far now…", but then disaster! He heard the noise of numerous horses coming towards him. Marcus managed to hide in a doorway and ducked down into a dark corner. He had still not gotten over his fear of the dark, but he knew he had little choice, as what appeared to be over fifty armed men rode towards him, and then stopped immediately in front of him.

He could hear them talking. They were organising a search of the city for him. Marcus sat upright. Fortunately, they could not see him in the dark. As he looked around, the same vicious-looking individual was still shouting orders to a very frightened-looking group of men. He instructed them to search every house and every alley in the city. Chillingly, Marcus heard him say that under no circumstances must this man be killed, nor must he be allowed to leave the island.

After they had left, Marcus slowly stood upright. He had been within a few feet of the Leader and could even smell his foul breath. He watched as the men dispersed in different directions, then he ran, and he continued running! As he turned a corner at the end of the street, he gave a shout of joy! He could see the harbour and there was a ship making ready to sail. As exhausted as he was, he managed to run faster. Marcus saw that they were about to remove the gangplank. He shouted as loudly as he could, "No. No! Wait!" He could hear the troop of men on horseback behind him. To his horror, he could see that the sailors had pulled up the gangplank, but still, he ran. The ship was now pulling away from the harbour. When he reached the harbour wall, and even though he was now completely spent and carrying a heavy bag, he jumped; he jumped for his life! He heard one of the sailors' shouts, "By all the Gods, the man's mad!"

Marcus crashed onto the deck of the ship. He lay on the deck, unable to either move or talk through sheer exhaustion and then the shock of landing on the deck of the ship. He realised he had no idea where the ship was heading. He said to himself, "I hope it is either Spain or Egypt, or even Carthage." Marcus looked up at the curious sailors staring at him lying on the deck. When he had regained his breath, he asked, "Where are you heading?" The sailors were obviously amused that someone would risk his life by jumping onto a ship but did not know where it was heading! One of the laughing sailors said, "Britannia, lad, Britannia!" Marcus screamed!

After a few minutes, a rather cheerful-looking man came to talk to him as he lay on the deck and said, "I hope you are intending to pay for your passage, or over the side you go!" Bizarrely, he accompanied his comment with a look of amusement! Marcus had no doubt that the man meant every word he had uttered. Marcus informed him that he had every intention of paying for his passage. The man, whom he assumed was the captain, looked disappointed. Marcus looked over the side of the ship as it pulled away from the harbour. He could see a troop of horsemen at the end of the harbour and a vicious-looking man shouting at them. He then saw Charis with a large cloth pressed to his face. It appeared to be covered in blood!

CHAPTER 14

STRANGE RESCUE

MARCUS CONTINUED LEANING against the side of the ship until he recovered his breath and felt able to move. He started to walk –slowly around the deck. It was a cargo ship, carrying wine to a place called Colchester. Marcus had never previously heard of the city. He paid for his passage and a little extra for his own cabin. He was shown down some rickety steps to a small cabin. Marcus was uncomfortable with the idea of spending too much time in such a small room, but he was aware that he could spend most of the journey on deck. He put his bag under his bunk and collapsed onto his bed. He lay there, exhausted, feeling the pain from the fall and exhaustion from the long run from the villa across every part of his body. However, he felt that as this terrifying day was now behind him, he should be able to relax and try to figure out the strange events of the day.

Suddenly, Marcus was thrown to the floor as the ship veered sharply to one side. It was obviously turning around. Marcus ran up the rickety steps and saw that the ship was heading back to port. Marcus went to the captain and said, "What are you doing?" The captain pointed to the port and said, "Charis is calling us back and this is his ship." Marcus could see Charis on the dock, waving the white cloth that had previously been held to his bloody face. The captain said, "If I were you, I would hide in the hold. I do not think they would look for you there." Marcus made his way to the ship's hold as quickly as possible. The hold was dark and filled with hundreds of wine barrels. Marcus hesitated as he looked into the hold. The captain said, "If I were you, lad, I would get a move on." Marcus climbed over the barrels as quickly as he could and found a small gap between two barrels. He slid into the space and waited.

Marcus could feel his heart pounding as he heard men enter the hold, climbing over the barrels looking for him. He closed his eyes and prayed as he heard the men getting closer to where he lay. Then, to his horror, he heard one of the men climb onto the barrel next to him. Suddenly, there was someone in front of him. He was amazed. It was a girl… the girl who had stood in front of the Nazarene! She lay down in front of him and covered him with her arms as the men drew closer. He closed his eyes, expecting to be discovered. After a few seconds, he opened his eyes and saw two men looking straight at him and heard Charis shouting, "Is he down there?" Miraculously, the two men replied, "No, no. There is no one here." They then turned around and scurried away over the wine barrels and through the hatch which led to the deck. The young girl smiled. Marcus could see that she was older than he had first thought. She looked to be in her early twenties, but Marcus had a feeling that she was much older than that. The young girl moved her arm, and said, "Remember, you are protected." Then she was gone.

Marcus waited until he felt the ship getting under way again. He climbed out of his hiding place and made his way to his cabin. As he passed the captain and some of the crew members, the captain said, "Get some rest. It looks as though you need it. We will talk in the morning."

Over the following days, Marcus had time to go over the strange events which had occurred during his escape from Charis. Marcus was puzzled. Did Charis kill his own father-in-law by merely pointing his finger at him? How could he—Marcus—have managed to survive the fall down the huge cliff face? Why did he ignore the old man's warning when he mouthed, 'Run'?

Marcus felt that over the past twenty-four hours, he had learned a very valuable lesson. Never ignore your feelings. The reality was that he had felt something was very wrong from the moment he climbed into the Charis carriage. He was, however, now safe on board this ship. Importantly, he now knew its destination. But, equally importantly, what on earth was he going to do in Britannia?

Early the next morning, a happy-looking captain brought his breakfast to his cabin. Marcus slowly pulled himself up in his bunk. Every part of his body hurt. Marcus said to the captain, "To what do I owe this honour? The captain himself, serving breakfast?" The captain smiled and said, "Do not get used to it. It will not be happening again! All other meals will be served in the galley. If you are not there, you do not eat." Marcus asked, "Is there any particular reason for you, personally, to have brought my breakfast?"

There was a long silence. It was as if the captain had something to say, but was not sure if he should say it, nor even *how* to say it. The captain pulled the chair over, sat next to the bed and said, "The way you came aboard the ship seemed pretty desperate to me. Have you broken any laws? I will not be having a thief or a murderer on board my ship." Marcus replied, "No…absolutely nothing like that. I promise you. I admit that I had to leave Cyprus very quickly. All I can say is that there was a girl involved." The captain, who was obviously no fool, said, "Caterina?" Marcus nodded and felt his jaw drop. He said, "How did you know that?" The captain replied, "Charis would not have called us back to port without good reason and when I saw him on the harbour wall with about twenty men… Let me tell you, Charis is not the type of man who goes wandering around at night with a troop of guards merely to take in the night air! No, he looked to me as though he was hunting for someone, and that someone, I guess, would be you?"

Marcus said, "He became very upset when I refused to marry his daughter." The captain roared with laughter! He laughed so much that he had to stand up and walk around the cabin. Marcus watched, bewildered, as the captain wiped away tears from his eyes and said, "Someone up there likes you, Mister! If you had gone anywhere else in the world, Charis would have tracked you down, but I reckon Britannia is one of the few places on earth where you will be safe."

The captain sat down again and said, seriously, "Charis is the wealthiest and most powerful man I have ever met. Let me tell you though, there is absolutely nothing in the world that would make me marry Caterina." Marcus asked, "Why?" The captain took a deep breath and said, "I have known Charis nearly all my life. He used to live in Larnaca, but that was before he bought that monstrosity of a villa in the hills. He was a lovely man. He was kind and generous. He became good friends with a man called Lazarus and joined some religious sect. Marcus, with a look of amazement on his face, interrupted and said, "Lazarus? Surely not Lazarus from Jerusalem?"

Marcus knew Lazarus well. Lazarus and his two daughters were regular visitors to Mary's house in Jerusalem. He wondered why Aristo had not told him that Lazarus was in Cyprus. He then realised Aristo probably thought it would bring too much attention to him. Aristo was always telling him to keep a low profile.

The captain said, "Did you know Lazarus?" Marcus answered, "Well…that is not important. Please carry on with your story." The captain said, "Charis was probably one of the most popular men in Cyprus. His daughter was a pretty young thing. Then, several years ago, they just changed. No one could understand it. They suddenly became mean and cruel. Charis's wife had died, and his father-in-law lived with Charis and Caterina. They were a happy family. They seemed very close, but then everything changed. Charis and Caterina were often seen making fun of the old man and, on at least one occasion, Caterina was seen to have slapped the old man.

It did not make sense. Why would Caterina slap him? She adored her grandfather."

Marcus asked, "When did this change take place?" The captain scratched his head and answered, "Oh, I do not know. Like I said, it was a long time ago." Marcus asked, "Was it about ten years ago?" Marcus could see that the captain was trying to work the timing out in his head and, suddenly, he answered, "Yes…Yes…That is right. I remember. It was Caterina's sixteenth birthday, and I was invited to the celebrations. It was a few weeks prior to them moving into that terrible villa. They were never the same after they moved. It did not seem that long ago. I was surprised when someone told me a few weeks ago that Caterina was celebrating her twenty-sixth birthday." The captain stood up and said, "Well, I will leave you in peace whilst you have your breakfast." Marcus thanked him. As he left the cabin, he turned and said, "Do not forget. If you want to eat later, you will have to go to the galley." Marcus nodded as the captain left, closing the door behind him.

Marcus was left alone with his thoughts. He had supposed that he had always believed in Gods and Devils and Demons. He had seen Paul do some remarkable things, but he now realised that he had never really believed; not *really* believed. Could it be possible that whatever was controlling Charis and Caterina—and he was in no doubt that something was controlling them—was just a coincidence, or had something actually followed him to Cyprus? He now knew that the 'something' was none other than Flavian. He remembered Flavian saying, "Sometimes I borrowed people." And the young girl that had hidden him was the girl at the Crucifixion. Then a question came to mind—was this the end of it, or would he meet Flavian again? The thought made him visibly shiver. Was there more to this life than he could possibly imagine? He decided to do the same as everyone else appeared to do and ignore it!

Marcus left his cabin and climbed the rickety stairs to the deck where he could take in the invigorating fresh air. The ship was long past Cyprus. His thoughts now turned to Britannia. He knew very little about the country, but he had heard a number of stories, emanating from there, which were not particularly encouraging. He had been told that the people were not civilised, and they had actually been described to him as 'savages'! He had heard that the climate was very different to that of Rome. Apparently, for most of the year, it was cold, and it rained very often. In extreme months, there was also the possibility of snow!

Marcus quite enjoyed the long journey to Britannia. It gave him time to relax. As most of the ship's crew were from Britannia, it put his mind at ease since the men seemed to be far from savages. They regaled him with stories from home. By the end of the voyage, he had made friends with most of the crew and he was looking forward to his new life in Britannia. As the ship moved in closer to the harbour, he gazed out at the impressive great white cliffs, wondering what he would encounter there.

CHAPTER 15

CAMULODUNUM (COLCHESTER)

By the time Marcus had reached Britannia, his mood had turned to melancholy. He knew nothing about Britannia apart from what the deckhands had told him, and he sorely missed his old life as a Centurion.

Marcus was carrying all his money. He had no fear of what might happen next, nor, indeed, any concerns regarding losing his money or even having his money stolen. He had simply given up on everything. He was without any hope or any expectations.

Marcus did not know any town or city in Britannia and he had no idea where to go when the ship landed. He assumed Britannia, like most countries, had good places and some unsavoury places where only bad people would dare to visit. He smiled to himself and thought Cephas and Paul would feel really at home in such places.

As Marcus was leaning on the ship's rail, contemplating his next move, he saw some heavy carts making their way to the ship. Marcus turned to one of the deck hands and asked, "What are the carts for?" The deckhand said, "Surprisingly enough, the cargo carts are for our cargo! You do not think we have travelled all this way just to drop you off, do you?" This comment was met with much hilarity! Marcus held up his hands and said, "All right... All right. It was a stupid thing to say! But can anyone tell me where the cargo is going to?" One of the men shouted, "Do you mean the Colchester wine?" Then another man shouted, "I think the Colchester wine is going to Gaul!" Then another man shouted, "No, the Colchester wine is heading for Rome." Marcus had not yet landed in Britannia but had already been introduced to sarcasm!

Marcus responded, laughing, "Dare I ask..." then, looking around at the smiling faces, he repeated, "Dare I ask, to whom do I speak to get a ride to Colchester?" One of the men came and put his hand on Marcus's shoulder and, pointing to the older man standing at the first cart, said, "That would be old Alfred. He is the man to see." Marcus thanked him and made his way down the gangplank. He watched as the carts came to a halt alongside the ship. There were at least twenty carts in all. Each cart had at least three strong-looking passengers. Marcus thought to himself that it would be heavy work unloading a shipment of wine and then loading it onto the carts.

As he made his first steps on dry land, he almost lost his balance and had to grab hold of one of the cargo carts to prevent himself from falling, much to the hilarity of the ship's crew members who were leaning against the rail. Marcus had heard that being at sea for many weeks can have a comical effect once you start walking on dry land again! He waved at the laughing crewmen and shouted, "Thanks for reminding me, men!" In the few weeks of the voyage, Marcus had got to know the crew quite well. He thought to himself that he would really miss their crazy sense of humour.

Marcus walked up to the old man in the first cart and said, "Are you Alfred?" The old man said, "Yes, I am. What can I do for you?" Marcus said, "I have just come off the ship and I was wondering if you needed any help unloading all that wine?" Alfred answered, "I have all the men I need, and I am not hiring any more men." Marcus said, "I do not want paid. I was hoping for a ride to Colchester." Alfred said, "If the ship's captain will vouch for you, then you have a deal. Let me tell you, though, those barrels are heavy. It will be hard work. Do you understand?" Marcus told Alfred that he had worked as a blacksmith and was used to hard work. Alfred pointed to the men who were getting down from the carts and said, "Join them and they will tell you what to do."

It was true that Marcus was not afraid of hard work. He had worked hard on the farm in Philippi, and he had worked as a blacksmith. However, he had never worked as hard in his life as he did in helping to unload the cargo of wine from the ship and loading it onto the carts. It took two and a half days of back-breaking work. As he helped load the last barrel onto the final cart, all the workers and deckhands gave a loud cheer! Whilst the labourers were roping and securing the barrels, Marcus walked back onto the ship. He said to the sailors, "I do not know why, but I am really going to miss you pack of scrawny dogs!" One of the men shouted, "And we will miss you. Who have we got to laugh at now?"

As he made his way across to the captain, the crew members patted him on his back. The captain shook his hand and whispered in his ear, "One day, you will have to tell me how you pulled off that disappearing act in the hold of the ship." Marcus said, "Maybe… one day…" and then winked.

Marcus made his way off the ship. As he went down the gangplank, he waved to the ship's crew and then climbed onto one of the wine carts. He kept watching the ship as the carts made their way up the hill, until finally, the ship disappeared from sight. Marcus felt a great sadness. He was alone... again!

Marcus, together with the small wagon train, made his way to Colchester, the capital city of Britannia, with more expectation and hope than he had had when he started with his companions on the journey from Dover. It took five days for them to reach Colchester. As the carts were extremely heavy, it was a slow journey and they had to stop frequently to rest the horses. Marcus, however, was not in any hurry and he used his time to make friends with the men, who were all from Colchester and seemed to be a jolly group. Some of them were retired Legionnaires and, on their arrival in Colchester, they were a great help. They found him a decent place to live and were able to give him advice on which area would be the best place to set up his own blacksmith's shop. Marcus knew he could not have had a better start to his new life.

Even though Marcus knew it was dangerous to make friends or to attract too much attention, he was glad the men he met on the journey from Dover kept in touch with him. He was amused by the nicknames that they had for each other. There was an incredibly tall man whom they called "Tiny", an overweight man they called "Slim" and a young man who took his time with whatever he was doing, whom they called "Speedy"! Tiny and Slim would often come into his shop, followed a few minutes later by Speedy. They would talk for hours about life in Colchester.

There were two other regular visitors to his shop—a young girl who came with her younger brother. They first wandered into his shop shortly after he arrived in the city. He was talking to Tiny and Slim at the time. Tiny saw them enter the shop and said, "Well, what do we have here? Two little dormice!" The young girl looked offended and said, "I will thank you to watch your tongue, Big Man." Her younger brother, who carried a wooden sword, said, "Be careful of whom you insult, Big Man." Tiny smiled and said, "Oh! My apologies." He then bowed and said, "My Princess! And such a brave young warrior."

The two children looked at each other with a triumphant grin. The young girl wore a blue hat. She was obviously very proud of it as she constantly viewed herself in the mirror which Marcus kept in the corner of the shop, adjusting her hat until she was completely satisfied. Marcus said, "That is a beautiful hat, Princess. I have just the thing for you." He went to the back of the shop and returned after a few minutes with a large red feather. Marcus said, "Here, Princess." and pinned it to her hat."

The young girl squealed in excitement. Slim said, "Well! Don't you look beautiful?" The two children became regular visitors to his shop but always seemed disappointed if Tiny was not present.

Marcus was forever grateful to Barnabas's brother for teaching him the blacksmith's trade, which meant that he was always able to earn a living. As a result, he quickly settled into his new life in Colchester. Overall, he got on very well with the residents and developed a very good relationship with them. In fact, he felt quite at home in Colchester, which had three Roman Theatres and the only Chariot Racing Circus in Britannia. It also had a Temple dedicated to Claudius. At times, he felt it was almost like being at home. To Marcus's surprise, he was actually a very good blacksmith. He was not normally good at repairing and fixing things, and whilst he was growing up, it was the household slaves who undertook all the menial work. He considered it unthinkable that he could be seen shoeing a horse. In fact, the only time he had held a hammer was on Crucifixion duty. However, he soon acquired an excellent reputation for his work.

Marcus was often called to work in surrounding towns and villages, and, on one occasion, he was asked to travel to Londinium (London). Even though it was a long journey, it was a city that he had always wanted to visit. At the end of the first day's journey, as he stopped to feed his horses, he saw a massive army appear on the horizon, approaching from the south, and heading in his direction. Marcus's first instinct was to run, but he knew that with the simple cart and horse that he had, he could never outrun them. He had no choice but to stay where he was.

As the army grew closer, from what he could see from the formation of the soldiers, it appeared that there were at least one hundred and twenty thousand fully armed warriors.

Marcus stood in amazement, as if frozen to the spot, whilst the massive Army walked by him. They just ignored him. It was as if he was not there! The warriors were painted blue and displayed the most brutal and ferocious expressions that he had ever seen on any face. It took a full hour for the Army to pass by and, in the middle of the warriors, he saw a woman riding a war chariot. She had long, fiery red hair and as she passed his cart, she turned her head and looked in his direction. She appeared to look straight through him. Her eyes seemed cold and hard. Marcus felt a shiver run down his spine. They obviously mistook him for a Britain, and they had more important things to do than harass a poor blacksmith. The most disturbing thing was that the Army passed by him without a sound. Marcus had been in many battles and dangerous situations, but this was the only time that he had ever felt real fear.

When the Army had passed, he decided to continue his journey and to spend the night in the next village that he came to. When he arrived, it was nearly dusk. There was only one name on the lips of each of the villagers—that of Boudicca. Marcus was told that Boudicca's hordes had attacked Londinium and massacred the population. The Roman Legion had apparently realised that they could not possibly defend the city and had fled, leaving the city totally undefended.

The carnage was, apparently, terrible. Marcus was told that over seventy thousand people had been slaughtered. After hearing the grim news, he decided to return to Colchester. He spent the night in the village inn and departed for Colchester the next morning.

All the way back to Colchester, Marcus could not dismiss the image of Boudicca and her cold, hard stare. He was still several miles away from the city when he saw smoke on the horizon. Colchester was burning. Even though Marcus had only lived in the city for a few months, he had befriended many of the city's inhabitants, including the men whom he had got to know whilst travelling back from Dover. After hearing of the fate of the population of Londinium, he feared for Colchester.

CHAPTER 16

THE BURNT FEATHER

As HE ENTERED what was left of the city of Colchester, all his fears were realised. The capital had been burned to the ground and there were very few survivors. The smell of death hung over the city. Marcus helped the few survivors to bury the dead, before making his way to his blacksmith's shop, which had been ransacked and burned. Marcus surveyed the damage. His shop had suffered less than most of the buildings in the city. The roof was still burning, but at least the stone walls seemed intact. Marcus set about the task of removing the still-burning roof, which had collapsed into his shop. After the fire was extinguished, and the wood removed, Marcus was horrified to discover five badly burnt bodies. One was that of a tall man with a sword in his hand who was obviously protecting his two friends from the Iceni onslaught. Marcus looked at the bodies of the dead Iceni warriors—both had several sword wounds and he noticed one had lost a hand in the fight. Marcus turned to the body of his friend and said, "Well done, Tiny." Marcus carefully removed the bodies of his friends and buried them in what remained of his courtyard. It was hard work, and it took him several hours. Through his labour, he tried to block out the constant sound of screaming as people from all over the city buried their loved ones. When Marcus had finished, it was dark, and he sat down on the ground near the graves of his friends. The sounds of screaming had been replaced by an eerie silence. The smell of the burning city combined with the smell of death was nauseating. Marcus tied his scarf around his face and sat staring into the sky which still had a red glow from the many fires that consumed the city.

After what seemed like several hours, but what was, in fact, no more than twenty minutes, Marcus slowly stood and then leaned against the wall of his forge, noticing it was still warm even though the fire had been extinguished hours earlier. In the front of his shop was a large oak tree. He looked at the tree, still smouldering. Some of its branches had fallen off and lay black and charred on the ground. As Marcus's eyes tracked the trunk of the tree, he noticed something at the top. At first he thought it was a small animal. He moved to get a closer look, wondering how it was possible for an animal to climb so high. He let out a large gasp. It was the bodies of two children, who had obviously climbed the tree to escape the carnage. One of the children wore what remained of a hat. Marcus recognised one of the feathers which decorated the hat. It was almost burned away, but there was no doubt. Marcus closed his eyes to block out the image, but it made no difference. The image of the burned feather was seared into his mind. He would never be free of it. Whenever he heard of a massacre anywhere in the world, the image of the burned feather would return. His face was covered in soot and ash and now, his tears ran down his face, making it look like a macabre mask. Marcus opened the graves of his friends and gently placed Princess and Little Warrior next to them. He took a sword from his shop and put it in the hand of the little Warrior and, what was left of the feather, he put in the hair of the Princess.

It was late and Marcus was exhausted, but there was one thing he needed to do. He went back into his shop. As he passed the bodies of the Iceni, he cursed and spat on them. Marcus examined the forge. He then pulled away a loose stone covering a hole at the base of the forge which he used as a hiding place for his money and the Artefacts, and found, to his relief, that it was all still there, untouched and intact. He then dragged the bodies of the Iceni warriors out of his shop and hung them feet first on the burnt oak tree. He then shouted, "Let the crows have you."

CHAPTER 17
GERTRUDE

OVER THE COMING weeks, Marcus worked alongside the survivors of Colchester in assisting with the rebuilding of the city. He soon discovered that the majority of the people whom he had known prior to the attack had been killed. Those who came into Marcus's smithy now were unknown to him. As with most people who have shared a traumatic experience, on the whole, the people who came into his shop were exceptionally friendly. There were, however, exceptions! There was one incident, in particular, which he had never forgotten, involving an individual whose name was Gertrude.

Gertrude was pretty, slim, and approximately five feet five inches tall. She had an engaging smile and an infectious laugh. She was obviously highly intelligent. She was one of the few women who carried a sword wherever she went and he soon realised that she would not be afraid to use it!

The first time she came into his blacksmith's shop, he was sharpening a sword. Whilst wandering around looking at some of the swords that were hanging on his wall, she stated, "I hear that you are a Roman." Marcus continued sharpening the sword, and, without looking up, answered, "Do you have a problem with that?" Gertrude slowly walked around his shop, carefully examining some of the tools he had made. She picked up a large hammer. Marcus said, "Be careful with that." Without looking at him, she put the hammer down and answered, "Why? What is the matter, Roman? It is not fragile, is it? Not much of a blacksmith, who makes fragile hammers." Marcus answered, "You will not find a stronger hammer anywhere. It is for you that I expressed concern. I thought you looked a little... delicate!" Again, without looking at him, she picked up a sword and held it outstretched, looking along the blade.

For the first time, Gertrude looked at him and said, "You have a secret, Roman." She moved the sword slowly through the air. Marcus responded, "What are you talking about?" Gertrude, holding the sword up in the air, replied, "The sword! How do you make it so light?" Marcus replied, "As you have already said, it is a secret."

Gertrude began to swing the sword around above her head at an incredible speed, then, throwing the sword into the air and catching it with her left hand, demonstrated that she was just as proficient with either hand.

189

She slashed out with the sword, missing his neck by no more than an inch. She followed by putting the sword under his chin. She was surprised to see that Marcus showed no fear. Gertrude stepped back a few paces, then threw the sword at Marcus. Marcus caught the sword with his left hand and, twirling it around, transferred it to his right hand and then back to his left.

Gertrude, obviously impressed with his swordsmanship, said, "Well, well… Methinks, not just a blacksmith, but a Legionnaire, and not just a common Legionnaire." She moved forward, put her hand under his chin and lifted it up, looking at his scar. She then looked down at his hand. Gertrude stepped back and said, "Also, a war hero. What rank?" Marcus was about to tell her to mind her own damn business when Gertrude said, "No, no. Do not tell… I think… a Centurion." Gertrude laughed. She could tell by the look on Marcus's face that she was correct, which made her laugh even louder!

Gertrude was one of those individuals who had both a smile and a laugh that were infectious. Marcus, looking at Gertrude, knew that he could very likely forgive her for almost anything. He asked, "Do you want to buy this sword, or are you just wasting my time?" Gertrude took the sword from his hand, and answered, "Well, yes. I rather think I will, but I actually came here to have my horse shod. How long will it take?" Marcus told her to come back in half an hour.

Gertrude moved across to a chair placed in the corner of the smithy and sat down. She said, "If you do not mind, I will wait." Marcus replied, "Please yourself" . Gertrude continued, "And… I will have a cup of wine whilst I am waiting." Marcus answered, "Sorry. I do not have any wine. You will have to make do with water." Gertrude looked surprised! "What? A Roman who does not have wine?! I will bring some with me on the next occasion I visit your smithy."

Gertrude stayed at the smithy for over an hour and talked constantly. She told Marcus how her husband and her young son had been killed by Boudicca and how she had managed to escape with her two daughters. Gertrude said that after her experience at the hands of the Iceni, she had decided to learn how to use a sword. She added that, surprisingly, she thought she was very good.

"Now, I do not, unfortunately, have anyone with whom I can practice," Gertrude said to Marcus, who responded, "I really do not understand at all why you cannot find anyone with whom you could practice your skills!" Gertrude laughed, and answered, "Because they are all big babies. Just because during our practices, I cut some of them a little, just a little, they all went home crying to their wives! I now have no one with whom I can practice." Gertrude paused for a second, looked at Marcus and said, "Until now!" Marcus continued, "Where did you cut them?" Gertrude smiled, and then drew a finger across her throat! Marcus answered, "Oh no. Oh no, girl. No chance!" Gertrude protested, "It was not my fault; they were just too slow and, anyhow, I only nicked them a little." Marcus's loud laughter was swiftly followed by Gertrude's.

The following day, Gertrude walked into Marcus's smithy carrying a large flagon of wine. Marcus told her that he did not drink wine. Gertrude smiled and answered, "Who said it was for you, Roman?" Marcus grinned and shook his head.

Marcus saw a lot of Gertrude. Whenever she was in town, she always found a reason to come into his smithy. She would sit down on his chair and pour out a cup of wine. Sometimes, she would stay for hours, talking about her life. Marcus came to really enjoy her visits and was disappointed on the days when he did not see her.

After a while, Marcus, reluctantly, agreed to practice sword-fighting with Gertrude. He took her into the yard at the back of his smithy. As she stood in front of him, she drew her sword. Marcus told her that in practice sessions, they should only use wooden swords. Gertrude's response was to laugh and shout, "Toys, toys, toys. I have not come here to play with toys!" Marcus smiled and answered, "You keep your sword, and I will make do with this." Marcus picked up a wooden sword from the corner of his yard and then said, "Let's go!"

Gertrude ran at Marcus, slashing her sword from side to side as she approached him. Marcus stepped to his left. Gertrude swung her sword at Marcus. He stepped to his right. Gertrude thrust her sword towards Marcus, who stepped to his left. Gertrude began to look frustrated and tried driving her sword towards his stomach. Marcus thrust his wooden sword towards Gertrude and, spinning his sword around Gertrude's weapon, flicked her sword into the air. It soared over her head and landed on the ground behind where she stood. As she turned and bent to retrieve her weapon, Marcus hit her hard on her bottom, knocking her over. Gertrude lay on the ground, looking extremely angry, then Marcus shouted at her, "Never turn your back on anyone!" Gertrude jumped up and ran screaming at Marcus, who stepped to one side. As her momentum carried her past him, Marcus pushed Gertrude into the wall of the smithy yard. Marcus, laughing, said, "You fight like a farmboy." Gertrude again slashed at Marcus, who dropped to one knee and pushed his wooden sword upwards towards her stomach.

As Marcus stood upright, he saw Gertrude's face change from anger to admiration. She said, "Wow, Roman, you will have to teach me some of those moves" . Marcus was pleased that he had beaten Gertrude through his skill and expertise with a sword and not because of any supernatural intervention.

Gertrude came to his smithy at least twice each week to practice. Marcus was impressed with the progress she was making and said to her, "I will make a Roman of you yet!" Gertrude laughed and said, "Over my dead body, Roman!" Marcus smiled, replying, "Maybe so, maybe so, farmgirl."

Gertrude would quite often bring her two daughters with her when she came to practice with Marcus. Her eldest daughter, Mildred, asked Marcus if he would teach her how to fight. Marcus laughed and told her that he would do so, but only if she agreed to use a wooden sword. He said that it was scary enough fighting her mother, with her sharpened sword. He added, "I do not want to risk losing an ear, or worse, twice in a day!" Mildred laughed and agreed. It turned out to be a very good decision. Mildred, even though she was only young, no older than fourteen, soon became so proficient that after one particular session, Marcus was left with heavy bruising on the side of his face and a pain in his stomach.

Mildred apologised profusely, although she could not help but grin. Marcus held up his hands and lied. He said, "Do not worry. It did not hurt." When Mildred had left, Marcus lifted his shirt to reveal heavy bruising on his stomach. Marcus closed the door of the smithy and screamed at the top of his voice.

Gertrude's younger daughter, Matilda, was a gentler girl. Marcus would often ask Gertrude, "Are you sure that Matilda is yours?" Gertrude would reply, "I have a softer side, Roman. It may be that it is you... you must bring out the worst in me!" She then burst out laughing!

Matilda liked nothing better than drawing or painting. Marcus thought that she was quite talented. She told Marcus that she would like to be a sculptor. One evening, after he had closed the smithy for the night, he rode out to Gertrude's farm. Gertrude welcomed him in her usual fashion—"Hello, Roman. To what do we owe this honour? You, a Centurion, coming all the way out here to my farm to see me?" Marcus laughed and said, "Do not flatter yourself, Gertrude. I have come to see Matilda." Gertrude looked slightly disappointed and went to fetch Matilda. After several minutes, Matilda appeared and said, "Hello, Marcus. Mother said that you wanted to see me?" Matilda was the only person in the household who did not call him 'Roman'. Marcus said,

"I have come to give you a gift." He opened his bag and produced a small hammer and a set of chisels, which he handed to Matilda and said, "No doubt you can now become the best sculptor who ever lived." Marcus never forgot the look of sheer delight on Matilda's face. Even after hundreds of years, the memory of it still brings a smile to his face.

One morning, Gertrude and her daughters came to his smithy and asked him if he would come out to her farmhouse and look at her plough. As it was already late, Marcus closed his smithy and accompanied Gertrude and her daughters back to their farmhouse.

After examining the plough, he told her that it was unrepairable, adding that he would make her a new plough, and if she came to his shop towards the end of the following week, it would be ready for her. Gertrude arrived the following week with a large cart pulled by two magnificent black horses. Marcus volunteered to accompany her back to her farm. He was mindful that people were looking at her cart, with the new plough loaded on the back, and also at the two black horses. He was well aware that the roads were dangerous places in first-century Britannia.

Initially, Gertrude seemed quite offended by his offer to accompany her back to her farm because of the possibility of an attack by robbers. She retorted, "I can look after myself. Let them try! You are probably the only one who could better me with a sword." Marcus replied, "What if there were two of them, or even three or four?" Gertrude thought for a moment and then, begrudgingly, nodded her head. Marcus tied his horse to the back of Gertrude's cart and joined Gertrude at the front. They had travelled approximately two miles when they were attacked by four men. One of the men threw a spear at Gertrude. Marcus leaned across in front of Gertrude. The attacker looked amazed when the spear missed; it seemed to turn in the air and go around Marcus.

Gertrude pushed Marcus out of her way and jumped from the cart, drawing her sword in one swift movement. She went down on one knee, as Marcus had taught her, and then drove her sword upwards into the robber's stomach. She quickly spun around and cut off the head of the second man. Marcus was slower to react as he was watching Gertrude in amazement and admiration. By the time Marcus joined the fight, there was only one robber remaining. Marcus drew his sword and swung at the robber only to miss him. The robber slashed at Marcus and failed. Marcus thrust his sword at the robber again, closely missing him. The robber thrust his sword at Marcus but missed. Marcus heard Gertrude, who was behind him, shout, "Oh, for goodness sake!" Marcus looked up and saw the robber's head flying. A smiling Gertrude looked at him triumphantly, saying, "I don't know how I could have managed without you! I actually didn't know if you were fighting or dancing!" All Marcus could say was, "He was very fast!"

On the way to the farm, both Marcus and Gertrude were lost in their thoughts. Marcus could not grasp what was happening. He was stunned that he was unable to land a blow with his sword. He knew that he was not allowed to kill or to save anyone, but he had always assumed it was a matter of choice, even though he was aware that the wrong choice carried terrible consequences. Marcus really did not understand what was happening. "Surely," he thought to himself, "if I am prepared to accept the consequences which such an action would have on my life—and, on this occasion, I was certainly willing to do so—am I really supposed to watch Gertrude suffer and die?" It now appeared that he had to live with the reality that not only was he not allowed to kill, but he was also unable to kill under any circumstances, even if it meant he had to witness the death of an innocent.

Marcus remembered his fight with Yusuf and his two companions and how, using his stick, he had been able to render them unconscious, which led Marcus to assume that he was allowed to defend himself, or others. Now, it seemed that his assumption was wrong.

On the journey home, Gertrude found it hard to conceal her anger. She was aware that Marcus would have had little trouble dealing with the four attackers. In fact, she was aware that he could have taken and overcome all four with one hand tied behind his back. Over the past few months, since they had become friends and got to know each other, they had, on many occasions, held 'training fights'. Although she was well known for her skills with a sword, Marcus could better her. In fact, quite often, she thought that when he was fighting with her, he was deliberately taking it easy!

As they arrived at the farm, Gertrude could not contain herself any longer. She shouted at Marcus, "That was the most ridiculous thing that I have ever seen! You looked like a pair of clowns." All Marcus could think of saying was, "I have killed lots of men in my lifetime. I think I have killed enough." For a moment, Marcus thought that Gertrude was going to explode. She shouted, "Enough! What do you mean? Enough! If people attacked you, then it does not matter if you have killed one person or killed a thousand! What have numbers got to do with it?" Marcus had no answer to give to Gertrude, partly because he completely agreed with her.

Marcus and Gertrude unloaded the new plough in complete silence. When they had finished, Gertrude did not invite Marcus into the farmhouse for a drink. She simply walked into the building without a word and closed the door. Marcus untied his horse from the cart and made his way home.

It was at least six weeks before Marcus saw Gertrude again. He was finishing shoeing a horse when Gertrude appeared and stood behind him. He heard her say, "Hello, Roman. I hope you still have my flagon of wine?" It amused him that even though they had got to know each other so well, she still addressed him as 'Roman'. Marcus turned around and was delighted to see Gertrude standing there, smiling at him as if she had never been away. Marcus said, "Help yourself to the wine. I will be finished in a minute." Gertrude found the flagon in the corner and then sat down, watching Marcus as he finished his work.

After a few minutes of silence, Gertrude said, "Have you heard the news? Boudicca has been defeated." She took a large drink of wine from her cup, stood up and threw what remained onto the floor. As she walked out the door, she said, "They are bringing some of the Iceni prisoners here, and they will be most welcome." Gertrude stopped at the doorway and said, "See you in the morning, Roman."

Gertrude had lost a lot of friends, a brother, a husband, and her young son to Boudicca and to the Iceni hordes when they had attacked Colchester, and, without mercy, slaughtered thousands of people. The city was practically undefended at the time. There were no walls and only approximately two hundred Roman soldiers to defend the city against the invaders.

Many of those who survived the initial onslaught sought refuge in the Temple of Claudius. They believed that the heavy wooden doors would protect them. However, Boudicca ordered that the Temple be set on fire. They also burnt the city to the ground. Gertrude said that the screams could be heard from a great distance. She had once told Marcus that she could never forget it and could still hear the screams.

Boudicca and the Iceni blamed the people of Colchester for the Roman invasion. They claimed that their Colchester King had invited Claudius into their country as an ally. Marcus could not understand the Iceni point of view. Boudicca's husband had made a pact with Rome, and when he died, Boudicca chose not to honour it. Marcus knew that it was not a good idea to break your word when you were dealing with Rome. He was well aware that when "you dance with the Devil, the Devil calls the tune".

When the inhabitants of the city heard that Boudicca had been defeated, and that she was dead, they celebrated for days. After the blood lust had ended, the following months in Colchester were difficult. It was an exceptionally dangerous and depressing place to be living. Day after day, prisoners from the Iceni tribe would be marched into the city. Some were executed immediately, while others were sold into slavery, but the most unfortunate ones were kept for entertainment.

Gertrude's anger and hatred for the Iceni knew no bounds. Although she was a very beautiful woman, her hatred and rage, when exhibited, made her ugly. Gertrude was more than happy to help organise the entertainment provided by the torture and punishments meted out to the Iceni soldiers. No one was spared her wrath, not even the children. Marcus told her that she should have pity on the very young ones. Her response was that he should save his sympathy for the children and the inhabitants of Colchester who were burned alive by the Iceni devils. Marcus did clearly remember entering the city after the attack and being told of the terrible atrocities committed by the Iceni people when they attacked the city. There was very little he could say to Gertrude which would help to assuage her anger.

Marcus had learned to accept that the world in the first century was a cruel place, and he was discovering, albeit with difficulty, that it was better to keep his opinions to himself. During this time, Marcus saw very little of Gertrude, which pleased him. Although he fully understood her rage, he found it difficult and very unpleasant to be in the company of someone filled with such hatred.

Marcus waited for a few weeks before visiting Gertrude, hoping that her anger would have subsided. Marcus took a large flagon of wine as a 'peace offering'. When he arrived at Gertrude's farmhouse, he could not believe how nervous he felt. As he stood outside the farmhouse door, he said to himself, "Why am I so nervous? What is the worst thing that could happen?" Marcus held the flagon of wine in front of him so that it would be the first thing that Gertrude would see when she opened the door. Marcus knocked on the door and waited. He was pleased when Gertrude opened the door, and it was immediately apparent that she was really pleased to see him. She swung the door open wide, and smiling, said, "Hello, Roman. It is good to see you!" She ushered Marcus into her cottage and he stayed until dusk, when Gertrude said, "You should not stay any longer. You do not want to be attacked and be forced into performing another ridiculous dance." Marcus smiled and laughed. "Oh, ha, ha. Very funny!" He was glad Gertrude appeared to be back to her old self.

The following day, Gertrude came to his shop and stayed for most of the day. He was pleased that she did not once mention the events and the atrocities in which she had been involved. For the first time, Marcus realised that his nature was changing. For some reason, the atrocities committed in Colchester had affected him more than he could understand. He had witnessed many massacres in his life and he had taken an active and enthusiastic part in many of them. He had always considered them to be part of his work in being a Legionnaire; something of which to be proud. After all, he considered that only a Roman life had any real value.

When he looked back over his life, he had real difficulty in believing he had ever felt that way. He remembered the time in Jerusalem when he had offered to kill Saul. John had asked him to sit down and told him that not only was killing wrong, but even wanting someone to be dead was wrong. Marcus remembered how ridiculous that had sounded at the time. He was now starting to see wisdom in mercy. He found it disturbing. It was as if there were three people living within him, all fighting for supremacy. The Centurion, proud, strong and arrogant—a man whom other men looked up to and even envied. There was a part of him that yearned for this old Marcus, but there was also a part of him that was ashamed of the man he had once been. Now, there seemed to be a metamorphosis taking place. He was uncertain of what this new man heralded and feared for the future and the type of man he would become. He decided, for the sake of his sanity, to try in the best way that he possibly could to forget the old Marcus and move on with his life.

Marcus's business was doing well. In fact, it was doing extremely well and increasing to such an extent that over the next few months, he was able to employ two young men. Marcus was not interested in either purchasing or using slaves. He was aware that this was because of the bad influence of Cephas and Paul! He recalled the time when Cephas had asked him to get Addayya a cup of wine. At first, he had felt insulted because Addayya was a mere slave. Then, through the wisdom and teaching of Cephas, he had come to realise that Addayya was not an inferior human being, but an individual who, like so many thousands of people in the Ancient World, and through no fault of their own, found themselves in the

205

wrong place at the wrong time. They were then easy victims for mighty Rome. Over the few weeks that Addayya and Marcus spent together at Mary's house, they had become quite close friends. Marcus came to regard Addayya almost in the same way as a little brother. He even suggested that Addayya accompany him to Philippi, but Cephas said that it was not a good idea.

Marcus, contrary to his expectations, was quite enjoying living in Colchester. He became friendly with the local inhabitants, and they seemed quite happy with the fact that he did not particularly want to socialise. Colchester was an important city to Rome. There was a constant stream of people travelling between Rome and Colchester and Marcus was able to keep well-informed on the news from home. He was deeply concerned to hear that life in Rome was becoming very dangerous for his friends. He managed to locate a group of merchants who were on their way back to Rome and he asked if they could deliver a letter for him to his friends. In his letter to Cephas, Marcus asked about his health and that of his friends. He asked whether they needed anything and, if that was the case, assured him that he would be pleased to send money to them.

Marcus would never forget the day he received the reply. He opened the letter with a mixture of excitement and trepidation. The letter began with good news. Cephas had promised to keep an eye on his family. Even though it was painful to read, as he missed his family and often thought of them, it was good to hear that they were all doing well. As he continued to read the letter, he was scarcely able to believe what he was reading. His good friend, Paul, had been arrested and executed. Cephas explained that they were in a very desperate situation and any help Marcus could offer would be gratefully received. Marcus immediately began making plans to leave for Rome as soon as possible. One of the young men he employed agreed to overlook the smithy, and Marcus asked a neighbour to look after his house whilst he was away.

As Marcus was making his way back to his smithy to make the final arrangements before he left, he heard a voice that made his blood run cold. He looked around, but the only person close to him was an old man. Marcus said to the old man, "Did you say something?" The old man smiled and said, "I must apologise for this rather unseemly grotesque body. It always amazes me why people let their bodies get into this condition. The problem is, I cannot take just any body, and this was the best I could do at such short notice." The old man gave a large sigh and said, "Oh well! I supposed it will have to do."

Marcus answered, "Flavian, will you get the hell out of my way, and out of my life?!" Flavian said, "My dear Centurion, I would like nothing better! Do you really believe that I enjoy your company? No! Assuredly not! I only require the Artefacts. Give them to me and I will leave you and your woman alone." Marcus said, "What woman?" Flavian laughed as he heard the fear in Marcus's voice. Flavian could smell fear; in fact, he could almost taste it. Flavian said, "Come now! You know who I mean… that rather striking warrior girl. I must admit, I underestimated that girl, and I can tell you, that does not happen often. I sent four good men to deal with her and she just swatted them like flies." Marcus could feel a rage building up inside of him and he screamed, "You leave her alone or I…." Flavian interrupted, "Or you will do what?" Marcus said, "I cannot give you the Artefacts." Flavian said, "Oh, do not tell me that the little girl told you not to part with them? Well, it is entirely up to you, but you have been warned." Suddenly, the old man shook his head, looked around with a bewildered look on his face and said, "Who are you? What am I doing here?" Flavian was gone!

Marcus ran to his smithy as fast as he could. As soon as he arrived, he started to saddle his horse. One of the young men who worked for him shouted, "Marcus, are you all right?" Marcus did not answer. As he mounted his horse, the young man said, "What is wrong? Where are you going?" But it was as if Marcus had not heard him. Marcus galloped away.

Marcus was never a great horseman. He could ride quite well, but he could never beat anyone in a race. Normally, he was happy to ride at a gentle pace, but now he galloped as if all Hell was chasing after him. He doubted that any man alive could have kept up with him. But it was too late. He knew that as soon as he approached Gertrude's farmhouse.

Everywhere was quiet and the barn was burning. Then he heard a scream. Marcus ran into the house. The first thing Marcus saw was Gertrude's housekeeper. She was crying and wailing. Then he saw the object of her distress. It was Gertrude. It was clear that she was dead. Marcus fell to his knees and screamed. He screamed for Gertrude and for her daughters. He screamed for his own family back in Rome and how he missed them and how much he longed to see them. Unexpectedly, long-forgotten memories flooded his mind. Memories of battles, massacres… an execution in which he was all too willing to participate. He remembered young men begging for mercy. He remembered ignoring those pleas, and now, as he stood over the body of Gertrude, he realised for the first time the full extent of what he had done. Not just to those whom he had killed, but to the mothers, fathers, brothers, and sisters who screamed when they heard the news that a Roman soldier had killed their loved one. As he was on his knees, he did something he never expected to do—he thanked God for the curse. He thanked God that he could never kill again.

Marcus struggled to come to terms with Gertrude's death; he blamed himself. He had stayed too long in Colchester. He had made it easy for Flavian to find him, and he had allowed himself to get close to Gertrude, making her a target. He knew that in future, he had to be much more careful around those he cared for and loved.

Marcus postponed his trip to Rome for a week. He felt that he had to stay for the funeral and to ensure that her family were all as well as could be expected. Gertrude's mother had moved into the farmhouse to take care of Gertrude's two daughters. In truth, there was nothing he could do for them, and he felt that he was needed more in Rome.

CHAPTER 18

THE STEWARD

MARCUS PULLED AWAY the loose stones from around his forge to reveal the bag which contained his money and the Artefacts. He transferred the money to a shoulder bag. Marcus gave last-minute instructions to the two young men who worked for him before he mounted his horse and galloped away.

He felt he needed to get to Rome as quickly as possible. It was the first occasion in a very long time when Marcus had been in a rush to get anywhere. Frustratingly, when Marcus finally arrived at Dover, he had to wait two days for a ship that was bound for Rome. In the meantime, Marcus managed to find lodgings which overlooked the harbour. He viewed the voyage with dread. Sailing in the first century was far from safe. He had considered taking the short trip across the Channel and then travelling overland to Rome, but he decided it would be quicker to travel by ship, a decision he would later live to regret.

When Marcus saw the ship, 'Phoebe', on which he was to make the voyage, his heart sank. It looked very much as though the ship would not make it out of the port in which it was moored! It looked at least a hundred years old! Marcus asked the captain if the ship was safe. His response was curt and he was clearly offended by Marcus's comments. He said, "Old Phoebe, the ship is called. Let me tell you that there is not a better ship anywhere. I have sailed to Rome more times than I care to remember on Phoebe, so you have no need to worry about her."

A deckhand showed Marcus to his cabin. Reluctantly, Marcus stashed his bag in his cabin and decided it was probably safer to spend as little time as possible there, as it was the last place he wanted to be if the ship went down. Marcus stayed on deck as the ship sailed out of the harbour and watched as Dover disappeared into the distance.

To Marcus's surprise, the ship provided quite a smooth voyage, and, to his great relief, they crossed the Bay of Biscay without incident and sailed smoothly past Gibraltar into the Mediterranean. Marcus, however, was far from convinced that the ship was safe and, as soon as he awoke each morning, he would hurry up on deck and spend the rest of the day there, even when the weather was bad.

Each morning, Marcus took his leather bag, which contained his money and the Artefacts and strapped it to his back. Even though the captain constantly assured him that the ship was safe, Marcus remained unconvinced. If the worst happened and the ship foundered, the last thing that he wanted was to have to run back to his cabin to retrieve his bag.

As Marcus wandered around the deck of the ship, he noticed that an older sailor appeared to be repairing a rowing boat on the deck of the ship. Marcus said to him, "If you do not mind me saying, would it not have been a better idea to have repaired that boat before we left port?" The old man laughed and said, "Don't you worry, Sir. We will not be needing this boat. Old Phoebe will take good care of us."

Marcus turned away from the old man, but then turned back and said, "What was that strange noise?" The old man answered, "Sorry, Sir, but I did not hear anything." Marcus said, "Surely you must have heard that strange sound coming from over there," Marcus continued, pointing to the horizon. The old man looked in the direction Marcus was pointing, scratched his head and answered, "Sorry, but I cannot see anything". He then turned away and returned to his work. As Marcus watched, the man appeared to be putting tar on the inside and the outside of the small boat. Marcus noticed that the small boat had neither a rudder nor sails and thought to himself, "God help us if we actually need that thing."

Marcus turned away from the old man and left him to continue with his work.

He walked to the side of the ship, leaned on the rail and was staring down at the sea when a crew member came up to him and said, "If I were you, Sir, I would get down below deck. It looks very much as though we have some bad weather ahead of us." Marcus followed the man's gaze. In the distance, he saw what appeared to be a storm. Marcus answered the crewman, "It will miss us and go to the right. The crewman answered, "Maybe, but I doubt it. It does seem to be heading straight for us."

As Marcus looked in the direction of the storm, he saw the clouds getting darker by the second and, to his dismay, it appeared that the crewman was correct—it was moving in their direction. The ship started to heave up and down and then swing from side to side, gently at first, but becoming more and more violent in its movements. He heard the same noise again. He could not establish what the sound was, nor from where it originated, but he was sure it was exactly the same sound that he was hearing again and again. Marcus was becoming increasingly worried. In addition, darkness had now fallen.

Marcus was now desperately holding onto the rail as the ship was rocked back and forth. He heard a huge crack, followed by fork lightning, and then by deafening thunder. Marcus was now being dragged from side to side as he desperately held onto the rail whilst the gigantic waves pounded the ship. He saw the captain shouting to him, but he was unable to hear what he was saying above the noise of the storm. The captain pointed— Marcus turned to see what it was that he was pointing at and saw that a large barrel filled with the ship's drinking water had broken loose and was now rolling around the deck and heading in Marcus's direction. Just in time, Marcus dived out of the way of the barrel as it crashed into the side of the ship where he had been standing, smashing a huge hole in its side.

Marcus frantically tried to grab the ship's rail but could not hold onto it. He was tossed around the deck, thrown backwards and forwards. He saw some of the sailors washed over the side of the ship, their screams lost in the storm. Marcus looked upwards and saw the ship's mast snap as if it were a piece of firewood. He heard the sound again. This time, he recognised what it was, although he shook his head, refusing to believe what he was hearing. Then a huge wave hit the ship and he felt as though a giant hand was lifting him up and throwing him into the sea. He was pulled down and down. Instinctively, he tried to remove his heavy bag as he was dragged down further into the depths. He heard a voice in his head laughing and saying, "I have you now…now I have you." It appeared to be the voice of Flavian! Marcus then realised what Flavian wanted. He wanted the bag that contained the Artefacts. Marcus thought to himself, "Oh no! Oh no you don't. There is no way you are having this bag!" Marcus strapped his bag tighter across his body.

Marcus felt as if he had been released from its grip and swam as quickly as he could towards the surface. As he did so, a huge wave lifted him up and up. He gasped air as the wave lifted him higher and higher. Marcus looked down and saw the Phoebe below him. Gigantic waves were pounding her and, suddenly, as though the ship could take no more, she rolled over and disappeared. Marcus again heard the strange sound. However, this time he had no doubt. He knew what he had heard—he had heard the Tempest laugh! The wave that had lifted Marcus collapsed and he found himself struggling to stay afloat. As suddenly as it had started, the storm ceased, the wind calmed, the sky cleared, and the sea became silent and still.

All around him, Marcus could see floating driftwood. It was the remains of the Phoebe. He felt a huge sadness. Even though he had hated every moment on the ship, now it was gone, reduced to a few scattered remains, floating on the now calm sea, he felt a deep sense of loss. he was thankful that he could not see the bodies of any of the crew. It was almost as if he had lost a friend. He knew it was a ship, just a ship, and that he was being foolish, but, nevertheless, he could now understand how sailors felt about the ships upon which they had worked and served.

After a few minutes, Marcus could see, a short distance away, the small boat that the old man had been repairing. He swam over to it and even though it was no more than twenty yards, he struggled to make it to the boat. Every part of his body was aching, whilst the weight of his rucksack threatened to pull him down. When he finally reached the sanctuary of the little boat, he hung on to its side for a few minutes whilst he regained his strength. Somehow, he managed to pull the rucksack from his back whilst clinging to the boat with one hand. He was afraid of letting go of his hold on the boat because he knew if he started sinking, he would not have the strength to swim another yard. Marcus threw the rucksack inside the boat, then summoned what remained of his strength and climbed inside. He collapsed inside the boat, curled up and immediately fell asleep. As he slept, he could feel the boat gently bobbing up and down. He had no idea where he was, but at this moment in time, he did not care.

Marcus had no idea how long he had slept. He awoke to the sound of men loudly calling to him. He opened his eyes and sat up to see a group of men standing around the boat. They were looking down at him, amazed at the sight of Marcus lying in the boat in front of them. He had lost most of his clothes and his body was a mass of bruises. He was also covered with a black sticky substance. It took a few moments for him to realise that it was the tar that the old man had been brushing onto the outside and inside of the small boat.

The men who had been standing around reached down to lift him out of the boat. Marcus screamed in pain. He had not felt such pain since he had jumped off the cliff in Cyprus. Marcus gritted his teeth. He later discovered that these were Sicilian fishermen, and they did not do 'gently'. They were, however, good men and took him to one of their cottages where he spent several days recovering.

The cottage, which was by no means small, belonged to a man called Tommaso. Marcus was immediately impressed by the cottage, but Tommaso apologised when he showed Marcus to the room that he would be staying in. He said, "It is a bit small and at night, the lights from the harbour can keep you awake, but if you really have trouble sleeping, I am sure that I can do something." Marcus breathed a sigh of relief. It had been over thirty years since he was locked in the tomb, yet he still had a fear of the dark. Marcus said, "Please, please, do not worry about it. This will be just perfect."

Marcus never managed to establish how many children Tommaso actually had in his care, as he was endlessly bumping into different ones! Wherever he went in the cottage, he would see a child he had never previously seen, who would smile at him and say, "Hello" . Marcus was fascinated by the cottage. it had at least seven bedrooms, which were always fully occupied by children!

The day before he was to leave Tommaso's house, as he walked along the beach, he saw one of the fishermen who had helped to rescue him. He was a young, tough-looking lad in his early twenties and as soon as he saw Marcus, he came over to ask him how he was doing and if his bruises were healing. Marcus, who still exhibited two black eyes, answered, "The bruises are still here, but fortunately, they do not hurt any longer." The lad nodded and said, quietly, "Good. That is good. I suppose you will be on your way soon?" Marcus answered that he would be leaving in the next couple of days. The lad, laughing, asked, "How are you managing with all those kids?" Marcus grinned and said, "Who are all those children? Where do they come from?" The lad shrugged his shoulders and said, "Orphans. Tommaso and his wife took in one lad a few years back. Now they just turn up, uninvited, and make themselves at home. Old Tommaso and his wife never turn any of them away." Marcus asked how he could afford to feed so many children and the lad answered, "Well, old Tommaso isn't short of money. It is him who owns the fishing fleet around here. It is only a small fleet, but it is enough to keep the kids fed." As the lad turned away, Marcus thanked him again for his part in his rescue.

Marcus made his way back to Tommaso's cottage. At the side of the building, he saw a young boy who looked approximately eight years old. He noticed that the lad had a large knife in his hand. Marcus sat down and said, "Hey, young man, what are you up to?" Marcus was not very good at talking to children and was not surprised when the lad did not answer him. The boy continued to ignore Marcus for several minutes, but then answered, "Tommaso said it was all right for me to carve my name on the stone wall as long as I don't do any damage, but I can't make any impression on the stone." Marcus answered, "Would you like me to help?" The boy nodded. Marcus took the knife from the boy, picked up a large stone and used it as a hammer and the knife as a chisel. Marcus smiled at the boy and said, "What is your name?" The boy answered, in a whisper, "Paolo." Marcus said, "That is a fine name, Paolo. We will carve your name nice and deep and then one day, your grandchildren will come here and say, "This is where our grandfather carved his name, with a strange man who survived a shipwreck." The boy laughed and said, "You must add your name, otherwise no one will ever know who the strange, shipwrecked survivor is." Marcus laughed, and said, "Well, that wouldn't do, would it?"

Marcus very carefully carved "Paolo and Marcus, shipwrecked survivor" onto the wall. Paolo had a huge smile on his face as Marcus got up to leave. Paolo stayed behind staring at the name carved into the wall.

Since the shipwreck, Marcus had found that he was easily exhausted, which was not surprising at all considering the way he had been thrown about on board the Phoebe. As he now found it difficult to breathe, he thought that when he was slammed against the ship's rails, he may have broken a few ribs. Marcus sat down on his bed and picked up his shoulder bag. He thought it was a miracle that it had not been lost in the storm, even though it had been strapped tightly to his back. He then lay down and fell into a deep sleep.

Marcus was woken by a loud knock on the door. Tommaso popped his head around the door and said, "If you want to eat, you need to come down now." Marcus thanked him and made his way down the stairs. He sat down at the kitchen table, which was occupied by a number of children, some of whom he had not previously seen. As they ate breakfast, Tommaso told Marcus he was going to Rome on business, departing early the following morning and that if Marcus wished, he was very welcome to accompany him. Marcus gave a weak smile. He was not looking forward to getting onto a ship again!

Early next morning, Marcus and Tommaso set off to the harbour, with Marcus warily looking up at the sky, whilst Tommaso constantly tried to reassure him that the weather was fine and there were no signs of a storm. Marcus answered that what he had just said was exactly what the Captain of the Phoebe had said before they set sail!

Marcus knew his fear was irrational, because he was aware that the storm which took the Phoebe down to the bottom of the sea had been supernatural. He kept trying to convince himself that he could not possibly have heard Flavian's voice as he was being dragged down below the waves or heard laughing in the storm. Marcus felt it was preferable not to tell Tommaso that the Phoebe was sunk by a homicidal demon which was chasing him.

As they boarded the ship, Tommaso said, "This is a good ship… a strong ship." He saw that Marcus was about to say something, but Tommaso held up his hand and said, "Don't tell me that what I have just said is exactly what the captain of the 'Phoebe' said!" Marcus laughed and replied, "No, I was about to say that this is a damn fine ship, and I was looking forward to the voyage." This comment caused both men to burst out laughing. Tommaso nodded to the ship's captain, which Marcus assumed was a signal for the captain to get the ship under way. As they made their way to their cabin, Marcus said to Tommaso, "I suppose that you will take the captain's cabin?" Tommaso shook his head and said, "No. The captain is in charge of the vessel, not the owner." He looked at Marcus and said, "Respect. Always show respect." Marcus had only known Tommaso for a few days, but already, he had tremendous respect for him.

Marcus asked him about the children and how he had got involved with looking after so many. There was a long pause before Tommaso answered and said that looking after orphaned children was never actually a plan. He looked uncomfortable for a moment and then continued, "It was on one of my business trips to Rome." Tommaso paused, then continued; "I met this strange man called Cephas." Marcus said, "What… Cephas?" Tommaso answered, "Yes. Have you heard of him?" Marcus replied, "Yes, but never mind that. Just finish your story." Tommaso looked as if he was going to ask Marcus a question, but then decided against it. Tommaso continued, "Cephas had just finished addressing a small crowd of people and we started talking. He asked me what I did for a living. I told him I had a small fleet of ships. Cephas said that I must be quite wealthy, and I answered that, well, I do all right. Then, to my absolute amazement, Cephas said, "You do know that the money you have is not your money. You are only a steward." I responded and asked, "Are you mad? Only a steward? What is that supposed to mean?" Cephas continued, "You only hold that money in trust. You are supposed to help people with it." I answered, "Who—who are the people I am supposed to help?" Cephas replied that I would know when the time came. I must admit that I thought it was all very strange. He does have a way of getting under your skin, Cephas does!" Marcus laughed and said, "You are not joking… but carry on with what happened next." Tommaso said, "Well, when I arrived back in Sicily, I told my wife what had happened and she said, "Well… Let us see what happens." I must admit to rather hoping that would be the end of the matter."

Tommaso looked at Marcus with a huge smile on his face and said, "I rather like having money and I did not like the idea of giving it away, but the next morning, I was walking through the town when I heard a lot of people shouting and then a small boy, carrying a large loaf of bread—well, the loaf was almost as big as the lad himself—ran straight into me. The baker then came running out of his shop with a big stick and thanked me for stopping the lad. The lad was now hiding behind me. I asked the baker what he intended to do with the stick and he answered that the boy had stolen his bread. I gave him some money and said that it would pay for his bread. He took the money and then raised his stick to beat the lad. I held up my hand and asked him, "What do you think you are doing? I have paid you for the bread." The baker replied, "The boy is a thief, and he needs to be taught a lesson." I then took the stick from the baker and hit him hard across the face with it. I thought Cephas would be proud of me." Marcus thought to himself that he did not think so. Tommaso carried on; "I took the boy home, and I thought I would give him a meal and that would be it! I was quite pleased with myself. I thought I had done what Cephas had said, and all it cost me was a loaf of bread and a meal, but, surprisingly, when the lad had finished his meal, he said that he was tired, and he would like to go to bed now. I was flabbergasted and asked him whether his mother and father would wonder where he was." He then told us that he was an orphan. At this point, my wife gave him a big hug and told me to take him to his room. Well, that is how it started."

Marcus was fascinated by Tommaso's story and urged him to continue. Tommaso said, "Well, the little lad settled in well. My wife even paid for tuition for him to learn to read and write. A few days later, two small girls came along and just moved in." He laughed and said, "You had breakfast with them yesterday" . Marcus said, "I remember them, but they did not seem that young." Tommaso said, "Well. It was a few years ago when they first came, and then after that, children kept coming and so I had to buy a bigger cottage to accommodate all these children. That is where all my money goes—on the children!" As Tommaso finished talking, the captain shouted across to him and he apologised and said to Marcus, "I had better go and see what he wants!" Marcus was left on his own, on the deck of the ship, thinking about the incredible story he had just heard. Marcus was disappointed that he did not have the opportunity to talk to Tommaso again as they would arrive in Rome shortly afterward.

CHAPTER 19
GIRL IN THE CUPBOARD

As HE DREW nearer to the city, his anxiety grew. On his arrival in Rome, it did not take him long to locate Cephas. He found him, surprisingly, in high spirits, living in a squalid part of town. He could not, however, believe his eyes. Cephas was old! They talked well into the night. Marcus told him about his life in Colchester and of his smithy. The conversation took a sombre note when Cephas told Marcus of the arrest and the dreadful treatment of his friends, not just those in Rome, but throughout the Empire.

Cephas sat quietly for a few minutes. He then stood, walked around the table and put his hands on Marcus's shoulders. "My dear friend, thank you for coming and for your very generous gift." Cephas patted Marcus on his back and, laughing, said, "We will ignore the fact that you cannot keep it anyway!" This comment was met with much hilarity.

Cephas smiled and said, "I have a surprise for you, but not for now. You will have to wait a little." Marcus was intrigued and answered, "Do not keep me in suspense, Cephas. What is the surprise?" Cephas laughed and said, "You are still like a big baby! You will just have to wait."

Marcus thoroughly enjoyed being with Cephas. Cephas, however, explained that Marcus needed to go home because it was far too dangerous for him to stay any longer in Rome. He told Marcus that his friends were all being arrested. Some were being sold into slavery, others were being thrown into the arena and torn to pieces by wild animals, and some were burned alive. Marcus protested, "I have never run away from a fight, nor deserted my friends." Cephas gently replied, "Marcus, your sword and spear are of no use here. We are well-armed with the weapons that we need." Marcus tried to answer, but Cephas put up his hand and simply said, "No, no, my good friend. You need to go home." Cephas made it clear that the conversation was at an end by turning away to talk to a small group of frightened-looking people who had just entered the room.

A few minutes later, 'the surprise' arrived. Marcus shouted out in delight. He was overwhelmed! It was Addayya! Marcus ran over and hugged him. Addayya introduced Marcus to his wife, Tamar, and their three children. Their eldest son was called Marcus! To Marcus's surprise, Tamar suddenly hugged him, sobbing loudly, and began to smother his face and neck with kisses, repeating over and over again, "Thank you. Thank you. Thank you."

Marcus started to feel uncomfortable. He glanced at Addayya and gently tried to push Tamar away, but Tamar clung onto him, sobbing louder. Marcus, not knowing what to do, patted her on the back, repeating, "It's all right… It's all right. What is the matter?" To Marcus's surprise, this had the desired effect. Tamar let go of Marcus, took a step back, then took hold of Marcus's hands, turned to Addayya and started sobbing again. Marcus looked around the room and, to his annoyance, Cephas looked amused at Marcus's embarrassment.

Tamar then made an announcement that completely shocked Marcus. She looked across to Addayya and said, "This is the man who risked his life to save me." Marcus looked closely at Tamar. He could hardly believe it, but she was the girl in the cupboard! Marcus was completely overwhelmed. It was now his turn to hug Tamar. He told her he had always wondered whether she had ever made it out of the village alive.

Tamar stopped sobbing, dried her eyes and told Marcus what had subsequently happened after he had been forced to leave the house where she was hiding.

She explained that she had stayed in the cupboard for hours. She had heard Marcus telling the other soldiers that the house was empty. She was terrified when she heard Marcus being ordered to leave the house. She had stayed hidden in the cupboard until it got very dark. Then, she very quietly sneaked out of the house. She said that she had nearly screamed and screamed when she saw the bodies of her family but remembered what Marcus had said to her—that she must be very brave.

Tamar continued, "I managed to escape just in time. When I thought I had got far enough away and that it was safe, I sat down, looked back and watched as they burned my village to the ground." Marcus asked, "What did you do? Where did you go?" Tamar continued, "The problem was that I had nowhere to go. All my family and my friends lived in the village. As far as I know, I was the only survivor. The Romans are very efficient." Tamar paused for a moment. Everyone in the room sat in silence. Marcus watched as Tamar struggled with her memories. Over time, he had learned to allow people to tell their story when they were ready, and at their own speed. He sat and waited. When Tamar had composed herself, she continued her story. She explained to Marcus that she had walked for a long time. She had been extremely frightened because her father had often told her how dangerous it was at night. She said that she was fortunate; she saw a light in the distance, but it was a long way away.

She continued, "I heard the Romans searching for anyone who had escaped the massacre of the village, and so I hid behind a tree. Then I heard a voice. I looked around but could not see anyone. It was strange because the voice was very soft, almost a whisper, but there was no one there." Marcus asked, "What did the voice say?" There was a long pause before Tamar answered. Very quietly, she said, "You are safe now."

Tamar paused as she turned and glanced at Addayya, who smiled at her in encouragement. Tamar continued; "Suddenly, out of nowhere, a young man was standing beside me. He said, "Come with me. My Master sent me to find you." We must have walked for about forty minutes. I could still hear the Romans in the distance. I cannot explain it, but I felt no fear. All the way to his master's camp, I kept asking him what his Master was like." Marcus asked, "What did the man say?" She said, "He told me that his Master was a very kind man and as long as I was with him, I would be safe. I would no longer be afraid."

Tamar looked around triumphantly at those listening to her, and said, "And I have not." Then, she continued her story. She said that as she approached the master's camp, she saw an elderly man coming to meet them. "He picked me up and hugged me and carried me back to his camp because he could see that I was very tired. We sat around the large fire in the middle of the camp. They gave me some food and asked what I was doing out alone, so I told them my story."

Tamar looked across at Marcus and told him that she would never forget the look of concern on their faces. As Tamar continued her story, she looked up at her sons who nodded and smiled, encouraging her to continue. It was clear that they were unaware of their mother's history. Tamar told them that after she had explained to the travellers why she was out on her own at night and what she was doing, they had excused themselves and walked a small distance away so she could not hear what they were saying, whilst they considered what Tamar had said to them. After a short period of time, they came and sat down next to her. Tamar said that they had looked very serious. They told her she must not tell her story to anyone else, and she must never again mention the name of her village. They explained that the Romans had put a Death Order on the village. "You will stay with us," the old man had explained. He looked around at the group, pointed to the young man sitting next to him, and said,

"This fine young man, sat here, is now your brother." He laughed, continued, and said, "That makes me your father."

She said that she had stayed with the family for many years until she met Addayya. She smiled at Cephas and said that one day she had gone to see the great Cephas. She smiled again and said, "Stood next to him was my very handsome Addayya." Tamar showed them two golden bracelets that she had been given as a wedding present by her new father. She then opened a small bag that she wore on her shoulder and took out a white stone. It looked like a marble stone, but it was pure white. There were no black lines in it as one would normally find in a marble stone. Tamar took a deep breath as if she was about to say something she found very difficult. She then continued, "When I first climbed into the cupboard, my sister tried to climb in with me, but there was not enough room. We could not close the cupboard door and so my sister said that she would find another hiding place. She kissed me on the cheek and said, "Do not worry, little sister. I will see you later." She then climbed out and that was the last time I saw her alive." All the time that Tamar was talking, she did not take her eyes away from the white stone. It took a while for her to compose herself, and then she continued. "When

I left the cupboard, I made my way out of the village. I saw my sister's body. It was clear that she had not died quickly. I told my new father how guilty I felt, and it was then that he gave me the white stone. He told me that whenever I felt guilty, I had to look at the stone and remember that I was innocent. In fact, it means more than that. It means that no charge can be held against me. So, whenever I feel bad, I look at my stone and I remember my sister for her beauty and for her bravery and how proud I am of her."

Marcus thought to himself how strange life was and how the consequences of one good deed could go on for generations. Because he had spared Tamar, she had grown up to be a beautiful, kind woman who went on to meet and then marry Addayya and to be blessed with three fine sons! He had no doubt that their story would go on for many generations to come.

Marcus then thought of all the bad things he had done during his life. Even though some of them may have been unintentional, the consequences could remain for many years. Marcus looked across at his friend Cephas who smiled weakly. Marcus thought to himself that Cephas always knew what he was thinking.

Marcus, Addayya and Cephas sat down and talked about their time in Jerusalem. Marcus told Addayya about his time in Cyprus and in Colchester. As Addayya and his family left, Marcus promised to visit them before he left for Britannia.

It was decided that Marcus would stay in Rome for a few more days and then make his way back to Britannia. It always amazed Marcus that even though Cephas was no longer a young man, he never seemed to rest. He was always the first to rise each morning, for which Marcus was grateful! It meant that he and Cephas could enjoy many conversations on a wide variety of topics.

Cephas spoke gently to Marcus. "You must be very careful. You must never spend too long in any one place. No more than ten years. In addition, you must build Cities of Refuge." Marcus replied that he understood. After ten years or so, people would wonder why he was not ageing. He did not, however, understand what Cephas meant by a 'City of Refuge'.

Cephas started to explain: "In the Torah…" he saw Marcus roll his eyes. "No, no. Listen to what I am saying. Soon everyone you know and love will be gone. You will be completely on your own. There will be times when you will need to run. In the Torah, the Jews had to build Cities of Refuge. These had to be within one day's journey of each other. Some existing cities still have houses for people who need a safe place to stay, especially if they are being pursued for crimes of which they are innocent."

Marcus thought for a moment, and then replied, "I do not understand. How does that apply to me? I cannot build a city." Cephas responded, "The idea came to me when you brought the gift, and I made that joke, because your money disappears as you are not allowed to get wealthy. What I propose is that we, your friends who are still here, can ask Mary Magdalene, John, Barnabas, and others who are with us, to each build a 'House of Refuge' in different cities.

"They can also then pass the message on, through the generations to come, that they must keep the Houses of Refuge as safe places for the Centurion. It will not be difficult for you to work out when you are getting near to your limit, and you can then send some money to the descendants of the people who love you. They will be able to ensure that should you need to run, you will always have a home which will provide safety and a refuge for you."

Marcus saw the wisdom in this and thanked Cephas. He stayed a few more days, during which time Cephas made a list of friends who would help Marcus and instructed him to contact them as soon as possible. The next morning, Marcus joined Cephas for breakfast, and after they had finished eating, Cephas suggested that they go for one last walk before Marcus set off for Colchester. Marcus readily agreed. He had a deep love for Rome, and he could not think of a better way of parting. As they walked down the busy streets, Marcus proudly looked up at the many Temples and the great buildings that adorned the magnificent city. He believed that to be born a Roman was the greatest gift that the Gods could bestow on a man. As they were walking, Cephas said to Marcus, "My friend, there is something I would like you to do for me." Marcus answered, "You know you only need to ask." Cephas said, "I would like you to go to the slave market early tomorrow morning." "Why?" asked Marcus. Cephas replied, "Just go."

They turned down one of Rome's narrow streets. They had not walked far when they heard a commotion; men shouting and women screaming. Marcus turned to see what was happening. Suddenly, a dozen soldiers surrounded Cephas and began dragging him away. In desperation, Marcus screamed for help and tried to fight his way through the soldiers to rescue Cephas, but it was too late. Cephas was gone, as quickly as if he had been swallowed up by the streets of Rome. Marcus just stood there, unable to move. It seemed unreal. It was as if he expected Cephas to come walking back down the street towards him.

GHOST CENTURION

Marcus walked through the streets for hours. He felt lost. To him, Rome had now completely lost its beauty. He was starting to see it in the way Cephas saw it—as hard and cruel. But, most of all, he saw it as lost. He recognised that it was lost, just as he was lost. If you are hard and cruel, but see yourself as good and glorious, then you are truly lost.

When he eventually arrived back at the house, his friends were relieved to see him. They had assumed he had also been arrested. As he packed his bag, they asked him to stay, but he told them that it had been Cephas's wish that he should leave. He told them he had one last thing to do, and then he would leave for Colchester. Marcus arose early the next morning and made his way to the slave market. Visiting the slave market was always an unpleasant experience. It was truly a terrible place, full of human misery. He wondered why Cephas had asked him to come here.

Marcus desperately wanted to leave the area, and it was only because of his friendship with Cephas that he stayed. After approximately an hour, Marcus was shocked to see a young family being dragged onto the large platform. The man and woman had clearly been beaten. At first, he did not recognise them, then, to his horror, he realised it was Addayya and his family.

Marcus was tall and always well-dressed. He looked intimidating; a man of stature. As he started bidding for Addayya and his family, not many of those present were prepared to bid against him.

After his bid was accepted, he was asked if he wanted them branded, or put in chains. Marcus told them that neither would be necessary. As Addayya and his family walked from the slave market, he told them to hurry. They made their way to Portus, a large artificial harbour on the banks of the Tiber. They were fortunate to find a boat heading for Cyprus. Addayya said that he felt he must stay in Rome with his brothers. Marcus looked at Addayya's wife and children. They looked terrified, and he could see from the expression on their faces that they were pleading for his help.

Marcus said to Addayya, "I do not like to say this to you in front of your family, Addayya, but you are an idiot! Fortunately, I have just purchased you and your whole family, and if I say you are going to Cyprus, then you are damn well going to Cyprus." Marcus saw a look of relief and joy on the face of Addayya's wife.

Marcus paid for passage for the family on the boat to Cyprus and gave Addayya's wife additional money for emergencies. He was not quite sure that he could trust Addayya.

Marcus asked the captain of the boat for something he could use to write a message. Marcus then sat and wrote a letter, which he gave to Addayya's wife. He told her that when they arrived in Cyprus, the family were to go to the farm where Barnabas and his family lived. He explained that the letter he had given to her confirmed that Marcus had set the family free. He turned to Addayya and said, "Again," which broke the tension and made everyone laugh. Marcus waited until the boat sailed away. He did not tell Addayya that Cephas had been arrested.

The truth was that Marcus no longer saw Rome as he had once done, as a beautiful city which embodied and illustrated the strength and power of the Roman Empire. Rome had, for him, now lost its beauty and attraction and he was ready to go anywhere except Rome. Marcus headed for Pompeii where he stayed for several days and then travelled to Naples where he spent a further few days, prior to sailing to Britannia.

Marcus arrived back in Colchester a very different man from the one who had left. Even with the minimal contact he allowed himself upon his return, he knew that people saw a difference in him. When he had left Britannia, he was a confident, successful businessman.

His confidence had been destroyed after witnessing the arrest of his good friend, Cephas.

Marcus had discovered that success was nothing to boast about, and failure was nothing of which to be ashamed. He now knew that one could only be successful at the pleasure of Rome.

CHAPTER 20

LAURA

MARCUS KEPT TO the advice given to him by Cephas and ensured he rarely stayed anywhere for much longer than ten years. Over the centuries, Marcus had lost contact with some of his Cities of Refuge. Cephas's family stayed in Rome, but after the sacking of Rome by the Visigoths, they disappeared from history. He had last heard of John's family in Greece in the seventh century. Of all his Cities of Refuge, there were now only two left.

Mary Magdalene's family had settled in Sicily. In 1947, he received a delightful letter from a young girl asking him if he was real. As much as he would have liked to have replied, he felt it was too dangerous to do so. The family of Barnabas continued to live in Cyprus. Both families were now totally unaware of their ancestry. They had no idea why this stranger would send money to them, and why they would have to keep a room always ready should it be needed by this strange man, known only as the Centurion.

He often thought of Addayya and his family. He knew that Barnabas's brother had taught him the trade of a blacksmith, and even though Marcus still regarded Addayya as somewhat of a fool, he knew that, fortunately, his wife was extremely intelligent. Marcus had every confidence that they would have a good and a happy life.

Marcus spent most of his time in England. He had found the English were the most civilised of people. They did not interfere in what you were doing, nor seek to know your life history!

In 1890, he had purchased a house in London, where he spent most of his time. Because of the English habit of "minding one's own business" and "keeping themselves to themselves", he felt safe enough to break Cephas's golden rule and he stayed longer than ten years.

Marcus had changed his name to Marcus Albright many years earlier. As he was only allowed to own two houses at one time, he maintained one house in Rome and one in London. He had tried to buy a third house in Paris, but when he went there with the intention of spending several months in the city, he discovered his house was occupied by a very angry Frenchman, who wanted to know what Marcus was doing trying to open his front door! When Marcus tried to explain that the house belonged to him, things became difficult, and the furious Frenchman threatened to call the Police!

Marcus calculated that at any particular moment in time, he was only allowed to retain three hundred thousand pounds, which was the equivalent amount he had when he was cursed. If he acquired even a single penny above that amount, the additional money would simply disappear. He ensured that whenever his money reached two hundred and fifty thousand pounds, he sent much of the surplus to either Barnabas or Mary's families and the rest he would give away to different charities.

Marcus did, however, have to earn a living. The days of the blacksmith were long gone! If he did not have employment, then his money would run out very quickly. Marcus was, however, fluent in four languages, and was highly respected in the fields of Classics, English Literature and Ancient History. He knew that even though he was an expert in so many fields, he needed to keep a low profile. He would find work as a truck driver, a postman and his latest career, as a supply teacher. However, this did, at times, raise some difficulties when he would meet Professors of Classics, or ancient history, when Marcus found it an irresistible temptation to show off his extensive knowledge.

There was, unfortunately, an incident with a Classics Professor, who fervently believed that Cicero was the greatest Philosopher who had ever existed until Marcus pointed out that he had stolen most of his material from his Carthaginian slave, whom he treated worse than he would a dog. The slave did not benefit!

The Professor had demanded to know how he had come by this nonsense. This was difficult for Marcus, as he could hardly tell the Professor that his grandfather had known Cicero well! As the Professor raised his voice and repeated that there was no record of Cicero having slaves, Marcus did not endear himself to the Professor by laughing and suggesting that he really ought to read more books about Rome and about slavery, adding that, if he did so, he might learn something! At this point, the Professor stormed out of the room, shouting obscenities in a most unprofessional manner.

Meanwhile, Marcus did have a friend. He had not had a real friend since Cephas. He had a lot of acquaintances, some of whom he had become very fond of, but no real friend. The house adjoining his had been re-let. A young woman—Laura—had rented the empty property. He had met her when she first moved in about a year ago. She was struggling to get her key into the door lock and Marcus had helped her.

Laura was a beautiful young woman, approximately nineteen hundred and fifty years younger than Marcus. She had beautiful shoulder-length, light brown hair with blonde streaks. She was one of those women who never missed a hair appointment and swore by her hairdresser, a man called Rupert, who had moved to the city from Manchester. Laura was always immaculately dressed. She was extremely intelligent and had an infectious laugh. She worked for a newspaper, was very ambitious and loved her profession. In a lot of ways, she reminded him of Gertrude. She had the same smile and, when she laughed, it was quite strange how similar her laugh was to that of Gertrude. Her ambition was to be a political correspondent. Marcus thought that should she ever achieve this ambition, then God help the Prime Minister!

Laura looked Marcus up and down and said, "What newspaper do you read?" Marcus, a little taken aback by the question, was unsure how to answer it.

"Er… The Times," he replied. Laura had a broad grin on her face, and said, "Well done," as if he had passed some sort of test. She added, in a matter-of-fact way, "That's where I work. What are your politics?" Marcus said, "I must confess, I start at the back page and work my way through the newspaper to the front page. I am not really into politics."

"Not into politics." She pointed to his house, and said, "Politics is about your house, your street, your school. What if you were attacked by a mob and there were no police, and you went to hospital and there were no doctors? You would be interested in politics then, wouldn't you?"

Marcus felt a little shell-shocked, and answered, "Well, if you put it like that, I suppose I should take more interest in who is running the country." He thought to himself, "My God, it is like talking to Gertrude."

Marcus asked Laura if she came from Colchester. She had a startled look on her face and answered, "No, but my grandparents came from Colchester." She asked how he had guessed. He told her that it was a lucky guess. It amused him that he was finally making friends with a Gertrude… a pleasant Gertrude! However, the fact that Laura resembled Gertrude only reminded him of how careful he had to be. As he had travelled around a lot over the last few years, he knew it was unlikely that Flavian had found him, and so he was probably safe for now, but he knew that he always had to be on the alert.

Marcus said, "I expect you are very busy, with just moving and all, but would you like to come in and have a coffee?" Laura replied, "Oh yes, please. I haven't stopped all day and my feet are killing me. I would love to sit down to a beautiful cappuccino."

Marcus screwed up his face and said, "Oh sorry. Just plain coffee, I am afraid." Before he could add anything else, Laura interrupted him and, putting her hands up, said, "Coffee will do very nicely." Marcus, looking embarrassed, added, "Sorry, no milk. Laughing, Laura said, "Black coffee; that sounds great."

Marcus made his way up the path to his house with Laura following him. He opened the door, ushered her in with a theatrical bow and said, "Welcome to my humble abode" . Laura laughed and stepping past him into the hall, said, "Well, thank you, kind sir." What she saw took her breath away. She stopped and looked around, scarcely able to believe what she was seeing. Marcus was a young man. He was well dressed, obviously well-educated, and not without money. No one living in a large house in this part of London could be described as poor.

Laura looked around the entrance hallway. It was drab—an old man's hallway. The wallpaper looked like something from the nineteenth century. The carpet was threadbare. There were no pictures of any kind on the walls, just a long boring old mirror. Marcus opened the door to the living room. Again, everywhere looked drab. There was a sofa and an armchair. In a corner stood an overlarge television, but, again, no pictures, no happy smiling Mum and Dad, or sweet little sister photographs.

Marcus opened the door which led to the kitchen, walked over to the sink and, turning around, asked, "Black coffee, it is then?" Laura looked around the room. The kitchen was quite large but very basic. There was a large table with a laptop and a stack of notepads on it. This was clearly used as Marcus's workplace.

As Marcus was making Laura her coffee, Laura asked, "How long have you lived here?" Marcus replied, "Oh, about a hundred and fifty years." Laura laughed. Marcus smiled. Laura continued, "Do you have family nearby?" "No. I am an orphan, I am afraid. Completely on my 'lonesome'," responded Marcus. Laura answered, "Oh, I am so sorry, Marcus. How terrible." Marcus said, "The way I look at it is that there are many people who are a lot worse off than me". Marcus then handed the cup of coffee to Laura, who replied, "What do you do for a living?" "Marcus said, "I teach Ancient History and Latin." Marcus sat down next to Laura and said, "You would not be very good at politics if you don't study history." Laura said, "How so? What's history got to do with politics?" Marcus smiled and said, "Well, that mob that was chasing me down the street. What is your politician's record on street crime? Does he even care about street crime? When I get to the hospital and there aren't any doctors, what is your politician's record on the health service? Remember, with politicians, talk is cheap; history counts." Laura took a sip of coffee; Marcus saw that she was about to say something but thought better of it. Marcus said, "Look, Laura, when you couldn't get your key in the door and I helped you, that was history and if you need help in the future, the probability is, because of that history, that you will come and ask me for help. That's life!" Laura laughed and said, "Life is not as simple as that" . Marcus interrupted and said, "The problem is that we make it too complicated because we do not want to know the truth." Laura said, "Well, I don't agree with that. I love the truth. I work for a newspaper." When she saw Marcus's smile, she paused, then said, "Well, not all newspapers tell lies." Marcus's smile grew wider. Laura laughed and said, "You pig, and I was just beginning to like you." Marcus and Laura talked late into the evening. Over the coming weeks, they met most days and became good friends.

Marcus was totally oblivious to the fact that Laura wanted to be more than friends. She could not understand why, even after they had known each other for several weeks, Marcus had not once shown any kind of affection; not a kiss... not even trying to hold her hand.

She was, however, convinced that Marcus had deep feelings for her. However, occasionally, she wondered if she was just fooling herself.

It was 6.00 pm and Marcus was expecting Laura. He heard the door open and then slam shut—Marcus never locked the door—he heard Laura shout, "It is only me." Marcus smiled as he continued preparing a cappuccino for Laura. He prided himself on his skill at making coffee for her. Laura wandered into his kitchen, as usual, talking about a dozen things at the same time. She sat at the table. As Marcus placed a coffee in front of her, she stopped talking for a second whilst she tasted it. "Wow, that's gorgeous," she said, as she carried on talking, even more quickly. Marcus smiled and listened attentively as she recounted her day. When she finally stopped for breath, she looked up from her coffee and asked, "How has your day been? Encountered any Syrian swordsmen trying to decapitate you, or Egyptian bowmen firing a flaming arrow at you?" she asked, laughingly. Laura had asked him weeks earlier about the scarring on his neck and on his hand. He had a huge grin on his face as he told her that a giant Syrian swordsman had tried to take off his head. "But," he had added, "I was just too quick for him." He stood up, demonstrating with an imaginary sword. She roared with laughter, and said,

"OK. What about the scar on your hand?" In a very serious voice, which then made her laugh even more, he pointed his hand upward to an imaginary archer in the distance, moving his hand as if following an imaginary arrow, screaming as if he had been hit, and holding his hand in pain. He then stood upright, tall, and straight, and, in a theatrical voice, stated that he simply snapped off the arrowhead, removed his scarf, wrapped it round his hand and carried on fighting. Thus he had become a hero of the Legion, and, subsequently, was given a medal for exhibiting such bravery. He then gave an elaborate, sweeping bow.

Laura laughed and pointed out that they did not award medals in the Roman Army. Marcus looked at Laura, his face very serious and said, "Really? Is that true?" Marcus told the truth with his words but lied with his laughter. He had learned a long time ago that making a joke and laughing was a good way of closing a conversation. Laura looked at Marcus and smiled, but it was a forced smile. She remembered when she had asked if she could look at his scars, and he had regaled her with his story of them being battle scars. She could not help thinking that the scar on his neck looked very much as though someone had tried to decapitate him. The scar on his hand showed clearly that something had

253

passed through his hand, as both sides of his hand were badly burned.

Obviously, she did not believe his hilarious and theatrical explanations, but she felt a certain unease about his story. It was a feeling she often encountered when talking to Marcus. There always seemed to be a story behind the story. She would frequently enquire about the lecture he had prepared for the following day. There were times when he would talk about characters from history or the classics almost as if he knew them; some with a fondness, even love, and some with a seemingly unreasonable hatred. His feelings for Brutus, for instance, seemed almost personal. How could someone living in the twenty-first century have a hatred for someone who lived in the first century?

Marcus would talk about some of the Kings of England with contempt. His description of several of them was that they were egotistical psychopaths. His opinion, often voiced, was that if one wanted to survive in the Middle Ages, the best way to achieve that was to stay as far away from them as possible. There were, however, exceptions, one being Alfred the Great, whom he talked about as if he had been a personal friend. Marcus called Alfred the Great's eldest daughter, Aethelflaed, "The Greatest Englishwoman" who had ever lived. He told her that the Lords, at the time, had to think of a new title to honour her, and the title they decided upon was Lady; Lady of Mercia. This is where the word 'Lady' had originated.

He added that apart from Alfred and several other exceptions, the best of kings were actually the worst. Laura looked puzzled. "How does that make any sense?" Marcus explained that they had abused the sovereignty which they had to such an extent that the barons had stripped them of much of their power. However, they were so arrogant that they did not learn, and, eventually, they lost all their power. "And that was the being of the great democracy we have now," he added.

Listening to Marcus, Laura thought that something was strange. It was not so much what Marcus was saying, but something in the way he related the events and the way he described that specific time in history which was really bizarre. He talked of walking along the Thames Embankment and of how it smelt appallingly of raw sewage. His descriptions of how the heads of traitors were impaled on London Bridge, impossible though it was, sounded as though they were being recited by someone who had seen the actual events. Marcus never spoke about his childhood. He never spoke about his mother or his father. Laura did not know whether he had siblings or cousins. Nor did she know where he was born. Whenever she asked about his family, he always found a way of shutting down the conversation.

Laura thought there was so much about Marcus that was strange and even mysterious. She had considered Googling his name, or even asking one of her reporter friends if they could find any information, any records, in fact, anything at all, about him. She then felt very guilty and ashamed for even considering such a thing. Should she actually enact any of these options, she thought that it would be such a betrayal of trust that Marcus would never forgive her, and she could not blame him.

Laura would quite often stay at Marcus's house until late into the evening. Marcus always enjoyed his time with Laura, and they would frequently go to the Marah Chain of Cafés. For some reason, he had always felt comfortable there. He could relax. He would always try to get a seat near the window and watch the world go by. When he drank his bottle of water and relaxed, he felt as though he was laying down some great burden. He was glad people's habits had changed over the years. They were now so much more suited to his lifestyle. At one time, if anyone had asked for a drink of water in a restaurant, people would have looked at them as if they were some kind of a miser! Marcus had often felt embarrassed and believed he needed to make excuses for only drinking water. Nowadays, of course, it is very common for people to go into a coffee house or café and spend hours chatting together and drinking bottled water. So often in his life, Marcus had experienced how quickly things can change.

It was a lovely Saturday afternoon and he and Laura were sitting in his garden enjoying the sunshine. Laura seemed to be in a strange mood, almost as if she was annoyed or had been upset and was too angry to talk about it. Eventually, Marcus said, "Okay. I give in. What have I done wrong?" "Nothing!" Laura said, without looking up. Marcus stood and started walking backwards and forwards along his garden path, as he tried to recall what he might possibly have done that had annoyed and upset Laura. When she had arrived at his house, she had seemed to be in such a good mood. That was only an hour ago. What on earth had he said or done in that time to annoy her so much? He walked up to Laura, and, in the gentlest voice he could elicit, said, "I am truly sorry if I have said or done anything, anything at all, to upset you. Please tell me; after all, we have been friends for a long time. Surely, we should be able to talk it through."

For a moment, Marcus thought that Laura was going to explode. "I don't want to be your friend," she screamed. "Or your mate or your pal. I have got all the friends I need." Laura slowly got to her feet. Marcus could see that she was trying her best to hold back the tears but without much success. Marcus was a kind man. He felt her anger and her distress. He had a real urge to tell her the truth, but how was it possible to explain to a girl who is in love with you, that you have been cursed and cannot have romantic feelings for anyone?

Laura wiped her face with her hands. She really did not want to cry or to seem pathetic. She was angry and, at the same time, disappointed with herself. She looked at Marcus and said, "Am I not pretty enough? Is there something about me that you do not like?" Marcus was searching for the right words, but he knew he could not say what she wanted to hear. "I don't know what to say. I don't know what you want." Marcus knew it was a lame thing to say, but he was genuinely stuck for words. Laura simply said, "More". She picked up her bag and, without another word, turned and walked out through the door. She was gone.

Marcus just stood and looked at the closed door unable to come to terms with what had happened. He waited for what seemed to him like an age. Laura did not come back.

Marcus was plunged into a new type of loneliness. He decided that what Tennyson had said, "…that it was better to have loved and lost than not to have loved at all…", was rubbish. In fact, it was absolute nonsense. In two thousand years, he had never felt as he did now. He should not have allowed himself to get that close to Laura. Any fool could have told him it would not work.

Months went by without Marcus seeing Laura. As she only lived next door, he could only guess she must be deliberately avoiding him. He often went to the café where they had been together so many times and he would sit for hours drinking his bottle of water and reading his newspaper. He would take long walks along the embankment. Sometimes he would stand outside her door, wondering whether to knock, but he could not see the point. Marcus now felt uncomfortable living in London. He thought that it was too soon to return to Rome permanently as he had only left the city as recently as a year ago. However, he did believe that he could risk returning for a short time. He was fortunate in that he had not yet rented out his property in Rome. So, as long as he kept a low profile, he believed it would be safe for him to move back into his house whilst he decided on his next move.

The following morning, he bought his newspaper and made his way to the café. After purchasing a bottle of water, he sat down at his usual table. As was his habit, he started reading the newspaper from the back—the two great loves in his life were sports and his work! He finally finished reading the sports section and turned to the front page. As he was not in any way interested in politics, he moved quickly through that section until a particular article caught his eye. The article was about Saint Peter. The name Saint Peter always annoyed him. He would say to himself, over and over again, that his name was Cephas, Cephas! When they translated the Bible, why did they change the names? Peter was not called Peter; he was called Cephas.

He knew, however, that it was the same with all Empires. If you lived within the Roman Empire, you had to speak Latin. For example, it was also typical of the English, in that, whenever they went abroad, they assumed everyone would be able to speak English. Centuries ago, when they had invaded Wales, they could not pronounce the Welsh names, and the inhabitants had to change their birth names to more easily pronounced names, such as Jones or Evans.

Marcus continued reading the article. Apparently, they had received permission to drill a tiny hole in the sarcophagus and insert a small camera to enable them to look at the body of St. Peter. Marcus was stunned. To the rest of the world, he was the great Saint Peter, but to Marcus, he was Cephas, his friend. It felt to Marcus as though they were crucifying Cephas all over again.

Marcus had often felt that grief was a strange beast. You thought you had conquered it, and buried it deep inside, only for it to rise up and bite you when you least expected it. So it was with Marcus after the death of Cephas. Marcus had never really grieved for Cephas. He could not understand why he felt this way. Perhaps it was losing Laura, or maybe the memory of Cephas's arrest, or perhaps it was prompted by the article he had just read.

He knew that there was no reasoning with grief. There was no real understanding of it. Marcus could feel it welling up deep inside him. He tried to push it down, but grief was determined to have its way. Marcus wept. He wept for Cephas. He wept for Laura. He wept for himself, and he wept for Yeshua. Yeshua did not deserve what he did to him. Like the breaking of a great dam, his grief overwhelmed him. He held his head in his hands and sobbed.

Customers in the café looked uncomfortable; one young girl came and sat next to him and asked if there was anything she could do to help him. The lady who

worked behind the counter came over. Marcus apologised. She told him not to apologise and offered to get
him a drink, which he politely refused. Marcus thanked
them for their kindness, got up and made his way to the
door.

Once outside, Marcus dried his eyes and hurried away.
He walked along the Thames Embankment, trying to
come to terms with what had happened in the café. He
decided to forget it—to put it behind him and move
on. In a few weeks, he would be in Rome, and all this
would be just another memory, no different from all his
other memories.

Marcus kept to his habit of buying his morning
paper and going to a café, where he would sit with his
bottle of water and read the newspaper. However, he was
still too embarrassed to go to his usual one, and instead,
had found an alternative café where he could have a glass
of water and enjoy reading his morning paper. After a
while, Marcus left the café and started his walk along
the embankment. About five minutes into his walk, he
heard a voice behind him. He turned around; it was
Laura. She was slightly out of breath, indicating that she

had seen him and had rushed to catch up to him. They stood and looked at each other. Laura broke the silence; "I hope you are being careful and watching out for any Syrian swordsman!" Marcus smiled, and said, "I am more concerned about those pesky Egyptian bowmen." Laura laughed.

Nervously, Marcus asked if she would like a coffee. Laura grinned and replied, "And a water!" As they walked back towards the café, Laura linked arms with him. It made Marcus feel good. He thought to himself that this was just like old times, but he knew that was not true. Things could never really be the same again.

When they arrived at the Marah Coffee Café, Marcus paused at the door. Laura asked if everything was okay. He looked through the doorway and saw the lady who had been so kind to him on the last occasion he had been here. He laughed and assured her that everything was great. She looked at him suspiciously. She had understood for some time now that Marcus would often laugh, purely to avoid confrontation.

He went to the counter and ordered a coffee for Laura and his usual bottle of water. The lady behind the counter smiled but said nothing of his last visit. Laura chattered away excitedly. She told Marcus that she had a new role at the newspaper—she was now working in the

Archives Section. Her job was to go through the history of the newspaper, back to its origins, and transfer it all online. She explained that, as a historian, Marcus would be fascinated.

There was a long awkward silence between them. It had been months since they had last spoken; it was Laura who broke the silence. She said, "Guess how old 'The Times Newspaper' is? Guess when its first edition was published?" Marcus replied, "I have no idea." Disappointed, Laura pleaded, "Go on… go on! Just one guess." Marcus replied, "1066". Laura looked disappointed. "Don't be so boring. You won't believe it," she said. "It was first published in January 1785 under the title of Universal Register and changed its name to 'The Times' in 1788."

Laura seemed almost triumphant as she relayed this information to Marcus. Marcus, however, responded with a sarcastic "Wow!" which Laura totally ignored, whilst proceeding to tell him of some of the fascinating stories she had uncovered. Marcus thought some of the news stories and articles she had unearthed were really quite interesting. She recited some of the headlines of the articles she had read, which had been published over a hundred years ago. Marcus was trying to recollect where he had been at that particular time. Some dates were easy to remember. He could always remember where he was whenever there was a war in progress.

At times of conflict, Marcus thought it advisable to live as far from the war zone as was possible. The last time he became involved in a conflict was in the English Civil War, with, for him, almost disastrous consequences. He had totally misjudged the situation. He had thought it was a local skirmish that he would easily be able to avoid. He did not favour any particular side. When he was with the Royalists, he would say, "God Save the King". When he was with the Parliamentarians, he would say, "To hell with the King", but most of the time, he was able to keep himself, and his opinions, to himself. He was aware that wars were very good for business. Even with the advent of guns and cannons, there was still plenty of work for a good blacksmith. He specialised in making pikes; a rather horrid, but profitable weapon, used in the Civil War. It consisted of a long spear with a rather vicious-looking hook at the end. He would quite often deliver the weapons to the soldiers near the battlefield.

It was one such occasion that taught him to stay as far away from a battlefield as he possibly could do! He had just delivered his goods and was feeling quite pleased with himself when someone shouted, "Quick! Move. The

Royalists are coming." He knew that the last thing he needed was to be found selling arms to the Parliamentarian Army! He mounted his horse and galloped away. He saw a large group of Parliamentarians ahead of him. In his time in the Legion, he had learned that there was "Safety in Numbers". So, he chased after them. As he rode through the trees, he saw thousands of soldiers. To his horror, as they cleared the woods onto open ground, he realised he was on a battlefield. There was nothing he could do other than to keep riding with the Parliamentary Cavalry.

Suddenly, thousands of Royalist Infantry appeared on the brow of the hill, about two hundred yards ahead of him. Before anyone could react, thousands of musket rounds tore into the Parliamentarian ranks.

The men to his left and right were shot from their horses. He could feel the musket rounds flying past him. He could hear the sound of the musket rounds bending in the air and going around him. It was as if they were hitting something solid in front of him, then being deflected and ricocheting away. He could actually hear the musket rounds 'ping' and rebound.

He was wearing baggy clothing and he could feel the musket rounds tearing through his clothes. He felt his horse shudder as it was hit by a number of musket rounds. The horse's front legs buckled beneath him, causing Marcus to fly over the horse's head and hit the ground heavily. As he lay there, winded, he saw his horse roll over and miraculously bounce over him.

He then heard a sound like thunder. To his horror, he saw hundreds of Royalist Cavalry bearing down on him. There was nothing he could do other than lie still and hope. As the Cavalry charged down upon him, the horses started to crash into one another as they desperately tried to avoid him. Some of the horses were knocked off balance, sending them and their riders flying to the ground. It was chaos as horses and men were bouncing over him. The riders who were able to remain on their mounts, whilst the horses were swerving to avoid hitting him, tried throwing their pikes at him. Each time, they missed. Some slashed out at him with their swords; again they missed. Sometimes, the swords cut through his jacket, and even his shirt was cut into pieces. One of the pikes landed inches from his face. He could clearly see the maker's mark on the pike—"MWM"—Marcus Weapons Maker.

Marcus lay flat on the ground. He could feel it shaking under him. It was the Royalist Cavalry on the retreat, and they were coming his way. Again, the horses were swerving to avoid him, but this time, it was not quite as chaotic as there were far fewer Royalist Cavalry. He lay there with his eyes closed, exhausted and trembling. He then heard the sound of men talking. The first voice said, "It's a bloody miracle." The second voice, "It's a bloody, bloody miracle." The third voice said, "I've never seen anything like it!" Marcus thought to himself that they really were an eloquent lot, these Parliamentarians.

Marcus opened his eyes to see that he was surrounded by approximately a dozen soldiers, all gazing intently at him. As he looked around, he discovered the reason for their obvious incredulity. His clothes had been ripped to shreds, without any obvious harm to himself. There were pikes sticking into the ground all around him. Some were just a few inches from his body. One, alarmingly, was between his legs. Around him were dozens of dead horses and dead men.

One of the Parliamentarians said, "Can you stand up, mate?" Marcus said nothing but merely nodded his head. As he sat up, one of the men held out his hand, and Marcus gratefully grabbed hold of it and was pulled up from the ground. As he stood upright, he saw that both of his jacket sleeves were hanging off. Both of his trouser legs were completely shredded, and even the heel of one of his boots had been sliced off. The men laughed as they saw his clothes hanging off him. One of the men said that it was the strangest thing he had ever seen. He added, "It does not seem natural!" Marcus was now starting to get a little alarmed. He was, of course, aware that 'so-called' witches were regularly burned at the stake. He looked down at his shredded clothes and said, "It is a good job I did not put on my best jacket!" At this remark, the men burst out laughing! Marcus had learned that humour could be very helpful in intense situations.

The Parliamentarians told him not to worry, that they would find him some fresh clothes and get him another horse. Marcus thought that he would rather walk home naked than spend another minute in their company! However, he thought it was wiser to keep quiet, to let them provide him with fresh clothing and a horse, and then to slip away. They invited him to sit with them and have something to eat, whilst they found him a horse and clothing.

As he was eating, he heard that the news of his miraculous survival was circulating around the camp. He could see men, in small groups, talking and glancing in his direction. To his great relief, one of the men brought some fresh clothing and a horse. The horse, to Marcus's dismay, looked very old and he was not sure if it would live long enough to get him home. He thought to himself, "Well—thank you very much, Parliamentarians! That is very generous of you!" Bizarrely, the horse had some small bells attached to its reins. Marcus asked, "What on earth are those bells for?" One of the men answered, "I do not know, but if you give me a minute, I will take them off for you." Marcus decided that he needed to leave as quickly as possible. He told the men that he quite liked the bells after all. Marcus changed into the clothing, thanked them, and rode away as soon as he could do so. When Marcus arrived back at the smithy, he was concerned to discover that the news of his miraculous escape had already reached home ahead of him. Again, he heard some of the people commenting that it was not natural.

Marcus remembered the promise he had made to himself after he had escaped from Flavian, which was to always trust his feelings. Now, every part of his being was telling him to get as far away from where he currently was and to do so as quickly as possible.

Marcus knew that he had to leave as inconspicuously as he possibly could. He packed a few of the tools from his blacksmith shop. Unfortunately, Marcus had got to know a girl named Bess and they had become good friends, although it was obvious that Bess was hoping for much more than that. Marcus did what he could to discourage her, even on some occasions being quite rude to her, however, the girl just wouldn't take no for an answer, even though it had been many years, Marcus couldn't get the image of Gertrude lying dead on the ground out of his head. Deep down, Marcus liked Bess but was terrified of what Flavian would do. He was just about to leave when Bess came out of the bakery and saw Marcus putting some of his tools in his saddle bag. She asked, "You are not leaving, are you?" Marcus tried to act as casually as possible and replied, "No. I just need to do some work at home." He tried to act as if he was not in any particular hurry and chatted to Bess about the items she had bought from the bakery, whilst all the while keeping an eye on the people who were now starting to gather in groups. Marcus was aware that they were watching him and were clearly talking about him. Marcus apologised to Bess and said, "Well, time flies. I have to be on my way." Then, inexplicably, Bess kissed him full on the lips. Marcus pushed her away and said, "What did you do that for?" Bess laughed and said, "Well, we have known each other long enough! Don't tell me you didn't like it." Marcus looked, panic-stricken, at the faces of the small crowd that was gathering, desperately looking for the tell-tale sign of Flavian's smile, then he shouted, "Flavian, she has nothing to do with me!" He realised that he sounded like a madman, then he looked at the shocked look on Bess's face, and shouted, "Leave me alone! Get away from me, you stupid girl." Marcus then jumped on his horse and rode quickly out of the village.

On the way back to his farmhouse, Marcus stopped every ten minutes or so to look through his spyglass to ensure he was not being followed. He could not see any sign of people following him but gave a sigh of relief when he finally reached his home.

Marcus stood at the farmhouse door and looked around at the trees and bushes which surrounded his property, trying to ensure that he was safe. He had a really bad feeling in the pit of his stomach... a really apprehensive feeling. He entered his farmhouse and went through into his kitchen. He pulled away the rug which covered most of the floor, revealing a trap door under-neath. As he opened the trap door, he heard someone shout, "Marcus, Marcus. Can you come out here? We would like to talk to you."

From beneath the trapdoor, Marcus pulled the bag, which contained his money and the Artefacts, and placed it on the table. He then opened the door. Outside, he saw four men on horseback. He could also see a large crowd in the distance, seemingly moving towards his property. Marcus recognised the mounted men as individuals from the village. He spoke to the four men, asking, "What do you want?" Marcus was well aware that there are men who fight in wars for noble reasons and others for the very worst of reasons. Marcus knew that there was nothing noble about these men.

He repeated his question. "What can I do for you, gentlemen?" Meanwhile, he was thinking to himself, "I know what I really would like to do with you all!" The men looked at each other and smiled, answering, "We would like you to come back to the village with us and talk about your adventures today. We heard that they were quite amazing." Marcus pointed to the large crowd, which was now only a few hundred yards away, moving towards his property, and asked, "How many people does it take to invite me to the village?" The same man who had spoken previously, and who was, obviously, their leader, answered, "We mean you no harm. We just want to talk. That is all."

Marcus laughed. He had met so many people similar to this man—Yusuf, Flavian and many others—who each thought so much of themselves, but who were, in actual fact, not worth 'a bag of salt!'

Marcus looked carefully at the faces of the four men. He was sure that one of them must be Flavian. The whole situation had a very familiar ring to it… He remembered the mob in the inn in Philippi, even though it was on a much smaller scale.

Then Marcus saw it—just for a second; it was hardly noticeable—Marcus almost missed it. He saw the leader of the group lick his lip—just for a second, the man's tongue darted out his mouth, but it was enough. Marcus replied, "I will tell you what I am going to do. I am going back into my farmhouse. I have a musket in there and if you are still here, outside my farmhouse, on my land in two minutes' time, I am going to shoot *you*." Marcus pointed directly to the man next to the so-called leader of the group, whom he considered to be, probably, the most timid of the group. The man stuttered and wailed, saying, "Why? What have I ever done to you?"

Marcus turned away smiling, as he went back into his farmhouse. Just before he closed the door, he said, "Remember… two minutes." He then pointed his hand in the shape of a gun at the men in front of his farmhouse, and said quietly, "Bang, bang!" As he closed the door, Marcus heard the timid man say, "To hell with this!" followed by the sound of him galloping away.

Marcus, however, was no fool. He knew that the situation was not over. He knew Flavian well enough to know that there was a lot more to come. Suddenly, there was a loud bang as a stone came crashing through the window of his farmhouse. Then a second, and then a third, and within seconds, every window in the house was smashed to pieces. Marcus stood, covered in tiny shards of glass. Remarkably, he was unharmed. Marcus could hear screaming and shouting outside. He was fully aware that there was nothing more dangerous, nor more terrifying, than a mob of people. One could reason with an Army, but there is no sanity to be seen nor reasoning to be found with a mob… especially one that is led by a devil.

Marcus prepared himself for the inevitable onslaught but it did not come. He reasoned that his threat to shoot one of them—which was definitely a lie and a serious under-estimation because he would happily have shot all of them—was, unfortunately, not possible, as he did not have a musket and because of the curse, he would not have been allowed to actually kill anyone. That part of the curse was, Marcus felt, sometimes very unreasonable and annoying!

The noise outside seemed to have subsided a little. Marcus went over to one of his windows and quickly looked outside. He could see the mob lighting torches. Marcus hurriedly moved to look out of the back window to see if that could be used as a means of escape. To his dismay, some of the mob had moved around to the back of his house and they too were lighting torches. As he moved away from the window, the shouting and screaming from outside reached a crescendo. This was followed by a flaming torch, which landed on his couch, immediately setting that alight. Another flaming torch came through and landed on his mat. Within seconds, there must have been twenty burning torches on the ground floor of his house. He could hear a thud coming from an upstairs room, followed by another thud, then another, as the mob threw burning torches through the windows of his upstairs rooms. Then, to his amazement, there was an extremely loud whooshing sound, like a very strong wind, and, unbelievably, he saw that the flames were being drawn back into the torches. Some of the flames that had been five and six feet high were completely extinguished. Then there was silence, from both inside and outside the farmhouse.

Marcus cautiously looked out of the window. He saw the mob looking at each other in stunned silence. They obviously did not know what to do next. He noticed that some of them looked nervous. He could see several of the men were making their way back to their horses and quietly slipping away.

Marcus heard a single voice coming from the mob, shouting, "Witch… witchcraft!" Marcus thought to himself, "There's always one!" Within a few minutes, the crowd were screaming and shouting "Witchcraft!" and working themselves into a frenzy. It was then that Marcus heard a piercing scream. He looked carefully out of the corner of the window and saw that the mob had set fire to a tree. However, he noticed that strangely, the mob were now no longer looking at his farmhouse, but had their attention fixed firmly on the burning tree. Then, to his horror, a figure appeared in the midst of the flames… it was Bess. Thankfully, she was dead. One of the men in the crowd shouted, "See what we do to witches here? We are coming for you, Marcus." Then Marcus heard a tinkling sound. It was difficult to make out where the sound came from above the noise of the mob. He strained his ears to listen. He then realised what the sound was—it was the sound of bells. Marcus quickly crawled over to the window at the front of the house. He peeped out of the bottom corner of the window and to his astonishment, he saw his horse was slowly and calmly walking towards the main door of the farmhouse. Amazingly, no one seemed to notice. Marcus quickly grabbed his bag and watched in fascination as his horse came closer and closer to his door.

He could also see that beyond the horse, the crowd of people were getting ready to charge his house. As the horse stopped just outside the door, Marcus made his move. He threw open the farmhouse door, ran across to his horse and mounted it. The mob stood, stunned, in absolute silence. As Marcus galloped away, they let out a loud collective scream and ran to their horses. In the commotion, one of the men tried to mount his horse, but the horse reared up throwing the man to the ground. The man stood up, pulled the reins and whispered into the horse's ear. The terrified animal stood still whilst the man remounted. The horse then carried its rider straight towards Marcus.

Marcus could hear the screaming and howling of the mob and the sound of their horses as they chased after him. He thought it was better that he did not look back, but rather concentrated on getting as far away, as fast as possible. The noise of the mob slowly diminished as he drew further and further ahead of them. Marcus smiled as he heard the bells on his horse ringing. He could not understand why, but for some reason, the ringing of the bells gave him a great deal of comfort. Marcus noticed that his horse appeared to be galloping at an incredible speed. He gently pulled on the reins for the horse to slow down, but it carried on galloping. Marcus leaned forward in his saddle, stroking his horse's neck, and said, "It is all right, girl. We are safe now. You can slow down", but the horse carried on galloping. Marcus did not want to pull too hard on the reins and risk causing the horse to fall. He knew that at this speed, a fall would almost certainly be fatal for the horse. He decided to cling on tightly as the horse continued running for over an hour without slowing down. As they approached a stream, his horse started to slow down and then came to a halt. Marcus dismounted and led the horse to the water. He was astonished that his horse was not even panting. He stroked his horse's neck, and it was not sweating. Marcus whispered into the horse's ear and said, "Hey, hey, girl. How are you even alive?"

Marcus tried to think of somewhere, some area to which he could relocate. He decided that there was no place, neither village nor town, in England, which would be safe for him. It appeared the whole country had gone mad. There was war everywhere. He made up his mind to travel to France. He was certain that there would never be a civil war or a revolution in that country. Marcus gently stroked his horse's neck and waited until it had rested. He decided to leave the bells on the horse's reins. He mounted his horse and slowly rode away, the bells tinkling.

Unknown to Marcus, Flavian's horse was starting to falter. Flavian used his whip to beat the horse, swearing and cursing as the horse fell to its knees. He just managed to jump clear as the horse rolled over on its side. Flavian kicked the dying horse... it wasn't the first time he had ridden a horse to death, but this time was particularly annoying. He shouted at the animal, "Die, you useless creature!" He pointed in the direction of Marcus and screamed, "Look! He's getting away!"

Marcus suddenly felt a jolt. He looked around in a daze. He heard Laura say, "Marcus. Are you all right? You seem to have left me for a moment. I have noticed that lately, you seem to be doing this more and more often." Marcus apologised and answered, "I think that I may have been working too hard lately. I am sorry. I may have drifted off a little there." Laura looked concerned and said, "You need to take it easy and not work too hard. Remember that life is too short for that." This comment made Marcus smile. Laura said, "What was that smile for?" He answered, "It's alright. I promise from now on that I will try to take it easy." Laura took a sip of her coffee and answered, "Just make sure that you do!"

Marcus was pleased that Laura would often visit his house after work. Excited about her day, Marcus would listen to her stories with interest, sometimes commenting, seemingly from a historical point of view, but actually, it was from memory. One afternoon, Laura called much earlier than normal. She had a very serious look on her face and was carrying a large brown envelope under her arm. Marcus leaned forward to kiss her on the cheek. She received the kiss without any emotion or encouragement. Her smile seemed to be forced. She brushed past him without a word and sat down at the kitchen table. She placed the envelope on the table. Marcus had a very bad feeling!

As Laura began to recount the stories of various conflicts she had discovered in her work going through the archives of The Times, Marcus found the subject very uncomfortable. He commented that she rarely arrived home this early and asked her if she would like a coffee. She nodded. Marcus was becoming more concerned. He asked if there was anything wrong. Laura took a deep breath. She looked up at Marcus, gave a weak smile, and, without saying a word, put her hand into the envelope, slowly removed three A4 photographs and placed them face down on the table.

Laura started to explain that whilst working in the Archives, she had come across an article relating to an event which was reported from the North of England, around the 1960s. Marcus held his breath as Laura, one by one, turned the photographs over. They were faint black-and-white photographs. Although the photographs were indisputably grainy, there was no doubt that they were photographs of Marcus carrying a young child. The remarkable thing was that he was standing in a lion enclosure with lions all around him, some of whom were lying down, others seemingly in the process of also dropping to the ground. The man was undoubtedly Marcus. The scars on his neck and on his hand were clearly visible. The photographs were dated 1963.

CHAPTER 21

THE ZOO

MARCUS SPENT MOST of the Second World War in Mexico, as far from the actual fighting as was possible. He would read the newspapers with deep dread and horror. His home city, Rome, was under Nazi rule. His adopted city of London was being bombed, almost continually. The situation looked bleak. Marcus was angry and extremely frustrated that there was absolutely nothing that he would be allowed to do which would assist them.

Marcus clearly remembered one afternoon in February 1920, at a London College, where he taught Latin. A group of students came to him and asked if he could explain something that he had said in the lesson he had just given. Marcus said that he was sorry, but they needed to go home as the caretaker was waiting for them to leave to enable him to lock up the premises for the night. One of the students said, "I am sorry, Professor. I know that you are very busy, but I was wondering if maybe we could go to the pub for half an hour." One of the other students then added, "Would you please come with us, Professor? We are buying!"

They all gave a cheer when Marcus agreed. Marcus thought that an excellent idea! As they stepped out of the College door, they were met by a freezing cold wind and there was about two inches of snow on the ground. They made their way, carefully, to the pub, trying their best not to slip on the hardening snow. When they finally arrived , they burst noisily through the door. Marcus noticed that the pub was full of young men. From looking at them, he guessed that most of them were ex-soldiers, who were now trying to ignore the noisy group of students. Marcus insisted on buying the drinks. He thought to himself, what else could he spend his money on?! Marcus took the order and went across to the bar. He said, "Five pints of beer, please, and a glass of water."

The landlord laughed, and said, "Water? Water! You do know that this is a pub?" Marcus was aware that almost everyone in the pub was now looking at him. He offered to pay for the water, which caused the landlord to roar with laughter. He said, "Pay for water! Who has ever heard of anyone charging anybody for water?! Perhaps I could bottle it and make a fortune!" This made almost everyone in the pub, including some of the students, laugh! The landlord then added, "Do not worry, lad. I will get you a glass of water and it will not cost you a penny. If I charge you for water, I will never hear the end of it!" The landlord then served the beer and the water without further comment!

Marcus carried the drinks across to the table, with two of the students assisting him. He sat down with his glass of water and was about to take a drink when a one-armed man came across from one of the tables, stood next to him and said, "Well, well, well! What is going on here?!" Marcus explained that they were from the local College and were about to start some course-work. The man growled, muttering, "Where were you in the War?" Marcus answered, "Well, that is none of your damned business, is it?" He then turned to his students and was about the speak to them when the one-armed man, who had obviously had too much to drink, said, "Let me guess. You have got a mysterious condition and stayed home with Mummy." The one-armed man turned around, demonstratively stretched out his arm and said, "Whilst all of us mugs were stood up to our necks in mud, getting shot at, bombed and gassed, this man was sat at home by the fire with his Mum!" The man then turned back to Marcus and said, "Do you know how you can tell a coward? You will ask him what he did in the War and he will tell you to mind your own damned business because he is too afraid to tell you."

Marcus may have appeared to be a teacher, but deep inside still lurked the proud Centurion. He could feel his heart beating faster and the blood speeding through his veins. His fists were tightly clenched. Marcus had an overwhelming desire to get hold of the one-armed man, rip off his other arm, beat him with it and then throw his bloody body outside in the snow.

Fortunately, a friend of the one-armed man came forward and said, "Hey, Bert, leave the man alone. Can you not see that scar on his neck? I wager that was made by a German bayonet. Damned lucky to survive, I can tell you. And just look at his hand, will you? It is clear it has been shot through. No, I reckon we should leave this man in peace." The man looked around the pub and said, "You all know my brother. He came back from Mons. Had a terrible time. You ask him about the Battle of Mons, and he will tell you nothing about the Battle. There is only one thing he will tell you about, and that is the Angel. The Angel of Mons. Over a thousand men saw it. People say that it was a mass hallucination, but that is rubbish! My brother saw it, as clear as day. He will not tell you a word about the War; he will only tell you about the Angel."

A second man spoke and said, "My mate, Fred," he looked around the room and said, "You all know Fred!" Marcus saw all the men in the room nodding, some looking quite emotional. Marcus realised that most, and possibly all the men in the room were damaged. Some of their scars were very visible, while for others, it was obvious that their scars were far deeper.

Marcus had fought in many battles, but he had heard of the terrible suffering in the trenches. Whilst the man was talking, Marcus was fighting to contain his anger. He kept glancing at the one-armed man. He could feel his anger getting the better of him.

As he was about to stand up, he felt a soothing hand gently brush his hair, then touch his cheek. Marcus felt all his anger and bitterness melt away. He looked up at the one-armed man and unclenched his fist. To be truthful, Marcus felt ashamed for thinking of hurting him. Marcus listened as the man continued to tell the story of his friend,

Fred. He said that when Fred came home, his wife welcomed him. She tried to hug him, but he gently moved her to one side, walked into the kitchen, and took off all his clothes. He just stood there, naked. His wife said, "What on earth are you doing? Put your clothes back on. Someone could come in at any moment." Fred merely picked up all his uniform, including his boots, and put them on the fire. He watched them burn. He went up to his bedroom and put on his civilian clothes. "To this day, he has never said a single word about the War."

The man then turned to Marcus and said, "If you do not want to talk, then we will all 'mind our own damned business'." Marcus saw that all the men in the room were nodding and saying quietly, "Yer, yer."

The one-armed man said loudly, "Well, you can think what you like and say what you like, but I am not staying here." The man then stormed out of the pub. One of the men shouted, "Show the man the picture!" The one-armed man's friend said to Marcus, "Before the War, my brother used to paint." Someone shouted, "Aye, and damned good he was too. Damned good!" All the men nodded in agreement. "Well," the man continued, "he cannot paint any longer. His hands, you see. They will not stop shaking. Damned shame. Anyhow, strangely, he managed to draw this." The man then took out his wallet and produced a folded piece of paper which he handed to Marcus. He said, "There you are. As clear as day. The Angel of Mons." As Marcus looked at the drawing, his jaw dropped. He then said, in a quiet voice, "Wow!" The drawing was obviously of a battlefield. The conditions looked appalling. Dead soldiers were hanging from the barbed wire. There were shells exploding all around. In the foreground, soldiers stood still, as if transfixed. They were staring at a figure of what appeared to be a beautiful young girl, who was hovering over the battlefield. Her arms were outstretched, and her face was radiant. She had tears in her eyes.

Bizarrely, Marcus could not shake the feeling that he knew the girl. The man said, "You will have to forgive Bert. It is not like him. He is usually the nicest, friendliest man you could meet. I do not know what has got into him." Marcus answered, "Do not worry. He has obviously been through a lot." Marcus stood up and went over to the man, to hand his drawing back to him, but the man said, "No. You keep it, lad. I saw the effect that the drawing had on you." Marcus answered, "But it belongs to your brother. You should keep it." This caused some of the men in the pub to laugh. Marcus turned to look at them and asked, "What is so funny?" One of the men said, "It is all right, mate. He has got thousands of them." Marcus looked at the man who had been doing most of the talking and said, "Thousands? What do you mean?" The man answered, "Well, that is all he does all day. He draws these pictures of the Angel." The man then turned and pointed to a picture on the wall, which was larger and much more impressive than the small picture that Marcus held in his hand. Both pictures were identical. Marcus thanked the man, then walked to the bar and gave the landlord some money. He said, "I would like to buy you gentlemen a drink." Marcus then returned to his seat and said to his students, "Right. Let's get to work."

After his experience of returning to London too early at the end of the First World War, and even though he longed to return to his home, Marcus decided after the Second World War had ended that he would wait until 1952 before he returned to his home.

When he arrived back in England, he was shocked to see the damage that had been done by the bombing. He was very fortunate; his London home was still intact. He managed to obtain a position teaching in a local college. Life returned to normal, or as near to normal as it could be for him. He was as happy with his life as it was possible for him to be, under the circumstances.

Marcus had learned that it was better for him to keep to a routine, but not to become too complacent. Unfortunately, in the early nineteen sixties, a young man stopped Marcus in the street and introduced himself as Alan, a former pupil. Marcus remembered him well. He was a clever lad, but he had a little too much to say for himself! Marcus felt very uncomfortable whilst talking to him. He was acutely aware that Alan actually looked older than he did. Marcus knew the time had come for him to relocate.

Relocating to other cities did not present a problem for Marcus. This had been his life for the past two thousand years. He had an agent who would look after his house, and, when necessary, find a suitable tenant. Marcus had already made enquiries relating to a vacant position at a university in Manchester. His application had been accepted.

Marcus arrived in the village of Crumpsall, a suburb of Manchester, early in 1963. He had lost count of the number of occasions he had thought it time to move and to make a new start elsewhere. Moving was not a problem to him; in fact, on the contrary, he quite enjoyed it. Travelling to other areas, or even other countries, was as near as he could get to an actual adventure! He had no family or friends, and moving from one place to another was exciting. He quite liked the challenge.

Each morning he would board the Number 81 bus which took him from Crumpsall into Manchester City Centre. He had settled well in Manchester. He loved the football and the Speedway.

One of the many things he really enjoyed and appreciated about the Twentieth Century was its entertainment. He loved watching television programmes and reading, especially books covering Ancient History. He would read about battles in which he had been involved and learned, retrospectively, why certain Generals had made decisions, which, at the time, often seemed strange or even ridiculous. He often put down the book he had been reading, thought for a moment and then said to himself, "Well, I did not know that. For all these years, I have thought that he was an idiot." He laughed, and said to himself, "I still think that he was an idiot, but perhaps on that occasion, he may have been right!" He enjoyed reading novels and read at least four each week, in addition to a number of nonfiction books. On the whole, he kept himself quite busy.

Marcus's circumstances were such that it was dangerous for him to socialise, but he soon discovered that alone, life can become extremely depressing.

He rose early each morning and went to the University where his Lectures were held. When he had moved to Crumpsall, he rented an apartment on Crumpsall Lane. He was very excited to learn that two famous footballers had also rented an apartment in the same building.

Each Saturday afternoon, Marcus made his way to the football stadium. He would spend Saturday evenings at the speedway. he clearly remembered reading an article about the speedway in a local newspaper and how it had attracted his attention and his interest. He had only gone to the speedway track to see what it was actually like but had watched the event with jaw-dropping fascination. He thought it was one of the most dangerous sports he had ever witnessed, not completely unlike chariot racing! Unless, that is, you had actually witnessed a chariot race, which was undoubtedly completely insane, composed as it was of a race, involving six men, who stood on flimsy chariots, racing around a stadium at unbelievable speeds!

Over the few years he spent in Manchester, he became quite a fan of the speedway track, which was situated in a very large stadium—part of The Belle Vue Complex on the east side of Manchester. Marcus would often go there during the day if he was not working. The complex also contained a large zoo and a funfair.

One of Marcus's passions was walking. He could not understand the modern idea of driving everywhere, even for the shortest of distances. When visiting the zoo, Marcus walked most of the way, getting off the bus after the early part of the journey, and making his way on foot, through Openshaw, along Grey Mare Lane to the Belle Vue Stadium. It would take him about an hour, but he thoroughly enjoyed the walk.

Marcus found it fascinating to see how things had changed over the years. It had been approximately two hundred years since he had visited this particular part of Manchester. He could not help but cast his mind back to the first time he had moved into the area in the Third Century. It was a Roman Garrison at that time and he had a very successful blacksmith's business in the Deansgate area of Manchester.

The Roman Fortress—which he would often visit as part of his work—was approximately half a mile to the south of his smithy. He loved spending time with the Legionnaires. The higher ranks were greatly impressed with his skills in making swords and personalised armour. He would sit for hours on a little wall just outside the main gate, talking to Legionnaires. When he was talking to the Legionnaires, he had, of course, to be extremely careful. It would be so very easy for him to make a mistake and to talk about his experiences and the various battles he had been involved in, but which had, in fact, taken place hundreds of years previously. However, being careful was now almost second nature for him.

As he arrived at the Belle Vue Stadium, he spotted a group of children who were hiding behind a wall. Marcus paused for a minute to see what they were doing. An older boy, a rough, unruly-looking lad, who looked about ten years old, kept bobbing his head around the wall, watching the security guard on the gate. The gate was about eight feet high and about fifteen feet long. The actual entrance into the zoo was via a turnstile at the gated entrance. Marcus watched the lads as he approached the entrance. One of the lads, who had obviously been waiting for the right opportunity, ran to the gate, closely followed by his friends. Once they reached the entrance, they scrambled up the gate with the speed and dexterity of a troop of monkeys! The guard, alerted by the noise, ran to catch them. It was too late. The boys were over the gate and running away in different directions. The guard could only watch the boys disperse, laughing as they ran, looking forward to their free day at the zoo. As he paid for his ticket, Marcus laughed, but the guard was not amused!

It was a beautiful sunny day as Marcus made his way around the exhibits. He could hear all the noise from the funfair—the screaming from the roller coaster and the excitable chatter and laughter from other rides! Marcus avoided the close proximity to the funfair as the music was normally played at an incredibly high volume. He regretted that he had to avoid any type of music, but it now always sounded unbearably out of tune. Even going to the cinema was difficult for him, in that, most films had a degree of background music. A colleague who loved pop music had asked him about his taste in music and about his favourite band. When he replied that he did not particularly like music, his colleague responded, astonished, that someone of his age did not like modern music. Marcus answered, "Why, how old do you think I am?" His colleague took a deep breath, looked at him, and replied, "Oh, I guess somewhere around twenty-six to twenty-eight." Marcus said, "Not bad, not too far out!" He did not like to tell him that he was born in Rome on the banks of the Tiber in the year 4 AD!

Marcus made his way to the lion enclosure. At the Belle Vue venue, the lions were kept in a large pit. Visitors to the zoo would lean over a high wall to look down at the lions in the pit below them. Marcus hated lions with a passion. He had witnessed—in the Arena in Rome—exactly what lions were capable of doing to humans. He had seen lions tearing people apart. There was one memory that, even after all this time, he still could not get out of his head. A young man and his family—his wife and two small children—were dragged into the arena. He remembered the young man desperately trying to protect his family by standing between them and the lions. Obviously, he was not able to protect either himself or his family. It had made Marcus feel sick to hear the crowd cheering when the lions attacked the children. Since that time, Marcus had hated lions. He knew his view was not popular. Some people saw them as magnificent beasts; others saw them as sleepy, lazy, or even cute! Marcus knew that they were none of those things.

As he drew near the lion enclosure, he was disappointed to see a large crowd, because occasionally, if there was no one else at the enclosure viewing the lions, he would throw stones at them. He was a very good shot! When he arrived at the enclosure, he leaned on the wall looking down on the lions. As usual, most of the lions appeared to be asleep.

In one of the areas nearest to the enclosure, there was a crowd of lads who were shouting at the lions, trying to awaken them. He heard one young boy—who was stood behind him—complain to his father that they were boring because they were asleep and not doing anything. His father assured him that they were very dangerous animals and they would probably soon awaken.

At the opposite side of the enclosure, a small boy, about eight years old, climbed up on the wall and started waving and shouting at the large male lion, as if he was trying to attract its attention. His mother leaned across, presumably to tell him to stop being silly and get down.

The boy ignored her and started dancing on the wall, at which point his mother moved to grab hold of him. The young boy quickly dodged his mother's flaying hands, and, in so doing, he lost his balance and in what appeared to be slow motion, fell into the lion enclosure. The lions were no longer sleepy!

Marcus looked at the place from where the boy had fallen and noticed a young man who turned towards him and grinned and then winked. The young man then turned and disappeared into the crowd. Marcus desperately wanted to follow him, but he did not want to leave the lion enclosure. Marcus looked down and saw that the boy had been fortunate; he had landed on a grassy part of the enclosure but appeared to have hurt his leg in the fall. There seemed to be a long silent pause, as if the people who had come to watch the lions could not quite believe what they were witnessing. Suddenly, the crowd screamed in unison. The boy's mother's screams could be heard above the noise made by the crowd.

A million thoughts went through Marcus's head. He had been told that he was not allowed to kill or save anyone. He had, however, witnessed in the past what lions were capable of doing to a small boy. He really did not want the boy's mother to see her son being torn to pieces by a pride of lions. He cast his mind back to the time when John had explained the curse to him. He asked John, "Am I not to save an innocent, a pregnant woman from the sword, or a baby from the fire?" John had grabbed him by the shoulders, moved his face closer to Marcus's face and said to him, "Listen. Count yourself as dead. You are a ghost. You are only to observe. You can play no part in human history." He continued, "However, you must pray for wisdom. You are always to do what is right, what is truly right, and not just what is right in your eyes. To do what is right will always cost you. It will cost you your friends, your relations, your reputation, and your wealth. It will cost you everything; even your life. Many others will take the easy path, but at the end, lose their soul."

There was a loud gasp from the crowd as Marcus jumped into the lion enclosure. He landed not far from the terrified boy and moved to stand between the lions and the child. The large alpha male slowly moved forward, preparing to attack. It paused as if it was unsure what to do next. It then let out a loud roar and six lionesses moved towards the alpha male lion, ready to join in the attack.

The crowd was silent, watching in horrified fascination. The silence was broken by a single scream from the child's mother. Marcus held out his hand as if to ward off the large alpha male. He moved slowly and deliberately towards the lions and shouted, "Parce, precor, mihi protected." All seven lions stopped, as if frozen in time. Marcus walked between the lions and the child, bent down and picked up the terrified boy. He turned back to face the lions and repeated loudly, "Parce, precor, mihi protected." There was an astonished gasp from the crowd, which had now trebled in size, as those nearby, having heard the noise and screams coming from the crowd, had come into the enclosure to see what was happening.

The giant alpha male lion started to lower his powerful head, lower and lower, until its great jaw touched the ground. Its front legs then started to bend. It looked almost as if it was bowing down, and then its hind legs slowly started to bend, until the giant beast was completely prostrate on the ground. Marcus quickly glanced around at the rest of the pride of lions and, as he watched, one by one, the lionesses started to lower themselves down onto the ground.

Marcus looked around the ring for the quickest way out of the enclosure. He spotted a gate at the far end. He could see several keepers armed with long sticks. Marcus said to himself, "Sticks? Sticks! Seriously, sticks?"

Marcus realised that to reach the gate, he had to walk through the pride of lions. He weaved his way through the prostrate lions and, to everyone's astonishment, he actually kicked some of lions out of his way. Once kicked, the lion would jump up and run to the other side of the enclosure and return to its previous position, prostrate on the ground. When Marcus finally arrived at the gate, the keeper quickly opened it with a look of absolute incredulity on his face. This was reflected in the faces of the other Keepers who had witnessed what had occurred in the enclosure. As he walked through the gate, still carrying the child, the watching crowd applauded. He was met by the boy's weeping mother and he handed her son to her. Almost without anyone noticing, he was gone.

As Marcus started his long walk home, he wondered what the consequences would be for breaking the rules of the curse. He felt unusually tired and weak, so much so that he called for a taxi to take him home. It was the first time he had been in a taxi in years!

For the next few weeks, having lived for two thousand years under a curse, Marcus lived in fear that he would now finish his life in hell. When he went to bed, he had no idea if he would wake up in his room or if he would suffer the consequences of breaking the conditions of the curse and somehow, be dragged down to Hell. It was a fear he lived with for many weeks. He was also frightened that he would be exposed. However, everything soon returned to normal. There was an article relating to the incident at the zoo, but no photographs appeared in the newspaper; not even a decent description. He remembered John's words that he must do what is right. He explained that it was not to make him feel good, nor for his own good, or glory, nor for his wellbeing, or for his advantage, but purely because to live under those conditions makes decision-making a lot easier. On his way back from the zoo, Marcus put his fatigue down to nothing more than stress. He had learned over the years that stress can have that effect.

It took a few weeks for Marcus to fully recover. He decided that it would be safer for him to stay away from the zoo. He knew that this decision did not make much sense. He would have loved to have gone back to the zoo and gloated and shouted abuse at the lions!

Over the next few months, Marcus realised that he had spent long enough in Manchester. He knew it was time for him to leave. He was sad to do so, but he understood that he had no alternative. He decided to take one last walk along Deansgate. It took Marcus approximately forty minutes to walk along Cheetham Hill Road, passing Victoria Station. Walking along this route brought a smile to his face. He remembered the large Roman barracks that had stood on this exact site. As he strolled down Deansgate, he felt a sense of apprehension that he could not explain. The memories of how it was in the Second Century came to him with strange, unnatural clarity.

Marcus had walked along Deansgate dozens of times and tried, unsuccessfully, to establish exactly where his workshop had been situated. As he continued along Deansgate, he paused halfway along the road. Inexplicably, he knew that he was standing on the exact spot where, so many centuries ago, his smithy had been sited. He shook his head. Although it was not rational, and there was no explanation for it, he could actually smell a forge, and, inexplicably, he felt as though he was back in the second century.

He remembered how, all those centuries ago, he had stood in this very spot and experienced a vision which, at the time, he thought was an hallucination. As the memories came back, he now recognised and understood that the vision he had seen all those years ago, was of 20th-century Manchester! At the time, he did not know what it was he seeing, but now he was aware that what he had seen were cars and buses. Central to the vision was a woman, who was smartly dressed, albeit in strange clothes, with blonde streaks in her brown hair.

The woman suddenly looked at him and said, "I will see you in Rome."

Suddenly, the smell of the forge was gone. He was back in the twentieth century, but the memory remained. He continued his walk along Deansgate. He was stunned and perplexed—who was this woman and what did it all mean? He stopped walking and stood for a few moments, almost in a daze. He shook his head, trying to clear his thoughts. He continued along Deansgate, trying to explain the vision he had just seen. He found himself at the site of the old Roman Fort. He sat down on a bench, which he knew was in exactly the same place as the small wall he used to sit on whilst talking to the Roman Legionnaires, so many centuries ago. He stood up to leave and the feeling of apprehension returned.

As he walked away, he looked back at the bench. He was shocked to see a vision of the same girl, with the blonde streaks in her hair, sitting on the bench, eating a snack and drinking from a paper cup. Then she was gone. Marcus made his way home, unsure of what was happening to him, why these visions were occurring and what they meant. He sat down in his apartment and wondered who this girl could possibly be and why she was appearing in his visions.

It was much too soon for him to return to London, as there would be literally hundreds of ex-students, in their thirties, forties or maybe even in their early fifties, who would very probably recognise him. Marcus decided instead to make his way to Rome. After any relocation, the first five years were always the best. There was no need to be concerned about possible discovery, nor anyone looking at you with suspicion.

On arrival in Rome, Marcus did what he always did when he was in Rome; he searched for his family. He knew how ridiculous it was to do this, but he always had hope. One of the strange things about having an extraordinarily long life was that he would meet people who were clearly the descendants of individuals he had met in his past. Sometimes, the similarities were startling. He knew that if you had larger ears, a long neck, or particular mannerisms, or it could quite often be the manner in which you moved, then there was almost a certainty that someone in the past had looked just like you and, very possibly, had many of the same mannerisms. Marcus would often amuse himself with the thought that sometime, way back in history, maybe even as far back as the time of the cavemen, someone had looked exactly like him. Marcus knew that there was very little hope—maybe a billion-to-one chance—

that one day, he would recognise one of his descendants. However, despite his pessimism, the day arrived when this hope was fulfilled.

It was the year 2019 and he was about to leave for London. He decided he would take a last stroll through the city. As was his habit, he stopped in a local coffee shop. He sat at a small table near the window, admiring the view. He still had a great love for Rome, but after the arrest and death of Cephas and all the wickedness that followed, he could now, to his regret, look back over the centuries and remember the city only for the many dreadful things he had witnessed. However, in so many ways, Rome was like a favourite son; no matter how appalling their behaviour might periodically be, there was always forgiveness.

As he sat drinking his water, he gazed around the room. At the table next to his was a young mother with two small children. He watched them for a moment, admiring the excellent way the children were behaving. On the next table along, there was a teenager using earphones who seemed to be in a world of his own. At the bottom end of the coffee shop sat an elderly man with a young woman, probably his daughter.

As he turned around, he saw a lady sitting just a few tables away from him. She was probably in her mid-sixties. She had black shoulder-length hair with grey streaks. She was elegantly dressed and seemed to be totally engrossed in the book she was reading. Marcus thought she was the most beautiful woman he had ever seen. She was his mother!

Marcus could not take his eyes off her. After a few minutes, the lady looked up and their eyes met. She lowered her book slightly and then smiled. Marcus returned the smile. The lady went back to her book and Marcus continued to stare. The lady looked up. She smiled again at Marcus, but, clearly, was starting to feel uncomfortable. Marcus stood up and walked over to her table. Her eyes followed him. When he reached her table, she put down her book and asked, "What can I do for you, young man?" Marcus was taken aback—she even sounded like his mother. For a second, he was speechless. He apologised for his rudeness and explained that she looked so much like his mother; he had actually thought she was his mother! As he explained that his mother had died many years ago, he could see her maternal instincts coming to the fore, as she invited him to sit down and join her.

He was stunned and ecstatic. He knew… he just knew that he had, at last, found his family. She told him her name was Sophia, and proudly announced that she could trace her family back to the eighteenth century. Marcus tried to look impressed. Initially, he had been worried—what if Sophia asked too many questions about his background? He was not quite sure how he would answer her. However, it soon became apparent that he need not have worried! Sophia was not shy and had no difficulty in talking and in maintaining conversation!

She told him all about her family and explained that her son and grandson would shortly be joining her. She said that she would love him to meet both of them. Sophia continued chattering, talking about her family, whilst Marcus sat in stunned silence. For Marcus, it was like a whole new world was opening to him. He felt like an orphan who had discovered that, after all, he had a family.

Sophia's son and grandson arrived and apologised for being late. They both looked at Marcus. Sophia made the introductions and explained who he was and why he was sitting with her. Her son, a tall, lean man, approximately six feet two inches tall, whose name was Francesco, sat down and asked Marcus where he came from and what he did for a living. At first, Marcus was a little disappointed, because Francesco did not look like anyone in his family. Then he started to talk! Almost everything he said was accompanied by a hand gesture. When he spoke about something that was tall, his hands went high. If he talked about something that was small, his hands went low. His hands did not stop moving for a second; they were in constant motion! Marcus smiled to himself. Francesco's mannerisms were exactly like those of his own brother.

Sophia's grandson, who had been introduced as Antonio, was staring into his milkshake. He dipped one finger into his milkshake and then put the finger in his mouth. He looked up, and his face immediately registered shock that his grandmother was watching and had seen what he had just done! She gave him a disapproving look, which made the boy glance guiltily around the table, to see if anyone else had noticed! It was during this transaction with his grandmother that Marcus noticed the similarity between Antonio and his own son. Initially, he could not quite identify exactly what the resemblance was between the two boys, but when Antonio looked up, he noticed his eyes. He had very dark brown eyes, exactly the same as his son, but it was not merely the colour alone; it was the intensity in his gaze when he was talking and interacting.

Marcus told Francesco that he taught Classics and was fluent in Latin. Francesco was excited, and very keen that together they should visit the many ancient sites in Rome. He turned to his son, explaining how great it would be to be able to visit these historical places with an actual Professor of Classics, who was also fluent in Latin. Antonio looked bored and unimpressed!

Marcus, however, apologised and explained that he was unable to spend any time with them as he was leaving for London the next morning. Francesco looked genuinely disappointed. Marcus promised that when he next visited Rome, he would call Francesco and he would be delighted for them to be able to tour the city together. They shook hands and exchanged phone numbers. He kissed Sophia on the cheek, and they said goodbye. Marcus left feeling elated, and, more importantly, as though he belonged. He had not had that feeling for a very long time.

CHAPTER 22

THE PHOTOGRAPHS

LAURA SAT AT her desk in the archive department surrounded by dozens of large boxes. She lifted one particular heavy box onto her desk. It had a label which had a handwritten date which read '1960s'. She opened the box to find a large brown envelope, and, scribbled in red ink was the word 'Rejected'. She leaned back, stretched her arms and gave a large yawn; it had been a long day. She took a drink of coffee and immediately regretted it; it was cold and weak. Laura looked at the time, and as it was almost time to go home, she lifted the envelope out thinking that as it had been rejected, it would only take a minute.

Laura sat in stunned silence as she examined the contents of the envelope. She looked over her shoulder as if she didn't want anyone to see what she was looking at, then carefully replaced the contents back into the envelope. She reached for her handbag, took out her phone and called Marcus. Marcus answered in his normal cheerful manner; "Hi, Laura. Good to hear from you. What can I do for you?" Laura said, "Are you busy? Could I nip round in about an hour?" Marcus replied, "Great! I will look forward to it. See you soon."

Marcus was in the kitchen preparing coffee for Laura when he heard the door open and Laura shout, "It's only me." As soon as he saw Laura, and the serious look on her face, he thought to himself, "Oh no. What's wrong?" He noticed that she was carrying a large brown envelope. Laura sat down as Marcus finished making her coffee. said he asked, "Good day at work?" Instead of answering, Laura said, "I have found something at the office that I would like your opinion on." Marcus placed the cup of coffee next to Laura then sat down, and said, "Mysterious; well, fire away."

Laura carefully opened the envelope and took out some A4-size photographs. She studied Marcus's face, looking, and hoping for some kind of explanation of the photographs she had just laid on the table. They appeared to show Marcus in a lion enclosure with a small boy. There were three photographs in all, and in the first photograph, it looked as if the lions were about to pounce. In the second photograph, inexplicably, the lions seem to be bowing down, and the third photograph clearly showed a close-up of Marcus carrying the boy to safety. His unusual scars were clearly visible.

Marcus stood in silence as he looked at the photographs Laura had laid out on his kitchen table. As the newspaper had not used any photographs alongside the article, he had assumed that there had not been any photographs taken of the incident. He had assumed incorrectly! The photographs Laura laid in front of him had almost certainly been taken by someone who was in the crowd, but, as the photographs were very poor in clarity, they were, seemingly, not used in the newspaper because they would not be sufficiently clear for the readers.

Marcus was very eloquent. He followed his usual path—a mixture of truth and humour. He examined the photographs very carefully, and then said, "Hey, have you noticed the man in the photograph looks an awful lot like me?" He then exclaimed, "Look! He has a scar just like mine." He turned to Laura and said, "What are the chances of that happening?" Laura replied, somewhat sarcastically, "Yeah, what are the odds? About ten billion to one!" Marcus laughed, then pointed to the photographs and then to himself. He asked, "When was this picture taken?" Laura looked a little embarrassed and responded, "About 1963" . Marcus let out a roar of laughter. "Oh, excuse me. When you get into your nineties, you get a little forgetful." Laura was perplexed. On the one hand, the man in the photographs was clearly Marcus, and, on the other hand, it simply could not be him.

Laura was disturbed by Marcus's response. She realised it would be pointless to carry on the conversation, but she was determined that this could not be the end of the matter. They continued talking until late in the evening. Laura gave a big yawn, stretched out her arms and said, "Well, time to go." She casually collected the photographs from the table and carefully placed them back in the envelope. Laura noticed that Marcus's gaze had never left the photographs. She stood up and kissed him on the cheek. She was taken by surprise that his face was as smooth as if he had just shaved, which she knew was not the case. It was late in the evening. By this time in the day, her previous boyfriend's face would have been rough and full of stubble. She thought to herself how nice and soft his face was to touch. She said goodnight and left.

Before she went to bed, she took out the photographs from the envelope and laid them out on her table. She then took the magnifying glass from a kitchen drawer and closely examined each photograph. It was Marcus.

Next morning, she arrived at her office early, took the photographs out of the envelope and laid them out on her desk. She needed to know where the photographs had come from, and who had taken them. The only clues were some initials and a date on the back of the photograph: "L.M." and "1963". She had no idea who "L.M." might be.

Laura stood up and shouted across the office, "Does anyone know who "L.M" is? He or she might be a photographer." She had a desk in the corner of a very large office, occupied by approximately twenty people. Most of them stopped working for a moment, looked blank and shook their heads. She turned around and stared at the photographs, wondering how she could find out who L.M. was. She heard a voice behind her. "I know who that is. It is Lucas Maloney." She turned around to see who it was who was talking to her. It was the mailman. She asked him how he knew Lucas Maloney.

The mailman answered, "Oh, he was a very nice man; a very nice man. Every Friday, *without* fail, (placing a lot of emphasis on the word "without"), he bought me a cake." Laura smiled and said, "Would you like me to buy you a cake?" The mailman replied, "I do not want a 'pity' cake!"

Laura answered, "It is not a 'pity' cake. I would like to buy you one because we are friends." He thought for a moment and said, "Okay, Laura, my friend. What is my name?" Laura was speechless. All she could do was to answer, "Erm, erm. Look—we are mates. We have known each other for years. Give me a break, please. Help me and I promise to buy a cake for you every Friday. Please."

Billy held out his hand, smiled and said, "Hello. My name is Billy." Laura shook his hand, said, "Pleased to meet you, Billy. What type of cake would you like?" Billy thought for a while and then answered, "You know that cake shop across the road?" Laura nodded. Billy continued, "On the counter, they have lots of cheap cakes. Well, I don't like them!" Laura roared laughing, and said, "Billy, you are nothing but a conman." She laughed again. "I promise, Billy. I will get you a lovely cake, every Friday." They both laughed as Billy pulled up a chair and sat down beside her.

Billy started to tell Laura about Lucas Maloney, an employee who had retired approximately fifteen years before. His role at The Times had been to decide which pictures to use in the edition. Laura thought for a moment and then said, "Why would he reject this? Surely this would be a big story?" Billy picked up the photographs, examined them carefully, and then said, "Well, the photographs are rubbish, very poor quality and, in addition, what is the story?" Laura answered, "That's the problem. I don't know! Does anyone know whether this

Lucas Maloney is alive or dead?" Billy smiled and said, "He is my uncle." Laura shouted, "Great. When can we go and see him?" Billy answered: "I will give him a ring later and let you know." Impatiently, Laura demanded, "Why wait? Why can you not do it now?" "Because," Billy answered, "my Uncle is an old man, and I do not want to phone him too early."

Laura nodded and said, "Fair enough, but please, let me know when we can see him." Billy promised he would pop down and see her before he went home. Laura thanked him and turned back to her work.

Laura spent the whole day wondering if she was doing the right thing. Marcus was her friend and she felt that, somehow, she was betraying him. She was sure Marcus would not like her checking up on him. Throughout the day, Laura tried to establish who had taken the photographs, but no one could shed any light on photographs taken in 1963. It was just too long ago. Laura was relieved when Billy came to see her and told her he had made arrangements to visit his Uncle that night at 8.00 pm. Billy told Laura he would pick her up at 7.30 pm. Laura made her way home. She felt guilty as she passed Marcus's house.

Laura poured herself a glass of wine, kicked off her shoes, lay back and relaxed. It seemed only a few minutes later that she heard a banging on the door. She had not realised that she had fallen asleep. She rushed to the door, apologising, and explaining, as she opened the door, that she had fallen asleep. Billy just laughed and told her not to worry. He led the way to the car.

They pulled up outside Lucas Maloney's house, more or less on time. Laura was still not sure if what she was doing was the right thing. Billy saw that she was apprehensive and merely said, "As we are here now, we might as well talk to him and see what he has to say. If you are not happy, then we can just forget it and go home. Alternatively, if you have changed your mind completely, and are not happy with this, then we could just go home now?" Laura nodded that they should go ahead as planned.

They got out of the car, walked up the pathway and rang the doorbell. It seemed an age as they waited for Billy's uncle to open the door. The door was opened by a surprisingly cheerful man. He insisted that Laura should call him Lucas. He invited them into his living room and refused to enter into any discussion until he had made them a drink. He brought in cups of tea and a great variety of biscuits. Laura soon discovered that he was a flirt, but in a harmless way.

Lucas Maloney started the conversation by telling Laura that she was very beautiful. After a short period of small talk, Lucas leaned forward in his chair and said, "Well, young lady, how can I help you?" Laura took a deep breath, looking nervously at Billy as she picked up the envelope placed on the floor next to her chair. As she took out the photographs, Lucas commented, "Well, I am intrigued!" Laura gave a nervous laugh. She laid the three photographs on the coffee table, in much the same manner as she had done at Marcus's house. She asked, "Do you remember these photographs?" Lucas picked up one of the photographs, examined it carefully, and then turned it over, looking at his initials and the date on the back. Lucas nodded, handed the photographs back, and said, "Yes, I remember them. I tried to get the newspaper to run them. Initially, they said that they were fake. So, I had them checked out. I took them to experts. Do you know what? Genuine; that is what they said. The photographs are genuine." I took them back to my boss and told him they were genuine, but he was not at all interested. Actually, I could not blame him, because the photographs were unbelievable!"

Laura asked, "Do you remember where these pictures were taken?" Lucas replied, "Manchester! I remember we worked with the news people up there quite a lot." Laura said, "Can you remember the name of the reporter who wrote the story?" Lucas shook his head and said, "He will be long gone by now. You have to remember that this was sixty years ago. Your only hope of getting to the bottom of this story is by going to Manchester, but even that is a long shot. As I said, it was a long time ago. Why all this interest? This story is finished!" Laura explained that she was putting the story online and she wanted to ensure that all the facts were correct. She surprised herself how easily she lied. But, neither of them believed her!

As she had finished her tea, Laura and Billy left the house. Once they were in the car, Billy asked Laura what was going on, as there was obviously very much more to this than she was actually telling him. She turned to Billy and said, "I am sorry. I like you, I really do, and I hope we can be good friends, but I cannot tell you anything at all about this matter…" Billy responded that she was not to worry and added that we all have our secrets.

The next morning, she phoned her boss and asked for two days leave. He was not completely happy with the short notification, but, in the end, agreed, providing it was no more than two days.

It was still early morning when Laura boarded the train to Manchester. Billy had already phoned ahead and made arrangements for her to meet an individual at the

Manchester Evening News. Laura had learned a lot about Billy over the last few days. If anyone needed anything at all, Billy appeared to be the one to ask. He seemed to know everyone! Whenever you walked into a room with Billy, it was as if you were invisible! People only saw Billy. There would be a 'chorus' of 'Hello, Billy', 'Hi, Billy', 'Thanks, Billy'. Others would just wave or stick up a thumb! Laura realised she had been so self-absorbed and buried in her work that she had missed much of the life that was going on all around her.

Laura arrived at Piccadilly Station in Manchester just before noon. She took a taxi to the offices of the Manchester Evening News on Deansgate. As she got out of the taxi, unaccountably, she paused for a second. She remembered that when she was a little girl, her father would take her horse riding and, sometimes, he would take her to the blacksmith's. She remembered the smell of the forge. She wondered what had brought that memory back. It was then she realised that, inexplicably, she could smell a forge. She looked around to see where that smell was coming from and thought, "This is crazy, absolutely crazy! There cannot be a forge anywhere around here. This is a city centre." She then clearly heard the sound of a hammer hitting an anvil. She looked at the building in front of her and, without even thinking, said, "Marcus, I will see you in Rome." She had no idea why she had said this. She looked around to see if anyone had heard what she had just said. She was slightly embarrassed at the idea of talking to herself. Just as suddenly as the sound and the smell came, they were gone.

Laura looked up at the tall building in front of her. Unknown to her, she was standing on the very spot where Marcus, much earlier in his life as Marcus Longinus, had sited his blacksmith shop. She did not realise that even though Marcus was two hundred miles away in London, she was closer to him now than she had ever been.

Whilst she was standing looking at the building, a young man came out and said, "Hi, are you Laura? My name is John. Billy asked me to keep an eye out for you." Laura was somewhat taken aback. She did not anticipate that Billy would have made arrangements for her to be met. She was very grateful, as it spared her the trouble of explaining to the receptionist the reason for her visit. As they went through the doors and made their way to the lift, John asked Laura, "How is Billy?" This did not really surprise Laura at all! It was a constant and ongoing surprise to Laura how many people actually knew Billy and would ask after him.

When they arrived at John's office on the sixth floor, Laura realised that John was not an office boy, or indeed a general factotum. He had a large, well-equipped office, and an adjoining office, which they walked through, where a young lady worked and vetoed anyone wanting to see her employer.

John pulled out a chair and gestured for Laura to sit down. He sat down next to her and said, "Okay, young lady, Billy has put me in the picture, but I am not sure what you think I can do." Laura took out the photographs and explained that she wondered if he could shed any light on the story behind them. John picked up one of the photographs, looked at the back, and said, "I do not know if you noticed when you came to my office, but there are not many people working here who are over one hundred years old." He paused for a moment and then saw the look of disappointment on Laura's face. He held up his hand and said, "Hang on, hang on, young lady. I have not finished yet." Apparently, Allan, who was one of our top reporters, documented everything (tapping his laptop) and so I have some eye-witness accounts." He turned his laptop around to enable Laura to see the screen.

As he was talking, he was tapping away at his laptop. He moved his laptop closer towards Laura. She leaned forward so that she could read the information on the screen. She was fascinated. There were at least ten statements. Allan had indeed done an excellent job.

All the statements had been given by individuals whom many would regard as trustworthy. The first statement was from a policeman, who saw the boy fall and watched in disbelief as a young man, who had been standing next to him, jumped into the lion enclosure, and put himself between the boy and the lions. The statement went on to say that he heard the man shouting at the animals in what seemed to be a foreign language. The reporter even went to the circus and spoke to a lion tamer and asked if it was possible that the man could have been a professional lion tamer and would know how to handle lions. The circus lion tamer's response was, apparently, unprintable.

When she had finished reading all the statements, she asked why, with this amount of available evidence, the Newspaper had decided not to go to print. John just gazed ahead and said, "I thought about that myself as I read the reports. The only conclusion I could arrive at was that the story was just so unbelievable. Unfortunately, all the witnesses are now long gone. The only survivor is the young boy, who, it goes without saying, is now an old man. I tracked him down for you."

He gave Laura a piece of paper with an address on it. Laura looked amazed. John said, "We do have Google in Manchester, you know!" Laura laughed and asked if he would mind printing a copy of the statements for her. John replied, "One step ahead of you, again!" as he handed Laura a file. Laura started flicking through the pages, repeating, "Great, great. Thank you very much for your help." She shook hands with John and, clutching the files and the boy's address, left John's office.

As Laura left the building, she turned right and walked up Deansgate. She needed time to clear her head, and to process the information she had just been given. She wandered aimlessly, thinking that all this surely, surely, could not be real. She bought herself a sandwich and a coffee and sat down on a bench just near to the ruins of the old Roman Fort. As she was eating her lunch, she thought to herself that she could not blame the editor for not running the story. John was correct—the story was just too unbelievable.

Laura was totally unaware that the bench on which she was sitting was situated in the same place where Marcus used to sit, nearly two thousand years earlier. As she drank her coffee from the paper cup, going over the story she had heard and the information she had been given, she was startled to hear voices all around and behind her. She turned around, but she was completely on her own! What surprised her was that the voices were not speaking in the English language but were speaking

Latin. Although she could not understand Latin, she was familiar with the language because it was Marcus's favourite language. He would often speak in Latin to her.

Suddenly, the voices were gone. A strange thought went through her mind but she had no idea where it came from—"There is nothing new under the sun!" When she had finished her lunch, she looked at the piece of paper that John had given her. She read out the name—Charlie Yates. She decided not to go to see Charlie Yates. She thought that all the evidence she had seen and amassed led to an impossible conclusion. She called a taxi to the station and caught the first train back to London. Whilst she was on the train, she read a magazine. She needed a distraction.

She arrived home in the early evening, had something to eat, took a shower, and went to see Marcus. She thought it was probably a good idea not to mention her investigation. She knew very well that he would only laugh and mock her. Laura avoided talking about lions, photographs, and scars. It was as though they were back to where they were before she found those stupid photographs. She was home, happy and relaxed.

The first person she met when she arrived at the office the following morning was Billy, who was keen to hear all the details of what had happened in Manchester. She merely gave him the file to read, whilst she carried on with her work. After he had finished reading the file, he said, "Wow! Do you know what I think?" Laura stopped working and turned around to face him. Billy continued, "As crazy as it sounds, I believe all of this did actually happen. But this was sixty years ago. Why is there all this interest now?" Billy stopped talking when he realised Laura was wrestling with something. The two friends sat together in silence. After a while, Laura spoke. "Billy, I need to know if I can trust you." Billy answered. "You know I have a lot of friends. I have, over the years, helped a number of people in different ways. Believe me, nobody likes a gossip. Whatever you tell me is safe with me."

Laura then told him the whole story, that the man in the photographs was her friend. She told him about the scars, and how they were identical to those of the man in the photographs. Billy thought for a moment, and then said, "Laura, do you know how crazy this sounds? Your boyfriend looks no older than he did in Manchester sixty years ago. What is he? Is he some kind of time traveller?" Laura replied, "Or, maybe he is ninety years old?" Laura quickly added, "I know… I really, really know how mental that sounds, and I absolutely know it cannot be him. Believe me, it is driving me insane, but it is, without any doubt, definitely him." Billy leaned forward, took hold of both of Laura's hands and said, "You know what, Laura? You need to know one way or another. You need to phone this Charlie and ask him to come to London. Then take him to your coffee shop to meet Marcus. Tell Marcus that Charlie is just an old friend. They will not recognise each other. So, it will all be over, and you can just go back to being friends."

Laura said, "What if they do recognise each other?" Billy answered, "Let's cross that bridge when we come to it." He added, "Look, Laura, I know you have strong feelings for this man, but unless this is resolved, it will always come between you both." Laura reluctantly agreed.

She phoned Charlie and asked if he would like to come to London. She explained that there was someone she would like him to meet, and whilst they were in London, she would show him the sights. He could then catch the last train home. She added, "I will pick up the bill!"

Charlie seemed excited. Although he had been to London many times, he always enjoyed it. Laura was pretty sure she knew Marcus's teaching schedule and so she arranged for Charlie to come on a week when she knew Marcus was free. Laura spent the whole week in an agony of indecision. She had such a feeling of guilt. If Marcus ever found out, would he ever forgive her? She could not blame him if he never forgave her. Despite this, she had to know one way or another. When the day finally arrived, Laura phoned Marcus and told him she was finishing early and would he like to go for a coffee? He seemed delighted. Billy had agreed to pick Charlie up at the station. She made him promise for the thousandth time that he would not mention lions or zoos to Charlie. She did not want him putting ideas into Charlie's head.

CHAPTER 23
THE CAFÉ

MARCUS WAS AWARE that she would not let this matter drop and would be looking for other ways to verify the age of the photographs. He understood he now had a serious problem. Weeks went by without any mention of the photographs, although Marcus suspected that Laura had not forgotten them. He had to admit to himself that each time she called in to have a coffee or phoned him to suggest meeting in the Marah Coffee Shop, he felt a little uncomfortable. When they were talking, he was constantly expecting her to reveal some new information she had collected! He knew from experience how she loved to be dramatic!

After several weeks had elapsed since the conversation, he started to feel safe. He had no doubt Laura had investigated further, but he was hopeful that, as it was such a very long time ago, she had simply not been able to locate any new information.

One rainy afternoon, Laura phoned him and explained she had finished work early. She asked, if he was not working, would he like to go for a coffee? He felt relaxed. He had almost forgotten about the emergence of the photographs of the incident at the zoo. As he had heard nothing further from Laura, he assumed that she was no longer pursuing the matter.

Marcus was quite looking forward to getting together with Laura. He put on his heavy raincoat and his silly flat cap, which always made her laugh. He stepped out into the pouring rain and made his way as quickly as he could to the café. He arrived before Laura and went over to the counter to order a cappuccino for her and water for himself. As he sat down at a table near the window, Laura arrived. He smiled. Laura stood at the door looking like a drowned rat. Shaking the rain from her umbrella, she came across to the table, her hair soaking wet. Marcus remarked that the umbrella did not appear to have done her much good! Laura answered, "Better wet than wearing that ridiculous cap of yours!" Marcus replied, "Vanity, vanity; all is vanity!" Her only response was to punch him lightly on the shoulder, as she whispered, "Shut up, you!"

She sat down and looked around as if she was looking for someone. Marcus inquired, "Are you expecting anyone?" Still looking around, Laura simply said, "Yes! There is someone I would like you to meet." She turned to wave to an elderly gentleman as he came into the café. Marcus smiled. The man did not look as bedraggled as Laura. He was wearing a deep flat cap, which he removed. He nodded, acknowledging Laura, and walked over to the table. Marcus thought there was something familiar about him. He suddenly had a very bad feeling. He was beginning to feel extremely uncomfortable. Laura introduced the individual to Marcus; "This is Charlie, from Manchester."

The waitress came over to their table. Charlie ordered a tea, which gave Marcus time to compose himself. Marcus was now in no doubt as to the identity of the elderly gentleman. He was the small boy whom he had rescued from the lions' enclosure so many years ago. Even though Marcus was feeling extremely anxious, he could not help but think, "Well done, Laura!"

He was stunned and amazed at how she had managed to find him, and then, how on earth she had persuaded him to come to London. Marcus decided the best way to deal with the situation was to 'play dumb', and to say as little as possible. He sat quietly and listened, as Laura made small talk. The situation did seem to be under control and was going well. It was clear that Charlie had not recognised him.

Charlie, whilst continuing to talk to Laura, glanced at Marcus and smiled. He turned back to Laura, but before he could respond to what she had said, he turned and looked again at Marcus, who was beginning to feel very nervous. Marcus could see the look of recognition appear in his eyes. Charlie looked closely at Marcus. He then leaned over to look at Marcus's neck. Charlie began to get very excited, pointing to Marcus's neck and saying to Laura in a voice that was a little too loud for a coffee shop, "It's him! It is him!"

Marcus sat in defeated silence, while Charlie told Laura the full story of the incident at the zoo. Laura listened to Charlie's account, occasionally glancing up at Marcus, who simply smiled weakly back at her. Charlie then turned to Marcus and said, "l looked it up," and turning back to Laura, repeated, "l looked it up." Smiling, and appearing to be very pleased with himself, he then turned again to Marcus and said, "He talked to the lions all the time he was in the enclosure with them. He kept talking to them." Looking at Laura, he continued, "I have got a very good memory; everyone says so." Charlie sat up straight as if he was about to make a statement of which he was very proud and said, "Parce precor, mihi protected. It is Latin; it means, 'Stop, I am protected'. Well," Charlie declared, "That is exactly what he said to them beasts and they just fell down. He even kicked some of them out of the way. No one believes me; no one."

Charlie looked at Marcus's face, and then, as if he suddenly understood that he was making things very difficult for the man who had saved his life all those years ago, he started to backtrack. "No, no. I am sorry, I can see now. You are not the man. You are not the one who rescued me."

All Laura could say was, "What?!" Charlie interrupted, "No, the man who saved me was much smaller, and had different colour hair." He stood up and said, "Very sorry, but I have a train to catch." He then hurried over to the door. Laura chased after him. Marcus did not move. He said nothing. The damage had been done, and there was no coming back from this. Marcus watched Laura and Charlie out of the corner of his eye. He saw Laura with her phone in her hand. Marcus looked away. He did not want to catch Charlie's eye. Laura came back to the table and apologised. She explained that she had to leave as she was taking Charlie to the station. Marcus just nodded. Then she was gone.

CHAPTER 24

RUN

Marcus rushed home. He was unsure how long it would be before Laura returned after taking Charlie to the station. Knowing Laura as he did, he knew she would not just abandon him at the station but would wait with him until the train arrived. This might give him a few hours' start. When he returned to his home, he packed as much as he could into a large backpack. He then made his way to the letting agency he had used in the past and asked them to advertise and organise the leasing of his house on a short-term basis. He also paid for a cleaner to ensure the property was made suitable for rental, and to also pack up all his clothing and donate it all to a charity shop. Marcus took a taxi to St. Pancras. He knew that Charlie was leaving from Piccadilly and so there was no chance of an embarrassing encounter.

Marcus caught the Eurostar train for Paris. He was aware that he was a long way from being out of the woods yet. He knew that he could dodge the F.B.I., C.I.A., M.I.5., or Interpol! But he also knew that the very last person anyone would want tracking them was a reporter! Once on the train, Marcus was able to relax. He made phone calls to the various colleges at which he was due to teach. He apologised and explained that he could not work for the foreseeable future as he had been called away on family business. They all told him not to worry, and that he was to take as long as he needed to settle his affairs. Marcus thanked them, leaned back, and closed his eyes.

This whole business had left him exhausted. It reminded him of the walk back from the zoo in Manchester, and how he had felt drained for weeks afterwards. He knew that on this occasion, he probably did not have weeks. He needed to come up with a plan. He decided to make his way to Rome. He knew that Laura was aware of his house in Rome because he had, foolishly, mentioned to her that he sometimes stayed there. He hoped she would not pursue him. After all, the idea of him actually being in his nineties was absolutely ridiculous; in reality, the truth was even more unbelievable.

Marcus stayed in Paris for a few days whilst he considered what would be the preferable and safest course of action. It was imperative to establish whether Laura was looking for him, and, if she was not, which he thought was unlikely, he would simply take up residence at his home in Rome. Choosing that particular alternative would not be ideal, as it had been only a few years since he had left Rome. In addition, he could not possibly work there again so soon, as he would very quickly be recognised.

Although it would not be an ideal solution to immediately move into his house in Rome, Marcus decided to keep watch on the property for two or three weeks, and then re-assess the situation. He considered going to work in America for several years. He had an American passport, an Italian passport, and a British passport. He had, however, learned not to rush into making decisions. He decided to stay in Rome for a while but to be circumspect with his movements around the city. After a sufficient period, he would then travel around Italy. This was something he had intended to do for the past few years. He would use his City of Refuge in Sicily.

The last time Marcus had stayed in one of his Cities of Refuge was in the 1890s in Sicily, at Mary Magdalene's descendants' home. He had fond memories of his time in Sicily. He had also spent some years teaching at Durham University. He loved Durham and its people. He was sorry to have left the city, but as he had spent ten years in Durham, he decided that it was time to move on. He had considered going back there after Laura discovered his secret but decided it was much too dangerous. Laura would soon have tracked him back to Durham.

He remembered Sicily, the happy time he had spent living there and the connection he had formed with Alonso, a small boy about ten years old. When Alonso was told by his parents of the secret surrounding their mystery guest, and made to promise not to tell anyone, Marcus thought that the boy would burst with delight and excitement. Over and over again, he said, "I promise, I promise", whilst holding his hands together as if in prayer. Alonso then took hold of Marcus's hand.

Marcus stayed with the family for about three months, and he could not recall a time when Alonso was not holding his hand. The boy was so excited that the legendary Centurion had come to stay at his house. They became good friends. The young boy wanted to know all about his history and the places and the cities in which he had lived. He wanted to know what it was like in Roman times. Marcus thoroughly relished and appreciated sharing his stories with the boy and his family. He enjoyed showing his scars and telling the family how he had acquired them. Alonso always sat completely still, listening wide-eyed, open-mouthed and in absolute silence to every word Marcus spoke. Over the years, Marcus had had to make many sad partings, but when the time came to say goodbye to Alonso, he found it particularly heartbreaking.

CHAPTER 25

I WAS PUSHED

Laura stood outside the café with Charlie and waved down a taxi. She tried to talk Charlie into returning to the café, but he shook his head. On the journey to the station, Charlie remained quiet. As they arrived at the station, the signs indicated they would have to wait an hour before the next train arrived. Laura offered to buy Charlie a tea, to which he reluctantly agreed. As they sat down, Charlie said, "I am so sorry. I really do not want to get him into any trouble." Laura explained to him that as he was the only survivor, there was no way that her newspaper or any other news outlet would use the story without his agreement. This seemed to satisfy Charlie.

He turned to Laura, asking, "What do you want?" Laura answered him, "Please, tell me what happened on that day at the zoo." Charlie said quietly, "My mum took me to see the lions at the zoo, but when we got there, they just lay on the ground. They were very boring and so I decided to wake them up by making a noise jumping up and down on the small wall around the enclosure.

Mum tried to grab hold of me and, as I tried to dodge her, I lost my balance and fell into the lion enclosure. He saved me." Laura said, "Charlie, are you certain that it was Marcus who saved you? After all, it was a long time ago." Charlie looked down at the table and started fiddling with the condiments, then, after a few minutes, he looked up and asked, "Do you promise, absolutely promise me that he will not get into trouble?"

Laura promised. Charlie said, "I can't understand it. He is exactly the same. He has not changed at all; the scars, his eyes. I remember his eyes, kind eyes. His hair is exactly the same and …" Charlie turned away. Laura said, "And what, Charlie?" "Nothing. It's nothing," said Charlie. Laura looked at him and felt guilty for the pressure she was putting on him. "Charlie, don't worry; even if you think it is nothing, just tell me."

When Charlie spoke, it was almost in a whisper. Laura leaned forward slightly so that she could hear what he was saying. He said, "I was very frightened. I think I wet myself a little. I hugged him so tightly that my face was pushed against his, and although it seemed a silly thing to notice, his face was smooth. My Dad, when I hugged him, his face was always scratchy."

Charlie paused for a moment and looked as though he wanted to say something more. Laura said, "What is it, Charlie?" Charlie hesitated. Laura added, "Is there something else you want to tell me?" Charlie said, "Yes, there is, but nobody would believe me. They thought that I was making it up, so that I would not get into trouble." Laura said, "What is it, Charlie?" Charlie looked at Laura as if he was about to tell her something important. He said, "I did not fall into the lion's enclosure." Laura said, "What?" Charlie said, "No. I did not fall in. I was pushed!" Laura said, "Pushed! Pushed! Who on earth would push a child into a lions' enclosure?" Charlie said, "See…See… You do not believe me! That is exactly what the police said to me."They said, "Who would do such a thing?" They did ask some other witnesses, but they all said that I was 'messing about' on the wall and I must have lost my balance and fallen into the lions' enclosure. They did not believe me! But I was… I was pushed, and I do not care if nobody believes me."

Laura was stunned. She had fought against all the evidence, telling herself over and over again how impossible the whole idea was—how absolutely ridiculous it was, but now, she believed, and she had to decide what to do next.

After seeing Charlie onto the train, she made her way home. She noticed that Marcus's house was in darkness. She was disappointed. She felt that the sooner they spoke to each other, the better it would be. As it was still quite early in the evening, she had hoped she could see him. She thought to herself that tomorrow, tomorrow they would meet.

When she arrived at her workplace the following morning, Billy asked her about the meeting with Charlie. She told him she did not want to talk about it yet. She was pleased when Billy, like the good friend he had become, told her not to worry and to take her time.

It seemed that her relationship with Marcus was in serious trouble. Now that she was in danger of losing him, she was starting to realise exactly how she really felt about him. As she travelled home, she rehearsed in her mind what she was going to say to Marcus. She was going to apologise, and apologise, and apologise again and hope that he would forgive her. She intended to tell him how much she liked him.

As she approached the house, she stopped. There were two men outside Marcus's house and they appeared to be putting up some kind of a sign. She quickened her steps and was shocked to discover that it was a 'To Let' sign that the men were erecting. Although it was very obvious, she asked the men what they were doing. Without interrupting their work, or even looking at her, they said, "Putting up a bloody sign, luv!" She asked the men who had instructed them to do so. Again, without looking at her, one of the men just tapped the name on the sign, 'Leyland Letting Agency'.

Laura went past the men and pounded on the front door of Marcus's house. One of the men said, "It is no use banging on the door, luv. It is empty—there is no one in the house." Laura ran into her house and telephoned the Letting Agency. She asked them about Marcus and if he had left any forwarding address. They replied that the vendor had been very specific in his instructions to them that they were not to reveal any personal details to anyone, under any circumstances. As she ended the call, the full realisation of what she had done hit her. She had hounded the man she loved and caused him to leave his home and his job, and to travel to who knows where. His only 'crime' had been to save the life of a child.

Laura wept as she had never wept before. When she had run out of tears, she came to a decision—she would find Marcus, even if it meant that she had to pursue him to the ends of the earth.

As she left her house, she instinctively looked up to see if there was a light on in Marcus's house. She knew that he never switched the lights off. She had once teased him and asked if he was afraid of the dark. Marcus had smiled but said nothing.

Laura knew that Billy was her best chance of finding Marcus. She dried her eyes, had a shower, and put on her make-up. She checked how she looked in the mirror. She did not want Billy to know that she had been crying. She had a glass of wine. She felt that she really needed it! She telephoned Billy and asked if she could call around to see him. Billy asked if everything was all right and Laura, trying her best not to cry, simply said, "No". Billy sounded concerned and told her to come over anytime she wanted someone to talk to, or simply for a change of venue.

Laura had promised herself that when she arrived at Billy's house, she was not going to cry. She cried! She swore Billy to secrecy. She then told him the whole story. She stressed that Charlie had confirmed without a shadow of a doubt that the man in the photographs was Marcus. She added that when she arrived home, she saw that individuals from a local House Letting Agency were in Marcus's garden and were erecting a 'To Let' sign. She had phoned the Letting Agency and was told that the owner was no longer living in the property and that it was now definitely 'To Let'. She turned to Billy and said, "He's gone, Billy, but who knows where?"

Billy said, "Are you really telling me that your boyfriend is at least ninety years old?"

Laura replied, "I really do not know what to think. It all seems so crazy." She then pleaded with Billy to help her find Marcus, telling Billy that she had no idea where to even start searching for him. Billy said, "Don't worry. We will work something out, but it's best you go home." He added that he might be able to contact someone who could possibly help. As Billy phoned for a taxi to take Laura home, he told her not to worry, and that he would talk to her in the morning. Laura thanked him. In fact, she kept thanking him until she got into the taxi. Before she closed her eyes and slept, she whispered, "Thank you, Billy."

Throughout the next morning, whilst she was working, she was constantly looking around, hoping to see Billy. Laura loved her work, but this morning she was so distracted that it was a great relief when Billy arrived with a huge grin on his face. He told her that he had a friend who was a genius computer hacker. Laura thought to herself, "Of course you have, Billy." Billy leaned forward, closer to her, tapped his nose, gave a wink, and said, "Least said the better!" Billy stood up and told Laura that he would pick her up later that evening. He added, "Don't worry—this man I know can find anyone, anywhere." Billy turned around and walked away, singing a 60's song.

Laura returned to her work, feeling guilty and wondering if she was becoming a terrible person. She was still hounding Marcus and it now seemed as though she was about to delve into his private life, and, to make matters even worse, she was encouraging someone to break the law.

That evening, Billy picked Laura up from her home and they drove to meet with Mike, who was, apparently, twenty-two years old, but looked about twelve! In the car on the way to Mike's house, Billy had told Laura that Mike loved to challenge governments, high-tech companies and even banks. He told her that Mike had never stolen anything and that he was always very careful not to do any harm, adding that he just liked the thrill of it all. Laura, however, felt more and more uncomfortable about the whole thing.

As they went into Mike's house, he asked for the photograph of the incident at the zoo, and for as much information as she had, or knew, about Marcus himself. As she recounted all the incredible details, Mike tapped away at his computer keyboard without commenting. When she had finished, Mike said, "First, I will check if he has a police record. Then I will look at his bank records. It is amazing what you can find out about someone simply by looking at their bank account. They may have used an ATM in Moscow, for example, or there may be strange money going into, or out of their bank accounts." As Mike explained what he was doing, Laura became increasingly uncomfortable and asked, "Surely, this is illegal?" Mike put his finger to his lips and whispered, "Shush!" Mike smiled, and then said, "Okay. Come see me tomorrow." Laura felt as if she had been dismissed. She glanced at Billy, who just shrugged his shoulders. As she left, she turned to Mike and thanked him. Mike, without taking his eyes off the computer screen, just grunted.

On the journey home, Laura asked Billy if he was sure that they were doing the right thing, and whether he thought it was a little dangerous. She added that she had no desire to end up in jail! Billy laughed and said, "Are you kidding? No is the answer to your question! It is not a little bit dangerous; it is very dangerous, girl. If we are caught, they will throw the key away." He laughed but Laura certainly wasn't laughing! For the rest of the journey home, she was completely silent, whilst Billy sang song after song as if he did not have a care in the world. As Billy pulled up outside her house, she looked sadly at the 'To Let' sign outside Marcus's house. Billy noticed and said, "Don't worry, girl. We're going to fix this." Laura was not convinced.

Working the next day was agony for Laura. She was on edge all day. In the afternoon, two policemen came into the office in which she was working. It is not at all unusual for members of the police force to visit any newspaper office, and although Laura was well aware of this, she was, nevertheless, convinced they had come to arrest her. She knew that her feelings and her fears were irrational, but Billy did not help! When she shared with him how she had felt when the police arrived at her office, he told her not to be silly. He said, "Mike would not reveal your name that easily. He would hold out for at least a week, no matter how much they tortured him." Laura tried, unsuccessfully, to smile and said, "Not funny, Billy! Not funny at all," which made Billy roar with laughter.

That evening, as they arrived at Mike's house, he let them in, and seemingly excited, hurried them into his office. He asked them to sit down and said, "You are really going to love this!" He placed several photographs on the table and said, "These photos are definitely genuine." Laura seemed frustrated and said, "Well, we already knew that" . Mike replied, "Sorry, but I have had to have them checked out myself. First: Marcus Albright is not Marcus Albright, and, unbelievably, I cannot at this moment find out who he actually is. Let us just leave that for now. This individual—for the sake of argument, let's call him Marcus—has a master's degree in Latin, Classics and Ancient History from Oxford."

Again, Laura said, "We know that." Mike replied, "No! All fake! I do not know how he did it, but he did." Mike continued, "However, we'll leave this for now. Currently, he is in Rome, in a house he purchased in the year… are you ready for this?" Mike waited for a response. Laura and Billy both nodded. "In the year 1946, the property was purchased by none other than Marcus Albright. Let us assume that he was about thirty years old when he bought the house in Rome; that would make him about 115 years old now." Laura looked shocked and stunned. Billy said, "You have to be kidding?" Mike answered, "There is more."

Laura held her breath as Mike continued. "I managed to get access to the records of the Colleges for whom he has worked, and looking at his work record, it appears that he is brilliant in all his subjects. He is fluent in Latin and Ancient English." He added, "How can anyone be fluent in Ancient English? He is also said to have a unique understanding of Classical History. On numerous occasions, he has been offered a position as a television historian, but he has always turned it down." Mike said, "That is not all. I checked for anyone with the same qualification, and I can tell you that this man has been around. He has taught in Rome, Milan, and London. I want to show you something." With that, he turned towards his computer, tapped on the keyboard, and an image appeared on the screen. Mike stood up and gestured to Laura to sit down in his chair. Billy pulled up a chair next to Laura and sat down. They both stared at the image on the screen. It was a photograph… a very old photograph. It was a photograph of a University Professor giving an award to a student. The photograph had been published in a local Durham newspaper. Laura and Billy did not see the actual name of the student, or the nature of the award. There were only two things that caught their eye. The newspaper was dated 1850, and the Professor in the picture was, undoubtedly, Marcus.

The silence was deafening. No one knew what to say. What is there to say when confronted with something which goes against all that you believe?

Mike said to Laura, "There are still a lot of gaps that I cannot quite fit together. I have no idea where he was before Durham, or where he went to after he left Durham. Try and think—has he mentioned any other town or city, anywhere in the world?" Laura thought for a moment and then said, "When we first met, he said something very strange, but it is probably nothing."

Laura continued, "We met when I was trying to open my front door. I had just moved into the house next door to Marcus, and I was having difficulty getting the door key into the lock and Marcus came to my rescue. I remember thinking how kind he was to help me. We started talking, and, suddenly, he asked me if I was from Colchester. It really surprised me because I do not have an accent or anything like that, but when I told him that my grandparents came from there, he had a strange look on his face, which I could not understand." Mike said, "Well, at least that gives us somewhere to start." He sat down and started to type on his computer. After a few minutes, he turned to Laura and said, "Sorry, we seem to have hit a dead end, but from what you have said, it would not surprise me if there *is* something there that we are missing." Mike was silent as he considered his next move. He turned to Laura and said, "I know that it is a long shot, but it might be worth going up to Colchester and showing his photo around and asking people if they know him. It is not too far away, and you never know!" Mike shrugged his shoulders and said, "I think that it is worth a try."

Laura turned to Billy and said, "What do you think, Billy?" Billy replied, "Well, it is like Mike said, 'What have you got to lose?'" Laura nodded and said, "Well,

OK, Billy, but only if you come with me." Billy protested and said, "Laura, I am sorry, but I am just no good at all that detective stuff." Laura looked at Billy, pleadingly, and said, "I just need some moral support. It really would be a great help if you were with me." Billy thought for a moment and then answered, "OK. All right. Just stop looking at me like a puppy that is on its way to the vets."

Billy arranged to pick Laura up early the next day and to drive them both down to Colchester, and she was waiting at the door when he called for her the following morning. On the drive down, Billy seemed really excited. He told Laura that it was like setting off on some great adventure and it was really thrilling to think what they might discover. He told her, excitedly, that he had once read a book about a girl who had found the Fountain of Youth, and maybe Marcus had found his very own Fountain of Youth! He continued, "Who knows, he may let us join him in it!" Laura, laughingly, answered, "That is very unlikely, and I am not really sure that going to Colchester is a good idea. Even if we do go, what are we going to do when we get there?"

Billy answered, "What if… What if?" He turned to Laura and said, "Just hear me out here, please. What if there is an actual Fountain of Youth at Colchester? After all, we have a young man walking around who is at least two hundred years old and no matter what the reason is for all this, it has got to be crazy. So", Billy continued, "until I hear something different, I am sticking to my theory of a "Fountain of Youth". Laura thought for a moment and replied, "Okay, Billy. Let us just suppose for a moment that you are right and there is a Fountain of Youth in Colchester. How on earth do we find it?" Billy said, "Simple! We just look for a lot of old people who look young!" Laura and Billy both burst out laughing!

Laura was really glad that she had persuaded Billy to accompany her to Colchester. She arrived in a far better mood, and even though she was not convinced that they would make any new discoveries, at least they were having fun!

As soon as they arrived and parked the car, Billy downloaded Marcus's photograph onto his phone. "You wait here whilst I go and talk to those two old people over there", he said, smiling and pointing to a young couple who were standing talking a few yards away from their car. Laura watched as Billy walked over to the couple and started chatting to them. After a few minutes, they were talking and laughing as if they had known each other for years. She watched as Billy showed them Marcus's photograph on his phone. They both shook their heads. Billy shook hands with them and moved across to talk to a small group of women who had just exited their car. Again, within a few moments, they were all laughing as if they were life-long friends! Billy, undiscouraged, moved across to another couple who had just parked their car and were leaving the car park. He repeated this with several people either entering their cars, ready to leave, or just arriving, going from one group to another. Then he came back to the car.

As soon as Billy sat down, Laura said, "For goodness's sake, Billy, what on earth did you say to all those people?" Billy smiled and said, "What do you think I said? I asked them if they had ever heard of H. Rider Haggard. Amazingly, they hadn't! I do not know what the world is coming to! Anyway, I explained that he wrote a book about the Fountain of Youth, and we believe that it is in Colchester. I added that as everyone around here looks so young, I suspect that he is right! I then showed them a photograph of Marcus and said, "For instance, this guy is about four hundred years old!" They did not recognise him, but all is not lost as they suggested I ask the gentleman who runs that shop over there." Billy pointed to a shop across the road from the car park. He then opened the car door and, turning to Laura, said, "I won't be a minute."

Before Laura could answer, Billy was gone. She watched as Billy disappeared into the shop, thinking that this was all a complete waste of time. Then she saw Billy reappear from the shop with a huge smile on his face. He opened the car door and got into the car. He sat there, in silence, with a huge grin on his face. Impatiently, Laura said, "Well? Well?" Billy did not answer. Laura said, again, but in a louder voice, "WELL?" Billy smiled at her. "The man in that shop knows everything about Colchester. When I showed him the photo of Marcus, he got very excited and then started laughing! When I asked why he was laughing, he apologised and said that he had never seen the actual man, but, remarkably, he had seen a scar just like the man had in the photograph I had just shown him. When I asked where, the man started laughing again." Billy turned to Laura and said, "Now, now, calm down." Laura said, "What do you mean? I am calm." Billy continued, "Well, I have not told you anything yet." Laura said, "Told me what?" Billy took a deep breath and said, "The man in the shop is somewhat of a history buff. He is always in the Colchester Museum. He told me that there is a sculpture in the museum of a Roman Centurion." Billy paused. Laura said, "AND…?" Billy continued. "The man in the shop said that the Centurion had the exact same scar."

Billy was taken aback by Laura's reaction. She shouted at the top of her voice, "No, no, no. Oh no, no, no!" Billy continued, "I don't think it would do any harm to go to the museum and take a look at the exhibits." Laura screamed in frustration, and then said, "When you were talking about the Fountain of Youth, I knew you were not serious, and it was very funny and, in fact, it helped me a lot! It was just what I needed, but the idea of a Fountain of Youth, as ridiculous as that sounds, is actually more believable than Marcus being a Roman Centurion, which would make Marcus… what…? When were the Romans here…? Four thousand years ago?" Laura turned to Billy, who had started to speak. "Well? Well?" Billy said, "It was actually less than two thousand years ago." Laura answered, "Oh, OK then, only two thousand years ago. That's all right then. I have got a grandfather older than that." Billy said, "You are being sarcastic, I hope?" Laura laughed. She turned to Billy and said, quietly, "We do have to go to the museum, don't we, Billy?" There were a few moments of silence before Billy answered, saying, "Come on. We can walk from here. It is only just around the corner."

Laura linked arms with Billy and said, "Thank you, Billy. I do not know what I would have done without you." They walked to the museum in complete silence, each lost in thought. When they arrived, Laura insisted on paying, much to Billy's discomfort. Laura smiled, and thought to herself, "Oh, Billy. You are just an old-fashioned man." They wandered around the museum until they came to a large sign that said, "Roman Colchester". Within a few moments, they saw what they had come to the museum to see. There were two sculptures—one was of a woman, with a sword in a scabbard strapped between her shoulder blades. Laura thought that she looked exactly like a frighteningly scary warrior. Next to the statue, there was a small plaque which read, "Gertrude". Standing alongside the statue of Gertrude was the sculpture of The Centurion. The sculpture was approximately two feet tall, and Laura and Billy had to bend down to examine it. After looking at it for a few minutes, Laura said to Billy, "Well, it could be anyone." Billy agreed but pointed out that he had a scar on his neck. Billy looked at the photograph of Marcus on his phone and said, "I must admit, the resemblance is uncanny." Laura said, "As it is very old, what looks like a scar on his neck might just be a crack in the stone." Billy answered, "You are most probably right, but to be sure, let's ask someone." Before Laura could answer, Billy had gone.

Laura stood for several minutes waiting for Billy to return. When he did, he brought with him a smart-looking young lady. Billy introduced her as the Curator. The young woman said to Laura, "I believe you work for The Times newspaper and would like to look at one of our exhibits" . Laura felt somewhat embarrassed and when the Curator was not looking, she gave Billy a look which made him go pale! Laura said to the Curator, "If you do not mind, would it be possible to have a closer look at the sculpture of the Centurion?" The Curator said, "It is a very interesting exhibit and was discovered quite recently at a dig just outside of the city. It was found alongside the sculpture of Gertrude." As the Curator was unlocking the glass panel, Laura asked, "How do you know their names?" The Curator lifted the sculpture of a female from the display cabinet and, as she handed it carefully across to Laura, said, "That is what is so exciting—the sculptures usually have either a personal name on them or the role and rank they undertook carved on the underside of each sculpture. The female figure you are holding is called Gertrude." The Curator then took the statue of Gertrude from Laura and placed it carefully into the display cabinet. She then picked up the second sculpture and handed it to Laura, saying, "Unfortunately, this sculpture simply said, "Centurion"." Even though the sculpture was quite heavy, Laura lifted it up to eye level to examine it, first looking at the scar around the neck. The Curator said, "It is fascinating, is it not? The scar looks like a battle scar." Laura answered, almost under her breath, "Probably a Syrian swordsman." The Curator said, "Indeed, and there is also the scar on the hand." Laura could feel her hands starting to shake and she carefully handed the sculpture back to the Curator, thanking her for her time. The Curator very carefully replaced the sculpture and said, "I hope that you found what you were looking for here?" Billy answered, "Yes, thank you very much. You have been very helpful." As they left the museum, Laura said to Billy, "Please tell me that we did not see what we just saw?" Billy said, "Now, now! Do not start jumping to conclusions. It might not be him." Laura, almost unable to control herself, said, "What on earth are you talking about—"It might not be him?" Did you see the scars? Exactly the same scars. Of course it is him!"

The drive back to London was made in almost complete silence. Billy was sorry that he had helped persuade Laura to go to Colchester. He had honestly believed that it was a wild goose chase but had hoped it would have stopped Laura from following Marcus around the world, ending up heartbroken. He had never believed the impossible narrative surrounding Marcus. He had thought that Marcus had just 'dumped' Laura and even now, with all the evidence, Billy was still having great difficulty believing it. As they drove into London, Laura asked Billy if he would mind calling at Mike's house. Billy smiled and said, "Anything you want to do" . As they pulled up outside Mike's house, Laura said to Billy, "You can just wait here. I will only be a moment." Billy said, "No problem. Take all the time you need." Laura got out of the car and made her way over to Mike's door. Laura knocked and waited. Mike seemed surprised when he opened the door and saw Laura. He smiled and said, "Laura, it is great to see you. How did you get on in Colchester?" Laura smiled weakly and said, "I am very tired. If you do not mind, please talk to Billy later and I am sure he will fill you in on all the details. I was wondering if you would please give me that address in Rome." Without speaking, Mike handed the address to her. Laura took the piece of paper, looked at it and then returned to the car. She turned to Billy and said, "Will you please take me home, Billy?" Billy asked her, "What are you going to do now?" Laura replied, "I am going to Rome."

The next morning, an anxious but hopeful Laura took an early morning flight to Rome. When she left the airport, she took a taxi to Marcus's house in Rome. Whilst on the flight, she had struggled with what she was going to say to Marcus, if and when she found him. How was she going to explain to him how she had located his Rome address?

Surprisingly, she was not as disturbed as she had expected to be on learning that Marcus was at least two hundred years old. It was hard enough, but the discovery in Colchester had completely pulled the rug from under her feet! She decided, however, to treat the information from Colchester as a red herring. She realised that she had been correct when she said that the Fountain of Youth was more believable. The Centurion sculpture was merely a coincidence. After all, the scars on the Centurion sculpture were probably quite common in the Roman world. It was a great shock, initially, but she reasoned with herself that she had already come to terms with the fact that Marcus was at least ninety years old. It is, in itself, unnatural to be ninety and yet to look only thirty years old. If it is not natural, it must, therefore, be supernatural! That was where the difficulty lay! Believing in the supernatural was the problem! It did not matter whether it was one, two, three or four hundred years! She, like a lot of people, enjoyed watching movies about vampires, werewolves and other scary creatures, but she did not count herself as being amongst the weirdos who actually believed these creatures exist, or had existed.

However, if one existed, why not two or even a hundred? How many people had she passed on the streets who were like Marcus?

On occasions, Laura, like a lot of people, went to church, but now, as she analysed it, she could see it was mainly for comfort, or out of habit. She did not actually believe in miracles, or in the devil. Laura took a deep breath and decided to watch a movie for the rest of the flight.

Before Laura left the Airport, she decided to have a coffee then take a taxi to Marcus's house. She had spent much of the journey trying to think of what she could say if Marcus answered the door. She knew that a simple "Hello" was not sufficient. As she sat drinking her coffee, she picked up a tourist magazine and, unsurprisingly, it was mostly about all the ancient sites to be seen in Rome. As she flipped through the pages, she stopped at an article on the Colosseum. Alongside the article, there was a picture of a Roman soldier. She wondered, could it be possible that Marcus was alive at that time? Laura shook her head and threw down the magazine, whispering to herself, "No chance." Laura left the rest of her coffee untouched and made her way to the taxi rank. She gave the taxi driver a piece of paper with Marcus's Rome address on it and, sitting back in the taxi, closed her eyes.

When the taxi pulled up outside Marcus's house, the taxi driver asked her if she wanted him to wait. Laura shook her head and replied, "No, but thank you", as she gave him a large tip. As the taxi drove away, Laura looked up and down the street. Across the road, she saw a large hotel. She thought to herself that if she was Marcus, that is exactly where she would be at this moment. She was sure Marcus would be aware that if she could find Charlie—and she did find him—then she could certainly find his house in Rome! She was also aware that the very last thing Marcus would want to happen would be to open the door and find her standing on his doorstep. "No, No," she thought to herself. "He is much too bright for that! He is up there, at one of the hotel windows, watching his house." She turned and walked up the path, admiring the house and the neighbourhood, and wondering what on earth was he doing living in London when he had a place like this?

Laura knocked on the door. As she had expected, there was no answer. She knocked again, merely 'for show.' She walked across the front of the house and looked through the window. She thought that it looked exactly as it would do if Marcus was actually living here. It was sparsely furnished, with no photographs or ornaments on display. She decided to walk around to the rear of the house. The back garden was beautiful. Clearly, Marcus was paying for a professional gardener to tend to it.

She looked up at the hotel and considered, just for a moment, phoning Mike and asking him to check Marcus's room number in the hotel, so that she could go to his room and surprise him. On reflection, she decided it was not a good idea! She thought of Paul Simon's song "50 Ways to Leave Your Lover". She knew that if she did that, it would definitely end any chance of a relationship.

Laura walked next door to talk to Marcus's neighbour. He was not particularly helpful. He smiled, as she described Marcus to him. She asked if he had noticed the scar on Marcus's neck. He replied, "You mean the one made by the Syrian swordsman, and the scar on his hand made by the Egyptian bowman." He then laughed out loud. Laura showed him the photo on her phone, on which the scars could be clearly seen. He confirmed that it was Marcus.

Laura thanked the neighbour. She did consider giving him her phone number and asking him to contact her if Marcus returned any time soon, but she decided against it. She did not want Marcus to think that she had a network of spies watching his every move!

As she considered what to do next, she came to the conclusion that the chase was over, but she thought it was important to let Marcus know how she felt, and that she was not a threat to him. As she walked to the front of Marcus's house, she stopped to write a short note, which she put through his letterbox. She then phoned a taxi, which soon arrived. As she was getting into the taxi, she turned in the direction of the hotel and waved. She hoped that the wave would be a message to Marcus, saying, "Hey! How are you? I miss you!", or, more simply, "Come out of that damned room and say hello to me. She realised the wave could be misinterpreted as sarcasm, but, she thought, "What have I got to lose?"

After being in the taxi for just a few minutes, she asked the driver to stop at a local coffee shop. She sat at a table near the window, ordering a cappuccino and a cake. Laura looked out of the window, took her phone out of her bag and placed it on the table, in the hope that Marcus had read the note and would phone her.

CHAPTER 26

THE HOTEL ACROSS THE ROAD

Marcus had checked into the hotel across the road from his house in Rome. He was fortunate; one of the rooms at the front of the hotel was vacant. It overlooked his house and had clear views up and down the road on which his house was situated. He was shown to his room by a young man, who carried Marcus's backpack for him in a disdainful manner. Marcus gave him a small tip!

Marcus looked around the room, checked that there was plenty of water in the fridge and pulled a chair over to the window. When he arrived, he had informed the lady on reception that they were to send all his meals up to his room at the appropriate times and he would eat there. He added that it did not matter what was on the menu because he was not a fussy eater.

Each day, Marcus would sit at the window of his room, a bottle of water in his hand, and watch his house. Marcus was a very patient man but spending six days looking out of the same window, at the same house, day after day, was driving him crazy. He had also become somewhat of a curiosity in the hotel. He was known as the 'weird man' who sat at the window all day. It was a common occurrence for the staff to go outside to see if the strange man was still at the window of his room. After two weeks, Marcus was questioning the wisdom of his decision. He was on the very point of giving up and going across the road and moving into his house. However, on the fifteenth day, early in the morning, a taxi pulled up outside his house. Marcus leaned forward, looking out of the window. He watched as a lady got out of the taxi. "Surely not!" Marcus thought. "Surely, surely not!" It was Laura.

Marcus watched as Laura paid the taxi driver. He quickly dropped down onto his knees as Laura, unexpectedly, turned around and looked across at the hotel. Marcus cursed himself over and over again, calling himself a fool and an idiot. He peered through the bottom corner of the window. He could see her staring at the hotel, although not specifically at his window. She looked along the front of the hotel before turning around and walking up the path towards the entrance to his house. She knocked on the door and then waited. Marcus watched, completely transfixed, as Laura knocked again. She paused for a moment, and then walked to the window. She spent a few minutes looking through each of the windows on the ground floor of his house. Marcus watched her, desperately trying to recall if he had left any clues that she could see, and which might possibly lead her to him. After a few moments, Marcus felt himself physically relax. As he knelt at the window, he thought to himself, "Dead end, baby. Dead end! Nice try. Nice try!" Laura turned away from the front door and walked around to the back of the house. Marcus started to feel uncomfortable. He did not like it when she was out of sight and he could not see what she was doing. Marcus waited impatiently. It seemed as if she had been gone for a long time, but it was probably only a few minutes.

Marcus drew a deep breath of relief as Laura walked back along the path to the road. He thought that she was giving up and he relaxed slightly. He was wrong! She paused at the end of the path and again looked up at the hotel. She appeared to be scrutinising each window. Marcus dropped down below the level of the window, thinking, "What is she doing?" He crawled on his hands and knees to the hotel phone, feeling ridiculous, and rang the Reception Desk. He told the Receptionist that a crazy woman, who had been convicted of stalking him in the UK, had seemingly followed him to Rome. If she came to the hotel, would the staff kindly inform her that he was not a resident of the hotel? The Receptionist asked if they should call the police, but Marcus said, "No, no, no, that will not be necessary."

Marcus crawled back to the window, peering out of the bottom corner. For a moment, he felt a wave of relief. She had gone. To be absolutely certain, he glanced up and down the street. Laura was about two doors lower down the street, talking to a middle-aged man and his wife. Unfortunately, Marcus recognised them. He had spoken to them on several occasions, which confirmed his tactics of not returning to the same city too early. However, Marcus was always positive. It had been two years ago, and he had only spoken to them briefly. It is also not easy to describe someone. What could she say? She could say that she was looking for a man, approximately six feet two inches tall, with brown eyes and black hair! In Rome, virtually everyone has brown or black hair! "Good luck with that!" he thought to himself. He reassured himself with the fact that she did not have a photograph of him.

Although he was at least fifty yards away, he had a good view of Laura and his neighbours. As he watched, he felt his blood run cold. Firstly, he saw her pointing to her neck. She was obviously describing his scar.

He saw his neighbours nodding and then she took out her phone. At first, Marcus could not understand what she was doing, then he remembered, and it all fell into place. It was a rainy day in London and they had spent some time in the café. As Charlie was leaving, Laura was talking to him at the door. She took out her phone as Marcus looked away. It must have been then that she took his photograph.

He saw both his neighbours nodding, and Laura started to write something down. Marcus guessed she would be recording their personal details, so that they could confirm her story. When Laura had, seemingly, gathered all the information she needed, she said good-bye to the couple, turned around and started to leave. She stopped outside his house, opened her bag, took out a notebook and started to write. She walked down the path and put a note through his door. She then made a phone call. Marcus watched as Laura waited at his door. Marcus wondered why she was continuing to wait.

A taxi pulled up outside his house. Laura walked up to the taxi and spoke to the driver. Marcus assumed it was to tell the driver of her intended destination. She suddenly turned, looked up at the hotel and waved. Marcus fell to the floor. He knew Laura well. She may have seen him, but it was more likely that the wave was her idea of a joke to shock him if he had been watching his house and seen her arrival. He waited for a few minutes before he walked over to his house. He opened the door, picked up the note and read it several times. It said: "Why did you run? You know I would not hurt you! Phone me. Love Laura XXX"

Marcus looked at his phone, transferring it from one hand to the other, trying to make up his mind whether to call Laura or not. He knew there were several reasons why he should not phone her. Although he had only been in Rome for a short time, he felt it highly unlikely that Flavian was nearby. His main concern was that Laura knew of his secret, albeit she would not be aware of the whole story of his life. Marcus was now fairly sure that he could trust her, but he was concerned at what might happen in a year or two years' time, when she realised that she could not have the future that she desired. Marcus pressed the call button on his phone. He had no idea why. He did it without thinking—the very action took him by surprise. Almost immediately, Laura answered. Marcus suspected she must have had the phone in her hand. Laura cried, "Marcus, oh, Marcus. I am so sorry. Please, please forgive me…" Marcus had to interrupt her. He said, "Me, forgive you?! You must be joking. It is me who is totally in the wrong." Then

Laura said something that made Marcus realise why he liked her so much! Even though she was obviously still crying, she said, "Well, I guess you are correct! It is your fault! I was only being nice!" They both laughed. Marcus asked, "Where are you? Can you come back to my house?" Laura laughed again and said, "I will be there before you! I am only around the corner."

As he left the hotel, handing the keys of his room to the lady at the reception, she smiled and said, "I hope that you enjoyed your stay. There is a lovely view from your window!" Marcus smiled at the joke, and said, "Yes, indeed there is!" Marcus laughed and said, "Goodbye."

As he stepped out of the door, he saw Laura standing outside his house. She smiled when she saw him. Marcus crossed the road, walked quickly down his path, and hugged her. Laura immediately apologised again, but Marcus put his finger on her lips and said, "Stop!" Laura nodded her head, and said, "I need to know." Marcus interrupted her, and answered, "I will tell you the whole story, but in time." Laura stroked his face gently, saying, "Take as long as you need."

Marcus opened the front door and stepped aside. Laura nodded in appreciation of the gesture and stepped into the house. She smiled to herself as she wandered around the house. It was exactly like his house in

London. It was sparsely furnished, with absolutely no paintings or photographs. In fact, there was nothing to brighten up the house, just a mirror… an old, ugly full-length mirror, very much like the one back in London.

When she had finished exploring the house, Marcus noticed that she looked unimpressed, which made him feel uncomfortable. All he could think of saying in his defence was, "I am not used to having guests." Laura smiled weakly and said, "Let's go out and get a coffee."

Whilst they sat in the café, they talked about the weather and the traffic in Rome. Marcus asked her about her journey from London. In fact, he talked about anything and everything, apart from himself. Marcus's problem was that he did not know where to start! After what seemed to him to be an age, Laura said, "I am not trying to push you into telling me your secret." She paused and continued slowly, "But it might be helpful if I told you what I know. You do not have to comment, or to say anything at all, but, if I am honest with you, I think it would be good." Marcus just shrugged his shoulders and lifted his eyebrows, indicating his agreement.

Marcus could tell that Laura was struggling with exactly what she was going to say. She took a deep breath and said, "I know that I am going to sound like a mad woman. So, stop me if I say anything that is completely way out there." She waved her hand over her head to emphasise her point. She then nodded her head, and whispered quietly to herself, "Okay". She leaned forward and said, "I know that you were in Manchester in the nineteen sixties, which makes you somewhere in your eighties. Of this, I have absolutely no doubt." Laura waited for some reaction; there was none. She continued, "I have also discovered photographs of a professor in Durham in the early nineteenth century. You are that professor! Of this, I also have no doubt." Again, she paused, waiting for some response. All Marcus could think of saying was, "Well done!" She answered rather loudly, "Well done?! Well bloody done?!" This caused some people to turn and look at them. "Well bloody done. Is that all you can say?" Laura leaned back in her chair and closed her eyes for a second. Marcus noticed that her lips were moving as if she was talking to herself. Laura was muttering to herself, "Keep calm! He is just a man. He is stupid." When she had sufficiently calmed herself, she said, "Well, that would make you, and stop me if I am wrong as Maths was not my best subject, about two hundred years old!" Laura looked at Marcus and said, moving her head from side to side, "Give or take."

Marcus said, "I thought we had agreed that you would give me time. You must remember that I have never had this conversation with anyone else, ever. I am sure you will understand." Laura put out her hand to stop Marcus from talking, and she continued, "No. Hold on. I am fully prepared to give you all the time you need. All I am doing now is telling you about what I know already." Marcus took a drink from his bottle of water as he gazed out of the window, wondering if Laura had any idea about the depth of the story that she had stumbled upon. Laura then said something that shook his whole world. Marcus had learned how to put on a poker face and he knew not to give anything away with a careless expression.

Laura continued, "I know about Colchester, or Camulodunum as you knew it, but who was Gertrude?"

Laura was struggling with the whole idea of Marcus being a Roman Centurion in first-century Colchester. She was just fishing. But, as unbelievable and impossible as it sounded, she now knew for certain. Marcus's expression, his bottle gripped tightly in his hand, his jaw dropped down, his eyes wide open, left her in no doubt. All she could do was put her hand over her mouth and say, "Oh, my God".

Marcus slowly placed his bottle of water on the table. Not for one second did he take his eyes away from Laura. She had a bewildered expression on her face, and kept repeating, "Oh, my God!", over and over again. Eventually, she took a deep breath, wiped a tear from her eye, and said, "What now?"

Marcus quickly looked around the café. There were about twenty people happily chatting away, totally oblivious to anything going on outside their own little world. Marcus glanced at each of their faces. The mention of Gertrude's name brought back the terrible image of her lying dead on the floor of her farmhouse. Even though it was a long time ago, the deaths of Bess and Gertrude were burned into his memory. He glanced around the café a second time, thinking to himself, "Is he here? Is Flavian here? Have I selfishly put Laura in danger?" Laura noticed Marcus was anxiously looking around. Initially, she assumed it was because of her revelation, but then she realised it was so much more than that. She leaned over and said, "What is it?"

Marcus said, "We need to go back to my house. We need to talk." There was something in the tone of what Marcus was saying that made Laura feel very uncomfortable. As they stood up ready to leave the café, she was about to say something to Marcus, but as he turned away, ready to leave, she decided to wait until they got home. As they left the café, Laura reached out to hold Marcus's hand, but Marcus pushed his hands deep into his pockets. Laura linked arms with him instead. Glancing at Marcus, she noticed this had made him look uncomfortable. She quickly removed her hand. As they made their way home, Marcus nervously kept turning and looking around. Laura wondered what on earth had frightened him. Suddenly, Marcus stopped walking, turned to Laura, and said, "Listen. I know this sounds strange, but would you mind walking just a little ahead of me?" Laura smiled weakly and said, "That is not the strangest thing I have heard today." She then stepped in front of Marcus and started slowly walking ahead. Marcus waited until Laura was about twenty yards ahead then started walking at the same pace as her. His mind was in turmoil. What should he tell Laura? He was definitely not going to tell her of his role in the Crucifixion. In fact, he decided not to mention anything about first-century Israel. His priority was to keep Laura safe, and, as difficult as it would be, he knew he had little choice. She had to know about Flavian.

When they arrived back at the house, Laura walked into the sparse living room, whilst Marcus ran up the stairs. After a few minutes, he returned with a scruffy old rucksack and sat down on the couch next to Laura, with the rucksack on the floor at his feet. Marcus had never forgotten what Cephas had said all those years ago, that

Flavian would keep well away from the Artefacts. Laura sat quietly waiting for some kind of explanation. There was a long pause whilst Marcus wrestled with trying to decide what to say to Laura and, indeed, how to say it. Eventually, Laura lost patience and said, "You obviously have something to say to me! So, come on, spit it out." Laura did not have any idea what was troubling Marcus. What Marcus said next came as such a shock that it actually took her breath away.

Marcus stood up and said, "Laura, you are in great danger. There is no easy way to say this. I know exactly how this will sound and so I am just going to say it out loud! There is a demon who is hunting for me, and he kills anyone who becomes close to me." Laura stood up and shouted, "What! What?! You have got to be kidding me. You are actually telling me that a demon is going to kill me?" Laura screamed in frustration and started pacing up and down. She then stopped, turned, faced Marcus, and said, "So! Let us get this right. You are telling me that…" She stopped and then shouted, "You are telling me that everything I believed about life is wrong! You know, little things like people living and dying!" She took a deep breath and said, sarcastically "Tell me! Are you a vampire?" Marcus answered, "Do not be ridiculous." Laura said, "Ridiculous! Oh! That's ridiculous! A crazy murderous demon… well, that's quite normal! A man who has been around for, what?… two thousand years… that is okay!" Laura slumped down on the couch. Marcus thought that she looked tired and lost for words.

Marcus sat down next to her on the couch and whispered, "Sorry." Laura did not respond. Marcus remembered what Paul had told him; "You can't run forever. One day, you will have to make a stand, and you will know when." Paul was right. Marcus knew.

Marcus stood up and started pacing around the living room. He did his best thinking whilst he was walking. Marcus knew that the last thing he could do was to tell Laura about his role in the Crucifixion. How would she react? How would anyone react if you told them that you were a 'Christ-killer'? Not just a Christ-killer but '*the* Christ-killer'! In addition, he could not tell Laura about the Artefacts. Marcus knew, however, that he had to stay close to Laura, and somehow lure Flavian out.

Laura watched Marcus pacing up and down the room. His lips were moving as he talked to himself. He would pause for a moment, nod his head and start pacing again. He then said to himself, "Right… Right…Okay."

Marcus walked across the room, sat down next to Laura and said, "I do not know where Flavian is. It is possible he already knows about you, and, in that case, there is no use in you going back to London. He would simply follow you." Laura said, "Well, what do we do?" Laura looked and sounded desperate. Marcus cupped her face in his hands, leaned forward, kissed her on her forehead, and said, "Don't worry; I have a plan."

Marcus smiled. He was aware his plan was dangerous, but he believed it had a small chance of success and he knew that he had to sound confident. He decided not to mention the curse just yet, nor that he had been warned he should not participate in any exorcism. After all, apart from him ending up in hell, what could possibly go wrong?! Marcus tried to sound as upbeat as possible as he spoke to Laura. He looked at her and said, "Well! This is what we have to do. We have to get Flavian's attention and go to Sicily." Laura said, "Sicily why Sicily?" Marcus said, "If there is one thing I learned in the Army, it was to pick your battlefield. I know a place where we can stay and be safe." Laura said, "Who do you know in Sicily?" Marcus laughed. He could hardly tell her it was a relative of Mary Magdalene. He answered, "An old friend."

Marcus took hold of Laura's hand and said, "You are going to have to trust me on this. There is a family here in Rome whom I met last time I was here. I told them that I was a Classics Teacher, and so I was fluent in Latin, so I offered to take them around all the historical sites in Rome. You and I will spend the whole day together, holding hands and looking as though we are madly in love, but it is really important that you always stay close to me". Laura raised her eyebrows and said, "All times?" Marcus looked a little puzzled for a moment and then the penny dropped! Laughing, he said, "Oh, I see! Well, when you have to go, take the rucksack with you".

After a few minutes, Laura said, "Well, whilst you are trying to work out a plan, I will make myself useful in the kitchen." Laura stood up and wandered into the kitchen, whilst Marcus made a phone call. She could hear him saying, "Great, great! See you in the morning". After a few minutes, Laura emerged from the kitchen and said, "No food in the freezer! No food in the refrigerator! The cupboard is empty, except for two cups, two plates and bizarrely, only one knife and one fork." Marcus answered, as if it was the most natural thing in the world, "I have to have two cups and two plates in case I drop one of them. Knives and forks don't break!" Laura was about to ask what would happen if an unexpected visitor arrived…as she had done! She then thought better of it, and said, "Well, I guess that means pizza!"

Laura saw Marcus was lost in his own thoughts. She knew that he was probably thinking over a thousand possible variations to his plan. As they waited for the pizza to arrive, she gave Marcus a cup of water. She smiled as she noticed that the cup had a chip in it.

Laura started to explore the house. As she moved from room to room, she discovered that each room was identical to the room she had looked into before that one! There were four bedrooms, and it was obvious that Marcus had gone into one shop and bought four of everything! Even the wallpaper and curtains were the same. Disappointed, Laura made her way down the stairs.

As she walked into the living room, Marcus greeted her with an excited look on his face. He said, "I have had an idea." As he stood there, grinning, Laura said, "Well! Go on." Marcus answered, "What is our problem?" Laura laughed and replied, "You have to be kidding me. Where should I begin? Oh, I know! A homicidal demon is trying to kill us. Oh…. Wait! Not us…. Me!!" Marcus ignored Laura's sarcasm, and excitedly answered, "Yes, yes, that's it, I have thought of a way of letting him know where we are currently. At the moment, we have no idea where he is, or if, indeed, he knows where we are now." Laura hesitated. She was not sure if she wanted to hear Marcus's plan. Laura said, "So?" Marcus answered triumphantly, "You get engaged." He then proudly continued as if it was the greatest idea anyone had ever had. "You get engaged to Marcus Longinus, a Roman Centurion, and put it all over social media." Laura gasped and said, "Are you mad? Please tell me you are joking!" Marcus, rubbing his hands together gleefully, answered, "No! What is the alternative? Cephas explained to me that Flavian is not omnipresent. Which means that he cannot be everywhere at once." Laura answered, disdainfully, "I know what omnipresent means." Marcus smiled and said, "Sorry, but the point is, he has to search for us, which could take years." Marcus sat down and waited for Laura to say something. As she sat down, she turned to Marcus and said, "Who is Cephas?"

If Marcus had merely answered that Cephas was an old friend from way back, Laura would have thought no more about it. However, the look of shock on his face, and his stuttering explanation of Cephas being someone he once knew, made Laura think Cephas was no ordinary friend. As Marcus carried on with his explanation, trying to explain how he knew Cephas, Laura put her hand on his shoulder and said quietly, "It's okay. I know that you have got a lot on your mind and so, leave it for now, but you must promise me that when we get to Sicily, you will tell me the whole story." Marcus nodded but said nothing.

The pizza arrived and Marcus did his best to pretend that he was enjoying it, whilst at the same time, drinking water from his chipped cup. Laura watched him as he ate and drank. She realised that in all the time she had known him, she had never seen him eat before, and now, as she watched him, she could not escape the feeling that something was wrong, although she could not quite work out what it was that seemed strange. Laura put down the bottle of Coke from which she had been drinking and asked, "Is everything alright?" Marcus answered, "Yes. I was ready for that; I was really hungry." He then gave her an uncomfortable, weak smile.

When they had finished eating, Marcus cleared everything away, whilst Laura opened her laptop. He then sat down beside her as she asked, "Are you sure you want to do this?" Marcus nodded and said, "We must end this. We must take him by surprise. We have to pick the battleground. We cannot live our lives in fear, not knowing when he will attack." Laura turned to her page on social media and said, "Right! What do you want me to say?" Marcus leaned over her shoulder, looking at the screen and said, "I would like to announce that today, a wonderful man asked me to marry him." Laura stopped typing, looked at Marcus and said, "Oh really? A wonderful man?" Marcus laughed and said, "What's wrong with that?" Laura grinned, and said, "Men… Men! Okay. Go on." Marcus smiled and continued. "His name is Marcus Longinus. He claims to be a Roman Centurion who is two thousand years old! We are having a wonderful few days in Rome and then we are going to Sicily to be married in a small chapel that Marcus knows." Laura stopped typing and said, "No one is going to believe that. In fact, everyone will think I am mad!" Marcus said, "It does not matter! The message is for one person only and he will believe it. Wait a couple of hours, then delete it, with an apology saying that your nephew typed the message as a joke. Flavian will think that you posted the message without my knowledge and that when I saw it, I made you take it down."

Laura turned to Marcus and said, "You are very good at this, aren't you?" Marcus said, "Good at what?" Laura turned back to look at the screen and said, "Deception" .

After a few minutes, Marcus heard Laura shout at her laptop, "Oh for goodness's sake. Get a life, will you?" Marcus asked, "Laura, what's wrong?" Laura just pointed to the screen. It had been only five minutes since she posted the news about the engagement, and Marcus could not believe some of the vile things that were being posted on the website! Marcus put his hands on

Laura's shoulders gently and said, "Two hours. Then take it down." Laura nodded.

Marcus continued cheerfully, "Hey, let's go out and get some fresh air and, if you are really good, I might buy you a drink." Jokingly, Laura saluted and said, "Please, Sir. I promise to be good." She added, "…And, whilst we are out, you can buy me my own cup." Marcus laughed and said, "Well, I don't know about that! Cups are expensive in Rome!" Laura grinned and playfully punched him on the shoulder. As they stepped out of the house, Laura felt the warm glow of the afternoon sun. She had only been in Rome for a few hours, and even though several of those hours had been traumatic, being bathed in sunshine and walking in the beautiful city of Rome, holding hands with such a good-looking man as Marcus, seemed to make it all worthwhile. However, she tried to suppress a deep feeling of foreboding which, even in the warm Italian sun, made her shiver.

After they had finished some basic shopping, they went into a local bar. Laura finally felt herself relax as she enjoyed a glass of white wine. As she watched Marcus drink his water, she was about to ask him why that was all he drank, but she thought to herself, "No…No more questions!" She had begun to realise that an answer from Marcus to every question she asked him just led to a thousand more questions. She was beginning to understand that sometimes, she had to just enjoy the moment. Marcus had promised to tell her the full story once they had reached Sicily. However, she could not help but notice how Marcus's eyes would continually wander, always looking at people sitting at the bar, and how he clung onto his rucksack. She asked herself, what could possibly be in that dirty old bag that caused him to treat it as if his life depended on it?

Marcus and Laura slowly made their way home. They enjoyed the warm Roman evening as they walked along the banks of the Tiber, Marcus remembering his childhood. It had always been his greatest fear that his memory would fade, because then he knew he would be truly lost. There would have been nothing in this world to which he could cling. His family was gone, the Legion was gone, Cephas and John had gone… He told himself that he would not lose Laura. It was time for him to start a new chapter… His last chapter.

Laura went to bed that night with her head spinning, thinking of all the events that had happened over the last few weeks. She could not help but wonder if it was all true or if indeed any part of it was true. She got out of bed and looked out of the window. She said to herself, "Rome! Have I gone mad? What on earth am I doing in

Rome?" She knew, however, that no matter how impossible it sounded, it was all true. Everything that Marcus had said, although it sounded crazy, was true. Marcus had said that it was too late, and that thing, Flavian, would follow her. She knew that her only chance was to defeat the thing and her only hope of doing so was with Marcus.

Marcus and Laura went for a morning walk and stopped at a small café for breakfast. Marcus noticed that Laura was watching him whilst he was eating. He looked at her and said, "What?" Laura answered, "Nothing. I was just wondering if you were enjoying your food?" Marcus was slightly tempted to tell Laura about the curse but decided it was not the time. They left the café and arrived back at his house at around eleven o'clock.

Laura noticed how excited Marcus looked as they got ready to meet Francisco and his family. As casually as she could, she asked, "Who are this family and how did you meet them?" Laura fully expected Marcus to say that he had perhaps worked with Francisco. She was well aware that he had worked in Rome. Marcus was combing his hair in the mirror when she asked him about Francisco's family. She saw his face change as if he was wrestling with the question and did not know how to answer it. Marcus then turned around and said, "Let's sit down for a second." Laura thought to herself, "Oh, please God, not another terrifying revelation."

When they were sitting down, Marcus saw the look of concern on Laura's face, and said, "No, no, no. It is nothing to be worried about. It is just that I think we might… well, just might… be related." Laura was about to say something, but Marcus said, "I am not going to say just yet why I think this might be so. I do not want to influence your judgment. I would appreciate your opinion when we get back home. You can tell me if you see any similarities."

Laura said, "Hang on! Hang on… just for one second!" She stood and walked around the room, obviously trying to process the information. Marcus watched her as she stopped for a moment, gasped, then looked at him as if she was about to say something but decided against it and started walking again. Eventually, she sat down and said, "Are you telling me that there is another two-thousand-year-old man or woman walking around, and that you have a whole family going back to the 'year dot?' Let me tell you, I am really struggling here with what you are saying! It was hard enough getting my head around the fact that I have a boyfriend who, let me say, is just a little bit older than me!" Laura held her finger and thumb close together to emphasise the point. "And now… and now… it appears that you think maybe half the old Roman Army is walking around! Is that what you are saying?" Marcus said quietly, "I have to say that I think you are being a little melodramatic!" As he looked at Laura, he could see that she was desperately trying to control herself. She closed her eyes and said quietly, "Is this whole story in any way *not* dramatic?"

Marcus said, "I saw an old lady in a café who looked remarkably like my mother. So much so that I was really startled, and, for a moment, I actually thought it was her. Of course, she was not my mother, but I went across to where she was sitting and introduced myself to her. Then, her son and grandson arrived and as soon as I saw them, I immediately noticed certain similarities to me in both of them. That's it! That is the whole story." Marcus gave Laura a few minutes to digest what he had said. Laura nodded and said, "Okay", but pointing at him, said, "No more surprises, and I mean it, I really mean it. No more surprises. Okay?" Marcus held up his hands and said, "Okay, Okay. I promise. No more surprises. Well….at least not today."

Laura checked her hair in the mirror then followed Marcus out through the door as they went out to meet Francesco. They arrived at the Piazza Navona just after noon. Marcus was pleased to see that Francesco had brought his family with him. Marcus smiled as he saw Sophia. He was very happy to see her again. He walked over and kissed her on the cheek, then introduced Laura. Sophia said that she was delighted to meet her, commented on how pretty she looked and said how much she was looking forward to this afternoon. Marcus turned and said hello to young Antonio. Then Francesco introduced him to his wife, Martina. She was a beautiful-looking woman. Marcus thought she was a wonderful addition to the family.

Francesco called the waiter over and asked Marcus if he would like anything to eat. Marcus declined and merely asked for a glass of water. For the last two thousand years, he had only been able to drink water. He must have drunk water in a million establishments and in almost every country in the world, but as he glanced at the menu, he decided that this was, without doubt, going to be the most expensive glass of water he had ever drunk! On reflection, he decided that this was very probably the most expensive glass of water in history! Francesco ordered water for Marcus and then Bourbon for himself, white wine for the ladies and a soft drink for Antonio.

As Marcus drank his water, he watched as Francesco finished his drink. He had to admit he was very jealous. He would love to have been able to taste Bourbon, Whiskey or Gin. He wondered how these drinks would actually taste. He glanced over to where the ladies were drinking their wine. Marcus knew he had to be careful. There were so many things which were now denied to him because he had no sense of taste. He was aware that if he thought about it too much and too often, it would be so very easy for him to slip into a depression. He turned away and drank his water, which was warm!

Marcus looked around at the Piazza Navona. He explained to the family that they were now sitting in the area that had once been the Stadium of Domitian, which later became known as Circus Agonalis. He pointed towards the great Fountain of the Four Rivers in the centre of the Square, at the Obelisk of Domitian. He said quietly to himself, "I remember when that was in the Circus Maximus." Francesco looked puzzled and said, "You remember? What do you mean? When was it moved?" Marcus took a sip of his water, and calmly corrected himself, "I'm sorry. Did I say I remembered? I meant to say, when I was a student at University, I remember studying about the Circus Maximus for the first time and thinking what a great pity it was moved. It would have looked much better in the Circus Maximus. It deserves to be there." He was pleased to see the whole family silently nodding in agreement. Laura had thought she had fully come to terms with the fact that Marcus was a Roman Centurion but for some reason, Marcus's describing of the ancient sights from memory gave Laura a feeling of both discomfort and awe. They finished their drinks and Francesco insisted on paying. Marcus was impressed that he did not collapse when he saw the bill!

They spent the whole day together. As they moved around the city looking at the incredible architecture and monuments, the family became more and more enthralled with what they saw and the historical details that Marcus related. Even Antonio asked questions at the various places they visited. Marcus took them to the Circus Maximus. He described how the Roman Triumph and a victorious Military Commander were honoured after battle. He explained that on the day of The Triumph, the Commander wore a crown of laurel. His robe was purple and embroidered with gold, which symbolised that he was near divine. Sometimes, they even painted his face red. He rode a chariot through the streets of Rome. The Roman General would have a slave on his chariot, who would continually whisper in his ear, "You're just a man."

His description was so vivid and passionate that Martina said it was almost as if he had witnessed it himself!

Laura smiled. Marcus knew he had to be very careful, and only recount to them information that was available in history books. It would be so very easy to say something that was not known by succeeding generations and then have an extremely awkward moment as he tried to explain how he had acquired that information.

Although they had lived for all their lives in Rome and were familiar with the statues and monuments, the presence of Marcus was similar to having their own personal escort, who was able to translate the Latin inscriptions and could explain the background to the monuments and expand upon the lives of the various people the statues depicted.

At the end of the day, the family invited them to dinner. They seemed disappointed when Marcus and Laura politely refused. Marcus had still not mastered the art of eating beautiful food, which, to him, continued to taste like stale bread, whilst at the same time pretending that he was enjoying it. The tragedy was that he would have liked nothing more than to spend the evening with Francesco and his family. Marcus and Laura said goodbye to the family and made their way back to his home. On the way home, Laura asked, "Why did you refuse to go back to their house? They looked very disappointed." Marcus, said, "Remember…. No more surprises."

Once they had arrived home, Marcus felt elated. He had had a wonderful day. He made Laura a cappuccino. As they sat at the kitchen table, Laura asked, "Tell me. Is there any reason why you drink only water?" Marcus gave a knowing smile! Laura said, "Okay, I remember. No more surprises" . Marcus took a sip of water and asked, "Well?" Laura answered, "Well what?" Marcus looked exasperated and said, "What do you mean, Well what? Did you see any resemblance between Francesco's family and me?" Laura laughed. "Are you kidding me? You all have the same hair, the same silly grin, and the same stupid sense of humour" . Marcus said indignantly, "I have not got a stupid sense of humour" . Laughingly, Laura answered, "What about the social media post—I just met a wonderful man?" Marcus said, "What's funny about that?" Laura cried out laughing, banging the table with her fist. She was laughing so much that tears flowed down her face. She was still laughing when she stood up, wiped her face and said, "I think I will go to bed now."

Marcus woke up early the next morning. He could hear Laura in the shower. He smiled as he realised the enormous changes that had taken place in his life. It was only forty-eight hours ago that he had been in the depths of despair and had felt as if he had lost everything and would have to start his life all over again. Now, he could hear Laura in the bathroom, and, for the first time, he had a plan. He made his way down the stairs and made Laura a coffee.

Laura stood motionless in the shower. The warm water felt refreshing, which is exactly what she needed. She had not slept well. Her mind had been leaping from one incredible story to another. She went over the sequence of events of the past few months and wondered whether she was being unbelievably stupid or unbelievably naive. Her mind went back to that day when she first saw the photographs of Marcus in the lion enclosure. Even though the photographs were old and unclear, she knew that, as impossible as it seemed, they were of Marcus, and, like Pandora, she had opened a box she could never close. She stepped out of the shower and started to dry herself. She thought, "I am here now, and I will have to get on with it."

Laura put on the same clothes she had worn yesterday as she had anticipated returning home, not staying overnight. She opened the kitchen door to find Marcus smiling, holding up a cup of coffee and saying, "Here you are… coffee… just how you like it." Laura grinned and thought to herself, "How on earth could he be so dammed cheerful in the morning?!" Laura grunted a thank you and then sat down. Marcus moved to sit next to Laura and said, "I thought we could go into town, have some breakfast and then do some shopping. You need a change of clothes. We will then come back here, pack, and set off to Sicily." Laura thought to herself, Sicily... Sicily; Marcus had described it as his battleground. She smiled, whilst thinking, "Ah, well... that's something to look forward to!"

Marcus saw Laura physically relax as they moved from shop to shop. He thought to himself that, whilst he hated it, obviously, Laura thoroughly enjoyed shopping and purchasing new clothes. Marcus followed Laura as she wandered around the shops, his mind on a variety of things. Unknown to him, a young man was watching their every move. The young man smiled, licked his lips, and said to himself, "I'll see you in Sicily, my friend."

After they had finished their shopping, Marcus and Laura both ordered a large breakfast, which Laura thoroughly enjoyed, and Marcus ate without comment. When they had finished, Laura said, "Well, what's the plan?" She swallowed a large gulp of coffee and said laughingly, "How is your water? It looks lovely." Marcus ignored her sarcasm. He was just glad that Laura seemed back to her old self again. Marcus said, "It is simple. We go back, pack and leave for Naples, then catch the ferry to Sicily. I hope you don't mind but I would like to call at a few places on the way." Laura put down her coffee, leaned forward and said, "What places?" Marcus answered, "Oh just a few places from my past that I had always intended to return to one day. As they are on our route, I thought we could take advantage of the opportunity." Laura was intrigued and interrupted Marcus. "'Past', do you mean 'past-past, or just a few years ago?" Marcus laughed and said, "Past-past" . Laura said, "Ooh great! Let's go." They stood and made their way through the café, carrying their heavy shopping bags and Marcus's rucksack, which, whilst he was with Laura, never left his side. He well remembered being at Flavian's villa in Cyprus and what had happened to Caterina's grandfather.

As they were packing to leave, there was a knock on the door. He carried on packing the last few items. As the individual at the door became impatient and banged even louder on the door, Marcus shouted, "Alright! Alright! I am coming." He opened the door and was surprised to see two policemen. They asked him his name and what he was doing in Rome. He invited them in and asked them why they wanted this information. The police officers simply said, "We will ask the questions, Sir."

Marcus was starting to feel nervous. He said to the policemen, "If you would excuse me for a moment I will get my girlfriend; she is upstairs" . He went to the foot of the stairs and shouted to Laura. When Laura came into the kitchen and saw the two men, she gave Marcus a puzzled look. Marcus said, "These two gentlemen are policemen." Laura said, "What's this about?" One of the policemen ignored Laura and said, "Could you give me your name and state your business in Rome?" Marcus told them his name and that he was a teacher of Classics and lived in London. Laura gave her name and simply said, "I am with him." Marcus told them that it was perfectly natural for a classics teacher to visit Rome regularly. They asked them if they could account for their whereabouts this morning. Marcus again asked them why they wanted this information but they demanded answers to their questions. Marcus then gave them a detailed account of their movements that morning. They asked him to confirm the name of the café where he had stopped to have breakfast and the name of the shops they had visited. The Senior Officer signalled to his colleague, who immediately left the house, presumably to check the information he had given to them.

Marcus asked him again why they wanted this information and what was the purpose of their visit. The police officer said, "Yesterday, you took Francesco Mancini and his family around some of our ancient sites." Marcus asked, "Yes, I did. What was wrong with me doing that?" The police officer replied, "There is nothing wrong with that, Sir. I just think it is a remarkable coincidence that the day after you, a stranger, took the family around the sites in our city, their son was snatched off the streets." It took Marcus a few moments to grasp what the police officer had just said. Marcus could only respond by saying, "What! Antonio?" Laura gasped and said, "Oh, no! Who would do such a thing?" The policemen turned to Laura and said, "That is what we are trying to find out."

The Officer noticed Marcus was packing and asked where he was going, Marcus replied that he was travelling to Naples, and he intended spending some time at Pompeii. The police officer continued to question Marcus for about thirty minutes. His colleague returned and whispered in his ear. The Senior Officer nodded and informed Marcus that his story had been checked and everything was in order. They apologised for having bothered him. Marcus responded that he fully understood that they were merely doing their job and walked them to the door. After they had left, Laura said, "Do you think that it could be Flavian? My God! Have we put that boy in danger? If he comes to any harm, I don't think I could live with myself." Laura sat down sobbing, and saying over and over again, "What have we done…? What have we done…? That poor, poor boy." Marcus sat next to her, took hold of her hand, and said, "Let's not get ahead of ourselves. We don't know for sure this is Flavian." Laura interrupted him and said, "Well, it's a dammed funny coincidence, don't you think?" Marcus said, "Agreed, it is likely, but not definitely; all I am saying is we will have to wait." Laura dried her eyes and said, "Wait… wait for what?" Marcus said, "Look, if Flavian has taken the boy, he has taken him for a reason; he wants what I've got in my bag." Laura stood up and shouted, "For God's sake, what have you got in that bloody bag?"Marcus fell silent. He knew this would be the worst possible time to tell Laura about the Artefacts—how could he do that without revealing that he was the Christ-killer? Marcus thought to himself that this was definitely not the time. Marcus said, "Look, he knows we are going to Sicily, so let's keep to the plan. If he's got the boy, and I do mean if, we will get him in Sicily." Laura said, "Wait a minute, wait a god-dammed minute… did you use this boy as bait? Did you see this coming?" Marcus said, "Of course not. I expected Flavian to show up and threaten me, as he has done before." Laura said, "Done before… what do you mean done before? When before?" Marcus was starting to feel uncomfortable, and said, "It was a long time ago." Laura said, "Yes, I am waiting."

Marcus realised that he had to tell her more, so he said, "Flavian threatened someone that I knew." Laura said, "Gertrude?" Marcus nodded. What happened to Gertrude?" she asked. Marcus said quietly, "Flavian killed her, but this time I am ready; this time, I won't be taken by surprise, Gertrude was on her own and unprotected." Laura put her hand over her mouth and kept saying, "Oh, my God, oh, my God."

Marcus said, "I think the sooner we get going the better."

After they left, Marcus phoned Francesco and asked if he had heard any news. Francesco was frantic with worry. Apparently, Antonio had just been snatched off the street by two men and bundled into the back of a car. Francesco said, "We don't know why, or by whom." Marcus asked Francesco to keep him up to date on what was happening and offered to do anything that he could to help. After the phone call, Marcus felt stunned. He just sat down in silence, his mind racing. Marcus did not know Francesco particularly well and felt it would have been inappropriate to go and see him. There seemed to be very little that he could do. As terrible as he felt for little Antonio, Francesco, and their families, he decided to continue with his plans and make his way to Naples, Pompeii, then on to Sicily.

As Marcus filled up his car, he was not looking forward to the journey. He hated driving. He only drove when there was no alternative. As he made his preparations, his thoughts kept going back to Francesco and his family.

It was approximately one hundred and fifty miles from Rome to Naples. They decided that if they got hungry, they would probably eat at fast food restaurants on the journey. They much preferred 'drive-through' restaurants, where they could sit in his car on their own. It was much quicker and they wanted to get to Naples as soon as possible. Marcus was feeling pretty much the same as he had on the last occasion he made this same journey. On that occasion, it was after Cephas's arrest, and his sense of loss had been indescribable, accompanied by fear and uncertainty.

He had such hopes for a new relationship with Francesco and his family. Simply being in their company gave him a feeling he had not experienced since the day he left for Jerusalem—of hugging his mother, of whom Sophia greatly reminded him, and Francesco, who was so very much like his brother, albeit not so much in his appearance, but certainly in his mannerisms. He remembered that as they had accompanied him on the tour of Rome, the little boy, Antonio, would constantly gesture with his arms and hands, pointing in the most excited manner at the things which attracted his attention. Antonio was so very similar to his own son that it was uncanny! In particular, he had the same eyes.

His disappearance shook him more than he could understand, and the full implications were just sinking in. Apart from the deep feeling of fear and sadness for the boy, he had a dreadful feeling of guilt, because he had overriding and selfish feelings of what he could potentially lose. If the boy was not found, how could he ever face the child's family again? The loss of the boy would always be between them, and the police officer was right—the coincidence of the boy disappearing the day after their tour around Rome was sure to leave a lingering suspicion.

He had hoped that maybe, in time, he could have revealed his secret. He had always longed to meet someone whom he trusted enough to explain to them who he was and what had happened to his life, someone with whom he could share his stories. In reality, however, he knew that he had now lost all hope of being part of a family again.

The last time he had made this trip, it had taken him more than four days. He had had a very slow horse, but if you are cursed to live forever, there seems to be no particular point in hastening. What surprised him on this journey was how very few things had actually changed. Wherever there had been villages in the first century, usually, they were still there. The villages were, overall, larger and with higher numbers of occupants, but the main roads were in the same place, with the same river or stream running through them and the same lakes and mountains.

On arrival in Naples, they booked themselves into a cheap hotel for three days. They then walked to the harbour and made enquiries about the ferry to Palermo in Sicily. They took their time walking back to the hotel and decided to have an early night. The long journey had left them exhausted.

The next morning, they rose early and made the short trip to Pompeii. He parked his car and made his way through the Herculaneum Gate, past the House of the Vestals. Laura wore the rucksack on her back as they walked around Pompeii, holding Marcus lightly by the hand. As she started to relax, she said to Marcus, "It is lovely to be here, but something tells me that we are not here to look at the sights!" Marcus said, "I have been here before." Laura answered, "When?" Marcus turned around looking in the direction of Mount Vesuvius and answered, "Just before that thing blew up, there was a girl…" Laura said, "Ooh, one of your earlier conquests? Tell me more!" Laura expected Marcus to laugh, or at least smile, but he had a strange look on his face. He looked offended. Laura said, "I am sorry, did I say something wrong?" Marcus answered, "Do not worry about it. I will tell you the whole story as we are walking along."

Marcus knew exactly where he wanted to go and what he wanted to see, starting, of course, at the Forum. As they stood looking at the magnificent ruins of what remained of the Forum, Marcus explained to Laura that this was where he had first met her. She was a beautiful slave girl, but her beauty was also her curse. Each morning, she would take her owner's daughter for a stroll. She had told me that this was the only time she felt safe. Her master was a brutal man.

Marcus continued, "I spent two weeks in Pompeii. I enjoyed watching the gladiatorial fights. I have always appreciated fighting—both watching and participating—the latter, most probably because I was very good at it." Laura smiled and said, "I have no doubt that you were!" Marcus laughed and said, "Well, I could tell you some stories!" Laura laughed and answered, "I will look forward to that!"

Marcus continued, "As I watched the Gladiators, I often thought that I could surpass any of them. I remembered that no one in my Legion could better me. I was almost tempted to put myself forward and make the challenge. But, on second thoughts, I knew that it would look suspicious if every spear hurled at me missed and every sword blow went wide of me. I often amused myself with the thought that if I was ever suspected of witchcraft, they might throw me to the lions, but the lions would not attack me! They would then try to burn me at the stake, but the fire would not burn!" He laughed to himself. Although he understood it was not a laughing matter, he decided it was better not to make a challenge! Laura gasped. This was a completely new revelation. She was about to say, "You mean, you cannot die?" when she realised, "Of course he could not die! He is two thousand years old. Oh… for goodness' sake!" She now realised she had never thought of it in those terms.

He pointed towards the Forum and said to Laura, "I remember seeing Livia on her walk near the Forum. I shouted to her, but she ignored me. I shouted again to her, but she carried on walking. I ran after her, caught up with her and touched her on her back. She flinched and pulled away from me. As she turned around, I saw her eyes were red and swollen. She had obviously been crying. I could also see that there was blood on her clothing and her back had been bleeding badly. I asked her who had beaten her and why and she told me it was her Master, and it was completely her own fault. He said that she had deserved it, adding that she was his property, and she had no right to refuse him. Marcus looked at Laura. He could see that she was trying to picture the scene in her mind. Marcus asked her, "Are you all right?" Laura nodded and said, quietly, "Please carry on. I want to know what happened." Marcus continued, "The next morning, whilst Livia was on her morning walk, I went to see her Master, who lived in a huge house overlooking the sea. The building was very impressive. It had the most amazing terrace and large windows. It was obvious that this was the house of an extremely wealthy man. I offered to buy Livia, but her Master looked amused. He asked, "Why should I sell it to you?" Laura said, "It? He actually called her an 'It'?" Marcus said, "The truth was that she was his property. I offered him twice the price of a slave, then three times the price, and then more, but Livia's Master laughed and shouted, "Stop, stop, stop," whilst roaring with laughter. Gesturing, he pointed towards his house. "Does it look as though I need your money? Do you believe that I would sell anything until I have finished with it?"

Laura could see that even now, and after all the time that had passed, Marcus still felt bitter at the memory.

Through clenched teeth, he said, "I cannot tell you how difficult it was for me to keep calm. All I wanted to do was to rip out the man's throat. The idea that he regarded Livia as an 'it', or a 'thing', completely infuriated me." Marcus shook his head and said, "I guess, in reality, he was no different to a million other slave owners. I contemplated stealing her away, but the more I thought about it, the more I realised it was a noble but foolish idea. It was unlikely that we would be able to escape and the penalty for Livia would be too terrible to contemplate."

Marcus was silent as they continued walking through the ruins of the old city. Laura was trying to imagine what it was like in the time that Marcus was here. She desperately wanted to ask him more about what life had been like in the city, but the story of Livia had completely captivated her. After walking for a few minutes,

Marcus said, "The next morning, I was having a meal at one of the trade vendors' stalls when I was surprised to hear someone shout my name. I turned around to see an old overweight man making his way towards me. I was delighted when the man was close enough for me to recognise him. It was Cassius, my good friend from the legion. As I threw my arms around my old friend, he said, Septimus was right; you really can't die. You have not aged a day. It is good to see you, old friend." Cassius invited me for a drink at a local inn. He watched as I drank water. He said, "We never knew if it was true. No one told us whether you had escaped from that tomb. We all assumed that you were dead, which was probably for the best." Laura wondered what tomb he was talking about.

"I told Cassius about Livia and that I would be leaving the city soon, but I did not want to leave her in the hands of her evil master. Cassius said, "I have an idea. I will buy her. You will give me the money, of course." Then he laughed. I said, "I told you. He will not sell her." Cassius answered, laughing, "Believe me. He will sell her to me."I knew that Cassius was a strange man. On the one hand, he could be the kindest and most gentle man you would wish to meet, and on the other hand, he could be one of the most terrifying individuals I have ever known." I said, "Thank you, Cassius. But be careful." We spent the rest of the evening reminiscing, before saying goodbye.

The great tragedy was that within a few weeks, the whole town of Pompeii was completely destroyed by the eruption of Vesuvius, which also decimated the neighbouring town of Herculaneum. I had always felt guilty since then because I knew I could have taken Livia with me and there would not have been any chase. The probability was that all those who knew her were almost certainly dead. Even if they had survived, the last thing on their minds would have been the disappearance of a slave girl… an 'it' or a 'thing'."

Marcus told Laura he had felt it was important that he visit Pompeii for Livia's sake, albeit just to say goodbye. He would have liked her to have known that even after all this time, someone remembered her. Laura said, "You did everything you could. There is nothing to feel guilty about. Absolutely nothing." Marcus gave one of those grins that meant that he disagreed with you and shut the conversation down. Marcus said, "Before we check out from our hotel, we have one last visit to make." Marcus took Laura to the museum. They enjoyed walking around, looking at all the exhibits. Most people enjoy looking at things that remind them of their past, providing that they were fortunate enough to have had a happy past.

The most popular exhibits in the museum were the plaster casts of the images of those who had been killed by the volcanic eruption. Unlike any other visitors to the museum, he was looking to see if he could recognise any of them. One of the first plaster casts was that of a young girl. It was Livia. Marcus felt as if a knife had stabbed him in the chest. He was devastated!

He was, however, fascinated to see that she was being held by an overweight older man. He smiled, and said, "God bless you, Cassius." As he looked at Livia, he was pleased that there was no fear showing on her face. She had a peace in death that she had never found in life. Marcus looked at Laura; she had tears in her eyes. They drove back to their hotel in Naples, both emotionally and physically exhausted.

He would never visit Pompeii again. He had said goodbye and made his peace with Livia. It was time to move on. They decided that they would leave for Sicily in the morning. Normally, when he felt that it was time to move, leaving the old life was almost always sad and sometimes traumatic. On this occasion, he was excited and felt that an adventure lay ahead. He liked the idea of stepping into the unknown. He had, however, recently been having more and more dark days and also a feeling of deep foreboding. He knew that it was a good choice to go to Mary Magdalene's house, which was in one of his Cities of Refuge.

CHAPTER 27
CITY OF REFUGE

MARCUS AND LAURA boarded the ferry to Palermo. He decided not to think of the oncoming battle with Flavian, which is exactly how he saw the inevitable meeting. He looked at Laura as she leaned on the ship's rail and marvelled at how tough she had proved to be and thought that many girls would have run a mile. Yet, here she was!

As they watched Naples slip away in the distance, he felt a real sadness, but he also had a great feeling of satisfaction. He had, for a long time, meant to return to Pompeii, to say his final goodbye to Livia, and to say sorry. He smiled to himself, thinking how much he had changed in those few short years between leaving the Legion and meeting Livia.

Marcus the Centurion was a cruel man. He would have had no sympathy for a slave girl. He knew he had changed and that it was due to the influence of people like Cephas, John and Paul. Previously, he had always looked back on his life as a Centurion with pride, but he now realised that he had only looked at himself on a very shallow level. He was aware that it is a dangerous thing to try to honestly analyse oneself. Quite often, the only difference between the 'good' you and the 'bad' you may solely and simply depend on those with whom you associate. He shook his head and said to himself, "I am a very different man now.

Marcus took the object out of his pocket. Doing this always made him feel better. He kept telling himself that he was a good man and he had always been a good man. After all, at great danger to himself, did he not rescue Tamar, the girl in the cupboard? He went to the bar, bought himself a bottle of water and a fizzy drink for Laura and went to where she was standing. He stood next to her and said, "When we get to Scilly, there is a place I want to visit." Laura said, "Should I be worried?" Marcus smiled and answered, "No. I promise. I think you will find it very interesting."

They felt the ship jolt as it arrived in Palermo. Marcus had a quick drink of water and said to Laura in a cheerful voice, "Well, let's get going." Marcus felt exhilarated as they collected the car and drove off the ferry. He was more excited than he had been for a very long time. After driving for approximately an hour, he pulled off the main road and into a small fishing village. He

415

parked his car in the local car park and they walked into the village. At first, he was disappointed. He had hoped that the village would have remained unchanged, and, of course, it hadn't, but a whole holiday village had now grown around the bay that he had been washed up onto. He hesitated, almost turning around and going back to his car, but then thought that as he was actually here, he would wander around the village for a while.

Laura said, "I assume you have been here before?" Marcus grinned, and said, "Just give me a moment."

After walking for a few moments, he was startled to see Tommaso's cottage. Initially, he did not recognise the cottage as a narrow road now ran in front of it. In addition, a new roof had been added and it now had large front windows. It appeared that the attic had been altered and two windows added. Although a number of changes had been made to the property, it was unmistakably Tommaso's cottage. Marcus stood staring at the building in amazement. He then saw a sign in the window which read, "Bed and Breakfast: Vacancy." He turned to Laura with a grin on his face. Laura said, "What?" Marcus, almost unable to contain his joy, said, "I have been here before, Wow." Laura said, "When?" Marcus grabbed hold of her and said, "In the second century." It was Laura's turn to say, "Wow."

Marcus walked up to the front door, hardly able to contain his excitement. He noticed a sign on the wall, next to the front door, which said, "THE STEWARD". Marcus nervously rang the doorbell. They waited for a moment and, as he was about to ring the doorbell a second time, the door was flung open. A young woman stood in the doorway. There was an awkward silence. For a moment, the young woman was obviously waiting for Marcus to say something. Marcus pointed to the sign and said, "Do we need to book in advance?" The young woman answered, "No. No." She dusted down the front of her dress and then said, "Please come in." They followed the young woman into the house, where she introduced herself as Serafina. Marcus and Laura were led into the kitchen. To Marcus's delight, he recognised the room. He stood and looked around the kitchen which had been fitted with modern equipment and yet, much to Marcus's delight, he could still recognise the room. It was the very same kitchen in which he used to sit with innumerable children, all noisily talking at the same time, whilst Tommaso tried, and often failed, to get some peace and quiet, before inevitably giving up and leaving the room, saying, "I will be in the garden if anyone needs me."

Marcus smiled at the happy memories entering the cottage had invoked. Laura did not take her eyes away from Marcus. He looked like a child on Christmas morning. Serafina asked Marcus to sit down at the kitchen table whilst she took a book from the kitchen cupboard. Marcus assumed it was the cottage register. Marcus told Serafina he had been told that his grandfather had stayed here at the cottage many years before. Serafina answered, "How interesting. I believe this was originally a fisherman's cottage. I was told that it is over four hundred years old. I do think it is strange that a fisherman's cottage came to have such a strange name as "The Steward". I will never know why. I keep thinking that I should change it to something more appropriate for a holiday let." Marcus quickly answered, "No, no. You must not do that. The name has such character. There is very probably a history behind that name." Marcus saw that Serafina had a puzzled look on her face and he quickly decided to change the subject.

Marcus asked if he could have the same room that his grandfather had stayed in. Serafina said, "Oh. What a lovely idea." She opened the Register of Occupancy and said, "Have you any idea what room your grandfather stayed in?" "I do not have a room number, but he told me that it was the room in the right-hand corner of the house," Marcus replied. Serafina said, "Well, if it is the room that I think you are referring to, then it is not really suitable for you." Marcus answered, "Why? What is the problem?" Serafina smiled and said, "Well, we can do much better for you. Your grandfather's room is only very small. It is really only a child's room. As it is the end of the season, and we only have a few guests staying with us, you can actually take your choice of rooms. If you wish, I can show you around. There is another reason why your original choice would not be suitable; it is directly above the room in which I practice." Marcus, intrigued, asked, "If you do not mind me asking, what are you practising for?"

Serafina, looking a little embarrassed, answered, "As it is the end of the season, my sisters come over to my home to practice—you see, we sing in a choir at the Cathedral—but the room you have chosen is just above my own room and my sisters can be quite noisy!" Marcus, with a smile on his face, answered, "That sounds great. You can all sing away and I promise it will not bother me at all." Marcus was, in fact, dreading it. Any music was painful for him to listen to and the idea of Serafina and her sisters singing at the top of their voices was, to him, the stuff of nightmares! Serafina, with a look of relief on her face, smiled. "Great, great," she replied. "Let me show you to your room."

As Marcus followed her along the hallway and up the stairs, he saw that the stairs had been renovated, but there did not appear to be many differences to the house from the time when Tommaso had lived there.

As they climbed the stairs, a vivid memory came to his mind. He remembered the last time he had walked up these stairs. A little wretch of a boy, about seven years old, who was walking behind him, kept smacking him repeatedly on his bottom with a toy wooden sword. Marcus turned around, telling him to stop. The boy apologised. Marcus continued up the stairs. Then 'Smack!' Marcus turned around again! The boy apologised again! As Marcus turned to continue his journey up the stairs, the child continued to smack him again and again. Marcus said, quite sternly, "Stop it." As Marcus proceeded up the stairs, it happened again. Marcus shouted, "All right! That is enough. I have warned you."

Marcus grabbed the boy and pulled him down onto his back and proceeded to tickle him. The boy screamed for mercy. Marcus said, "No mercy. I sentence you to be tickled until you die."

He heard a voice from behind him. It was Tommaso's wife, "Marcus, what on earth are you playing at?! Leave that poor boy alone, you big bully." Marcus let the boy go, watching as the little wretch ran away toward the end of the hallway, where he turned around and stuck his tongue out at Marcus. All Marcus could think of saying in his defence was, "I am sorry, but he hit me first." Even as Marcus uttered these words, he realised how pathetic they sounded! He just quietly stood there and listened as Tommaso's wife gave him a telling-off! She told Marcus that the children had been through a lot and did not need a great brute of a man pushing them around. Marcus apologised again, and then, humiliatingly, he was dismissed and sent to his room!

Serafina saw Marcus smiling and asked him if everything was okay. Marcus said, "Yes, Yes, I was just thinking about my grandfather walking these very same stairs." Marcus followed Serafina along the upstairs landing that led to his old room. Marcus, full of anticipation, could not wait for Serafina to open the door. She paused for a moment and said, "I do not want you to be disappointed. It is quite a small room, and you are welcome to change rooms anytime." Serafina looked at Laura and, pointing to a door a little further down the hallway, said, "That will be your room. Please follow me. I am sure you will be comfortable in it." As Laura and Serafina made their way to Laura's room, Marcus stepped into his room. It was actually larger than he remembered. It was obvious that at some time, the room had been extended. It was now en-suite and had fitted wardrobes along one wall. The window was much larger. But… it was still his room.

Marcus sat on his bed and memories came flooding back. It did not seem possible that it had been two thousand years ago that he had sat in this very same room. He got up and looked out of the window. He gasped as he looked out at the bay, and, over to the west, he saw the mountain range. He said to himself, "The same view… exactly the same view! You can change buildings and roads, but only God can move mountains."

Marcus decided to take a walk with Laura to his car to collect his bag and then wander around the village. He went to Laura's room and knocked on the door. As she opened the door, Marcus could see that she had a huge smile on her face. He could see how excited she was as she started talking. "You must tell me everything about the last time you were here." Marcus laughed and said, "Nothing would give me greater pleasure. Let's go for a walk and I will tell you all about my little adventure." Laura gave a cry of delight, Marcus gave a theatrical bow, then took Laura by the hand and said, "If you will allow me." He turned and led a smiling Laura down the stairs. As they passed Serafina on their way out, he told her that it would probably be a few hours before he returned. She answered that she would most likely be practising with her sisters when he returned, and she would leave the front door unlocked. She added that he was to enter and make himself comfortable.

As Marcus and Laura walked around the village, he thought to himself how remarkable it was that Tommaso's house had survived when everything else appeared to have changed. They had a meal in a small café they found in the village and then walked towards the beach. As they made their way along the beach, Marcus told Laura the story of the Phoebe and the shipwreck and how he believed that Flavian had tried to drown him. Laura said, "How could you possibly know that? Did you see him?" Marcus turned towards Laura and said, "No, but although I know that this will be difficult for you to believe, I heard him." Laura took a long time to answer and then said, "What do you mean, you heard him?" Marcus looked down and watched as the gentle waves washed onto the beach before he replied, "In the storm, I heard it laugh. I heard the Tempest laugh." Laura said nothing. There was nothing to say.

They made their way to the spot where he believed he had been rescued. They stood there for a long time, looking out at the sea. They both watched the blood-red sun as it sank slowly below the horizon. Marcus almost expected to hear a sizzling sound as the hot sun touched the cold Mediterranean Sea. He could not bear to think of the Phoebe and all the poor souls who had lost their lives that day. He pushed his hands deep into his pockets as they walked to the car park to retrieve his bag. It had been a long day and they were both tired. He then remembered that he was in for an uncomfortable night as Seraphina and her sisters would be at the cottage, singing. "Ah well," he thought, "I can always put my head under my pillow!"

They arrived back at the cottage just as it was getting dark. The door was unlocked, as Serafina had arranged. As they walked into the cottage and passed Serafina's room, he could hear Serafina excitedly chatting to what appeared to be several girls. From the noise emanating from the room, he guessed that Serafina must have at least three sisters. As they climbed the stairs, they could hear one of the girls starting to play the piano, not playing a particular tune, but, rather, tinkering with the keys, whilst the other girls were chattering away, seemingly all talking at the same time!

Marcus paused on the stairs for a moment. Something felt different, but he could not identify what had changed! He could not put his finger on exactly what was different, but whoever was tinkering with the piano stopped. Laura looked at him. She said, "Is anything wrong?" Marcus answered, "Oh, it's nothing. I am just tired, I guess." Laura kissed Marcus on the cheek and said, "Well, I will see you in the morning." Marcus watched as she entered her room, then realised that the girls were about to start singing. He rushed to his room as quickly as possible and jumped into his bed fully dressed, apart from his shoes. He seriously regretted not staying out longer, which would have avoided him hearing the sound of the four girls singing at the top of their voices, making, to him, what sounded like the most dreadful noise.

Marcus pulled the pillow hard down over his head. He then heard the piano being played. To his amazement, he realised what had happened on the stairs. The difference he had felt was the piano. It was in tune. At least, it sounded in tune. As Marcus had never heard a piano played previously, nor indeed heard any musical instrument played for two thousand years, he quickly removed the pillow from around his head, sat up and listened as the piano was played. A word came to his mind—melodic. He was not sure if that was the correct word. He had never had the need to use this word! He did know, however, that the sound of the piano playing was, without doubt, the most beautiful sound he had ever heard. Marcus sat on his bed completely spellbound. Then he heard Serafina singing.

When he was in Rome, he had attended street theatres and enjoyed some of the theatrical productions. Quite often, a lady would sing during the course of a production or a play. Although he had heard some beautiful renderings of a variety of songs, Marcus had never heard anything, nor anyone, to compare to Serafina. It was not merely that her voice was beautiful, but it sounded pure and clear in a way he knew he would never be able to explain. Her sisters joined in, all singing in perfect harmony.

Marcus thought to himself, "Is this what I have been missing all these years? Is this what all music sounds like?" Then, as the girls harmonised, he heard Serafina's voice rise above those of her sisters. It had a power and a beauty which he knew was completely unique. Suddenly, there was a knock on the door. Marcus said, "Come in"; it was Laura. She had tears streaming down her face. She said, "I just had to come. Have you ever heard anything as beautiful as that?" She lay on the bed next to him, both of them totally enthralled by what they were hearing.

The girls practised for hours. When they had finished, Marcus wondered why, after all these years of music sounding so painfully out of tune, could he now hear the girls singing so beautifully. He saw that Laura was asleep with a smile on her face. Marcus lay next to her and tried to keep in his head the sound of the girls singing. That night, he slept well.

CHAPTER 28
SERAFINA

THE NEXT MORNING, Marcus and Laura arose early and went for a walk along the beach. They stopped at the same café where they had eaten the previous evening. Marcus ordered a large breakfast for himself and Laura. They both ate whilst considering their next move. As it was a lovely, bright, dry day, they decided they would walk through the village. Of all the times Laura had spent with Marcus, she thought these were the best of times. She loved walking with Marcus whilst he regaled her with wonderful stories.

When they arrived at Tommaso's cottage, they found Serafina busy in the kitchen. She smiled when she saw them and asked if they had slept well. She added that she hoped her singing practice the previous evening had not disturbed them too much. Laura said, "Oh my goodness! No, it was the most wonderful singing I have ever heard." She looked at Marcus, expecting him to say something. Marcus said, "Oh, yes, it was beautiful." Serafina looked a little embarrassed and thanked them both.

Serafina asked them if they had any plans for the day. Marcus said that he did have an idea in mind, and he wondered if she could help him. Serafina answered, "Of course. What can I do for you?" Marcus explained that his grandfather had told him that there was some graffiti scratched into the wall in the garden at the back of the house. He added that his grandfather had said that it looked very old. Marcus continued, "It sounds fascinating to me, and I wondered if you would mind if I had a look at it?" Serafina wiped her hands on the front of her apron and answered, "Of course it is OK. Would you mind if I came with you?" Marcus said, "It would be my pleasure."

Serafina led the way into the garden. Marcus followed. Once in the garden, it took a few minutes to familiarise himself with the layout. Marcus stood for a few minutes and then said, "My grandfather said it was over there," and he pointed to a large thorny bush. They walked over, but they could not see any markings anywhere on the wall. Marcus was very disappointed. Serafina said, "Wait a moment. No problem." She disappeared into the cottage and appeared a few minutes later wearing a large pair of gardening gloves and carrying a pair of secateurs. She knelt down and said, "Now... let me see." With that, she started chopping away at the thorny bush. Marcus offered to help, but Serafina said, "No, no. You will cut your hands to ribbons." She then pulled the bush away from the wall and, with a look of triumph, said, "Done it!"

The wall was covered with what appeared to be a combination of very old, broken cement and dirt, which had, apparently, been undisturbed for centuries. Serafina leaned forward and started scraping and rubbing the wall, brushing more of the dirt and broken cement from its surface. As the wall was cleared, they could see what appeared to be writing across the surface. Serafina read what was written on the wall; "Paolo and Marcus, Shipwrecked Survivor." There was a moment of silence, followed by Marcus adding, "I wonder what became of poor Paolo."

Marcus realised that he had unintentionally spoken out loud and added, "And, of course, Marcus, whoever he was." Serafina smiled, and said, "I do not think you have to worry about Paolo. I am sure he had a good and happy life." She then stepped back to enable Marcus to see the writing on the wall. She added, strangely, "It must have been very difficult for you, Marcus. But remember, 'All things work together for good…' and always remember that you are protected."

Marcus was about to ask her what she meant by that comment, but before he had a chance to speak, Serafina stood up and said, "I will leave you alone." She went back into the cottage. Laura looked at the writing on the wall, then at Marcus, and said, "What just happened? What did she mean?" Marcus said, "I honestly don't know." Laura knelt and touched the stone. She said, "I can't believe you wrote this all those years ago." She added, "It's like magic."

Marcus, lost in his own thoughts, pondered on Serafina's strange comment. Marcus and Laura stood staring at the writing on the wall for a while and then followed Serafina into the cottage. She was sitting in the kitchen and signalled for Marcus and Laura to sit down and join her. She asked if he would like a drink of any type, but Marcus declined, whilst thanking her for all she had done for him. "I felt quite guilty watching you chopping away at that thorny bush!" he said. Serafina laughed and answered, "You are most welcome. As I said, there was only one pair of secateurs."

Marcus and Laura went to their rooms, packed their few belongings and went downstairs to say goodbye to Serafina. He took one last walk through the village and then made his way to the car park. Marcus put their bags into the boot and they climbed into the car. As he was

431

about to drive away, he saw a florist shop. He said, "I think I would like to buy Serafina some flowers." Laura said, "What a wonderful idea!" She laughed and said, "I will pick the flowers." They got out of the car, walked over to the florists and bought a large bouquet of flowers. They made their way back to Tommaso's cottage, but when they arrived, they were surprised to find an older lady in the front of the cottage intent on some gardening. As Marcus walked up the path, the lady said, "Excuse me. Can I help you at all?" Marcus replied, "No, thank you. It is OK. I have just brought these for Serafina as a thank you for all she has done for me." The lady said, "There is no one called Serafina here." Marcus looking puzzled said, "I do not know what you are talking about. She works here. I left here approximately an hour ago." Marcus could see that the lady was beginning to look concerned as she responded, "This is not a 'Holiday Let' house and I have lived here for fifty years." Laura was about to say something, but Marcus held his hand up and said, "Our apologies. It's alright. It's just a misunderstanding, that is all." Laura looked a little exasperated but said nothing.

The lady thought for a moment and said, "It is strange though…", as she carried on with her gardening. Marcus said, "Strange. What is strange?" The lady said, "There is a legend attached to this house that goes back a long time. Longer than anyone can remember. Some people say it goes back thousands of years, but that is probably an exaggeration. You know what people are like."

The old lady ceased talking and started to pull up some weeds from the flower beds. Marcus said, impatiently, "…and you were saying?" The lady answered, "Oh, yes! I have only been away a few days and look at the state of the garden." Marcus said, "Yes. Yes… What were you saying about the legend?" The lady looked up from where she was removing the weeds and answered, "Oh! Yes. Where was I? Ah… that is it… the legend! They say that an Angel has been seen here. There have been many, many sightings. Anyway, when you said that name…" Marcus interrupted her and said, "Serafina?" The lady answered, "Yes. That is it. 'Serafina', that is what they call her." Marcus said, "Have you seen her?" The lady said, "No, but I know when she is here. You will not understand, but I can feel her presence when I am in the cottage. It is difficult to explain, but I feel safe." Marcus nodded and said to himself, "Safe. Yes, safe. That is a perfect description and exactly how I felt all the time that I was here." Marcus stood still. Suddenly, everything fell into place—her beautiful singing voice and the fact that he could hear it in tune; her sisters, whom he never actually saw, and how she seemed to be aware of the inscription on the wall. In addition, her comment that he was 'protected'. It all now made perfect sense. Marcus turned to the lady and said, "I am sorry to have bothered you." He then handed her the bouquet of flowers and said, "These are for you." The lady looked stunned, but before she had time to speak, Marcus took a rather confused and stunned-looking Laura by the hand, turning to make their way back to the car. As they made their way through the small winding streets of the village, Laura said, "What on earth is going on? Where was Serafina? Who is that old lady? What is this about an angel? What's going on?" She stopped walking, and said, "For goodness' sake, say something!" Marcus said, "I have got a million things going through my head at the moment—just give me a minute to work things out." Laura said, "Just so that you know, I am struggling here." Marcus said, "I know, but hang on; you are doing great."

They got to the car park without saying another word. As they pulled out of the small car park, Laura could see Marcus's lips moving as if he was talking to himself, trying to understand exactly what had happened at Tommaso's cottage. He remembered some of the strange things that Serafina had said... in particular,

"All things work together for good…" What on earth did that mean? Also, she had told him to remember that he was protected. Protected from whom? Protected from what? Did this mean that Tomasso's cottage was a House of Refuge, something of which he had been unaware? All he knew was that it was a 'stepping stone' that he needed, after being chased from London and from Rome to his City of Refuge in Sicily. He had to admit that being protected was comforting.

As they drove to Mary Magdalene's descendants' house, a memory came back to him. He thought to himself, "No. It cannot be…" He desperately wanted to stop the car to confirm his idea, but he was driving on a busy country lane with nowhere to stop. As he approached a bend in the road, he hoped to see beyond it a place where he could park but shouted in frustration as he rounded the bend and saw only the road stretching for miles ahead of him. Laura said, "What's the matter?" Marcus answered, "When we stop, I will show you."

Marcus had to drive for twenty minutes before they came to a picnic area. He pulled into the car park, jumped out of the car and opened the boot. He pulled out a small bag and put it onto the bonnet of the car. Laura got out of the car and watched, fascinated. He rummaged through the bag until he found the article for which he was looking. He pulled out a small plastic folder and carefully took out a folded piece of paper. As they got back into his car, he turned to Laura and said, "Have you heard of the 'Angel of Mons'? Laura answered, "Of course I have heard of the Angel of Mons! I work for The Times Archive Department." Marcus continued, "Just after the First World War, I met this chap whose brother was badly shell-shocked at Mons. All his brother did each day was to draw pictures of the Angel of Mons."

Marcus nervously opened the folded piece of paper to reveal the drawing of the Angel. It was Serafina! Marcus turned the drawing over. On the back was the name "Serafina". He handed the drawing to Laura, who looked at the picture and then, as Marcus had done, turned it over. She put her hand over her mouth in disbelief and said, "Oh, my God."

Marcus explained that he had always assumed that because the name was written in a shaky hand and the drawing had faded, that the name read simply "Serafin", which made sense as "Serafin" is a name often used in the past to describe angels. Now, as he sat in the car park, he could clearly see that there was most definitely an 'A' on the end of "Serafin"—it read "Serafina"!

He had dismissed it, but, thinking back, when he was about to kill the girl in the cupboard and instead had let her live, he now knew that he was not being merciful, or indeed kind; it was Serafina. He remembered, as he drew his sword, the same soft hand on his brow and hearing a gentle, beautiful voice, Serafina's voice, which said, "She looks like your daughter." Marcus the soldier had, inexplicably, lowered his sword. He looked at Laura, but he could not read her face. Her expression seemed a mixture of surprise, shock, joy, and wonder. He asked if everything was all right.

Laura turned to him and said, "You cannot keep doing this to me." Marcus replied, "What… Doing what?" Laura shouted, "This! Every day, you share some impossible revelation. My mind is going crazy. It is hard enough for me to get into my tiny brain that you are a two-thousand-year-old Centurion…Listen to me…! I cannot believe that I am even saying it." Marcus interrupted her and said, "You definitely do not have a tiny brain!" Laura screamed, "Do not do that. Don't you dare to patronise me! What I am saying is that you have to tell me the full story. I mean, it is hard enough to come to terms with the idea of a Devil following you around, but now I find that there is an angel who keeps popping up from time to time! I mean, for God's sake!" Laura sat back in exasperation. There was quiet for a few moments, then Marcus said, "Believe me. I know how hard this is for you and I promise I will tell you everything when we get to my friend's house."

Marcus and Laura sat in the car in complete silence, both lost in their thoughts. Laura stared at the drawing, turning it over and over again as she looked first at the drawing and then the name on the rear of the paper. Marcus stared out of the window of the car. Eventually, without comment, Laura handed the drawing to Marcus, who put it back into his bag and placed the bag on the rear seat of the car. Marcus had learned to accept that, sometimes, there are no answers. Sometimes things cannot be 'worked out'. Often you just have to move on. Marcus put the car in gear and slowly pulled out of the car park

CHAPTER 29

MARY'S HOUSE

As HE DROVE along, he felt a rush of excitement at the idea of meeting the descendants of Mary Magdalene. Of all the people he had met over the course of his life, Mary Magdalene had been one of his favourite people. He was now looking forward to meeting her descendants. He remembered clearly those first few weeks after he had learned of the curse. He had no alternative other than to spend additional time with Cephas and his friends as they were the only ones with whom he felt safe.

Marcus had become more and more aware that his friends in the Legion were increasingly suspicious of him and speculating about the changes in his behaviour. He had overheard some of his friends talking. They were saying that he was not the same person that he used to be, and that he had changed. Marcus had always had a great sense of impending danger, and over the years, he had learned not to ignore it. He had no alternative. He was forced to leave his beloved Legion.

It was Mary who seemed to have the least difficulty in forgiving him, even admonishing Cephas and John, which Marcus always found extraordinary, especially as he was aware of how Mary felt about the Nazarene. It would be wrong to say that Mary loved Yeshua. She adored him. One day, Marcus had asked her how she could not hate him for what he had done to Yeshua, especially as she loved the Nazarene so much. She gave an answer which he could not understand—"It is because of my love for Yeshua that I can forgive even you."

As he spent more time with Mary, he realised she was like a 'mother hen', constantly helping and looking after people. She succeeded in making Marcus feel that he belonged, and, eventually, he became good friends with Cephas and the whole household.

As Marcus made his way to Catania, the city where Mary's family lived, he tried to remember the last time he had travelled along this road. He did not keep a record of time or dates, nor log each day of his long life, preferring instead to live in the 'here and now'. He did know, however, that it was over a hundred years since he had been in Sicily. Looking back and reflecting over time, it had been such a very long road that he had travelled. For him to now look forward to a future, which, seemingly, stretched endlessly into eternity, was impossible.

He found it easier to call the past yesterday and to call the future tomorrow.

When they arrived at Catania, he parked his car approximately a mile from Mary's house. He told Laura that the house was about a mile away, which prompted her to ask, "Why on earth are we parking here if it is a mile away?" Marcus answered, "I have to confess that it has been a while since I was last here and this being the case, I think it would be better if I checked it out before we go barging in there." Laura answered, "Just as a matter of interest, how long has it been since you were last here?" Marcus thought for a moment and then said, "It is hard to tell. I do not really keep track of time, but I guess it was probably over a hundred years or so." Laura said, "What! What?! One hundred years ago? Did you think for one moment that your friend would still be alive?!" Marcus laughed and answered, "Of course not, but I have a long-standing arrangement with the family. You will see that it will be OK. I will, however, go down to the house and have a look around, just to make absolutely certain." Marcus got out of the car and started walking. After he had walked a few yards, he stopped, turned around and said to Laura, who was still in the car, "Well, are you coming?" Laura got out of the car looking slightly bewildered. Marcus waited

441

until she was beside him as they made their way down to his City of Refuge.

Mary's house was situated on the very outskirts of the city, which was itself located on the slopes of Mount Etna, an active volcano. Marcus thought that it was a strange place to live, even though the lava flow from the volcano was very slow, which gave people ample time to move once it became apparent that an eruption was imminent. He had been told that, in the past, Sicilians had even had time to dig trenches to divert the lava flow. He was, however, not sure how successful that had been. He thought to himself … at the end of the day, it is still a volcano!

Marcus and Laura made their way to Mary's house, enjoying the sunshine as Marcus familiarised himself with the area. As they came nearer to the house, Marcus noticed that several new businesses had been created, including some small street cafés. Laura said, "I could murder a nice cup of coffee now." Marcus said, "Well then! A coffee you shall have." They were fortunate in that they were able to find an empty table at one of the cafés from which Marcus could see Mary's house. Marcus ordered a cake and a coffee for Laura and a water for himself. An older man who served them noticed that

Marcus was looking at Mary's house. He introduced himself as Alberto, the café owner.

Pointing towards the house they were looking at, he said, "Do you see that house? Let me tell you something about that house. If it were not for that house, I would not be here today! In fact, a lot of the people walking around here would not be alive today, if not for that house." Marcus was intrigued and asked Alberto what he meant by that statement. Alberto explained: "This whole area was badly bombed during the war." He gestured with his hands towards the surrounding houses –"All these houses were on fire. Only that one house escaped. My Mama and Papa, together with many of our neighbours, were all welcomed into that house. It has big deep cellars, safe from all the bombs." He then said, "Bless that house," and crossed himself.

Marcus remembered the house, but he could not recall it being that large. It was sizable—that was true—but not as big as Alberto described it. Marcus drank from his bottle of water whilst Laura sipped her coffee. She looked at the house, fascinated. Alberto turned to Marcus and said, "Why are you interested in that house?" Marcus answered, "That's where we are going. That's my friend's house."

As they sat with their drinks, Alberto kept popping over to tell them more of the history of the area. As they watched the house, they saw a lot of activity with people walking up and down the road, children playing games, and neighbours chatting. Marcus saw only one person actually leave the house.

Marcus decided that as the house looked safe, he would take a closer look at it. He said to Laura. "Whilst you are enjoying your cake, I am going to have a look around the back of the house." As Marcus got to his feet, Laura said, "Has anybody ever told you that you are really weird?" Marcus laughed and answered, "All the time…"

As he approached the building, he noticed it was surrounded by a high wall. He followed the wall, walking around the outside of the house. At the back of the house, there were miles of open countryside, and a path leading across the meadows, which—as far as he could see—led up to the summit of Mount Etna. Marcus walked along the path until he could so position himself that he had a good view of the back of the house. What he saw amazed him. Two large wings had been added to the house since his last visit. There were also two medium-sized outhouses.

From what he could see, the house itself looked very well-maintained. All the upstairs windows had new white window frames, with neat white blinds, operated by bright scarlet cords. At the rear of the grounds was a spring with water gushing out into a fast-flowing stream, which meandered through the grounds. Marcus could not believe what he was seeing. He was aware that land on volcanic slopes was very fertile, but the grounds of the house were full of fruit trees, with an extraordinary amount of fruit. Along the edges of the stream, there were approximately a dozen heavily laden olive trees. The stream flowed out of the grounds into the property of the house next door, which, in turn, flowed into the grounds of the next house. This continued for as far as Marcus could see. He noticed how the stream seemed to bring the whole area to life. Everywhere that the stream flowed were the most heavily laden fruit trees that he had ever seen.

CHAPTER 30

GRACE

MARCUS AND LAURA stood at the front of the house that belonged to the descendants of Mary Magdalene. Marcus felt a little nervous. The house had a large purple front door. Next to the front door was a long, rather comfortable-looking chair. He took a deep breath, walked up the path and knocked on the door. He waited for a few minutes and then knocked again. A woman answered the door. She was about five feet ten inches tall with long black hair which she wore looped over her left ear. Marcus was completely stunned. He just stood there with his mouth open. It was Mary Magdalene!

What had drawn Marcus to Sophia was that she reminded him of his mother. Gertrude was obviously an ancestor of Laura. However, in all of his long life, he had never seen such a likeness. He knew the woman standing at the door in front of him was not Mary Magdalene, but he could not tell the difference. She appeared to have the same stance, and the way she rested her hands on her hips was identical. Marcus realised that he had been standing there with his mouth open! He quickly apologised. The woman at the door looked puzzled and asked him how she could help him and what did he want?

Marcus smiled at her politely, looked at Laura then looked back at the lady at the door. Mary Magdalene had always made him feel like a small boy who had been caught with his hand in the cookie jar, and this encounter was no different! He apologised again. He told her that he was looking for a lady called Grace. The woman at the door continued to look at him, suspiciously, as he stood at the door carrying his scruffy rucksack. She asked him who he was, and how he knew Grace. Marcus totally ignored the woman's questions and asked if Grace was in the house. The woman was totally unmoved and asked again, who was he, and what did he want? Marcus took a deep breath, and nervously took a step backwards. "My real name is Marcus Longinus, Centurion in the Roman Army, and this is my City of Refuge."

It was now the turn of the woman at the door to be dumbstruck. Marcus waited for her to process that information. When she had regained her composure, she said, "I don't believe you. The story of the Centurion is just a family myth. He does not exist! How dare you come to our house with such stories! You will upset my grandma." Marcus took off his rucksack and as he was reaching inside it, he said, "I have proof. Your grandma wrote me a letter." Marcus took out the letter and handed it to the woman. She read the letter. Marcus looked at Laura who was starting to look a little nervous. Marcus gave a smile of encouragement.

They looked at the letter.

17. 5. 1946.

Dear mr centurion,
Are you real can you please come and visit me, Lots
and lots of love

Grace Conte

She turned it over, looked at the back of it and then returned the letter to Marcus. She said, "That's not from my grandma. It is not her handwriting." Marcus felt exasperated. He said, impatiently, "Of course, it is not her handwriting. She was only about nine years old when she wrote this. She was a child. She wrote like a child. She thought like a child, but now she is a woman. She has put away childish things." The woman looked unimpressed. She said, "You can wait here until Grace gets back. No one comes into this house unless Grace says so." She pointed to the chair on the porch and told Marcus that he could wait there. She turned around and closed the door.

Laura said, "Okay! That went well." Marcus smiled confidently and said, "Don't worry—it will be alright."

Marcus and Laura sat down, relaxed, and had waited approximately twenty minutes, when a rather striking-looking older lady walked up the pathway. Marcus stood up, ready to introduce himself. As he did so, the door opened and the woman who looked like Mary Magdalene came out and quickly repeated Marcus's story to the older lady who had just entered the house.

Grace turned around and said, "I am very pleased to meet you. My name is Grace and this lady here is my daughter, Sarah; and you are…?" She paused, waiting for Marcus's response. Marcus answered, "It is wonderful to finally meet you. My name is Marcus, and this is Laura."

Grace said, "Would you like to come into our home? We are ready for you." Marcus replied, "What do you mean, you are ready for me? How did you know I would be coming?" Grace replied, "My dear, dear boy. We have always been ready for you."

Sarah protested, asking her grandma, "How can you be so sure that he is the so-called Centurion?" Grace smiled and simply said, "You will see." Grace led Sarah,

Marcus and Laura into the kitchen and asked them to sit down. She then asked Sarah to, "Get the boy a drink." Sarah was about to ask Marcus what he would like to drink when Grace interrupted; "He will have a glass of water." She turned towards Marcus and smiled knowingly at him. Sarah asked Laura if she would like a drink, and Laura, rather nervously, said that a coffee would be fine. Grace asked Sarah to look after Marcus and Laura, explaining that she would not be long. Their eyes followed her as she left the room.

After a few minutes, Grace came back into the room carrying what looked like an artist's folder. She put the folder on the table, placing it down gently, as if it contained something very precious. She smiled as she opened the folder. It contained several sheets of paper. Before he had a chance to look at the papers, Marcus heard Sarah gasp. As he glanced across at the papers, he could see that the first sheet contained a drawing. The drawing was very good and extremely accurate. It was a drawing of him.

Marcus picked up the folder and carefully went through the other drawings in the folder, laying them out on the table. Whilst he was doing this, Laura leaned on his shoulder, saying over and over again, "Oh, my God!" There were approximately ten drawings in all. After looking at them for a few minutes, Marcus glanced across at Grace and asked, "Alonso?" Grace nodded.

Grace explained that her grandfather, who became a fine artist, had drawn all the sketches laid out in front of them. She explained that as she was growing up, he would tell her stories of the legend of the mysterious Centurion, and how no one believed his story. Grace continued, "But I was captivated by the story and that is why I wrote that letter. I asked my grandfather what you looked like, and that is when he sketched these likenesses."

As Sarah went through the drawings, looking carefully at each one, she kept glancing at Marcus. She asked, "These pictures are over a hundred years old. How is this possible?" At this point, Grace interrupted her and explained that there would be time for explanations later. She asked Sarah to show Marcus to his room. Grace turned to Laura and said, "I have a room for you in the East Wing."

Marcus followed Sarah into the hallway, up the stairs and along the upstairs hallway to one of the new wings that had been added since his last visit. Marcus was impressed, and thought to himself, "Money well spent!"

The addition to the house was not merely a room, but a suite, comprising of a kitchen, a living room and a large bedroom and bathroom. Marcus looked at Sarah in surprise when he noticed that the bed was made up and there was a bottle of water on the bedside cabinet. Sarah said, "Every day for as long as I can remember, we have changed the bedsheets and put fresh water on the cabinet just in case the Centurion came to stay. I must admit I never believed this day would come." Sarah looked at him suspiciously, and said, "I am still not totally sure that it has!" Marcus smiled and said, "To be honest, I cannot blame you. It is an incredible story." Sarah said, "I will leave you to unpack..." and, looking at his rucksack, added, "...it should not take you long!"

Just as Sarah was about to leave the room, Grace entered with Laura. She was carrying a small suitcase, which she lifted onto the table. She looked at Marcus and said, "I hope you do not mind, but I noticed you did not have much in the way of luggage. To be quite truthful, and I am sorry to say this, but what you are wearing now really does need burning." One thing Marcus quickly learned about Grace was that she was honest and always spoke the truth, even though sometimes it was not what the recipient necessarily wanted to hear!

Marcus said, "We have some bags in the car." Grace ignored Marcus and opened the suitcase, stepped back, and said, "These are for you. Get changed and I will see you downstairs shortly." As she was about to leave the room, she stopped at the door. "Oh, and bring those disgusting things with you," she said, pointing to the clothes he was wearing. She turned around and left the room. Sarah and Marcus laughed. Laura looked stunned! Sarah explained that her grandma always insisted that everyone must always look smart and clean.

Marcus and Sarah looked at the contents of the suitcase and discovered it was full of new and obviously, very expensive clothes! Remarkably, they were all Marcus's size. Sarah told him that she would leave him to get changed and would see him later downstairs.

Marcus changed, picked up his old clothes and made his way down to the kitchen. He was surprised to see the whole family sitting around the kitchen table. Grace did the introductions, starting with Enrico, Sarah's husband, then Roberto, their son, who was nine years old. He appeared to be very excited and immediately blurted out, "Are you really the Centurion? Mum said you did not exist." Sarah looked embarrassed and told Roberto to be quiet. Enrico said, "You owe us no explanation. If you want to tell us your story, that is fine, but only do so in your own time. All we know is that we have been receiving large sums of money, going back hundreds of years, from some mysterious benefactor, whom, we assumed, went by the code name Centurion."

Marcus waited a moment whilst he considered what he should say, and, once he had his thoughts in order, exactly how he should respond. He most certainly did not want to reveal that he was in charge of the Platoon who had carried out the Crucifixion of the Nazarene.

After a long pause, Marcus decided not to tell them too much. After all, it was such an incredible story, who could possibly take it all in at one telling? Marcus started to recount to them part of his story. He looked at Sarah and said, "Do you remember when you opened the door to me, and I just stared at you? I think that is what made you very suspicious of me. I do not blame you. You see, you reminded me of one of your ancestors." He waited for them to say something. It was Sarah who broke the silence, "Who? Who do I remind you of—can you tell me who she was?" Marcus looked at her, waiting for her reaction to his answer, and said quietly, "Mary of Magdala."

Little Roberto was the only individual who did not let out a loud gasp, followed by complete silence, before they all started to talk at the same time. "THE Mary

Magdalene? The one from the Bible?" "Are you seriously saying that you are two thousand years old?" They continued asking questions and talking over each other. The questioning grew louder and continued to such an extent that Marcus could not tell who had asked which question. Laura sat quietly thinking to herself, "Well… Just when you think you have heard it all, he hits you with a new revelation!"

Grace tapped on the table and very calmly said, "Give the man a minute, please. Quiet… calm down." Marcus nodded a thank you to Grace, then looked nervously at Laura who responded with a weak smile. "Yes, Mary of Magdala from the Bible. She was my friend, as was Cephas, whom you call St Peter." There was another loud gasp from around the table. "It was he, Cephas, who thought of the idea of building a City of Refuge," Marcus added, as he gestured around the room. "This fine place is my City of Refuge. Cephas said that I should continue sending money, through the generations, to the families of the people that I trust. Mary was an obvious choice."

Enrico asked, "So you are saying that my Sarah looks like Mary Magdalene?" Marcus answered, "One of the things that has always fascinated me throughout my long life is the likenesses I see in people. Not merely between father and son, but likenesses that go back generations. Believe me, I have seen many, but never, and I mean never, have I seen such a likeness as I see here. When Sarah opened the door, and just for a moment, I really thought it was Mary. Not merely because of her appearance, but because of her deportment; the way she stands is exactly the way that Mary stood. I am aware that I have only just met Sarah, but even her personality, and certainly the way she speaks, appears to be the same as that of Mary."

Enrico asked, "What do you mean by 'same personality'?" Marcus, smiling at Sarah, answered, "Oh, you know! Stroppy, bossy, protective, and totally, totally, loyal. As well, of course, as being one of the loveliest individuals that I have ever met! I did, however, very quickly realise that there was absolutely no way I was getting through that door unless Grace said it was okay." This last comment caused everyone to burst out laughing.

Roberto asked Marcus the question that he suspected all young boys would ask. He said, "Tell me, tell me, were you in any battles and did you kill anyone?" At this point, Sarah said, "Roberto!" Marcus looked at Sarah as if he was seeking approval. Sarah said, "Remember, he is just a little boy." Marcus said to Roberto, "Yes, I have been in lots of battles." He then showed Roberto several of his scars and told the child how he had got them. The little boy listened, completely spellbound. Roberto then asked, "Who was the most fearsome enemy that you have ever faced?"

Marcus thought for a while and answered, "The Persian Bowmen . Well, I was never really sure whether they were archers mounted on horses or Persian cavalrymen with bows. Anyway, they would ride straight at you, at an unbelievable speed, firing dozens of arrows. They would then ride past you, and you would think that the danger had gone, but you were wrong! As they were riding away, they had the ability to turn almost completely around in full circle on their saddles and, facing the rear of the soldiers they had just passed, firing off dozens of arrows into their backs. Then they were gone. You did not have the opportunity to strike back."

Roberto said, "Wow!" Marcus continued, "And that is where the saying, 'parting shot' comes from." Roberto said, "I do not understand. What do you mean 'parting shot'?" Grace said, "A parting shot is when someone who is leaving says something to someone else, as they are walking away, that is not very nice. It can be like 'An arrow in the back'! Remember, it is never a good thing to deliberately hurt someone."

Over the coming weeks, Marcus became familiar with all the members of the family and felt comfortable living at Grace's house. He was glad to see Laura build up a strong friendship with Sarah. Over the years, he had learned that "comfortable" was better than "happy" and better than "joy!" "Happy" is dependent upon circumstances. "Joy" can be fleeting, but comfortable ticks all the boxes. Comfortable means that you feel welcomed and wanted by everyone in the house. Comfortable means you are relaxed in other people's company and people are relaxed in your company.

It was on the first evening after Roberto had gone to bed that Grace asked Marcus and Laura to join them around the kitchen table. Marcus had a very good idea what it was that they were about to say. When they were seated, Grace looked around the table to ensure everyone was ready. Marcus thought it was rather like a head teacher before a school assembly. Grace then turned to Marcus, gave a reassuring smile and said, "I cannot tell you how delighted we are to have you and Laura staying with us." Grace's smile widened, and she said, "But what brings you here?" Marcus then told them the whole story of Flavian across the centuries and the recent suspected abduction of the little boy. Marcus looked around and saw the concerned look on their faces. Grace gently placed her hand on Marcus's hand and said, "Don't worry. That thing cannot harm you here." Marcus said, "To be honest, we are not sure if Flavian has the boy or if he even knows we are here." Grace answered, "One thing you can be certain of is that he knows you are here, and he will come."

Over the next few days, Marcus spent a lot of time with Grace. He asked her about the huge cellars. He told her that he did not remember them from the last occasion he was here in the house. Grace then told Marcus a remarkable story. She said, "When Mussolini came to power in 1922, my father could see that there was going to be trouble. He said we had to prepare, and so he, and several men who were his friends, dug out and built the cellar under the house. It took them ten years. He also planted all the fruit trees at the back of the house. We have everything we need: we have safety, we have fruit and vegetables, we have five goats for milk and cheese, and we even have our own vineyard." Marcus told her that he was very impressed.

Grace continued with her remarkable story. She explained that there had been a terrible night, at the end of the War, when the city was bombed. All the houses were on fire. "Somehow, our house escaped the bombs. I was only a child, but I ran out into the streets telling people to come to our house. I was shouting to them that it was safe, and they should come and join us. Some people came and were saved; some did not. Those who did not join us said that they did not need my father's cellar, but they were wrong. They perished." Marcus noticed that even though it was so many years ago, Grace was crying at the memory of it. They both sat in silence.

Marcus looked at Grace and realised she must be incredibly old, yet she was still very beautiful. In fact, he thought that she was, without any doubt, one of the most beautiful women he had ever met. Marcus had met a lot of women who were physically attractive, but he had learned in many instances, that the more you got to know them and the closer you actually were to them, the less attractive they became. He had also known several women whom many people would consider to be quite plain, who had found the secret of true beauty. He looked at Grace and saw her tears. Real beauty was running out into a burning street whilst bombs were falling and trying to persuade people to come into your shelter where they would be safe. Beauty is when, years later, you still weep for the proud and arrogant ones who perished. Marcus quietly left the room leaving Grace to her memories and her grief.

Marcus enjoyed three wonderful weeks at Grace's house. During this time, Marcus would regularly call Francesco to ask if he had any news about Antonio. Quite often, Laura would sit beside him hoping for some good news, but Marcus would shake his head. Laura would be unable to say anything; she would just stand up and go to her room.

Grace said, "If he has him, he is just playing with you. That thing will contact you—give it time—and keep busy… there is plenty of work to do around here." Marcus took Grace's advice and helped in the house, the gardens and the small vineyard. He even enjoyed helping milk the goats and learned how to make cheese. All the time, little Roberto was close by. Little Roberto never stopped asking questions about what it was like to be a Roman soldier. Late one evening, whilst Marcus was sitting at the kitchen table, chatting to Enrico, and thinking that his life at this moment was just too good to be true, Sarah came into the kitchen with a worried look on her face. Enrico asked Sarah, "What is the problem?" She turned to Marcus and said, "There is a man at the door, and he is asking for you."

Marcus looked at Laura. He could see the worried look on her face. They had left the house on only one occasion since they arrived, and that was only to retrieve his car, which he had left a mile up the road. The car was now parked in the garage. Marcus asked, "Who is he and how does he know that I am here?" Sarah ignored the question, glanced at her husband, and then looked back at Marcus. She said, "He asked for the Centurion." Enrico asked the questions that they all wanted to ask, "Who is he and what does he want? How does he know that the Centurion is here?"

Sarah tried to assure Marcus that no one would have mentioned his presence, and she had no idea how anyone would know anything at all about the Centurion. Marcus tried to reassure her that he completely trusted everyone in the household. He thought back to when he first arrived. The only person he had spoken to was Alberto from the café, and he was sure he had not mentioned where he was staying. He definitely would not have said anything about being a Centurion! He concluded that the only way to solve the mystery was to speak to the man. He asked Sarah to bring the man into the house. He added, "Let us see what this man has to say." Sarah shook her head, and said, "I am sorry, I cannot do that. Grace will not let him in. She said if you want to speak to him, then you have to go to him."

Marcus said, "If that is the case, then tell him to get lost." Enrico added, "A good decision! There is nothing he could possibly say that we would want to hear." As Sarah left the room, Marcus felt uneasy. He asked Enrico if Grace had ever, as far as he was aware, previously refused entry to anyone? Enrico thought for a while and said, "Yes. It does happen, but not very often. My opinion is that if Grace will not let them in, then keep well away from them."

Marcus stood up and paced slowly up and down the room. For some reason, it helped him to think. Sarah came back into the room. He hoped that she would tell them the man had gone, but he knew life was never that simple! He was not, however, prepared for what Sarah had to say. As Marcus sat down at the table, Enrico asked, "Well, what did he have to say?" Sarah had a puzzled look on her face. She turned to Marcus and said, "I gave him your message. He did not seem surprised that you did not want to see him." He said, "Antonio wants you to come; Antonio from Rome."

Laura looked across at Marcus, who looked as if he was in shock at what he had just heard. Marcus said, "Well, this is it—this is what we have been waiting for." He turned to Laura and said, "Don't worry; it will soon be over. It will be alright."

CHAPTER 31

ANTONIO

Marcus looked around at the shocked expressions on the faces of Enrico and Sarah. Marcus asked if the man was still outside the house and Sarah nodded. Marcus could not believe how calm he felt. Laura and their small group of friends made their way to the front door.

In front of him stood a rather unconcerned young man, with a neat beard, who held out his hand and said, "Hello. My name is Jason, and I assume you are Marcus Longinus, the Brave Centurion, also known as Marcus Albright."

The young man stood there with his hand still extended. Marcus said to him, "I would put that hand down, if I were you, before I cut it off." The young man put down his hand and said, "Come, come now. I am sure we can deal with our little problem in a civilised manner." Marcus, raising his voice, responded, "Tell me where the boy is now. You have no idea what I am capable of doing." The young man laughed, grabbed his beard and started to pull at it, crying out in loud mock screams, and shouting "Ow, Ow. Stop—it hurts." He roared laughing. He suddenly stopped and smiled, putting his finger to his lips, and said, "Our little secret," and winked.

Marcus felt a shock run through his body. Long-forgotten memories were awakened. He felt his knees weaken. Enrico said to him, "Are you alright? What is he talking about?" Marcus did not answer him, but shouted across at the young man, "What if I just phone the police and tell them that you have the boy?" The young man, again, merely smiled. He gave Marcus a piece of paper with an address on it and said, "Come to that address at midnight. If the police come first, then the boy dies. If you do not come by midnight, then the boy dies."

He added, "Listen. Nobody needs to get hurt. We can all get what we want. You can come away with the boy—be a hero." He turned to walk away, then paused and said, "Oh, by the way. You were right. He is one of yours. The boy, I mean. Your blood. Your DNA. Thank you so much for introducing him to us. We have been waiting for a long time to find your particular Achilles Heel." Marcus watched him walk away whistling some infuriating tune. Even after he was out of sight, Marcus still stood at the door, watching.

The household gathered together in the kitchen. Grace was the first to speak. She said, "What are you going to do?" Marcus answered, "I do not know, but, obviously, I will not allow the boy to get hurt." Grace said, "This man does not care about the boy. He does not care whether the boy lives or dies. He cares only about himself. Remember, he is evil, and all evil men are weak. You have to look for his weakness. He will try to put on a show of strength, but do not be fooled."

It was ten minutes to midnight when Marcus stepped out into the street on the way to his rendezvous with the man, Jason. He had with him a small but powerful torch, for which he was grateful. It was a very dark cloudy night. There was no moonlight and rain was in the air. It was so dark, that he knew if he had not brought the torch, he would have struggled to find his destination.

When he arrived at the address he had been given, he saw that it was a large house which was boarded up, and all of it, including the brickwork, appeared scorched and blackened. Marcus did what he always did when in a potentially dangerous situation—he walked around the building to check it from all angles and to see where the doors and windows were positioned. The building had obviously been on fire at some time in the past. Marcus wondered if this was one of the houses that had been a victim of the bombing. If that was so, he wondered why it had not been rebuilt. The war was a long time ago.

When Marcus was satisfied that there was no escape route from the back of the building, he made his way to the main entrance at the front of the house. Just as he was about to knock, the door opened. Jason, the annoying young man with the infuriating smile, greeted him at the door. Marcus thought to himself that once he had the boy back safely, Jason would pay for what he had done... He would make him very, very sorry...

Marcus stood at the door and looked into the house. It was dark and cold. It looked like a tomb. Marcus said, "I am not going in there." Jason said, "Why on earth not? Oh, I see; it's dark. What's wrong with the dark? All the best things happen in the dark." Marcus said, "Very funny. Now get some light in there." Jason answered, "Okay! Whatever you wish. Anything for the brave Centurion." Jason then turned around and started lighting candles which were scattered along the length of the hall. When Marcus considered the hall to be sufficiently lit, he entered the house.

Jason led the way into what had probably once served as the living room. The fire damage was extensive. The ceiling, at some time, had completely collapsed and all the debris had simply been pushed into one corner. The room was dimly lit by six candles. There was a chair in the corner, underneath the boarded-up window. In the semi-darkness of the room, Marcus could just make out the shape of a mattress on the floor.

In the middle of the room was a small table with a single chair. On the chair sat a young boy. It was Antonio. Jason walked over to a corner of the room and sat down on a chair. Antonio said in a calm voice, "Hello, Marcus. It is good to see you again. I hope that you are well?" Marcus walked over to the table. He was surprised to see that the boy looked fine. He looked clean, his hair was brushed, and there were no apparent signs of injuries.

Antonio spoke again, but this time in a strange, yet familiar voice. Antonio said, "I feel quite offended that you do not remember me. After all, we were once so very nearly family!" Antonio turned toward Jason and said, "Caterina, say hello to Marcus." Jason looked at Marcus, and, speaking in Caterina's voice, said, "Hello, Marcus. I was so disappointed when you left me. We could have been so good together."

Marcus turned to Antonio and said, "Flavian!" Antonio stood up and gave a theatrical bow in Marcus's direction. Marcus said, "I remember you in Cyprus, when you stole Charis's body." Turning to Jason, Marcus said, "You are not Caterina. You are both just 'things' who steal the bodies of other individuals. Caterina and Charis are long dead. You cannot harm them any longer."

Antonio shrugged his shoulders and seemed disappointed. He said, "It was so sad when you left. Poor Charis just could not cope without me and he went quite mad. Caterina, poor girl, threw herself off the same cliff that you fell off. Unfortunately, it was with a very different result!" Antonio then lifted his right hand high in the air, bringing it down sharply towards his left hand, as a gross imitation of Caterina's fall, whilst, at the same time, mimicking Caterina screaming. Then, clapping his hands together loudly, shouted, "Splat!"

Marcus said, "Aristo kept me informed of the events in Cyprus and, apparently, after you left that family alone, Charis became, once again, a kind generous man, loved by all who knew him. Caterina married and had five children and eighteen grandchildren and lived to the age of eighty-three. All proof that you are a liar."

The thing that was in Antonio gave an annoying smile and said, "Of course, I am. It is so much more fun to lie, do you not think?" "Wherever is the fun in telling the truth? Where is the challenge in telling the truth? To tell a good lie, one has to be clever—devious even. It is a battle of wits, although admittedly, as time goes on, it becomes less and less challenging, therefore, less fun. Did you know that you can lie to people and they know that you are lying, but they still believe you? Well, politicians do that all the time! It takes all the fun out of lying, if you ask me. However, my favourite lie is the 'old white lie'. It always amazes me how cheaply people sell their integrity."

The thing inside Antonio smiled at Marcus. The smile sent a shiver down Marcus's spine. The thing continued, "I have had my eye on you, Centurion. It was me that organised the little riot outside your farmhouse during that lovely English Civil War and, of course, that poor one-armed man in the public house just after the First World War. I actually got quite excited when I heard what you wanted to do to him—yes, I can hear your thoughts –what was it again? Wait, do not tell me, let me think… Ah, I have it. I remember. You wanted to rip his arm off and beat him with it and then throw his body into the street. For a moment, I thought I had you back! Just like old times!" Marcus said, "What do you mean—'Have me back?' I was never yours." The Demon replied, "Oh… Really…? Do you believe that?" "Let me tell you. You were completely mine, but I started to lose you when you found that girl in the cupboard and then at Golgotha, I lost you completely." The Demon sighed and said, quietly, "Like so many others." It paused for a moment, then continued; "Do you remember me in the zoo and that little push on the obnoxious small boy? I must admit that there was a part of me that was rooting for the lions, however, it was not to be! Never mind." Marcus said, "What could you possibly gain from watching a small boy being torn to pieces by a pride of lions?" The thing replied, "Apart from the sheer fun of it, you mean? Can you not guess?" It gave a huge sigh and continued; "You humans are not very bright, are you? It is intended to get you to break the terms of the curse, of course. You are not supposed to save anyone's life and you cannot fight in any War and, be honest now, when the Second World War started, you remembered the one-armed man and how ashamed you were for not fighting for your country and you very nearly broke the rules of the curse."

It went on, "This is how it is supposed to work. You break the rules—you go straight to Hell and I can then get the Artefacts and destroy them. When you jumped into the lions' enclosure, I thought I had got you. Then, He forgave you."

Marcus said, "What do the Artefacts have to do with me? I am sure you must have had plenty of opportunity to steal them. How could I possibly stop you from doing so?" The thing said, in amazement, "You do not know, do you? Now that does surprise me. You are the Guardian of the Artefacts. I cannot touch you or the Artefacts." Marcus, puzzled, answered, "Guardian? Why me?" The thing responded, "Oh no! Can you humans not ever say anything original? Moses replied, 'Why me?', Isaiah said, 'Why me?' Whenever He asked any of you useless humans to do the simplest task, the response is always the same old whining, 'Why me?' The answer is… I cannot tell you because he does not tell me!

I was waiting at Tommaso's cottage, but you had those ladies protecting you." The Demon saw the look of surprise on Marcus's face at what he had just said and laughed loudly! "You did not know! Oh! You humans! What did you think when you survived jumping from that cliff at Charis's house? Did you think that you could fly?" The Demon roared laughing. "No, no, you fool. Serafina caught you. It was Serafina who stood in front of you during the Civil War. Or did you think that the bullets were just bouncing off you? It was Serafina who blew out the torches in your quaint little cottage." The Demon was now laughing so much that he was unable to speak. After managing to control himself for a moment, he continued; "Tell me. Did you really think that those lions were bowing down to you?" The Demon stopped laughing. He said, in a very low voice, "Serafina has always got in my way, but hear this, Centurion, you will be mine!"

Marcus decided he had heard enough and said to Antonio, "Okay, Antonio. Come with me and I will take you home." Antonio replied, "I cannot do that." Marcus asked, "Why can't you come with me?" The boy, pointing towards Jason, replied, "He won't let me." Marcus turned towards the young man sitting on the chair. It pleased Marcus that he saw a fleeting look of fear in Jason's eyes.

Marcus shouted across the room to Antonio, "Do not let this thing stop you, Antonio. Believe me, I can snap this thing like a twig." Antonio stood up, calmly walked around the table, and then suddenly charged at Marcus with his hands outstretched, hitting him fully in the chest and knocking him across the room. Antonio let out a loud scream. The voice of Flavian spoke through the boy, "So, you think you can snap me like a twig? When are you going to learn, Centurion? You are no match for me."

Marcus got to his feet, remembering what Grace had said—"Evil is weak. It has no power over you. Look for its weakness and you will find it." Marcus made a show of dusting himself down, and then said, "It does not take a lot of strength to push someone over when they are not expecting it. Would you like to try that again?" The boy was silent and did not move. Marcus said, "I didn't think so." Flavian's voice came from the boy's lips, "He is mine, Centurion. He belongs to me." Marcus said, "Well, I might go down the road and get the local Priest to come back here with me." The boy gave a hideous laugh, and the Demon within him shouted, "The boy will be dead before you even leave the room."

While the Demon was speaking, its voice resounded in Marcus's memory. He frantically went back through the long years he had lived. He knew he had heard that voice before, long before he had met Flavian in Cyprus. The remembrance suddenly came back to him as vividly as if it were yesterday. Marcus laughed out loud. It was not a forced laugh! It was a laugh that came freely when you remembered something amusing from your past; a laugh that comes totally unprompted! Marcus smiled as he said, "I remember you. It was in Ephesus. You were trying the same trick on a little boy, and Paul, with absolute ease, cast you out! He cast you out as if you were absolutely nothing, and you cried like a baby." Marcus started to mock the Demon, mimicking a baby crying,

"Boo hoo, Boo hoo. Oh please, Paul. Don't cast me out, please, please. Boo hoo."

The Demon in the boy gave a loud blood-curdling scream. Marcus was unimpressed. He knew that it would not harm the boy because it wanted something. Marcus walked across to the corner where Jason was sitting. Jason was now looking a lot less confident. Marcus suddenly slapped him hard across the face, overturning the chair, and knocking Jason to the floor. Marcus picked up the chair and said, "Do you mind if I have this?" He took the chair and moved it over to sit at the table. He gestured to Antonio to sit down. The boy sat down. Marcus said, "Okay, crybaby. What do you want?" Marcus waited.

The Demon spoke, "You have certain Artefacts in your possession. I want them." Marcus looked at Antonio and felt a deep sadness for him. As he looked into the child's eyes, he could see a frightened little boy, which reminded him of his own son, and made what he had to say next all the more difficult. He replied, "No." The Demon screamed, "He is like your son, your family. He is your flesh. He is your blood. He carries your genes! How can you say no?"

Marcus answered, "I do not know why you want the Artefacts, but I should imagine that they are quite powerful, and I do not believe I am a so-called Guardian, because we have already established that you are a liar. I am not going to give you that power. I can tell you this, however—if you do not set the boy free, although I know I am not permitted to perform an exorcism, because if I do, then I will be sent straight to hell, nonetheless, Demon, mark my words, I will cast you out and I will drag you straight to hell with me."

There was a long pause before the Demon spoke; "Bring me the Artefacts and I will give you ten." Marcus said, "What are you saying?" The Demon answered, "I will free ten if you give me what I want. Two days, just two days. No more. Bring the artefacts to the old barn." Marcus asked, "Which old barn?" The demon replied, "Ask Grace." Marcus looked at the boy and said to him, "Do not worry. He will not harm you. I promise I will be back in a few days, and I will then return you to your family." The Demon said, "Oh… how sweet!" Marcus shouted, "I want to hear the boy." Marcus saw the boy's face relax and then he heard Antonio's voice; it was quiet and nervous. Antonio said, "Please help me. I want to go home." Marcus answered, "Just be brave for a few more days, then this will all be over, I promise." One of the hardest things Marcus had ever had to do was to leave Antonio. He made his way to Grace's house. He knew he had little choice other than to leave the boy.

CHAPTER 32

THE PLAN

As MARCUS GAVE an account of all that had happened at the house, he watched Grace's face to try and get a clue to what she was thinking, but her face was almost entirely without expression. Marcus thought that she looked old, and even though he was well aware that she *was* obvi-ously very old, this was the first time he had thought that perhaps this was all too much for her. When Marcus had finished speaking, everyone turned to Grace. Looking tired, Grace put her hands on the table, and seemingly with great effort, pulled herself to her feet. She walked to the window and stared into the night sky. It was Laura who spoke first. "Grace, are you alright?" Grace turned around, and with a weak smile on her face, she said, "Just a little tired, my dear, as I am sure we all are. It's been a long day, and I am sure we all need to get some sleep." With that, she looked around the table, gently nodded, then left the room.

That night, few slept. Marcus replayed the meeting with Flavian over in his mind, Laura worried, and Grace prayed.

The next morning, they all gathered once again around the kitchen table, strangely everyone looked tired except Grace, she looked and acted years younger than the previous evening. She turned to Marcus and asked, "What do you plan to do?" Marcus replied, "I was hoping you could advise me. I know that on the one hand, he wants the Artefacts, but on the other hand, he can't go near them, so my guess is that he will have someone there to help him. I am pretty sure if I can get near to him with the Artefacts, I can destroy him. It's a plan... not a great plan, but it's the best I have got!" Grace said, "Actually, it might work! You have the advantage as you have the Artefacts." Laura asked, "What are the Artefacts? I have been very patient, and you promised me you would tell me the full story, so now I think it's time, don't you?"

CHAPTER 33

NOT ONE SPARROW FALLS.

MARCUS LOOKED AT Laura and then realized that she would not be satisfied until she had heard the full story.

Marcus sat down at the table, opposite where Laura was sitting, and said, "It is difficult to know where to begin." Laura replied, "Well, why not start at the beginning? Exactly where and when were you born?" Marcus looked around the room and asked, "Are you all ready to hear this?" They all nodded. Marcus paused, took a deep breath, waited for a moment and then began to tell his story. "My grandfather was a Roman Centurion. He was with Julius Caesar when he crossed the Rubicon. When my father retired, I took his place in the Legion. The stories of how I acquired my scars, of the Syrian Swordsman and the Egyptian Archers, were true." He paused for a moment. Although he thought that everyone in the room, with the exception of Laura, was aware of elements of his story, he understood that some of the things he was about to say would come as a shock.

Marcus looked at Laura and said, "I loved being in the Legion. I was a Centurion by the time I was twenty-six years old. When I was twenty-eight, the Legion was sent to Jerusalem." Laura interrupted. She started to say, "Surely you don't mean at the time of…" and then her voice trailed away. Marcus prepared himself, wondering how these individuals—his friends, and most of them closer than friends; rather more like close family members—would receive what he was about to say next.

Marcus said to Laura, "Of course, you have worked out that I was in Jerusalem at the time of one of the most important events in human history. During my time in Jerusalem, I held various roles and positions, all of which encompassed the keeping of the peace and protection of the interests of Rome. Occasionally, I carried out the supervision of executions.

"It was the time of the Jewish Feast of Passover, and we were on high alert. There were thousands of people from all across the known world who had come to Jerusalem for the Passover. I know Herod was very nervous." Marcus paused for a moment and looked at the shock on the faces of those around the table. Only Grace smiled at him and nodded her head in encouragement. Marcus continued, "I was given the duty to oversee the Crucifixion of three criminals, which I duly carried out. It was no different to the dozens of executions that I had previously supervised.

"As you have probably guessed by now, one of the criminals was the Nazarene." Laura stood up and said, "You mean Jesus. Are you saying that you killed Jesus?" Marcus answered, "As far as I was concerned, it was just another execution, no different than any other, but that night, something changed."

Laura let out a loud gasp and sat down. Marcus could see that she had something she wanted to ask, and he waited in silence. After a short time, Laura said very quietly, almost in a whisper, "What was he like? Jesus, I mean." Marcus leaned back in his chair, as if he was trying to assess the best way to answer Laura's question. After what seemed to be an age, Marcus continued, "He did not look like anybody special.

He looked completely ordinary; the same as any other Jewish male at that time. He did not look in any way like any of the paintings or the statues you will have seen. He looked very Jewish, with long black hair and Jewish pigtails."

Marcus then leaned forward, looked around the room and said, "I have always been good at languages, and in every town and country I went to, I always took the trouble to learn the local language. It is surprising how useful it can be, and what I can find out when people standing around me do not know that I can understand the language they are using and what they are saying!" Marcus laughed at the memory. He added that on one occasion, this fool was boasting and saying how he would love to kill Pilate. "You should have seen his face when I had him arrested." Marcus took a sip of water, and then continued. "My Commander asked how I knew what the man had said. He seemed astonished when I told him that I could speak a little Hebrew and some Aramaic."

Laura was surprised to see that Marcus seemed quite proud of himself. "The next thing I knew was that Pilate wanted to see me. I made my way to Pilate's Palace. When I arrived, I was surprised to see that Pilate's wife was with him. I was told that the Nazarene was speaking to a large crowd, and Pilate's wife wanted to hear what he said. I was tasked with accompanying her and translating what the Nazarene had to say." Marcus took another sip of water and continued. "We travelled on horseback for a few hours until we came to a gigantic crowd of people. There must have been about twenty thousand people there in the middle of nowhere. We sat down on the grass and listened to the Nazarene. Laura said, "What did he say?" Marcus answered, "Crazy stuff." Laura seemed exasperated, and asked again, "What did he say?" Marcus replied, "Well, it was very strange, because although he spoke very quietly, everyone could hear him. I was sitting next to Pilate's wife. The Nazarene would speak, and I would whisper the translation into Pilate's wife's ear. Then she would gasp! I would listen to more of what he was saying and translate that for her. She would gasp again." Laura repeated loudly, "What did he say?" Marcus answered, "Okay. Give me a minute. I am trying to tell you." Marcus took a deep breath, and said, "The Nazarene was telling them not only to give their money to the poor, but to sell what they had and give that money away, and also to give shelter to the homeless." Marcus leaned back and said, "Can you imagine him saying to the Church today that the congregations must give away their money and take in a refugee? They would crucify him." Marcus smiled at the thought, adding that this was a man who would allow prostitutes to shower him with kisses, who would walk away from important people and yet dine with the poor and with the most appalling people. He added, "I was surprised he lasted as long as he did."

Marcus took a sip of water and said to Laura, "Have you ever wondered why I only drink water?" Laura said, "I had wondered, but I just assumed that it might be a health thing."

"I used to love wine. I would drink it by the barrel. That night, after the executions, my friends and I went out with the full intention of getting absolutely blind drunk. However, as soon as I tasted the wine, I vomited all over the floor. It has been the same ever since. Water is the only liquid that my stomach can tolerate. My only enjoyment in drinking, and I know that this sounds foolish, is watching other people enjoy a drink as I try to imagine what it tastes like to them." Laura remembered the first time Marcus made her a cappuccino and how he had asked her to try to describe the taste.

Marcus continued with his story. He said, "Can you imagine it? I was sitting there with my vomit all over the floor and then the most dreadful noise started—all the men had started to sing some song about the Legion. I cannot possibly describe how excruciating it sounded to me. That is why I never play any music."

Marcus took another drink of water and looked around at the sad expressions on the faces of his friends. "Do not feel sorry for me," he said and, holding up his glass of water, added "I have got used to it. Anyone can get used to anything in time. I admit I sometimes succumb to temptation. On one occasion, after you had left for the night, I made myself a cappuccino. I took it into the bathroom and knelt on the floor with my head over the toilet bowl." He looked around and saw their smiling faces, obviously trying to imagine the scene. Marcus said, laughingly, "I kid you not. I was not going to risk vomiting all over the kitchen floor."

Marcus told them about the time he worked in Durham when a huge Scotsman insisted on buying him a whisky. Marcus continued, "I had often wondered what whisky tasted like, and, for the reason I have already explained, I politely refused his offer. But, at his insistence, and as he mentioned that I was insulting Scotland, I succumbed and I promptly vomited all over his kilt!" Although they all laughed, they were devastated and sad for Marcus. Laura thought that Marcus had a wonderful gift of being able to turn tragedy into comedy. She had seen him do this so many times. She assumed that this was how he had survived over the long years since the curse.

Marcus continued, "Although I would love to drink all the wonderful beverages that the world now has to offer, I decided, on the way back to my quarters all those centuries ago, that trying them would not be a good idea! I stopped on the way to my quarters to have something to eat. Chicken? Yes, I think it was chicken. I remember the chicken was quite hot, but when I put it into my mouth, it was cold. I remember thinking to myself how very strange, but that was not the worst of it! It tasted like stale bread. Since then, everything I eat tastes like stale bread." He looked around the table, and said, "That's the worst of it. I want to taste chicken again."

Marcus got up and walked to the window, looking out at the noisy street below. He said, "As you can imagine, I arrived at my quarters feeling quite confused, but things were to get much worse. Next morning, as I was preparing to shave, I saw that my chin was smooth. I have never shaved since. I realised then that I was the victim of a curse."

Laura said, "Let me get this straight. You crucified Jesus, and you are the victim?" Marcus said, "Do you want to hear this story or not?" Laura held up her hand by way of an apology.

Marcus continued, "Nowadays, people think the idea of a curse is ridiculous or even funny, but let me tell you, until quite recently, a curse was taken seriously. I have seen many people burned at the stake, for allegedly 'planting curses' on someone." He looked at Laura and saw that she seemed sorry for her last comment.

Laura thought that Marcus seemed to visibly relax as if he felt he had overcome some great hurdle. He continued, "Mary took me to meet Cephas, whom you know as Peter, and Y'hochanan, whom you know as John." He paused, as it appeared that Laura was going to speak, but then she seemed to change her mind. Marcus carried on. He described how it was Cephas and John who had explained the curse to him. He could only drink water and all food would taste the same to him. He could never become rich or lead an Army or go into politics. He could neither kill anyone nor save anyone. If someone fired an arrow, threw a spear, or even launched a punch at him, they would miss.

Marcus looked at Laura and said, "Animals are not allowed to hurt me. If I kill myself, I go straight to hell. I am forbidden to perform an exorcism." He left out the part about him being unable to fall in love. "I shall never grow old. My body stays the same as it was on that day of the execution. I need never to shave. Do you know what I do every morning?" Laura gently shook her head, Marcus said, "I rub my chin just to see if the curse has been lifted. Do you know what would be the first thing that I would do if it was lifted?" Laura replied, "No." Marcus smiled and said, "I would make myself a beautiful cappuccino."

Laura said, "I am surprised that Peter and John would speak to you, considering what you had done." Marcus responded, "I can understand you think that way. If it had been the other way around, and they had killed one of my friends, I would never have forgiven them. I think it actually took a long time for them to completely trust me; especially Cephas. He made it very clear from the very beginning that he wanted nothing to do with me."

Then Marcus looked at Sarah and everyone in the room followed his gaze. He said, "It was Mary—wonderful, wonderful Mary—who won them round." Sarah looked uncomfortable and said, "I am not Mary." Marcus smiled and continued with his story. "Surprisingly, we became good friends. At first, I had a very difficult time adjusting. Friends in the Legion were beginning to notice that I had changed, and things were becoming dangerous. Since then, I have become a lot better at concealing my secret." Marcus looked at Laura and said to her, "You were the first one in a long time to suspect anything, and that was only through a bizarre set of circumstances."

Marcus ceased talking. It was as if he was not with them any longer but lost somewhere in the distant past. Laura could hear a dog barking and children laughing and playing together outside. Marcus's friends, sitting around the table, were quiet. They waited for Marcus to come back to them. In his mind, Marcus had to travel backwards in time, back from the dusty roads of Philippi, the grandeur of Ancient Rome, and the brutality of Colchester. It took a while for him to speak. They waited in silence.

After a while, Marcus continued; "All this here," he said, looking around the room and gesturing with his hands. "It was Cephas's idea, all of this. He told me that soon, all my friends would be dead and gone, and that I would be all alone in the world." Marcus explained to them about the Cities of Refuge in the Torah and how these cities had to be built no more than one day's travel apart to ensure that the people who were being persecuted could always find a House of Refuge. Marcus stopped and said, "This here, this house," and gestured to his friends around the table, "...you good people. This is my House of Refuge.

"I tried to keep in touch with the descendants of my friends, sending money to them whenever I could do so. Unfortunately, I lost track of Cephas and Y'hochanan's families when the Vandals sacked Rome and I lost touch with Paul's family, who had settled in Syria, during the Crusades.

I have met, spoken to and been friends with innumerable people over the centuries, all good, sensible, honest and intelligent individuals, but Cephas was by far one of the wisest men I have ever had the privilege of meeting. It was he who advised me not to stay in any one place for too long. That was one of the last things he ever said to me." Marcus stopped talking for a moment. His friends could see that he was upset and struggling to maintain his composure. They waited until he regained his self-control. "I was with Cephas when he was arrested and I have never forgiven myself for what happened all those long years ago. We were just walking through the streets of Rome when the Roman soldiers came out of nowhere, just grabbed him and took him away."

Laura said, "I don't understand. How is this your fault?" Marcus answered, "He was grabbed by the Praetorian Guard. They were a group of mercenaries with no loyalty to Rome. As they were taking him away, I noticed that one of the soldiers did not even have his hand on his sword. At the time, I was over sixty years old, but I still had the body and the mind of a thirty-year-old, and nobody could have bettered me with a sword. I could easily have overcome that soldier, which would have taken the others by surprise. I could have killed them all and then taken Cephas away. I could have taken Cephas away! I could have saved him, but Cephas saw my intentions. I could read his lips." Marcus stopped talking—it looked as though the memory was still too painful for him to continue. Laura could clearly feel Marcus's sorrow. She wiped a tear from her cheek, leaned across the table and took hold of Marcus's hand, asking, "You said that you could read Cephas's lips, just as you were about to rescue him?" Marcus nodded. Laura continued, "What did he say?" Marcus looked at Laura and replied, "He said no. I realised later that because of the curse, I would not have been able to rescue Cephas anyway because I was not allowed to kill anyone, but this knowledge did not do anything to ease my guilt."

Laura listened intently as Marcus told her of his life and of his journey throughout the centuries. He told her about Pompeii and Colchester. He explained and described to her the glory and the brutality that was Rome. Marcus told them about the girl in the cupboard and how that one act of kindness had changed his whole perspective on life. He added that for many years afterwards, he used the 'girl in the cupboard' almost as a counterbalance for all the bad things he had done in the past. Over time, he had, however, realised that the bad things stay with you. He felt that for him, there was no redemption. Even though Cephas would argue differently, Marcus felt he would carry the burden of his deeds, and that his life was one long struggle trying to come to terms with his behaviour at the execution of the Nazarene.

491

Marcus talked for over an hour. The group of friends sat in silent fascination. After he had finished, Marcus watched Laura, dreading the question which he knew would come. He could see her going through what he had said and working it out in her mind. When she spoke, it was like waiting for very bad news that you hoped would never come, but then you hear the knock on the door. Laura said, "What I do not understand is exactly how many soldiers were there with you when you crucified Jesus?" Marcus said, "Ten." Laura thought for a moment, and continued, "Were *they* cursed?" Marcus answered, "No." Laura asked, "Was Jesus not brutally flogged and tortured?" Marcus replied, "Yes." Laura asked, "Were those who did *that* cursed?" Marcus answered, "No".

Laura continued, "So! You're telling me that all these people, who did these unbelievably terrible things to Jesus, were not cursed? Not, of course, forgetting Pilate, Herod, and the Priest. All of whom were much more culpable than you. Surely, this could only mean that you did something terrible, even more terrible than anyone else at the Crucifixion." Laura added, "Marcus. What did you do?"

Marcus said, "Have you not heard enough? I have told you my story. Can you not leave it be? It is all in the past, I am a different person now." Laura answered, "You promised me that you would tell me the full story."

As Marcus started to relate his story, there was silence, and Laura felt something change. At first, she could not quite identify the change and then she realised what it was that had happened. She looked around to see if anyone else had noticed. Grace also seemed to be aware that something strange was happening, and looked around, puzzled.

Everywhere was silent. There was no noise—dogs had stopped barking, the laughter of the children had ceased, birds were not singing, and the traffic had stopped. All was hushed. She could not even hear a fly buzzing. It was as if the whole world had stopped to listen. Laura could not have explained it, nor would she share this with anyone else, because she, herself, could hardly believe it. She felt it deep within her soul, and she knew that even the Angels had paused and leaned forward to listen.

Laura looked around the room. She noticed that Grace appeared to have her eyes fixed firmly on Marcus, but, as Laura followed Grace's gaze, she realised she seemed to be looking at someone or something just behind Marcus, although there did not appear to be anything there.

Grace thought to herself that this was the greatest moment of her life. She had longed to meet the Centurion. She had sat next to her grandfather for hours, listening to the wonderful tales that he would tell about his time with the Centurion. She had even written a letter to him. She remembered how disappointed she had been that he had not replied, even though she understood why he had not done so. No one believed the story of the Centurion. The story was just too incredible, but she believed… she had always believed, and now, here he was, sitting only a few feet away from her, telling the most amazing stories that anyone could ever have heard. Here was the Centurion, friend of the Apostles, and yet, it was not the Centurion who held her gaze, but rather she was completely transfixed by the figure standing behind the Centurion. It was the figure of the most beautiful young girl she had ever seen. Her face and her whole body glowed. She looked to see if anyone else could see the young girl, but it was clear that they could not see her. Grace was about to speak, when she saw the Angel put her finger to her lips, signalling Grace to stay silent, and then she was gone.

Marcus said, "It was about two days prior to the Crucifixion. Pilate had sent for me and, on the way to his Palace, I passed the Temple. The Nazarene was sitting on the Temple steps with a few of his followers. This was unusual. I had seen him on many occasions, but it would be normal for him to be surrounded by a massive crowd, so much so, that one could hardly see him in the midst of them all. I had a clear view, and he looked directly at me! Let me tell you, it is a brave man, or a fool, who maintains eye contact with a Roman Centurion.

"Then, whilst he was still looking at me, the Nazarene said to his followers…," Marcus paused as if the memory was still raw and painful. The whole room was now in complete silence. The friends sitting around the table started to notice the silence and complete stillness. Stefano pushed his chair away, stood up and walked to the window. Laura noticed that when the chair was pushed back, there was no noise accompanying it, only silence. Marcus continued, "The Nazarene said, 'Not one sparrow falls.'" Marcus looked at Laura and said, "Can you imagine how angry that remark made me feel?" Laura answered, "I am sorry, but I do not understand why that would make you angry." Laura looked at Marcus's face and it appeared that even now, the memory still seemed to upset him Marcus seemed to pull himself together. He answered Laura, and said, "What the Nazarene was saying was addressed to me and he was saying that I," Marcus raised his voice, "I", he shouted, "I, a Roman

Centurion, could not kill even a sparrow without his permission!"

Marcus continued, "I thought to myself, 'Who does this person think that he is?'" Marcus looked around the table, and said to Laura, "Have you any idea how powerful Rome was at that period in history? We laid waste to cities! Carthage was destroyed. All its great Temples and fine buildings were torn down. The stones were taken away, and the land was salted so that it could never rise again. If you want to see Carthage, go to Rome. A lot of its older buildings were built with Carthaginian stone. I, myself, was considered a hero, because I found killing easy, and, here, in front of me, stood a Rabbi, telling me, telling *me*, that I needed his permission to kill a sparrow! Fortunately for him, I was on my way to meet with Pilate, and, as no one could keep Pilate waiting, I left. Had it been otherwise, I would have finished him with my sword there and then."

Marcus looked around the table at his friends who were listening closely to what he was saying. The subsequent events were something that he had never previously shared with anyone. Even now, he still did not want to reveal this part of the story. He tried to control his mounting anger, which was not at the Nazarene. His anger was because he now felt cornered, with no way out, and that always made him angry. There was a time when he would have turned over the table and stormed out, but he was not that person any longer.

He remembered, when he was on the ferry, reflecting on his life and how much he had changed. At one time, he did not control his anger; his anger controlled him. He would go out at night and, controlled by the wine he consumed, he would be totally at the mercy of his passions; anger, jealousy, hate and greed. He thought to himself that he had been a pitiful man.

Marcus was now ready to disclose a secret that he had never revealed to anyone. He looked at his friends seated around the table, who were as close to being a family as he had ever had since he had been separated from his beautiful wife and children so many centuries before. His worry was how his friends would react and what their response would be to his confession. He could not blame them in any way if they cast him out and wanted no further contact with him.

Marcus took a deep breath. "As no executions were planned for this particular day, I had been assigned to other duties. However, at the last moment, I was ordered to take a troop of soldiers to Golgotha to crucify some criminals. We made our way to Golgotha and started the preparations for the executions. We waited approximately two hours before we saw the soldiers and the condemned men making their way up the hill. The size of the accompanying crown took my breath away."

Marcus hesitated for a moment, drank more water, shrugged and carried on talking. "Most of the crowd had dispersed by the time they got to Golgotha. When I saw the Nazarene, I could not believe it. We all knew this man—he was practically untouchable. We were told that he had a million followers, and yet, here he was, almost on his own. I watched, as they nailed the three men to the crosses.

As they were about to hoist the crosses upright, I stopped them. I bent over the Nazarene as he lay on the ground, nailed to the cross, and I said, 'Do you remember me?' and then I punched him." Marcus stopped. He hoped that they had heard enough, but Laura, quietly, said, "Go on." Marcus continued, "When you crucify someone, you need quite a lot of equipment—hammer, nails, and a large pair of pliers. I took the pliers, went over to the Nazarene and said, 'Please can I have your permission to pull out your beard?' I then pulled it out."

He heard Sarah let out a loud wail. He looked at Laura. She had her hand over her mouth, and tears were running down her cheeks.

Laura had, over the last two hours, gone through the full range of emotions. She had gone from incredulity to joy and then to sadness. When Marcus was talking about the arrest of Cephas, she had felt pity or even love. Now, all he saw in her face was horror. Laura wiped the tears from her eyes, and then she became aware of children playing outside. She looked at Marcus and said, "How could you?" The question hung in the air for several minutes before Marcus spoke. He replied, "I didn't. Rome did."

Laura, answered, "Oh, Come on! The old line that 'We were just obeying orders.'" Marcus responded, "Oh, what an excellent position you are in! It is wonderful to be sitting here, comfortable and smug, making judgements about the past, but remember, I have seen your past. I saw you, yes, you, or at least your ancestors, throwing children to wild dogs and laughing. When I said it was Rome, I meant it. You do not realise how the teaching of Cephas, Paul and Y'hochanan changed the world." Marcus stood up and started to pace up and down the room. Everyone else just sat silently, except Grace, who quietly walked over to Marcus and hugged him. Grace, only Grace went over to Marcus. Grace always understood. Grace always loved, unconditionally.

Laura watched in silence as Marcus and Grace returned to their chairs and sat down. He said to his friends in the room, "I am not trying to justify what I did. I am just trying to help you to understand. Each one of you here now, you are here because of the teaching of Cephas, Paul and John." He looked at Laura and said, "You do not live far from Parliament." Laura nodded. Marcus asked, "Have you ever noticed that the Parliament Building has an inscription around its exterior?" Laura said, "No." Marcus explained, "It is in Latin, and it is the prayer of the Nazarene." He continued, "All your laws, your Magna Carta, and your Bill of Rights are based on the teachings of the Nazarene. You do not understand. You have had two thousand years of the teachings of the Nazarene and these teachings changed everything. Up to that time, I had only ever had the teachings and example of Rome."

Marcus could see that Laura was beginning to understand. Marcus continued, "In the nineteenth century, it always amused me how men liked to be addressed as 'Gentlemen'. 'Gentle-Men'. I could not believe it! Do you know what would happen to a Gentleman, a 'Gentle-Man' before the teaching of Cephas? He would have been robbed and killed." Marcus looked around the room and said, "That was Rome. Rome was barbaric, as indeed was the rest of the known world."

Marcus continued, "Before I came here, I stopped in Rome for a few weeks and I saw men dressed up as Roman soldiers, with tourists putting their arms around them so that they could take 'selfies'. If you dared to put your arm around a real Roman soldier, you would have lost that arm. I know, having heard what I have just said, that you may think I am a bad person." Marcus paused to allow them time to process all the information he had given them and all that he had said to them. He looked at them, watching their faces, waiting, and hoping for a sympathetic response.

It was Laura who was first to speak. She said, "We do not think that you are a bad man. I do accept that we can, perhaps, sometimes come across as smug and self-righteous, but I, for one, do not judge you. When I look at you now, I do not see Rome. Rome is gone. All I see is a kind and considerate man whom I have travelled across Europe to be with."

Marcus continued, "I do not consider myself to be a bad man, at least, not anymore. For a long time, I struggled with what I had done and, to be honest, there are times when I do still struggle." Marcus then told them of Tamar's remarkable story, of how she had escaped from her village and how she was miraculously found during the night by a stranger and taken care of and adopted by a new family. He added that her new father had given her a white stone to show that she was innocent and loved. He explained that she always kept the white stone with her.

Marcus then said, "But now I have this." He reached into his pocket and pulled out an object. Everyone leaned forward to see what he was holding. Marcus held out his hand, which was closed in a fist and his friends were unable to see what he held. When he saw that everyone was watching him, he opened his hand. There was a loud gasp from everyone in the room. In his hand was a white stone. Laura was the first to speak. She said, "Is that…" She paused, as if she could not believe what she was seeing. She repeated, "Is that Tamar's stone?" Marcus just nodded and answered, "When Addayya and his family got on the boat to Cyprus, I waited for over an hour for the boat to set sail. I felt I had to make sure that Addayya did not get off the boat. Then, just as they were pulling away the gangplank, I heard someone shout "Wait!" and, to my surprise, I saw Tamar running down the gangplank. She ran over to me and hugged me. She said, "I have something for you." She gave me her white stone. She said that she did not need it any longer."

Marcus rolled the stone around in his hand for a few moments, as if deep in thought. Then he looked at Laura and said, "She told me that whenever I was feeling bad about myself, to take out the stone and to remember that there is always forgiveness." He continued, "Ever since then, I have always kept this stone with me."

Laura asked, "Please, can I hold it?" Marcus handed the stone to Laura. Laura held the stone as if it was the most precious thing on earth. She held it tightly in her hand and then held it against her chest and closed her eyes. Marcus knew that she felt at one with Tamar. Marcus saw her eyes fill with tears. He reached across and gently held Laura's hand, saying, "You keep the stone." Laura opened her eyes, wiped away her tears with her free hand and said, "No. I could not possibly…." Marcus interrupted her and said, "No. You keep it. I do not need it any longer. I know that Tamar would have loved you to have it." The whole room was in complete silence.

Laura stood up and said, "If you don't mind, I would like to take a little walk, as I am sure you will understand I have a lot to process." Marcus offered to accompany her, but Laura said, "No, I will be alright if I take the bag with the Artefacts in. I am sure I will be safe, and when I get back, you can tell me about the Artefacts, though I think I can guess what they are." Marcus simply nodded.

CHAPTER 34

THE ARTEFACTS

LAURA STEPPED OUT into a lovely warm Sicilian evening. She had been in Sicily for less than twenty-four hours and she was already falling in love with everything she saw of the country. She was glad that Marcus had found Grace's house. As she walked over to Alberto's café, she kept going over and over in her mind all the things that Marcus had told them as they listened to his story.

When she reached the café, Alberto came out to greet her. He gave her a hug, as if they had known each other for years. She sat down and ordered a cappuccino. Laughing, Alberto said, "Remember, no charge." Laura smiled and thanked him. She was not really in the mood to argue. Whilst Alberto was making her coffee, Laura could not help but picture in her mind the terrible things that Marcus had told her. The realisation that her ancestors had been so cruel suddenly became too much for her and she wept. She wept as she had not wept since she was a little girl. She tried her best to control herself, but she just could not stop crying.

Alberto brought her coffee, saw her crying, and said, "Hey, hey, little girl. What's the matter?" He sat down next to her, looking concerned. Laura apologised and said she could not understand why she was so upset. Alberto said to her, "Sometimes things build up and build up and suddenly, without warning, it's like a dam. It just explodes and there is nothing you can do until all the tears have gone. Do not worry about anything. Take your time." Alberto told her he would leave her in peace, but if she needed anything, she was to tell him.

Laura managed to control her tears. She could not understand how she had broken down in that manner. She had always considered herself to be a strong woman. Whilst she was wiping her eyes, to her delight and surprise, Alberto appeared with a delicious-looking strawberry cake. Laura laughed and thanked him. Alberto sat down next to her and asked her if she was OK. She said, "You know what, Alberto? I do not think that I am." Alberto thought for a moment, then pointed to the little church down the road from his café and said, "Go and see Pastor Matteo. He is a wonderful man. He is very wise, and he will help you. Whenever people here have problems, they go to see Pastor Matteo."

Whilst finishing her cake, Laura considered what she should do next. The more she thought about it, the more she decided it was a good idea to go to see this Pastor Matteo She thanked Alberto and made her way down the road towards the little church, wondering if it would still be open; it was, after all, nine o'clock in the evening. As she made her way to the church, she hoped, in a way, that there would not be anyone there and she would then be able to leave.

As she approached the entrance, she saw that the door was open. She took a deep breath and, reluctantly, walked into the building. Once inside, she saw a man at the top of a ladder trying to change a light bulb. It was a very high ladder, and the man was on the very top rung, singing at the top of his voice. Laura assumed it was a maintenance man. She was frightened of interrupting and startling him, causing him to fall and so she stood there and waited.

Eventually, the man on the ladder noticed her, and said, "Hello. Can I be of service to you?" As he came down the ladder, Laura was surprised that he knew her nationality, and asked him how he knew she was English. He smiled and said, "The rucksack. In Sicily, no one goes into a church with a rucksack! Now, how can I help you?" Laura said, "I would like to speak to the Pastor. Is he around here?" The man wiped his hands on his trousers, held out his hand and said, "Let me introduce myself. I am Pastor Matteo, maintenance man, cleaner and gravedigger, at your service!" Laura smiled nervously and shook his hand. She told him her name, and said she would like to speak with him, but then looking at the ladder, said, "If you are busy, I could always come back." Pastor Matteo glanced at the ladder, and laughingly said, "Oh that. Don't worry about that! Most of my congregation have been in the dark for years! So, how can I help you?"

Pastor Matteo sat down on a nearby pew and urged Laura to do the same. Laura sat down and said, "I know I don't go to church as often as I should…" Pastor Matteo interrupted, "How often?" Laura answered, "Well, to be honest, not since Sunday School, but I have heard the Gospel preached hundreds of times, and I have also read the Bible lots of times, but…" Laura paused. Pastor Matteo said, "But?" After a few moments, Laura continued, "Someone told me something that I am finding very, very difficult to believe and I wondered if you could help me with some actual facts." Pastor Matteo responded, "If I can, then of course, I will do so."

Laura started, "I was once told that when Jesus was crucified, someone pulled out his beard. I have never heard or read that anywhere, and so it cannot be true, can it? If it is not true, then it means that I cannot

507

believe anything else that the person who told me has said!" Pastor Matteo got up from the pew, walked over to a bookshelf, and picked up a Bible. He came back and sat down next to Laura. Laura watched as he opened the Bible and read: Isaiah 50:6: "I gave my back to those who struck, and my cheeks to those who pulled out the beard."

Laura felt as if someone had just slapped her. She said, "Why doesn't anyone know that? Why is that not in the New Testament?" Pastor Matteo said, "I'm sorry, but I have no idea. It is, as I have just shown you, in the Old Testament—and I could show you different versions, from earlier manuscripts of the Bible, through to those printed today. It is in all the versions." Pastor Matteo paused for a moment, then said, "What a lot of people do not realise is that there is not really an Old Testament and a New Testament, but that the Bible is just one story, centred on just three days. All that goes before those three days is looking forward to those three days, and all that comes after is looking back to those three days."

Laura was thinking hard about the verses Pastor Matteo had read and of the implications of this revelation. She said, "Who would have done that? Who would have pulled out Jesus's beard?" Pastor Matteo said, "I don't know, and I would not like to speculate." Laura responded, "Oh dear me… for goodness sake, man, speculate. If you get it wrong, I promise you that no one is going to shoot you!" She then apologised for her sharpness, and continued, "Do you think it could have been the Roman Centurion?"

Pastor Matteo was silent for several minutes before he answered. He said, "I suppose that would make the most sense. I doubt it would have been the Temple Guards, or the Soldiers who flogged him, and so, that only leaves the Centurion. What I have just said, however, is highly speculative." Laura asked, "If it *was* the Centurion, why did the Gospel writer not mention him? It does not make any sense." Pastor Matteo said, "Well, there is one possibility, although it is very unlikely."

To Laura's frustration, Pastor Matteo stopped talking. Laura said, "Yes, yes, and…?" It seemed an age before Pastor Matteo spoke. "It may be that this Centurion, somehow, met up with the Apostles, and they forgave him. You see, that is what they would do, and, very often, they would not mention past sins. Paul, for example, was responsible for rounding up early Christians. We have no idea what atrocities, if any, he committed, but we know that prior to his conversion, the Disciples feared him, and they would not do that without very good reason. All this is speculation, and, as I have said, it is not mentioned in the Gospels. After the four Gospels, Peter's denial was not mentioned again."

Laura could hardly believe what she was hearing. She said, "So, you are saying that it is possible?" Pastor Matteo replied, "This is just wild speculation, and it is somewhat pointless, if you do not mind me saying so?" Laura replied, "No, no, Pastor. You have been a great help. I will leave you in peace." As Laura was about to leave, Pastor Matteo said, "Before you go, may I pray with you?" Although she felt a little uncomfortable, Laura agreed. Pastor Matteo took Laura's hand and said, "Dear God, through your Grace, please keep Laura safe in your House of Refuge, and protect her from evil. Amen." Once again, Laura wept uncontrollably. Pastor Matteo said nothing. He merely waited until Laura was able to compose herself. She dried her eyes and apologised. Pastor Matteo told her she had no need to apologise and said, "Would you like to tell me what it is that is troubling you?" Laura replied, "Yes, Pastor, I think I would, but you must promise me that you will never repeat what I say to anyone, although I do very much doubt that you will believe me."

Pastor Matteo assured Laura that her secret was safe with him. He sat in complete silence as Laura told him of the kidnapping of little Antonio, and the story of the

Centurion. When she had finished, Pastor Matteo said to her, "When you get back to the house, will you please tell your friend that tomorrow night, when you go to the old barn, I would like to come with you." Laura looked uncertain, and said, "I am really not sure about that. It could be dangerous." Pastor Matteo said, "Tell your friend I will join you around eleven forty-five tomorrow night."

He looked at the rucksack and said, "Is that where the Artefacts are kept?" Laura nodded. Pastor Matteo asked, "Do you know what they are?" Laura replied, "I am sorry, but I do not know." Pastor Matteo asked if she would mind if he held the rucksack. Laura responded, "No, of course not. Please go ahead." She handed the rucksack over to him. Pastor Matteo took the rucksack, held it to his chest and closed his eyes as if in prayer. After a few minutes, he handed it back to Laura. Silently, she turned around and left.

On her way back to Grace's house, Laura went over in her mind what had happened and what she had heard. She felt as if her whole world had been turned upside down. All the talk of Devils and the supernatural! Surely, it could not be true? She felt that she really did not know what to believe anymore.

When she arrived at the house, it was Grace who opened the door for her. As Laura stepped through the doorway, Grace gave her a hug and asked if she was all right. Although she felt emotionally drained, Laura nodded and gave a weak smile. Grace said, "You have had an awful lot to cope with and you are doing very well." Grace took the heavy rucksack and led Laura back upstairs. As they walked through the door of Marcus's room, he smiled, walked over to Laura and gave her a kiss on the cheek. He asked if she was okay. She nodded. She wanted him to say something encouraging, such as, 'The worst is over', or 'It's all right now', but he did not do either. Grace handed the rucksack to Marcus.

Marcus carried the rucksack over to the table and sat down. Laura followed Marcus to the table and sat down opposite him. She looked at the small group of friends already seated and could see that they were just as anxious as she was to see what was actually in the rucksack. When Marcus saw that everyone was ready, he stood up to open the rucksack. He told them that he had not opened it for at least ten years.

He struggled with the combination lock and then lifted the flap back, exposing what was inside.

Laura noticed that the atmosphere in the room had become very tense. Marcus pulled out what looked like a bundle of rags. As he started to unwrap the rags, she saw that it was, in fact, a single piece of cloth with four tassels. To everyone's amazement, they could see that the cloth was wet. It was wet with blood. Laura let out a loud gasp as she saw the blood on Marcus's hand from where he had handled the cloth. When he had finished unwrapping the cloth, he stood back to enable everyone to look at the Artefacts on the table. They looked at the items displayed in front of them with astonishment and disbelief. A hammer lay on the cloth, together with a large pair of pliers and what looked like the head of a spear. Blood appeared to be coming from the spear and pooling on the table.

It was Enrico who said, "Are these items what I think they are?" Marcus nodded. Sarah said, "Whose blood is that?" Marcus answered, "Your guess is as good as mine. All I know is that after every Crucifixion, one of the soldiers on duty collects the items and returns them to the barracks. This same procedure was followed on that day.

On this occasion, I packed up all the tools that were used in the execution, which included the hammer, a pair of pliers and my spear. I took them back with me to the barracks. The next morning, I noticed that the spear had blood on it. Normally, I would have blamed my Egyptian slave, but fortunately for him, I had witnessed him cleaning it the previous evening. I wiped it dry. On the following day, there was, again, blood on the spear. This was repeated for the next few days, until I took off the head of the spear and wrapped it up with the other items you see in front of you. This is how they have remained since then, exactly as you see them before you on the table."

Marcus shook his head and said, "When I left the barracks, I took them with me. I really cannot say why I did not just leave them behind, but once I had them, I did not know what to do with them. It just did not seem right to throw them away. I thought of giving them to a Church or a Museum, but I did not know how I could explain how they came into my possession. I never take them out to look at them. They bring back too many bad memories. Every now and again, when the bag in which they are stored starts to rot, I transfer them to a new storage bag. That is the only time that I ever touch them."

Laura asked, "How were you able to carry the rucksack containing these through airport security? Why did they not show up on the X-ray machine?" Marcus grinned and said, "They never do." Everyone was silent and lost in thought.

Laura asked Marcus what he planned to do next. Marcus replied, "What else can I do? I am going to go to the old barn tomorrow night, and, if necessary, I will hand the Artefacts over in exchange for the boy and the others." Laura asked, "What others? What others?" Marcus explained, "We made a deal. He said that he would release ten others."

Laura said, "There is something I need to tell you. When I left here with the rucksack, I do not mind telling you that I was not in a good place. I am sorry, really sorry. I mean, I do believe you; I really do believe every word you said, but at the same time, I found it really hard to believe any of it! I know what I am saying sounds crazy, and that it makes absolutely no sense whatsoever."

She looked at the faces of the people sitting around the table. To her relief, they all nodded to show that they understood. Laura took a deep breath then said, "I felt that I needed someone to talk to and so I went to see Pastor Matteo." Grace interrupted, and said, "Pastor Matteo is a good man." Laura continued, "I just wanted to know if he had heard the story of the beard, and even though I believed you, I wanted to know beyond doubt and to have it confirmed for my own sake. Of course, he told me it was true and, I am afraid to say, I broke down and wept." She looked at Marcus and said, "Please forgive me, but I told him the whole story, and he said that he would come with us to the old barn tomorrow night." Marcus leaned across the table, took Laura's hand and said, "Do not worry. I am glad he is coming."

Grace stood up and, looking at Laura said, "Well, I think we will all agree that is enough drama for one night. We will all have a large cup of coffee and get this girl to bed. She must be exhausted."

While they were drinking their coffee, Marcus was lost in thought. It really did not matter that Pastor Matteo now knew his secret. It did not actually matter if the whole world knew his secret, because he really did not expect to survive tomorrow night. He was completely exhausted. He felt, and was sure, that he looked like the marathon runners he had seen on television, who were so absolutely drained as they approached the finishing line that they were, literally, staggering, not running and other marathon runners were catching them up as they stumbled towards the end. Marcus was exhausted. He felt that for the whole of his life, he had been chased by Hell, and that Heaven was always just out of reach.

As Laura finished her coffee, she knew Grace was right—she was exhausted. She smiled at Grace as if to say thank you for her kindness and for her understanding. She again apologised to Marcus for breaking his confidence and sharing it with Pastor Matteo. Marcus told her that it no longer mattered. Grace was correct. Laura was tired. She was more tired than she could ever remember having been previously, but she knew she would have trouble getting to sleep. She laughed to herself; after all the revelations she had heard today, who would be able to sleep? Amazingly, when she finally got into bed, she felt a calmness. She remembered when she was a little girl, how she had always felt safe and protected when her father had tucked her in for the night. As she closed her eyes, she felt Pastor Matteo was praying for her. She whispered, "Thank you, Pastor Matteo." She had no bad dreams, nor even the slightest bad thought.

CHAPTER 35
THE OLD BARN

LAURA AWOKE FEELING remarkably refreshed. She had a shower and decided to go for a walk. Even though Catania was a beautiful town, she was so lost in her thoughts that she saw very little of it. As she went over again in her mind what had happened, she felt a flicker of fear as she remembered the last thing that Marcus had said to her. He had said that now, it didn't matter that Pastor Matteo knew. She said to herself, "What does he mean, that it does not matter now? Why does it no longer matter? Why does he no longer need Tamar's white stone?" She knew that Marcus had done all he could and that for two thousand years, he had fought to keep his secret safe. She could not understand how or why the secret was now so unimportant. She felt the flicker of fear turning into full -blown panic. What was he expecting to happen tonight? She walked around the town for an hour, examining his statement from every angle. She thought that there could be only one explanation… Marcus expected to die.

About a mile from Mary's house, Laura suddenly stood still in the street. She realised she had left without the rucksack. She felt a terror creeping into every part of her body. She shook her head and said herself, "You stupid, stupid girl." She looked around. Then, muttering, followed it with, "Damn! Damn! Damn! What am I looking for?" As she looked at the faces of people in the street, Laura said to herself, "What does he look like?" A young man passed her and smiled, then touched his hat as if in some kind of salute. Laura felt a shiver run down her spine. Her first thoughts were to return to Mary's house as quickly as possible. As she hurried along the pavements, every few yards, she would turn her head to see if the young man was following her.

As she hurried along the street, Laura passed a young woman dressed in a nurse's uniform. When she was several yards away from her, the young woman suddenly started screaming, "Run, run, run!" Laura ran as fast as she could. As she ran, she could hear the young woman laughing. Laura stopped at the end of the street, panting heavily. She turned to see the young woman walking away.

When she finally arrived at Mary's house, she let out a huge sigh of relief. There was a small boy sitting on the steps leading up to Mary's house, singing in Italian. As Laura smiled at him, the boy's face suddenly changed and took on a hideous grin. Speaking with a strong English accent, the boy said," I can have you anytime I want, bitch." The boy then continued singing in Italian as if nothing had happened. Laura scrambled past the boy and banged hard on the door. Thankfully, the door was opened immediately by Grace. With a look of concern on her face, Grace said, "Oh, Laura. Where have you been? We were all so worried about you. It is too danger-ous for you to be out." Before Grace could answer, Laura grabbed hold of her as if her life depended upon her, crying out, "Oh, Grace. Thank God, thank God!" Grace hugged Laura and said, "It's alright. You are safe now." Grace then turned to the boy who had stopped singing and was now smiling. Grace said, "See you tonight. Now go." The boy walked away, whistling.

As Grace pushed the door shut, Laura started to sob uncontrollably. Grace looked Laura in the eye and said, "Laura, I don't know what happened, but I think I can guess. The point is that you have to pull yourself together. You must not mention this to anyone. Everyone here is extremely on edge. We do not want them to be more nervous than they are already." Laura nodded her head in agreement, dried her eyes and went to her room, where she lay on the bed and sobbed.

It took Laura an hour to calm herself. She wanted to plead with Marcus and to beg him not to go to the old barn tonight. She thought that perhaps Pastor Matteo could go instead. Laura knew that what she was thinking was nonsense. She was aware that nothing on earth would stop Marcus from going to the old barn tonight. A thought suddenly occurred to her. I need the 'old' Laura! The 'old' Laura was strong! She thought to herself, "What is happening to me? What on earth is happening to me? I have not cried in years and now I am crying like a baby. What Marcus needs now is the old Laura; the strong Laura." "

Grace met Laura at the kitchen door where she whispered, "Are you alright?" Marcus and the rest of the household were sitting around the table. Marcus got up to greet her. Over the course of the evening, Marcus seemed to be trying too hard to be cheerful. He was also very successful at avoiding any mention of the old barn—they talked about the weather, sport and politics… anything but the barn!

Pastor Matteo arrived at 11.30 pm. Grace welcomed him into the house. He looked at Marcus, held out his hand and said, "You must be Marcus? I have heard a lot about you." Marcus shook his hand and said, "Thank you for helping Laura. I really appreciate it." Pastor Matteo asked Marcus what the plan was for tonight and what he expected to happen. Marcus replied, "It's quite simple really. I hand over the Artefacts. 'It' releases the boy and ten others and then we go home. That's the plan! As for what I expect to happen, well, let's just say that we 'Expect the Unexpected.'"

Pastor Matteo said, "The Artefacts?" Marcus answered, "I suppose you would like to see them?" Pastor Matteo smiled, and said, "Yes, if you do not mind. That is why I came a few minutes earlier." He glanced around the room, and said, "Most people just call me Matteo." Marcus invited him upstairs to show him the Artefacts. As Pastor Matteo followed Marcus upstairs, it was obvious that he was so excited. Matteo still struggled to believe that what he had been told by Laura was possible. Could this really be the Centurion who crucified Christ? Did the Centurion actually make friends with his heroes, the Apostles? He knew that one way or another, he would know the truth tonight. Marcus led the way up the stairs to his rooms. He could hear Pastor Matteo breathing heavily behind him. Marcus showed Pastor

Matteo into his dining room and asked him to sit down at the table.

Pastor Matteo walked into the room, his gaze focused on the parcel which occupied the middle of the table. Marcus had already separated the wrapped Artefacts. He had decided all that would be needed would be the spearhead. Marcus picked up the parcel and said, "I want you to prepare yourself for what you are about to witness, and, I will add that there is no earthly explanation for what you are about to see."

Marcus then carefully unwrapped the spearhead. Pastor Matteo looked at it with a look of absolute disbelief. He glanced at Marcus and said, "The blood. Is it his blood… but how?" Marcus replied, "Who, how, why and what, that is not for me to answer. All I can tell you is that I used this spear to pierce the Nazarene and the blood on it cannot be wiped away." There was a long silence. Marcus waited. He knew that Pastor Matteo wanted to ask a question; he watched as he struggled to find the correct words. Pastor Matteo looked at Marcus and said, "I want you to know that I have faith." Marcus smiled and replied, gently, "Yes, I know." Pastor Matteo said, almost guiltily, "When you pierced him, was he really dead?" Marcus said, "I am an experienced Centurion. I have witnessed and carried out many executions and I can tell you the theory that he was still alive is born out of desperation and believed by fools." Marcus wrapped up the spearhead and then, turning to Pastor Matteo, said, "Let us go now." They then made their way down the stairs engrossed in conversation, with Pastor Matteo excitedly asking questions about his long life, which Marcus appeared happy to answer. He felt a great relief to be able to finally talk to someone about his past. It had often been extremely frustrating when he had been forced to stay silent, even when speaking with the most intelligent of individuals, who would be relating absolute nonsense about historical events that he, personally, had actually witnessed.

Whilst Marcus and Matteo were talking upstairs, Grace had made Laura and Sarah a coffee and told them that they were not to be afraid, and they were to remember that whatever they met or saw tonight, they—all of those who were there tonight—were the stronger! "We must not believe anything that the 'thing' says. It knows only lies." When she had finished talking, she handed out torches. She added that where they were going tonight would be dark. Laura turned her torch towards her face, and, curious to see how powerful the light was, she switched it on! The powerful beam dazzled her so much that she nearly dropped the torch. Grace said, "You do not need that in here!" Laura felt slightly embarrassed and apologised.

A short time later, Marcus appeared with Matteo. Laura noticed that Matteo looked stunned and had tears in his eyes. Marcus explained that he had taken one of the Artefacts out of the rucksack, wrapped it in a red cloth and given it to Matteo to carry. It was clear there was only one Artefact in the red cloth. Grace handed a torch to both Marcus and Matteo, then, looking at Laura, said, "Don't shine them in your faces. They can be quite bright." They all laughed, whilst Marcus wondered why Laura looked slightly embarrassed.

Marcus and Laura stepped out into an unusually dark night, accompanied by Enrico, Sarah, Matteo and Grace. Marcus thanked God for Grace. The old barn was a fifteen-minute walk from Grace's house. They walked past Alberto's café, then turned off the main road and onto a small track. As they turned onto the track, they switched on their torches and were startled by the strength of the light. The light from the six torches, lit together, split the night.

The old barn was clearly visible, and it was easy to see why it had been abandoned. There were a number of holes in the roof, probably resulting from one of the many eruptions from Mount Etna. It was apparent that the old barn was generally in a poor state of repair. As they approached the barn door, Marcus paused and said, "Just wait here for a moment." He made his way to the back of the barn, thinking to himself that old habits die hard. He was surprised to see that the back of the barn was relatively undamaged. It was very obvious—as there was no exit through the rear of the barn—that it would be easy to get trapped inside. Satisfying himself that he knew the layout of the building, he re-joined the others at the front of the barn. Marcus paused for what seemed like an age, while the rest of the group looked at each other wondering what was causing the delay. Grace stepped forward and whispered in Marcus's ear, saying, "Don't worry, our torches will light that place up." As Marcus put his hand on the door, he said to them, "If you want to leave, now is the time to do it." Grace answered, "Oh, for goodness sake, get on with it, man!"

As the door swung open and the light from the torches pierced the darkness across the barn, the group was hit by an enormous wall of sound. The sound was of wailing and screaming. The barn was occupied by a huge crowd—what appeared to be about a hundred people—who were now screaming, shrieking, yelling and wailing with high-pitched voices, whilst running around the barn, pushing each other over as they tried to hide from the light. Some were cowering behind each other in the corners of the barn. They were all screaming, "Turn off the light! Turn off the light!" Marcus had to raise his voice to be heard above the noise. He shouted in a loud voice, "No! The light is not going off—get used to it." The screaming died down to a loud moaning and wailing sound.

Marcus looked at his small group of friends. Laura and Matteo looked a little frightened. He smiled as he looked at Sarah as she stood with her hands on her hips, just as her wonderful ancestor, Mary Magdalene, had done so often all those many centuries ago, whenever she was protecting or defending people in need. The look on her face was one of defiance; she showed no fear. Enrico moved to stand next to his wife, putting his hands around her waist and whispering something in her ear that made her smile. He could see Laura was clutching something in her hand. He guessed it was Tamar's white stone.

Marcus watched the wailing mass of people spitting and hissing like snakes, desperately trying to cover their eyes from the light, and, at the same time, encircling Marcus and his friends. Amongst them was a man dressed in the uniform of a New York policeman, a young woman in a nurse's uniform, young boys, young girls, and men and women of all shapes and sizes. They all had one thing in common... they were possessed!

The smell of vomit and urine was almost overwhelming. It was obvious that many of the crowd of people now in the barn had been captive for a long time, judging by their condition, but others not quite so long. The man in the policeman's uniform and the nurse charged at Laura, causing her to scream. Grace, considering her age, moved at a remarkable speed and placed herself between Laura and the attackers. They retreated from her, cowering as they moved away. Marcus spotted Antonio at the back of the barn. He had a wicked grin on his face. Marcus shouted, "Why are all these people here? You told me just eleven." Marcus, of course, knew why—it was because the thing that possessed Antonio was a bully. Years had shown Marcus that evil always manifests itself as a bully. Hitler was a bully... Mao was a bully! Marcus had met thousands of bullies in his long lifetime. He had met millionaires with fat cigars boasting that "You are either a predator or prey; a winner or a loser." He realised that he had known this his whole life. It explained so much, including why he sometimes, inexplicably, would cross the road when he saw particular individuals coming towards him, even though he did not know them.

He remembered Cephas and how he loved to be in his company. It certainly was not for his sense of humour, and it was not merely for his wisdom and the good advice that he gave him. He realised it was because he was clean. Marcus could see that throughout his whole life, he had, unknowingly, gravitated towards the clean. Laura was beautiful, intelligent, and funny, but he knew that was not why he liked her. He liked her because she was clean. Marcus looked at the great crowd in front of him who were wailing and moaning. He was surrounded by unclean people. He thought to himself, "I am going to cleanse you all."

Marcus shouted to the thing inside Antonio, "What do you want? The Thing replied, "You know what I want: the spear." Marcus signalled to Matteo, who walked over to Marcus and gave him the red cloth which contained the spear. Marcus removed the wrapping. He held the spear aloft and shouted, "Here it is. Come, come and get it!"

As Marcus produced the spear, the crowd of the unclean let out a deafening scream and retreated from where Marcus was standing now holding the spear aloft. Marcus laughed, and, with the spear still held aloft, moved towards them as they continued screaming, whilst desperately trying to move further and further away from him.

Marcus shouted again to the thing inside Antonio, "Come on. What are you waiting for? You want this; come closer!" The thing inside Antonio screamed, "I don't want it." Marcus said, "Well, in that case, what is all this about? What do you want?" The thing replied, "Pick out the ten you want to release, then leave here, take the path that leads up the mountain and throw the spear into the volcano." Marcus responded, "Let me get this straight. You expect me to climb a mountain of nearly ten thousand feet in the middle of the night?" The thing said, "No. You only need to walk up the path for half an hour and you will see a vent. Throw it in there."

Marcus gazed at the pitiful mass of wailing, moaning, spitting people, many of whom were vomiting at the very sight of the spear. Marcus made a decision. He glanced at Grace, who smiled and gently nodded. The nearest captive to him was the New York policeman. Marcus took a step towards him and touched the side of his face with the spear. The man immediately fell to the floor screaming. Marcus saw he had blood on his face from the spear. The man seemed to be writhing in pain. Suddenly, a putrid green smoke started to pour from his eyes, followed by an ear-piercing scream. To his astonishment, the scream did not come from the man's mouth, but from the green putrid smoke. More smoke streamed from his mouth, this time, a dirty ink colour. Then a different scream, this time it was a low-pitched sound. This was followed by more smoke, different smoke, this time a sickly yellow, coming from his ears; then another scream, followed by another. Marcus realised, to his horror, that each colour represented a different demon. Suddenly, the demonic smoke shot screaming up into the air and out through the holes in the roof. Marcus turned his attention to the woman in the nurse's uniform. He laid the spear on her arm. Again, she screamed as different coloured smoke poured out from her body, some of the demons screaming, others begging to be left alone.

Marcus saw the panicking mob move toward the barn door. He screamed to the others to close the door and not let any of these things escape. He, Matteo and Enrico rushed towards the door and slammed it shut. He then moved in front of the girls. After ensuring that the girls were safe, Marcus moved through the mob, slapping people with his spear. As he passed through the crowd, the individuals he touched fell down, like puppets who have had their strings cut. As they hit the ground, they started screaming, all adding to the bedlam which was going on all around them. As they fell, they caused others to fall over them. Marcus started to move back towards the mob. Moving from side to side, like a sheepdog, he started to corral them into the corner of the barn, all the time, continuing to hit them with his spear. Eventually, there was only one left—Antonio.

Marcus walked over to the boy and looked into his face. He saw terror! The thing within the boy said, "You will be in hell tonight." Marcus responded, "See you there then!" He saw the boy's eyes widening as he reached forward and gently touched his face with the spear. The boy fell to the ground and a thick black screaming smoke left his young body.

Marcus turned around. It appeared that all the demons had fled. Of the crowd in the barn, some were lying down and weeping and some were sitting down, looking dazed. Matteo and Enrico opened the barn door. The girls were now moving among those lying on the floor. One particular woman, dressed in a nurse's uniform, looked exhausted, yet she was still trying to help others. Marcus thought to himself, "I may end up in hell, but I have no regrets." It was then that Marcus saw three young women ministering to the crying victims. Marcus looked at Grace to ask who they were, but he could see that she was speaking to a young lady who had her back to him. He could see that the young lady had gently placed her hand on Grace's cheek. The young lady leaned forward and kissed Grace on the other cheek. Grace's face glowed. Marcus suddenly recognised the young lady. He shouted, "Serafina!" He was then distracted by the lady in the nurse's uniform who came to thank him. When he looked again, Serafina and her three sisters had gone.

Grace came up to Marcus. He saw that she looked tired, so Marcus put his hand on the back of her head, gently pulled it down and kissed her on the forehead. Grace said to Marcus, "You and Laura need to leave. The police and ambulances are on their way here. We need to get these people to the hospital." Marcus agreed, but then said, "What did Serafina say to you?" Grace smiled and said, "I think that it is between me and Serafina. Now you need to go."

Marcus went over to talk to Antonio and asked him if he was okay. He was not. He was still in shock. Marcus found it hard telling Antonio that he had to leave. The boy nodded bravely and whispered, "Thank you". He hugged Marcus. Sarah came over and whispered to Marcus, "You go now. I will take care of him."

Marcus, Laura, and Grace stepped out through the barn door into the beautiful Sicilian night. All the heavier cloud cover had disappeared. The sky was clear with a bright moon. When they got to the end of the track and onto the main road where the street lighting illuminated their way home, they turned off their torches and silently walked back to the house. As they arrived, they heard the police sirens wailing as the police cars made their way to the barn. Marcus thought of the woman in the nurse's uniform and the New York policeman. He wondered how long they had been captive, but most of all, he thought of Antonio. He wondered how long it would take the boy to recover from such an experience.

Grace opened the door for Laura and smiled. She asked her if she was all right. Laura nodded and tried to put on a brave face. She said, "I will be ok." She then gently closed the door. Laura walked over to the bed and fell on it. She was completely spent. All of her courage and all of her strength was gone. She wept and wept until she could not weep anymore. She fell asleep, still dressed, with her shoes on.

When she woke the next morning, she ached all over. She got up, washed her face and looked in the mirror. She would normally have been horrified at the sight. Her mascara had run down her cheeks and her face was swollen with tears. Normally, she would never miss having a shower, but today, she just did not care how she looked. She sat on the bed and looked at the clock. It was still early—6.00 am. She had a desire to run to Marcus's room and bang on the door. But she thought to herself, "Oh, don't be silly!" She went into the bathroom thinking to herself, "A positive Marcus is going to take me out to breakfast and I am going to look gorgeous, beautiful… bloody stunning!" As she stepped into the shower, she shouted, "To hell with you, Flavian. This lady has got a date!"

An hour later, Laura stood admiring herself in the mirror. Even though it was early, she wore a long blue evening dress and high heels that matched her dress. She turned around inspecting herself, saying, "Not bad, not bad at all, even if I say it myself."

Laura could hear her heart beating as she made her way down to the kitchen. She was met by Grace in the hallway. Laura made every effort to keep calm as she asked Grace, "Is Marcus here?" Grace answered, "I am sorry, Laura, but he is not here." There was a pause. Grace continued, "He had to go out. He said he had to buy a razor. He needed to shave."

The 'thing' which had possessed young Antonio slowly floated towards the hole in the roof of the old Barn. The 'thing', which chose to go by the name of Flavian, looked down onto the barn floor. The devastation caused by the mass exorcism looked very similar to the aftermath of a great battle, which, of course, it had been.

Flavian knew that this was not the end! It was very, very far from being the end!

The 'thing' had left the body of the young boy, Antonio, a second before the Centurion touched him with the spear. The spear with the blood of the Nazarene was, to Flavian, the most powerful weapon in all of Creation. He was aware that for him to come into contact with the Artefact would condemn him to the darkness forever. Fortunately, he had been clever... far too clever for a simple human.

Flavian had expected some type of betrayal. Betrayal was, after all, one of his greatest successes in all his dealings with humanity. He had taught them well! Outside was the fool, Jason, who was already inhabited, but there was still plenty of room! A young man such as Jason could accommodate many... in fact, Jason could accommodate a legion of demons.

As the 'thing' entered Jason, he collapsed with exhaustion. The 'thing' thought to himself, "Let the weakling rest."

Flavian started to make plans. He was aware that he was not allowed to kill the Centurion. For some reason, he was protected. Flavian smiled to himself. He had, a long time ago, convinced the world that he was much more powerful than he actually was. For any human to believe that he was as powerful as the Creator of the Universe just showed that many humans are exceptionally stupid.

Flavian had never been far from the Centurion. He was in the mob outside the farmhouse during the English Civil War. He had seen the Centurion escape on a horse with bells on its bridle. The horse actually had bells on its bridle and the idiot had no idea what they meant! Flavian thought to himself, "Oh, how the Nazarene likes his symbolism."

Flavian shouted up to the heavens, "Nobody understands it! Nobody cares! I have fooled them all!" The truth was that he was bitter about the escape of the Centurion on that stupid horse with the bells. Flavian has quickly taken possession of one of the idiot's horses. He had galloped as fast as a horse could possibly go, but he could not get anywhere near to the old nag with the stupid bells. Eventually, Flavian's horse dropped down, dead with exhaustion. It was a pity. If he could have slowed the Centurion's horse long enough for the mob to catch up—Flavian smiled to himself and said, "Well, that would have been fun."

Milton Keynes UK
Ingram Content Group UK Ltd.
UKHW010620210624
444344UK00002B/10

9 781805 415480